19.71

"Damn you, Arabella, don't you understand?

"I will not marry you, not ever. But if you push me far enough, I will make love to you."

For a moment Arabella was speechless as her breath caught in her throat. This was the passion, the wildness, she had only glimpsed by the river. Her blood heated, and the excitement began to pound within her, as the vision of what it would be like to see such passion unleashed teased her.

"How far?" she whispered.

"What?" Nando's voice was hoarse.

"How far will I have to push?" Arabella's shallow, quick breathing made her sound winded.

The grip of the fingers around her wrist loosened and became a caress as Nando's thumb began to rub the throbbing pulse point. "Not far, Arabella. Not far."

Dear Reader,

Welcome to Harlequin Historicals, where we hope you'll find a lot to be thankful for this November.

Fans of Bronwyn Williams will be pleased to see that Dixie Browning and her sister, Mary Williams, have written another book in their popular Outer Banks Series. In *The Mariner's Bride,* young seaman Rogan Rawson marries a woman for the sole purpose of keeping an eye on his wayward stepmother, only to discover that nothing is ever that simple.

You will also find *Season of Storms,* from Kate Kingsley (our one hundredth book by the way). It's the tale of a wayward son of the Creole elite and an independent heiress. Readers of contemporary romance will recognize the name Laurie Paige. In the author's first Harlequin Historical, *Wedding Day Vows,* an Englishwoman trades her release from Newgate prison for her hand in marriage.

Last, but not least, I would like to mention Nina Beaumont. This first-time author lives in Austria, and her wealth of knowledge and experience lend a powerful flavor to *Sapphire Magic,* the story of a cynical Austrian count and the woman who melts his heart.

Please keep an eye out for *Historical Christmas Stories 1991.* The collection features Lynda Trent, Caryn Cameron and DeLoras Scott. You won't want to miss it!

Our best to you and yours during the upcoming holiday season.

Sincerely,

Tracy Farrell
Senior Editor

Sapphire Magic

Nina Beaumont

Harlequin Books

TORONTO • NEW YORK • LONDON
AMSTERDAM • PARIS • SYDNEY • HAMBURG
STOCKHOLM • ATHENS • TOKYO • MILAN

Harlequin Historicals first edition November 1991

ISBN 0-373-28701-1

SAPPHIRE MAGIC

NINA BEAUMONT

is of Russian parentage and has a family tree that in-
cludes the Counts Stroganoff and a Mongolian Khan.
Born in Salzburg, she grew up in Massachusetts and
in 1970 moved to Austria, where she now lives in the
country with her husband and an overly friendly
schnauzer.

An avid history buff, she enjoys traveling, which gives
her the opportunity to utilize the five languages she
speaks. She also loves music, books and the French
Impressionists.

Her writing keeps her more than busy, but she also
finds time to work as a translator and teach adult
English classes.

To my mother,
who gave me all the possibilities, with love.

And my special thanks to Eileen Nauman
for her friendship, her practical advice and her
support and encouragement in good times and bad.

Chapter One

Vienna, Austria, 1814

The minute she opened her eyes, Arabella threw aside the feather tick and bounded out of bed. Skipping across the room, she jerked the rose velvet curtains aside and flung the casement window wide open. The first rush of cool air, which the September sunshine had not yet had a chance to warm, flowed in, smelling vaguely of smoke and fresh bread. Arabella grasped the window frame lightly and pushed her bare feet off the floor to lever herself across the wide sill. Her face tilted upward, she inhaled deeply.

Only a small patch of brilliantly blue sky was visible above the multistoried, narrow houses. Oh, but what a blue! Certainly no sky at home in England had ever been painted with that incredible azure color. She was sure of it. It was bold and beautiful and seemed to be making a statement about the world beneath it.

"Vienna," Arabella whispered. The name tasted as sweet on her tongue today as it had on the morning she had leaned out this window for the very first time two weeks ago. Just as sweet as one of the luscious pastries the city was so famous for. Even the fact that she had already encountered less attractive aspects of the city could not detract from the pleasure of an adventure she looked forward to from the moment she opened her eyes every day.

It was early yet, and the few sounds that drifted toward her third-story window were distinct in the morning stillness. The clatter of dishes from a kitchen window. The pigeons cooing under the eaves. The regular thump of something heavy being loaded onto a wagon. The whinny of a horse from around the corner. Smiling, Arabella closed her eyes and let the sounds blend to a comfortable picture inside her.

The snatch of a whistled song that was her signal caught Arabella's attention, and she wriggled a bit farther so she could see down into the cramped little square.

The towheaded boy who was apprenticed to the baker on the ground floor was wrestling an unwieldy basket overflowing with rolls, bread and buns onto a cart. He sneaked a look upward, and a smile appeared on his thin face. He sent Arabella a surreptitious wave and glanced over his shoulder to make sure his master, who was so quick to box his ears, was nowhere near.

Arabella returned both the smile and the wave, giving little thought to how she looked in her white lawn nightgown, her thick, black braid hanging half unraveled over her shoulder, and leaned a little farther out of the window, trying to decide what she would have for breakfast.

The boy threw another glance over his shoulder and began the daily ritual that had developed since Arabella's arrival. Quickly he pointed to one sort of roll after another, peeking upward after each gesture. When he reached the raisin buns, Arabella nodded vigorously and reached for her reticule.

Dropping a coin inside, she looped the end of a ball of string around the drawstrings and lowered the purse to the street, the blue velvet incongruous against the gray-brown stone.

Within a minute, a warm raisin bun lay where the coin had been, and Arabella rewound the ball of string, the transaction completed to the satisfaction of both parties.

Behind Arabella a door creaked open and there was a gasp and a rattle of crockery before her maid's voice sounded. "*Mon Dieu.* Get away from the window, Arabella. You will fall out."

Within seconds Jeanne had grabbed a handful of nightgown and had hauled her charge back into the room. Opening her mouth to scold, she was effectively silenced when Arabella threw her arms around her and hugged her fiercely.

Slipping an arm around Jeanne's plump waist, Arabella offered her a piece of the bun with her free hand. "Have you had breakfast yet?" Her smile was impish.

"Must you do this every morning?" Jeanne grumbled. "Can't you wait until I bring you your breakfast? If Lady Castlereagh found out what a hoyden you are, she'd pack you off back to London and be done with you."

Arabella playfully squeezed the soft roll of flesh that bulged above Jeanne's apron. "You can't fool me, old woman." She chuckled gently. "If I suddenly became the meek, well-mannered young lady everyone has been trying to make me into for the past nineteen years, you'd hate it more than anyone."

Jeanne gave up resisting the smile that was already deepening the creases in her cheeks and returned the hug. "*Eh bien,* keep your little morning game, for all I care." She shook her finger at Arabella. "Just make sure you don't sail down to the street along with your reticule."

"Don't worry." Arabella patted Jeanne's cheek as she leaned against the table to take a sip of her morning chocolate. Her mind already on the day ahead, she felt too full of energy to sit down to breakfast. As early as it was, she had no time to lose, for the day never had enough hours.

Before she left the house Arabella knocked on the door of Lady Castlereagh's sitting room, as she did every morning.

"Will you be joining us for our sight-seeing today, Lady Castlereagh?" She asked, wincing inwardly as the lie slid easily from her lips, but she refused to feel guilty.

During the past five weeks, which they had spent in Antwerp, Brussels and then Paris, Arabella had become fond of Lady C, as she had taken to calling her to herself, so she disliked lying to her as she disliked any kind of deceit. But even though the easygoing, good-natured Lady C was neither the strict keeper nor the inveterate matchmaker her father would have preferred, Arabella hesitated to tell her that the hours she supposedly spent admiring the architecture and art of Vienna were in reality spent in a squalid orphanage.

"Not today, my dear, but do go ahead. Just make sure you take Jeanne with you, won't you?" Lady Castlereagh smiled and reached for a chocolate. "I'm told there are even Turks about!"

When they left St. Peter's Square, Arabella and Jeanne walked quickly down the Graben, past the richly baroque column commemorating safe delivery from the Black Death. They did not pause in front of the elegant shop windows underneath the colorful canvas awnings, nor did they stop to admire the Gothic splendor of St. Stephan's.

Walking arm in arm through the maze of streets, they soon reached their destination—a run-down building that nestled in a narrow, sunless street near the ramparts by the river. Here the city walls looked dark and forbidding, bearing little resemblance to those near the imperial palace, the Hofburg, where the enterprising Viennese had turned the ramparts into an elegant promenade.

As they climbed the steps, Arabella wondered if Jeanne could ever understand that she needed the time here at the orphanage, so full of children hungry for a smile, a touch. Needed it to offset the frivolousness of her social activities.

It was early afternoon when they started back to St. Peter's Square. The sunshine was inviting, and they decided to take the long way and stroll along the top of the ramparts.

The stone walls had served their purpose well during the centuries when Vienna had been repeatedly threatened by Turks and the warlike peoples from the Eastern plains. But now that they were no longer an essential point of defence, their broad walkways were *the* place to promenade a new gown or a new lover.

The walkways were seamed by trees and bushes, and colorfully painted benches were bright punctuation marks among the greenery. Arabella felt Jeanne's steps slow.

"Shall we sit for a while?" Arabella asked.

Jeanne sent her a grateful look, knowing that Arabella with her boundless energy would not have chosen to sit down just then.

Many of the wider sections of the ramparts had cafés nestled among the greenery with tables both inside and on flagstone terraces. The bench where they sat afforded them a view of such a café, and Arabella lifted her nose to catch the delicious fragrance of freshly roasted coffee and almond milk. Musicians strolled among the tables and even Jeanne fell under the spell of the violins and accordions that had just the right touch of melancholy and began to sway a little in time with the music.

There was a feeling of gaiety about the elegant crowd, but it was not the brittle, slightly artificial gaiety Arabella had seen in Paris. Here it was lighthearted and spontaneous. She felt like laughing out loud with her pleasure in it all.

Finally Arabella could sit still no longer, and they walked on. When a curve of the ramparts offered a fetching panorama of the city on one side and a particularly inviting café on the other, Arabella decided that after their long walk some refreshment would be appealing.

Jeanne caught her wishful glance. "Don't you dare go in there by yourself," she whispered.

Arabella's wishfulness gave way to determination. "There are several unescorted ladies sitting there."

"There are unescorted *females* sitting there," Jeanne huffed. "I would not wager a sou on the certainty of their being ladies."

"Oh, come now, Jeanne." Arabella gave her a little conspiratorial nudge. "No one knows us, and all I want is a cool drink. I am not planning on making a spectacle of myself."

Jeanne jerked down the ends of her shawl and crossed her arms over her generous bosom. Glowering at her charge, she blocked her path and filled her lungs to rebut any arguments that Arabella might have to offer.

But Arabella did not argue. Instead she disarmed Jeanne with a guileless smile, and under the guise of taking her companion's arm, insinuated her hand under Jeanne's elbow, tickling the older woman's well-padded ribs mercilessly. Jeanne barely managed to mask a yelp of surprise and although her eyes flashed sparks, she could not prevent a chuckle at Arabella's sleight of hand.

Giving in with a small sigh, Jeanne let Arabella sweep them by the potted shrubs that separated the terrace from the walkway.

Count Ferdinand Berg leaned against the white counter running the length of the café. His slender fingers, bare but for a signet ring of gold and lapis, toyed with a tall glass of *Einspänner*—sweet, aromatic coffee with a dollop of whipped cream—barely tasted. A casual observer would have said that his posture was lazy. Only someone who bothered to look more closely would have seen the tension in the long-boned hands, the restlessness in the clear gray eyes.

He was bored. And as always when he was bored, Count Berg was irritable. But the life he led had long since forced him to acquire the discipline to mask such inappropriate emotions, so no one noticed. Not his young friend Count Hugo Lemdorf, who lounged against the counter beside him. Not even the pretty blonde at a nearby table who monitored the direction of his gaze carefully, never missing an opportunity to send him a coquettish smile.

With half an ear Berg listened to the boyishly enthusiastic comments about the ladies present that Hugo insisted on sharing with him, caring not a whit for the overabundance of feminine beauty around him. His eyes swept coolly over the gay, chatting crowd, and with all the passion he usually hid so well Count Berg wished himself elsewhere.

After nine years in the Imperial Austrian Army, nine years of almost ceaseless war, he was back in Vienna. The last campaign he ever hoped to fight had been over six months past. Yet still he was not a free man. He had been kicking his heels in Vienna for four months now, constantly badgering General Prince Schwarzenberg, his commander, to grant him leave to return to his estates, which were scattered through Styria, Bohemia and Hungary. Instead the prince had insisted that his presence, as representative of one of Austria's oldest and most noble houses, was absolutely necessary during the congress that was gathering in Vienna in September to rearrange Europe after the fall of Napoleon.

A flare of discontent rose within him. His life was full of empty social occasions that disgusted him with their subtle intrigues and their wanton flirtations. At least in the army, life was clear-cut. At least there the brutality and cruelty were open and honest. A man knew precisely who his enemies were. Berg had always thought that it was easier to cover his back in a cavalry charge than in a Viennese salon.

He longed to be home, in the endless meadows and forests of the Berg estates. Surrounded by vivacious chatter, he wanted a silence broken only by the song of a bird or the swish of a scythe. Among clouds of French perfume, he wanted air that smelled of damp pine needles and freshly cut hay. He wanted to feel whole again after years of being fragmented between the battles of the field and the battles of the boudoir, which had left him empty and cynical.

Berg's gaze slid away from the blond woman with the flirtatious smile. Suddenly he straightened as if an invisible hand had pulled him up by the high, stiff collar of his immaculately white uniform tunic.

He would never be able to pinpoint the first thing he noticed about her. Perhaps it was her height. Despite the distance separating them, he knew that the top of her head, even without the dashing high-crowned aquamarine bonnet she wore, would easily reach his chin.

She stood just beyond the potted shrubs that separated the café terrace from the walkway, her full lips curved into a smile that was just a little wicked; the smile was echoed in her dark eyes. Then a hint of the girl's voice floated over to him—the gentle rasp of velvet on naked skin. A shiver slithered down his spine.

"A small wager, Nando, my friend? That girl in the blue bonnet, is she French or English?"

Hugo's voice penetrated Nando's consciousness, and he realized that the girl he had been staring at was the subject of his friend's speculation. Berg's eyes glinted with sudden annoyance at himself for the rush of fascination he had felt.

"Why don't you tell me, Hugo?" he drawled. "You're the one who's been studying the ladies of our charming city with such unerring perseverance."

The young man stroked his reddish-brown mustache with his thumb and good-naturedly ignored Nando's sarcasm. "Her French is impeccable. Her dress is the latest fashion. But her companion's dress is quite outlandish." He leaned his head closer to Nando's and murmured, "I have it on the best authority that only Englishwomen wear corsets these days."

Nando laughed without real amusement. "Hugo, if you applied the same seriousness to the study of military strategy as you do to female fashions, you would make a formidable general."

He himself cared not a whit what women wore. After all, the silks and satins, the jewelry, the perfumes were nothing more than trappings to get the women into some man's bed, Nando told himself caustically. Preferably a man who could offer wealth and power as well as prowess in the boudoir.

He watched the girl take a seat and put a hand on her companion's arm. Her smile had exchanged its wicked gleam for a sweetness that seemed too natural to be contrived. Nando would have laughed cynically had someone told him that his expression softened under the silky dark blond of his fashionably long mustache as he forgot what direction his thoughts had taken and lost himself in her smile again.

"Either she is an Englishwoman with a French dressmaker," Hugo continued, "or she is a French *emigrée* recently returned from exile in England." He propped his soft, round chin on his fist and cocked his head to the side with the pose of the true connoisseur. "I'd say the latter," he mused dreamily. "Yes, that natural elegance and poise just have to be French."

"Good Lord, Hugo, don't you have anything better to talk about?" Nando exploded. "Must you persist in mouthing such absolute drivel?"

The laughter at a nearby table stilled at his outburst, and Hugo stared, his soft mouth hanging slightly open in amazement. Where was the melodious, mild baritone with which Nando habitually masked the most biting comments? Hearing him raise his voice was something utterly new. The only place he had ever heard Nando amplify the volume of his mellow voice was on the battlefield.

"Forgive me, Nando," Hugo stuttered, a flush creeping up his neck. "I didn't mean to irritate you."

Nando felt a stab of remorse. It was hardly poor Hugo's fault. He had no right to use his friend as a lightning rod just because that girl had touched some long buried, long forgotten source of tenderness in him. A spot he did not want touched. For just a moment it crossed Nando's mind that perhaps he wanted it too much. But he wouldn't think about that now.

You are being stupid, Nando castigated himself. *She's beautiful and that's simply reminded you that you haven't had a woman for much too long.*

Still Nando's eyes stole over to her again for just a second to absorb her smile as the dry earth absorbs the tiniest raindrop. Then he clapped a hand on Hugo's shoulder, meaning to pull him away from this place. But before he could say anything, a scrap of conversation from a nearby table floated over to him.

"The girl in blue over there. I've heard..."

Nando stood there as if he had taken root and did something he would have found despicable if he had been thinking clearly. He eavesdropped.

"That's Arabella Douglas, a family connection of the Castlereaghs. She must be a poor relation, for she has no title." The woman's voice held an assurance that indicated she had gone to some trouble to get her facts straight. "Yet."

"She's quite lovely," her male companion said, masking his enthusiasm with a slight cough.

The woman sniffed. "She's probably husband hunting. After all there are more unmarried, titled men in Vienna right now than in any European city."

"I've heard a rumor that she spends every morning in some orphanage," another female voice chimed in. "Can you imagine actually doing something like that *willingly?*"

"These English with their self-righteous ways," the first woman snorted. "If it is true, the chit probably thinks she can impress some well-meaning man with her charity." Her laugh was full and throaty with an undertone of malice. "Why should she be any better than the rest of us?"

The sound of the woman's laughter startled Nando into an awareness of what he was doing. He whirled around and cuffed Hugo on the shoulder again.

"Come on," he snapped. "We've been standing around here like idiots long enough. I need some exercise."

Nando slammed his barely tasted coffee down on the counter and stepped inside the café to deposit the coins he had fished from his pocket with the comely cashier, not bothering to even acknowledge her inviting smile. But once outside again, his steps slowed as if he had no will to control them.

The girl in the aquamarine bonnet looked beyond her companion's shoulder, and her gaze caught in his. Blue, he thought. But what an incredible shade of blue! Like the richest, darkest sapphires with a hidden fire that would change with the light. There was magic there. Magic that would insinuate itself into a man's blood and make him weak.

"Where to now, Nando?"

Hugo's voice brought him back to the sun-bathed terrace, and Nando remembered how much deceit beauty could conceal. And yet it cost him to tear his eyes away from the seductive blue depths.

"Anywhere," he rasped.

In deference to Jeanne, Arabella chose a table that was partially concealed from the walkway by a latticework screen and with a regal nod thanked the waiter who placed tall, iced glasses of almond milk in front of them. Slowly she began to remove her gloves finger by finger.

Alerted by an odd feeling she couldn't have described, Arabella raised her head and glimpsed the most remarkable eyes she had ever seen. Gray. But not a tame dove gray. No, these eyes were the vivid, hard gray of an ice storm. Then the ice seemed to melt a little and something entered those eyes. Not quite a smile, but something heated that touched Arabella deep inside where she had never been touched before, igniting a fire she had not known existed.

Then as suddenly as it had receded, the ice returned and Arabella watched the officer pivot around sharply and stride down the sanded path, his highly polished black Hessian boots below tight red breeches kicking up little clouds of dust. She watched him until he was out of sight, and all other thought fled from her mind.

Chapter Two

"Are you Arabella Douglas?"

The question sounded almost like a challenge, and Arabella excused herself with a polite murmur from a desultory conversation she was engaged in with a elderly gentleman.

"Yes, I am." Arabella turned to find herself facing a young woman with an elaborate coiffure of ash blond curls.

Arabella submitted to the open examination and indulged in her own, finding the young woman not unattractive in a long-nosed, aristocratic sort of way. "Well?" she asked after a short while. "Do I pass muster?"

"I think yes," the blonde said. Her mouth curved and the smile softened her features. "I'm Lulu Thürheim, and as you may have guessed, my bluntness is notorious."

"I'm pleased to meet you." Arabella had heard the name and knew that the three Thürheim sisters were well-known in Viennese society for their elegance and their forthright wit. "I find bluntness a very pleasant albeit seldom enough habit." Arabella could not repress a grin at Lulu von Thürheim's surprised look. "So if you tell me what your criteria are, perhaps I can help you decide whether I pass muster or not."

Lulu tilted her head to one side and tapped one high cheekbone with her fan. "I'd like to know if you are a fake."

Taken aback, Arabella's hand flew up to her chest. "Do you mean whether I really am Arabella Douglas or an impersonator?"

"No, there seems to be no question about your identity," Lulu continued with perfect equanimity as she flipped her fan open and fanned herself with languid elegance. "But elsewise opinion is divided. Are you truly such a Samaritan that you sacrifice your days for some filthy orphanage—" she shivered delicately "—or have you merely found an especially clever way of blowing your own horn and making the rest of us look like Philistines?"

Arabella felt the blood leave her face. "Do you mean people know about that?"

"My dear, there are more spies in Vienna than fleas in a dog's coat. Nothing, absolutely nothing, remains a secret for long." Lulu's pale brown eyes narrowed and rested assessingly on Arabella's face. "Were you planning on keeping this strange pastime of yours secret? Why, for heaven's sake?"

Arabella took a deep breath. "This pastime of mine is why I was sent off to Vienna in the first place."

Lulu motioned for her to continue.

"My father decided that my 'confounded good works' as he called them were keeping me from my duty of finding a suitable husband." Arabella shrugged. "So he cajoled Lady Castlereagh into taking me with her to Vienna, hoping that here someone will take me off his hands."

Lulu laughed. "I know the problem well. But now that I've reached the ripe old age of twenty-six, my father has become resigned to the idea that he will be paying my dressmaker's bills for the rest of his life. So now I'm generally left in peace to hone my tongue on all and sundry." She tucked her hand into Arabella's arm. "I think, Arabella Douglas, that we will get along famously."

They strolled off together toward the music room where someone was tinkling on the piano. Lulu seemed to know everyone and had something to say about each one of them.

Arabella followed Lulu's comments with a detached interest, but her attention began to wander. At the core of her restiveness was a memory of gray eyes. The memory that had stayed with her since that moment in the café several days ago. She found it a new and not very comfortable experience to have a man ceaselessly occupying her thoughts. But that moment when the ice in the blond officer's eyes had melted and the heat had touched her still lay curled within her like a living thing.

Every time Lulu pointed out some dashing officer in the dazzling white and scarlet uniform of the Austrian Army, Arabella snapped to attention and found herself searching his eyes to see if this was the one with the eyes of fire and ice.

Finally Lulu asked, "Are you looking for someone particular?"

Briefly Arabella considered a denial, but then settled for a half-truth and moved her shoulders in a shrug.

Lulu smiled. "Indeed? I shall wait for you then near the main ballroom in the Hofburg tomorrow." She squeezed Arabella's arm. "All the men wearing uniform will be unmasked."

Arabella felt a flutter of excitement as she entered the red and gold ballroom with the Castlereaghs.

The approaches to the Imperial palace had been so clogged by carriages that they had been forced to walk the last part of the way, preceded by two lackeys to clear a path for them with long sticks. Inside, the crush was even more intense. And when Arabella saw the doorman who took their invitations surreptitiously handing them on to someone else in exchange for some coins, she knew why.

She had already decided that Lulu von Thürheim would never find her in this incredible crowd when a tall, thin figure in a pink domino touched her arm.

Introductions were made, and the Castlereaghs seemed to be content to leave her in Lulu's care.

Despite the half masks that most of the ladies wore, Lulu seemed to recognize everyone worthy of note, and by the time the ball officially began with the ritual, stately polonaise, Arabella had entered into the spirit of Lulu's irreverent commentary.

The long line of dancers was led by Tsar Alexander and the Empress of Austria.

"An oddly matched couple," Lulu whispered.

They were oddly matched indeed, Arabella thought. The Tsar of all the Russias was tall, blond and going to fat, while the empress, whose dark head barely reached Alexander's elbow, was so emaciated that her heavily rouged cheeks looked quite grotesque.

"Do you think he's wearing a corset?" Arabella whispered, and they broke out in giggles, drawing disapproving looks from the other spectators.

The polonaise was interminable, so to pass the time until the general dancing would begin, Arabella and Lulu maneuvered their way through one glittering, overcrowded ballroom after another. When Lulu stopped to exchange a few words with someone, Arabella slipped into one of the smaller drawing rooms, grateful for the comparative coolness.

Shining black boots and a tantalizing flash of scarlet moved past her, and Arabella's head snapped upward. The broad-shouldered figure in a tunic of pristine white stopped in front of a window and Arabella went still. He turned to speak briefly to someone, affording her a glimpse of a chiseled profile. She held her breath without knowing that she held it.

When the air finally whistled softly through Arabella's parted lips, it stumbled along in a jagged rhythm. Unaware of her unnatural stillness, unaware of the tripping heartbeat that unsettled her breathing, she waited for him to turn around.

Suddenly, Arabella felt the pressure of Lulu's hand on her arm. Her eyes never leaving the figure at the window, she whispered, "Do you know him?" She was disregarding every tenet of propriety, but Arabella could not seem to make herself care.

Lulu smiled. "So he's the one. Yes, I know him. Shall I introduce you?"

Arabella disregarded the question. "His eyes. Are they gray?"

"Yes." Lulu gave her a shrewd glance.

Arabella's heartbeat tripped anew and clogged her throat, interfering with her breathing again.

"Perhaps it would be a kindness not to introduce you," Lulu murmured.

Arabella's eyes widened until the dark blue was only a narrow rim around huge black pupils. She knew her friend's words should make her apprehensive, but she was only afraid he would disappear before she could look into his eyes again.

"Nando has that effect on women," Lulu said with a smile that was older than her years. "Fortunately I was afflicted at a young age when one recovers easily."

Nando. For a moment Arabella silently tasted the name. "How long have you known him?"

"Forever. Our families own adjoining estates in Bohemia, and we all spent at least part of every summer there." Lulu smiled at a fond memory. "Nando broke his leg the summer he was twelve. Keeping him company while he convalesced was almost fatal to my young heart. I was eight." She laughed softly. "The quantity of charm he possessed even at that tender age was rather formidable."

Lulu glanced at her friend and gave her arm a little squeeze. "Are you all right?"

The touch brought Arabella back to the crowded drawing room. She was making a perfect fool of herself, she thought, and her chin lifted in defiance of her feelings. She did not care a whit for propriety, but she would be damned if she would act like a witless goose for the sake of one man's eyes, be they ever so beautiful.

* * *

Nando stood at the high window and stared out into the night, willing himself to block out his surroundings. They revolted him—the laughter, the chatter, the music, the air, heavy with the smell of too many candles and too much perfume.

He was tired. It was not the satisfying fatigue that comes after a day of hard riding. It was the exhaustive weariness that comes from too many days filled with tedious social obligations and too many nights of uneasy sleep, haunted by those incredible dark blue eyes, holding such sweet promises. Nando grimaced at the memory, reminding himself again to remember that such promises were never kept. That was a lesson he had learned the hard way a long time ago. And yet . . . Nando let his lids drop.

But his eyes flew open at the rustle of a velvet whisper behind him. Shifting to the side, he focused on the reflection in the window. The images were distorted in the uneven glass, but just a few steps behind him he could see two dominoes, two masked faces.

Nando narrowed his eyes, trying to make out their features. Then a corner of his mouth quirked in a smile. That bow mouth above the small, pointed chin could only belong to his old friend, Countess Lulu Thürheim. His eyes moved to her companion. Suddenly the weariness, the boredom were gone and a heady anticipation took their place as all his instincts came to life.

Lowering his arms from their crossed position, he spun smartly on his heel. Closing the gap with three long strides, Nando bowed over Lulu's hand with an exaggerated click of his heels. "My respects, Countess," he drawled.

Lulu swatted her fan against the high, stiff collar of Nando's white dress tunic. The mother-of-pearl sticks clattered against the gold braid and snagged in his hair, which was the color of dark honey. As he straightened, she flicked at a thick strand.

"What's this?" she demanded. "You look like a Jacobin with your hair long like that. Or have you been in the cavalry so long that you're growing a mane just like one of your horses?"

Nando grinned at her. "Don't you get impertinent with me. Remember I'm one of the few who know your real name."

Lulu wrinkled her nose at the reminder of her hated first name, Ludovika. She had taken her share of teasing about it from Nando and his brother. "Odious as always, I see." She shrugged. "Nando, may I introduce..."

But she stopped, seeing that her words were lost on her companions. She stepped back and surveyed them, but they were staring at each other so raptly that neither noticed her movement. With the barest touch of envy, Lulu watched the two for a minute then moved away.

There were the eyes she had been searching every face for. The gray that had been stormy in the afternoon sun had taken on a silvery sheen in the bright candlelight.

The heat was there just as she remembered it, warming her skin. Arabella wanted to protest his shameless scrutiny of her face, only half hidden by its white silk mask, knowing that he would see the eagerness, the agitation, everything that the rules decreed she should conceal under a smooth demeanor. But she made no attempt to dissemble. Yes, she even welcomed the gaze that roamed her skin with almost unbearable slowness. The gaze that was a caress in itself.

The warmth grew heady and began to spread languorously throughout her body, as if he had touched her. She lifted her chin in defiance of all the strange, new emotions that ran through her.

There were the eyes that had been haunting his sleep. The candles in the crystal chandelier above them were golden flickers in the sapphire depths that glowed with a warmth that precious gems could never have. By force of habit Nando wondered how much of the warmth was real, but he found himself brushing away the question as he discovered that he didn't really want an answer.

Nando let his gaze glide slowly over her face, absorbing the flushed dewiness of her skin. His fingers itched to tear the silky mask away, to touch the skin he was certain would feel like satin. Her lips were lightly parted in surprise, and when his gaze slid downward to rest in the hollow of her throat, he saw that a pulse was beating wildly, proclaiming her agitation. But she did nothing to hide it. On the contrary, her chin rose, allowing the bright candlelight from the chandelier to fall on her neck.

A tenderness arose in him, acknowledging the artless way she conceded her vulnerability, but he blinded himself to it. Perhaps she was young and not yet well schooled in the arts of seduction, Nando told himself. A pity that he was not in the market for innocence.

But then she smiled, and the radiance of her smile was like a bright shaft of sunlight blotting out the artificiality around them. He could not relinquish this moment. Not just yet.

Chapter Three

"My name is Arabella Douglas."

"I know." Nando stared into her eyes for a long moment before he remembered his manners and bent over her hand, his lips stopping the regulation inch above her gloved fingers. The white satin gloves carried the faint perfume of lily of the valley, and he found himself wondering if the rest of her would be fragrant with the same scent. Merely the thought made his body respond.

"You do?" Arabella forgot to remove her hand from his when he straightened. "How?"

"Someone at the café mentioned your name." Nando couldn't help but smile at the artless way her eyes grew round and dark with surprise, even as the sinister voice inside him denied the authenticity of her innocent expression.

"But how..."

Nando shrugged. "Vienna is like a big village. Everyone knows everyone else's business."

"I must be the exception then," Arabella concluded with a small sigh. "Not only do I not know your business, I don't even know your name."

"Didn't Lulu tell you?" Nando's eyebrows slanted upward.

"Yes—" Arabella smiled at him "—Nando."

Again, Nando found himself lost in the smile she gave so freely. He straightened, dragging his cloak of discipline around himself with some difficulty. "Ferdinand von Berg."

"Ah, Ferdinand. That sounds very stern and haughty." Arabella pursed her lips in a playful smile. "I hope no one ever calls you that."

Nando pushed away the memory of his father and the lectures and whippings that had come his way every time he had caught his father's eye. "No," he said. "Not any more."

Arabella saw the shadows come into his eyes and regretted her flippant words. Her hands curled with the desire to touch him and drive the shadows away. Instead she turned aside to look for Lulu, but there was no sign of her friend.

Shrugging, Arabella looked at Nando. "I imagine that Lulu simply became tired of waiting for us to stop staring at each other."

The simple statement took Nando by surprise, an emotion he was unable to conceal. Damn her, he thought. He hadn't expected this. He didn't know what he had expected, but it hadn't been this disarming straightforwardness, this—this innocence. For a moment his suspicious mind wondered just how she used that directness for her devious female ends. But then Arabella smiled at him, and he found himself holding his arm out to her, asking her for the next dance and feeling ridiculously pleased when she assented with a smile that held no apparent coquetry.

They danced one dance and it merged into the next and the next without needing question or answer. They did not speak at all, allowing this first encounter to be limited to discovery that was purely sensory. Discovery that teased their nerve endings with its very tenuousness.

The touch of gloved fingers. The brush of silk against wool. The faint scent of leather and tobacco. The innocently seductive fragrance of lily of the valley.

Arabella felt her blood heat. The pulse that throbbed at the base of her throat was multiplied tenfold, the cadence converging at a point deep within her, making her light-headed.

Nando's thought of what it would feel like to put his mouth on the fluttering skin of her neck made his body come to life.

And then there was her mouth—lush and moist and the color of sun-ripened raspberries with a smile so enchanting, so radiant that for one insane moment Nando felt that she was the sun and he was a planet created solely to revolve around her.

With a kind of desperation Nando called on every ounce of his self-control to temper the turbulence within him, telling himself he wanted neither the excitement nor the sweet enchantment she offered.

Arabella had been watching Nando, fascinated by the easy yet precise way in which he moved, his apparent discipline, his control, the way he looked at her with a smile that was maddeningly distant and rarely seemed to reach his silver eyes to warm them. Every little chink in the armor of restraint he had erected around himself was doubly interesting—the moment when she had felt his fingers above her waist spread and lower toward her hip; the way his eyes darkened and warmed when he let them rest on the traitorous pulse in her throat.

A blaze had licked at the ice in his gaze, but the ice had won. For now, she told herself, for now, certain with all the romantic idealism of her nineteen-year-old imagination that the warmth she would give him could melt the ice. All of it.

"Is something wrong?" she asked softly, seeing his frown.

"No." Nando smiled his cool smile, the armor safely in place again. "Should there be?"

Arabella shrugged and sent him a smile. "I don't know. You looked . . . discontented."

Nando absorbed her smile. There was something so sure, so confident in it that he wondered if Arabella was as in-

nocent as he had first thought after all. The thought sent a
new wave of heat through him.

"No, I'm not discontented." Nando's fingers closed
briefly over Arabella's, and he forgot that just a moment
ago he had denied wanting her. "I am well pleased."

They found themselves near a grove of potted orange trees
that had been set up in one of the ballrooms and Nando
drew Arabella away from the dance floor. He suddenly
wanted to hear her voice, to savor her smile away from the
distraction of her gracefully moving body.

"Are you enjoying Vienna?" he asked as they made their
way through the crowd toward the audience chamber where
a lavish buffet had been laid.

"Very much. I think it's a lovely city."

"Doesn't it bore you after the brilliance of London?"

Arabella looked up at him in surprise. "Brilliance?" For
her, London was a gray place where her days had been determined by a distant father and a beloved mother who lived
her life in some faraway region of her memories. It was in
Vienna that she had felt truly free for the first time in her
life. "I don't know about brilliance, but I find Vienna more
appealing."

Nando shook his head that anyone could find a city he
had experienced only as a nest of intrigue appealing.

"So tell me about yourself," Nando invited as they
walked on. "You have me at a disadvantage. I know nothing about you but your name, and I'll wager that Lulu filled
your ears with tales of my misspent life." Deliberately
Nando did not mention what else he had overheard in the
café about her and wondered how long it would take her to
vaunt her charitable activities.

"I'm afraid she was remiss." Arabella shook her head. "I
didn't even know your last name until you told me," she
reminded him. Then she sent him a mischievous smile. "But
I do know that you used to spend your summers in Bohe-

mia and that you broke your leg the summer you were twelve."

Nando gave her such a blank look that Arabella was almost tempted to go on and tell him what Lulu had said about his charm. She bit her lip and felt the warmth suffuse her face and neck at the thought.

"Do you still? Spend your summers in Bohemia, I mean." Arabella said the words a little too quickly, confused by the heat within her.

Nando wondered if her charming discomfiture was real or if she had long gathered all the pertinent information about him and was playing an especially clever game. But when he answered her, his voice was gentle and carried some of the sadness he felt for those long-gone, carefree summers. "Not for a long time, I'm afraid."

"What do you do? Except fight in wars and very valiantly, too, I see," Arabella asked, pointing her fan at the Cross of Maria Theresia, the highest Austrian medal of valor, that hung at the closure of his collar.

Nando frowned, thrusting away the memory of how he had earned that medal. How with six hundred men he had held off four thousand Frenchmen at the battle of Leipzig a year ago. But at what cost? What cost?

Arabella watched Nando's eyes darken and the lines around his mouth deepen with remembered pain and regretted her blithe words with a distress that was almost physical. He hated all this, she realized with a flash of insight. He hated the wars he had to fight. He hated the careless gaiety of this ball.

"I'm sorry," she whispered.

The pain in Nando's silver eyes gave way to puzzlement.

"I have reminded you of things you would prefer to forget."

Nando retreated from the sympathy in Arabella's eyes and said nothing.

They wound their way through the crowd in silence, unaware of the striking picture they presented, unaware of the many eyes and whispers that followed them.

"You don't look like all this appeals to you." Arabella made a circular gesture with her fan. "Why are you here?"

Nando stopped and half-turned toward Arabella. Again he was caught in the magic of her sapphire eyes, and he wondered if they had bewitched him.

"I was looking for you." The words slipped out of their own volition, taking him unawares. For a split second Nando hoped that he had only thought those revealing words, but the acknowledgment in Arabella's face told him otherwise. He knew he had spoken the truth and yet he felt betrayed, exposed as he braced himself for a flippant, flirtatious remark.

But there was no triumph in Arabella's voice or her eyes. Not even a smile. Only a deep, quiet understanding. "Yes," she said, "so was I. Ever since that afternoon in the café." And silently she added, *Perhaps I've been looking for you forever.*

Nando shook his head and his mouth curved in a rueful smile that for an instant was mirrored in his eyes. "Tell me, Arabella Douglas, are all Englishwomen so straightforward?"

Arabella's heart tripped against her ribs as she felt his half smile take its effect on her like a powerful drug. She feigned a lighthearted smile and dragged her gaze away from his face, feeling an urgent need to pull back from a situation that was getting out of her control.

"Is that an elegant way of telling me I've been indiscreet?" With a flick of her wrist Arabella flipped her fan open and moved it a shade too quickly as they moved on.

"Indiscreet?" Nando arched a dark blond eyebrow. "No. Frank is perhaps the better word."

"Yes," Arabella agreed, "I've always had a problem with lying."

"Then you will be hard put upon to maneuver properly on Vienna's slippery parquet." Nando's tone was dry. "The intrigues will devour you alive unless you fight them in kind."

He was mocking her now, she knew, but Arabella was grateful. Grateful that the intensity of the moment that had put her insides into a spin had dissipated.

"Is that what you do?" she demanded. "Fight them in kind?"

Nando smiled, admiring her quick wit. "I don't need to. I've taken myself out of the game."

"Well, I haven't joined the game yet." Arabella's chin tilted upward. "So I should manage very nicely."

There was a crowd near the foot of the staircase and Arabella saw that the group was clustered around a tall man with curly blond hair and overlarge gold epaulettes on his blue uniform tunic. As he turned in their direction, she recognized Tsar Alexander of Russia. He was laughing at a woman who hung on his arm, a petite blonde wearing a gauzy, almost transparent white gown instead of a domino. Suddenly a dark-haired man with an extravagantly curled mustache detached himself from the group and sauntered toward them.

He planted himself in their path and they would certainly have collided with him had not Nando yielded and stopped. The man did not step aside to let them pass, but remained there, so close that Arabella could distinguish the perfectly cut diamonds on the sunburst-shaped medal that glittered ostentatiously on his chest.

A broad hand came down on Nando's shoulder, and Arabella registered the flicker of dislike in Nando's eyes and around his mouth before it disappeared under an icily polite mask.

The dark-haired man wore the blue and white Russian uniform, but when he spoke, his French was flawless. "We meet again, Count Berg," he said with a joviality that somehow rang false. "You must introduce me to your companion. You always seem to have the good fortune of having the loveliest ladies on your arm." His black eyes glinted with excitement.

Arabella could feel the gathering tension in Nando's arm, just as she could feel the almost palpable animosity between the two men.

She hastened to speak before Nando could say anything. "You must respect the mask, *monsieur.*"

"Must I indeed?"

"Indeed."

"May I introduce myself then?"

"If you wish." Arabella's shrug was infinitesimal.

"Prince Nikita Volkonsky, aide-de-camp to his Imperial Majesty Tsar Alexander of all the Russias, at your service." He paused, as if waiting for his words to take effect, then asked slyly, "Will you tell me your name now?"

Arabella's smile took on a touch of impertinence. "No."

Of course, she knew of the prince. She even recognized him belatedly now that he had told her his name, for he had been Tsar Alexander's ambassador in London. She also knew that he had the reputation of a libertine. London had buzzed with gossip about him and his escapades.

"No? *Eh, bien,* then I shall have to waltz with you until your lovely head spins and you won't be able to keep a single secret from me." Without looking away from her face, he said, "You permit, Berg?"

Nando knew that he had no way of preventing Volkonsky from dancing with Arabella without causing a scene. "I permit, Volkonsky," he said tightly, "but only if the young lady permits as well."

Arabella had absolutely no wish to leave Nando's side, but she knew it would be poor manners to refuse a dance except for a very good reason. She bent her head in assent. "But only if you return me to Count Berg after one dance."

Volkonsky raised a dark eyebrow. "*Mon Dieu,* such constancy. You've made quite a conquest, Berg. Obviously I shall have my work cut out for me."

Arabella had barely slipped her hand from Nando's arm when Volkonsky summarily swept her up.

"Tell me, *belle dame masquée,* who are you?" Volkonsky demanded as soon as they reached the dance floor. He whirled her expertly.

"I won't tell you."

"Are you certain?" The pressure of the hand at her waist increased a little.

Arabella instinctively withdrew from the pressure. "Quite certain. A lady has the right to refuse a gentleman anything." She emphasized the word "gentleman" just enough to make it almost an insult. "At least where I come from."

Volkonsky threw back his attractive, dark head and laughed, his teeth very white in his swarthy face. "Then you must be English. Only an Englishwoman could be so abominably stubborn."

His hand moved toward the silk ties of her mask. "Have we perhaps met in London?"

Arabella was too quick for him, slapping his hand away with her fan. "This *pleasure* has been denied me until now," she snapped.

Volkonsky's obsidian eyes narrowed slightly even as anticipation deepened his smile. "The kitten has claws. All the better."

"Do not rejoice too early, prince."

"Will you take some refreshment with me?" he asked, all good manners once again when the waltz had ended.

"I've promised Count Berg, prince, and I remember my promises," Arabella said. "Do you remember yours?"

Volkonsky pulled his sensual lips from his teeth in a smile that could only be described as feral and bowed slightly. "Indeed, *mademoiselle,* I remember my promises very well."

* * *

Nando seethed as he watched Arabella and Volkonsky walk toward the dance floor, and his anger was not directed at Volkonsky alone. How had that chit of a girl managed to weave a spell around him so quickly? How had she gotten through his guard so easily?

"My, my, you don't look very pleased, my friend."

Nando turned his head and the sight of the smug smile on Lulu von Thürheim's face prompted him to bark, "Don't you dare to say a word." His movements were jerky as he turned away and folded his arms across his chest.

Lulu pursed her bow mouth and tapped her fan against her cheek, her unperturbed gaze resting on his face.

"Well, what is it?" he demanded. "You may as well say whatever you have to say, since I know you won't give me any peace until you do."

"I wish you wouldn't glower so, Nando. You have an audience."

Nando turned to look at her, and Lulu gestured with her eyes to the group at the foot of the staircase. The men were still talking animatedly among themselves, but the blond woman on Tsar Alexander's arm was staring in his direction, her nearsighted eyes narrowed in concentration, her soft full lips pressed together tightly.

Biting back an oath, Nando stared at Princess Katharina Bagration, knowing exactly the degree of malice that would be in her limpid aquamarine eyes. He had not seen her for a long time and he was gratified that her white and gold beauty had begun to look a little worn.

It confounded Nando that he had once had the poor taste to fall in love with the princess, whose transparent gauze gowns with their overgenerous décolletage had long ago earned her the sobriquet "the naked angel". But he had been young and naive and had believed the sweetly whispered promises. The pain she had caused him was long gone, but the mistrust of women she had sown in his heart eight years ago was still strong, although to be fair to Katharina,

Nando would have had to admit that other women had admirably reinforced that particular conviction.

Deliberately Nando turned away from her, giving no visible sign of recognition.

"Well, Lulu?" he prompted. "Aren't you going to tell me all about Miss Arabella Douglas?"

"Didn't you ask her? What happened to your glib tongue, my friend?" Lulu teased. "Or were you so busy looking at her that you forgot to use it?" she mocked gently.

Nando tightened his grip on his arms until he could feel the pressure of his fingers even through the wool of his tunic. The need in him was suddenly so sharp that he could taste it.

"Yes, I asked her," Nando answered tightly, "but she didn't tell me," he finished softly, as the realization struck him that despite all the openings he had given Arabella, she had not talked about herself at all.

"She has come to Vienna with Lord Castlereagh and his lady. Apparently her disinterest in London's bachelors has driven her father to despair and he sent her here hoping that she will find a husband in Vienna." Lulu grinned. "Perhaps *you* would like to call at the British delegation in St. Peter's Square tomorrow?"

Slowly Nando exhaled and looked at her. "I have no intention of calling at the British delegation or anyplace else for that matter. As you should know, my dear Lulu, I am not in the market for a wife." There was no room in his life for this, he told himself angrily. It would dominate him and make him weak. And he had sworn long ago that he would never let a woman make him weak again. Yet the need for this girl he had known but an hour was so basic, so vital that it took his breath away.

"Suit yourself, my friend," Lulu said with a little, secret smile, pleased that Arabella had managed to get under Nando's skin so thoroughly.

"So I shall."

* * *

Nando's face was an impassive, icy mask as Arabella approached on Volkonsky's arm. But then she saw the muscle twitch in his cheek and she knew that he was not as indifferent as he looked.

"It has been a highly instructive experience, prince." Arabella sent Volkonsky a patronizing little smile and turned to stand at Nando's side.

Volkonsky laughed and released her elbow with a lazy bow. "It would appear that you have the superior tactics, Count Berg. Austrian coolness seems to fare better than Russian fire." His full lips lifted in a sneer. "Sometimes."

"Indeed." Nando stiffened his back further and fought to keep his face expressionless.

The two men faced off, well remembering that they had stood like this before with a woman between them.

"A matter of compatibility, perhaps," Nando remarked with a tight smile. "The English, too, are known for their coolness."

Volkonsky's glance flickered over Arabella assessingly, taking in the flashing eyes, the flushed cheeks. "Not really a valid generalization, my dear Berg." He turned his black eyes toward Nando. "Just how vast is your experience with Englishwomen?"

Nando shifted away from Volkonsky, his body language involuntarily responding to the heavy-handed bait.

Arabella observed the two men, repulsed by the way they squared off like two barnyard roosters, yet somehow perversely fascinated and flattered. Suddenly she wanted to get away from both of them. They were dangerous to her peace of mind, each in his own way. And she wanted to punish them. Volkonsky for his impertinence. And Nando for fascinating her and making her so vulnerable.

Spotting Lulu, who stood a few steps away talking to the fat, charming Prince de Ligne, Arabella decided on a tactical retreat.

Imperiously, she looked from one man to the other. "I leave you to your little debate, *messieurs*. Don't bother letting me know who wins."

Flicking her domino with one hand to avoid brushing Volkonsky's white kidskin breeches, Arabella turned, wishing for all the world that she had eyes in the back of her head.

Chapter Four

A fool. He was a fool, Nando told himself, to stand here staring after Arabella, providing the gossips with grist for their mill, the informers with tidbits for the reports that Prince Metternich and his minister of police, Baron Hager, would read with their morning coffee. But there was an urgency in him that refused to be deprived of the pleasure of looking at her.

Nando watched Arabella slip into the conversation with the old prince with apparent ease. Then the old man nodded to him, and telling himself that it would be impolite not to pay his respects, Nando moved forward.

Pleasantries were exchanged, then someone hailed the prince. Suddenly Lulu, too, was gone, and Arabella and Nando found themselves alone once again.

Arabella knew she had been furious only a few moments ago, but the anger became a faint memory when she looked up into Nando's face and found amusement warming his eyes.

"That was very elegantly done, you know."

Arabella raked him with her very best haughty look. "Good. I've always wanted to make an elegant exit." But even as she spoke, the laughter was already bubbling up inside her. She raised a gloved hand to her mouth to smother it. To no avail.

As he listened to Arabella's uninhibited laughter, Nando caught himself on the verge of believing her easy charm. "I shall forgive you if you dance one more waltz with me," she promised between giggles.

"Forgive me? For what?" Long ingrained habit had Nando stiffening once more.

"For making me feel like a fool," Arabella retorted. "Or how do you think it felt to have you and that popinjay of a Russian prince squabbling over me?"

Nando hid his surprise and wondered what kind of woman she was not to enjoy being fought over. He decided that Arabella was lying, albeit charmingly, but nevertheless he offered her his arm.

They had just reached the dance floor when the music stopped. After a minute the orchestra played an extravagant flourish, then another. Midnight had arrived and with it the moment for the ladies to remove their masks. Laughter and chatter rose around them as many of the gentlemen reached for the ties to see whom they had been dancing with.

But Nando remained perfectly still and watched as Arabella very deliberately caught his gaze and, without moving her eyes from his, reached up and loosened the silken ties. Her gesture was smooth and sleek and sensuous, as if she were removing far more than a mask. The scrap of white dropped away.

Nando felt his breath catch in his throat. She was even lovelier than he remembered, and his eyes drank in her beauty as a man in the desert reaches out for water. He wanted her. He'd wanted her from the very first moment, and he had only begun to realize just how much.

"Well," Arabella demanded, impatient with Nando's silence, "aren't you going to ask to keep the mask as a favor?"

Nando's lips twitched, both at Arabella's words and at the way she bit her lower lip once she'd realized what she had said. "Do you want me to?"

Arabella looked at him. Any other man she would have
answered with a shrug and a light word. Any other man
would not have received the tactless, telling invitation at all.
"Yes," she whispered.

"May I?"

Nando reached for the mask and their fingers brushed
and, for a moment, held, sending a jolt of awareness
through their blood. But only Nando recognized the cur-
rent that flowed between them and felt the danger. While
Arabella would have lingered to taste more of the hot
sweetness she had never before encountered, Nando withdrew—abruptly, awkwardly, as if from a source of sudden
heat. Crushing the silk mask in his hand a bit more forcibly
than necessary, he stuffed it into the gold-braided cuff of his
tunic.

Accompanied by an enormous, bearded servant in a fur-
trimmed red cossack uniform, Prince Volkonsky called on
Arabella the next day. With an exaggerated bow, he handed
her an extravagant bouquet of exotic flowers that had no
fragrance.

"May I venture to hope that I did not cause you any distress last night, Miss Douglas," Volkonsky said, glibly
skirting an apology. Obeying the imperious flick of her
wrist, he sat down in the chair opposite her. His black eyes
seemed guileless in the early afternoon light, the tone genuine.

"You caused me no distress, Prince." Arabella allowed a
faint smile to touch her lips. "At best you brought embarrassment on yourself."

Volkonsky cringed as he remembered Princess Katharina
Bagration's mocking laughter after he had returned. "It was
your loveliness that made me lose my head, you know." He
leaned forward and lifted the hand that lay on an embroidered pillow to his lips.

Arabella listened politely to his effusive compliments and
allowed her thoughts to drift to Nando.

* * *

A look at the clock told Nando that he still had time before he had to leave for his interview with Chancellor Prince Metternich. He elbowed the window open and sat on the wide sill as he fiddled with the closure of the sleeves of his lawn shirt. The sound of a barrel organ drifted up to him from around the corner. The melody limped along, as if the organ grinder was letting his crank rest a moment before beginning each upward curve.

The tune reflected his state of mind perfectly, he thought, as he dug the heels of his hands into his eyes. Would he never be able to get that girl out of his head?

The picture Arabella had presented—her chin tilted up stubbornly, her sapphire eyes flashing—teased his memory, and Nando smiled despite his annoyance with himself. She had done a masterful job of reducing Volkonsky, and him as well, to the stature of small boys scuffling over a plaything.

Nando wondered if Miss Arabella Douglas realized what a stir she had created. He had watched Princess Katharina Bagration as she repeated the scene in her whispery, little-girl voice for the benefit of her coterie of tame followers. There had been not only maliciousness aimed at him and Volkonsky in her eyes and words, but a very basic jealousy of the younger, more beautiful Englishwoman.

A draft ruffled his hair as the door opened to admit his manservant. Nando turned his head toward him, but remained seated on the windowsill. "What do you think Prince Metternich wants from me, Franz?"

A stranger might have thought it an odd question for an aristocrat to ask his manservant, but Franz was hardly what one would describe as an ordinary domestic.

The two men had grown up together on the rambling Berg estates, and after Nando had once pulled the older boy out of an icy river, they had become inseparable. When old Count Berg had decreed that Nando take his dead brother's place in the army, Franz, who should never have been anything but a farmer, had chosen to enter the army as well, to serve his friend and master as an orderly. He had long since returned the favor Nando had done him.

"A diplomatic mission perhaps, my lord."

Nando snorted.

"The prince is not well liked by the Austrian nobility. Perhaps he needs your help."

Nando's eyebrows rose quizzically. "My help? Why should he? Metternich rules the emperor, and the emperor rules the rest of us. What more can he need? Besides, why would he ask help of me, of all men?"

Franz lifted a broad, fleshy shoulder in a shrug. Even after eight years he well remembered the look on his master's face when he had returned from Princess Bagration's apartments, a much older and much wiser man. Helpless, he had watched the young count drink himself into oblivion that night, heard his stumbling words as Nando talked the pain from his soul. The pain of finding the woman he loved with all the passion of his twenty-two years in the arms of the dapper diplomat Metternich.

"I am but a peasant. Who am I to understand a diplomat whose brain surely has more twists than a mountain stream?"

Nando grinned at Franz's analogy and stood up, reaching for the tunic that Franz held. "Yes," he agreed. "That and the clarity of a cesspool."

Outside the air was mild, with none of the chill wind that often blew down from the mountains at this time of the year. Needing to walk, Nando dismissed the carriage.

Although he would have denied it, the unrest, the unfulfilled needs still churned within him. The same unrest, the same needs that had driven him out into the cool October night yesterday.

But the night air had done nothing to cool the heat of his blood. Nor had the willing body of the young widow whose apartment he occasionally frequented slaked the desire edged in anger that whipped through him. Back in the street a scant hour later, Nando had known that the turmoil in his blood had not been stilled. The physical release had done nothing to allay the sharp need within him.

If he had been honest with himself, Nando would have admitted that this need had little to do with the desire he felt. It was Arabella's innocence, her simplicity that he coveted, even though it was their very existence that he denied so vehemently.

The desire still raged inside him today, though its contours had blurred a bit in the warmth of a sunny afternoon. Shaking his head at his own folly, Nando quickened his step.

Prince Clemens Metternich rose from behind the large desk and advanced to greet his visitor.

"It is most kind of you to come and see me on such short notice, Count Berg. I thank you." The chancellor's speech still carried the razor-sharp vowels and clipped tone of his native Germany.

Nando murmured some meaningless courteous phrase and assessed the diplomat with a steely stare. The fine-boned, aristocratic face had a few more lines than it had had eight years earlier, but nothing else had changed—from the elegant head with its short, lightly powdered curls to the snowy white cravat at his neck. From the graceful movements that stopped just short of being effeminate to the pale eyes of indeterminate color that revealed only what Metternich wanted the world to see.

He led Nando to an artfully arranged group of exquisitely upholstered chairs. Nando scorned the chair Metternich offered him, recognizing that if he sat there, he would have the afternoon sun that poured through the high windows directly in his eyes.

"What did you want to see me about?" Nando demanded.

A smile touched Metternich's thin lips. "You believe in going straight to the point, I see."

"I'm a plain man, prince. Unlike so many others, I have never had a taste for equivocation."

The words were said blandly, but Metternich was a keen judge of men, and he heard the animosity under the simple aloofness. Just as he heard the steel beneath that deceptively soft Austrian idiom he had never quite been able to master.

Metternich made a steeple of his fingers and tapped the tips of his forefingers against his chin. This would not be easy, he mused. He had expected hostility, but he had hoped the years had taken the edge off the younger man's antagonism. Too bad. His plans had no room for personal considerations.

"Yes, as you have said, you are a plain man. Perhaps you are therefore unaware of certain exigencies of diplomacy. Especially in such difficult times," Metternich added. He would have given a great deal not to have to resort to this, but he had no choice. The English were being so damnably clever, and all the reports he had received about last night's ball seemed to indicate that this opportunity was simply too good to allow it to slip by.

Nando said nothing. Leaning back in his chair, he forced his muscles to relax, schooling his features to polite disinterest, even as his mind worked to divine what this serpent wanted from him.

"It is in the interest of His Majesty the Emperor and of our country that we act expediently. That we be well prepared to do so at all times." The chancellor paused to let what he had said sink in. "To achieve this we need as much information as possible."

With supreme willpower Nando pressed his shoulders against the chair when he wanted to spring up and disarrange the carefully smooth facade before him with a few well-placed cuffs.

"In this endeavor we need your help," Metternich went on, slickly including himself in the inner circle of emperor and fatherland.

Nando willed himself to keep silent. He saw through the game now. He knew that both Metternich and Baron Hager had intricate nets of informants in all walks of life and now they apparently wanted him to join their ranks. Grimly Nando fought down the bile that rose in his throat at the mere thought that Metternich believed him capable of being an informer. But he would wait, Nando told himself. He would let the snake squirm a little longer before he cut him off the hook with an appropriately caustic word.

Metternich cleared his throat and waited.

The silence stretched and became deafening. With every passing second, Nando relaxed a bit more in the assurance of the discomfort of the man opposite him.

"Eh bien," Metternich finally said, "I see I shall have to be blunt. We need certain information that we believe only you can obtain for us."

Nando's stomach muscles tightened, but he invited the diplomat to proceed with a lift of his brows.

"You were observed last night, my dear count, with a lady who may possibly be able to supply us with information we need urgently. Perhaps all that will be necessary is a little—" his thin lips curved slightly and the heavy lids hooded his colorless eyes "—subtle persuasion from you."

Nando's eyes narrowed. He couldn't possibly mean...

"Our attempts to penetrate the English delegation have been singularly unsuccessful. Perhaps with your help..." Metternich finished the sentence with an elegant wave of his hand.

Suddenly the discipline and control were gone. The rage Nando felt welling up in him would be mirrored in his face, he knew, but he cared not. Rage that this excuse for a man dared to reach for Arabella, who was young and innocent and needed protection. Nando didn't stop to remember that he didn't believe in innocence. But the moment passed so quickly and was swallowed up in such an explosion that he would never be able to remember the sequence or the nature of his emotions.

"How dare you?" Nando stood and tensed all his muscles to keep his hands at his sides. He would have given a great deal to look at those pale eyes over a pistol at twenty paces.

Metternich rose as well. "I have asked for nothing dishonorable, count."

"Only that I seduce an innocent to get you your bloody information." Nando spat out the last word.

"In service for the same country you wear that uniform into battle for," the prince returned smoothly.

Nando fixed his gray eyes on the smaller man for a long, long moment. "At least on the battlefield the lines are drawn clearly."

"I regret, count, but there are no clear lines on the battlefield of diplomacy."

"No, I don't suppose there are. The world is a chessboard for you, and no sacrifice is too large to secure a victory."

"Indeed, Count Berg." Metternich executed a curt little bow in acknowledgment. "Preventing a checkmate of one's king is all that counts in the end."

"Indeed, Prince Metternich," Nando mimicked. "If that is the case, then perhaps you should enlist the help of the Duchess of Sagan. I hear that Lord Charles Stewart and Sir Frederic Lamb, who certainly should have access to more information than Miss Arabella Douglas, both spend an inordinate amount of time at the Palm Palace."

A quickly controlled flicker in the diplomat's light eyes at the mention of his wayward mistress was all the reward Nando got, but it was enough. Without further ceremony, he whirled to leave the room.

Nando's hand was on the elaborate brass door handle when Metternich's voice stopped him.

"It's a pity that you choose not to take such a pleasant assignment, Count Berg. Someone else will garner the rewards you spurn."

Nando felt his heart pound against his ribs as he turned, but he had himself under control and his tone was mild. "I advise you strongly, prince, to change your plans."

"Are you threatening me?" Metternich bristled.

"Threaten?" Nando dismissed the word with an elegantly casual movement of his hand. "Advice, prince. Merely some well-meant advice."

"And I have a piece of advice for you, my dear Count Berg." Metternich's fingers toyed with a jewel-encrusted letter opener shaped like a small Florentine dagger, but his colorless eyes did not veer from Nando's. "You are a hero of the wars, so your lacking sense of duty to the interests of the Crown in this case might be forgiven. But do not obstruct those who serve unquestioningly."

"I have always allowed my conscience to be the ultimate judge in all matters, Prince Metternich. I do not expect to change my ways now." Nando stared at the smaller man across the sun-filled room before he turned and closed the door softly behind him.

Much later, when the sun had long set, Nando dismounted in the courtyard of the Berg Palace. He had ridden like a madman for hours to get the foul taste of the interview with Metternich out of his mouth, and the arousing images of Arabella out of his mind.

But his blood still ran hot in his veins and the need for Arabella Douglas still burned.

Chapter Five

The days were visibly shortening as October entered its second half, but on sunny days the afternoon air held a seductive mildness all the sweeter because the first frost lurked just beneath the surface every time the sun went down.

Arabella sprinkled sand on a letter to her mother, displeased that she dared to write only about trivialities like the festivities she and the Castlereaghs had attended and their move from their cramped quarters to the luxurious Dietrichstein Palace on the Minoriten Square. It troubled her that she could not share what was most important to her—her work at the orphanage and Count Ferdinand Berg.

Propping her chin in the palm of her hand, she frowned as she followed the dance of the dust motes on a sunbeam. Since the ball at the Hofburg, Arabella had seen Nando only from afar. He had not called on her. Nor had he sent flowers. He hadn't approached her to exchange a few words or to ask for a dance. In fact he acted as if the magical moments they had spent together had never been.

At first Arabella had believed that she had offended him at the ball and that he possessed more masculine pride than Volkonsky. Then she had sadly come to the conclusion that he was not interested. But as time went by she had begun to realize that Nando was far from indifferent to her, and that she found even more disquieting.

He watched her. Again and again she had seen him follow her with his eyes across a crowded room. And he watched the men she spoke and danced with just as carefully. Once—just once—their eyes had met when she happened to turn aside from the pleasantries she had been exchanging with Prince Nikita Volkonsky. A fire had burned in those stormy depths, and it had taken Nando a long moment to put the screen of ice up again. But still he made no move toward her and the unfulfilled expectation was slowly driving Arabella insane.

"The courier is waiting downstairs. Are your letters ready, Arabella?"

She turned to face Jeanne and ignoring the question asked, "Have you ever wished you were a man, Jeanne?"

"A man? *Quelle idée!*" Jeanne shook her head. "But you used to say that all the time when you were small. Before your father sent you away to your grandmother's for the first time."

A smile touched Arabella's mouth as the memory surfaced. Yes, she remembered that first stay in Surrey when she had learned that being a girl need not prevent her from doing amusing things such as romping with the stable boys or climbing trees. She had made a promise to herself then never to let her sex keep her from doing anything she wanted.

Arabella lowered her eyelids against Jeanne's sharp gaze and compressed her lips to hide the smile that bloomed as the idea took shape within her. There was no reason that being a woman should prevent her from pursuing what she wanted, she told herself with aplomb. And she wanted Court Ferdinand Berg.

Lulu glanced at Arabella. "I take it that Nando still hasn't spoken to you."

"Mmm."

"My God, but that man is stubborn." Lulu sighed and rolled her eyes heavenward. "He watches you like a hawk, you know. You and every man you exchange more than two words with."

"I know." A thin line formed between her black eyebrows. "And I am about to do something about it."

For a few moments the only sounds in the room were the gentle gurgle of tea being poured and the musical chink of silver against fine Viennese china.

"Well?" Lulu prodded.

Their eyes met over the gold rims of their teacups and Lulu detected the mischievous but determined twinkle in the eyes of the young Englishwoman. Would Nando's bitterness be able to withstand this girl's incredible gusto for life? For his sake, she hoped not.

"You wouldn't happen to know if he rides regularly, would you?"

Lulu grinned. "I think midmorning is a safe assumption."

Both women laughed and Arabella leaned forward to clasp Lulu's hand. "Am I being very outrageous?"

"Marvelously so. Extreme problems call for extreme solutions."

Arabella laughed aloud with relief that the waiting was over and reached for a chocolate pastry.

Lulu watched Arabella bite into the pastry with such pleasure that she was reminded of a sleek black cat licking a bowl of cream. Even though she had always preferred portraying life in her pastel watercolors or her diary to participating, Lulu felt a touch of envy. Being an observer of life would never be enough for this vibrant creature, she thought. Arabella wanted to taste it firsthand. All of it.

Never one to postpone action once she had reached a decision, the next morning Arabella was on the steps of the church of St. Anna, which stood diagonally across from the Berg Palace. She slipped inside the door, not wanting to loiter on the narrow street in view of the doorman in the green and white Berg livery. A shiver traveled down her spine as the chill, damp air from the old stones and the scent of incense and wax enveloped her, and it occurred to her that she was terrified. She couldn't remember anything ever mattering quite as much. Perhaps it never had.

Her fingers worried the drawstrings of her reticule as she waited for the huge oaken doors of the palace to move.

It was a discreet palace as Viennese palaces went. Its plain front of pale yellow plaster held no statues, no fantasy figures, no baroque ornaments. Only the elegantly simple stucco decorations above the tall windows relieved its classical severity. Arabella smiled in approval. She found that the lack of frivolity fit Count Ferdinand Berg very well.

Just as the bell above her marked the quarter hour, she heard the clank of an iron bolt followed by the creaking of the heavy doors across the way. Arabella moved down the shallow steps, stopping before she reached the cobblestones.

Sultan was just as anxious for a gallop as he was, Nando thought. The familiar warmth of horseflesh between his thighs, the animal's barely tamed energy, the pleasantly pungent smell—all soothed his abraded nerves. Lately it seemed that only the hours he spent astride Sultan lessened the tension that had taken up permanent residence within him. Tension created by the vision of Arabella Douglas that was branded into his brain.

He raised his face a little toward the cool wind that swept between the houses. The movement of something blue to his right caught his peripheral vision, and Nando straightened and turned his head.

Arabella stood straight and perfectly still on the church steps, the wind ruffling her blue cape. Their eyes met and held, but neither of them moved.

Nando felt the warmth of something resembling relief course through his veins. The easing of the expectant tension when the waiting is over and the battle begun. But the moment of abatement was brief and the excitement, the danger began to pound within him.

There were no smiles, no acknowledgment. It was as if they had both reached a decision to bypass all the prerequisite social gestures. But they knew. They both knew.

The stallion grew impatient and Nando gentled him with his hand. With a calmness he did not feel, Nando nudged his mount toward the church steps.

Arabella watched him approach. The fire had melted the ice in his eyes, but there was no smile, no welcome, no tenderness on his face. Yet she felt a fierce pleasure blaze to life deep within her as Nando came closer and she wondered if it burned within him, too.

Looking down at her fingers, which had twisted the drawstrings of her reticule into a braid, Arabella opened her hands palm upward. The interlaced cords lay across her hands like an offering. "This is your fault. I was terrified that you would ignore me."

Nando could not resist the artlessness of Arabella's gesture, the candor of her smile. He slid his large two-cornered black hat from his head and tucked it under his arm. "Like I've been ignoring you for the past weeks?" The beginnings of a self-deprecating smile lurked at one corner of his well-shaped mouth.

Arabella inclined her head.

"But I haven't been ignoring you." Nando paused and narrowed his eyes. "And well you know it."

"Yes, I know," Arabella admitted. "But I don't know why."

Nando ignored her implicit question. "What are you doing here?" he demanded.

She had prepared a little speech, but it seemed deceitful to speak anything but what she truly felt. "I . . ."

"Yes?" Nando prompted with unexpected gentleness.

"I was going to ask you if I could ride one of your horses, but that was only an excuse." Arabella let the pent-up air out of her lungs. "But what I really wanted was to see you.

To ask you why you've been avoiding me." She returned to the question he had not answered.

Nando shook his head, bemused at her openness. "Hasn't Lulu warned you about me?"

She nodded, at the same time tilting her chin upward.

Nando saw the devil in her eyes, the youthful fearlessness, and all the reasons he should cast Arabella out of his life before she could become a part of it emerged with perfect clarity in his brain. He knew that he had nothing to offer her. Nothing but pain. The brief pleasure they could give each other would count for little in the long run.

"I have nothing to give you, Arabella."

The bleakness in Nando's eyes took away some of the joy, some of the certainty Arabella felt. But still hope remained.

"Not even a horseback ride?" she asked gently.

Arabella's eyes were so clear, her smile so genuine. Nando wanted that impulsiveness, that eagerness as he had not wanted anything for a very long time. A taste, he bargained with himself, just a taste.

"Would you care to keep me company when I ride tomorrow?" Nando capitulated and finally the lines around his eyes crinkled in a real smile.

"Yes," she said softly. Then Arabella grinned impishly. "But only if we really ride, not just a tame, civilized trot along the main path of the Prater."

Nando looked at Arabella, wondering if she was aware of the vitality, the promise of sensual delight that she radiated. Suddenly an unreasoning jealousy shot through him. Jealousy of all the men who had sunned themselves in her glow during the past weeks while he had shut himself out in the cold.

"You should be careful about what you wish for." Nando's tone was surly, as if he were already regretting his invitation. "You just might get it."

"I never wish for anything I don't want."

Her lighthearted laugh caught Nando by surprise and he resisted its charm. "Just what is it that you want?"

Arabella went very still. She should say something witty now, she thought. Something light and coquettish. But the words would not form on her tongue.

"Don't you know?" Arabella asked softly and her eyes roamed Nando's face with its eyes that were a shade too hard, its mouth that was a shade too sensitive.

Then her laugh chimed again, and Arabella danced down the remaining steps, but instead of turning aside to trace her way to the ramparts, she stopped and turned her face up toward him.

"Tomorrow?" she whispered, suddenly afraid that Nando had been only teasing her.

Relentlessly he pushed back the joy that threatened to surface and nodded curtly. "Tomorrow."

Arabella turned and skipped away, remembering only after a while to slow down to a more ladylike pace.

Sultan seemed to sense his master's need for a quiet moment, for he stood uncharacteristically still as Nando watched Arabella make her way down the narrow street. Just as she turned the corner, a dark-clothed figure slid out of a doorway.

Nando stiffened, and his instinctive movement had Sultan prancing again on the cobblestones. The dark figure cast a furtive glance over his shoulder at the sound and quickened his pace.

"Damn the swine." Nando wished he could spit out the vile taste that suddenly appeared in his mouth. "Damn Metternich." He had been watching Arabella so carefully during the past weeks, afraid that Metternich would follow through with his threat and send another would-be seducer after her. But he had not expected this kind of stealth. For a moment Nando wondered if his imagination and his hatred for Metternich were running away with him.

"Damn it," he swore again, and this time his anger turned toward Arabella. He hated this feeling of protectiveness. He hated feeling that he was responsible for her innocence and her safety, for they made him vulnerable. And that did not sit well at all with Ferdinand von Berg.

Arabella and Nando exchanged no more than a few polite words as they rode sedately to the nearest city gate that opened onto the Glacis, which stretched for almost half a mile between the walls of the inner city and the outlying districts. It was crisscrossed with tree-lined paths, and its extensive meadows were used as a playground by Viennese children and as a drill ground by the army.

"Shall we ride here?" Nando asked.

Arabella eyed the well-cared for, sanded paths with the leisurely moving carriages and riders without great enthusiasm. A fast trot would be the most to hope for here, and she wanted so badly to urge her horse into a gallop that she could already taste the wind on her lips.

"I thought you promised me something less tame and civilized." Arabella tipped her head to the side as she looked at Nando.

"I didn't promise. You demanded," Nando reminded her dryly, doing his best to ignore the ebullience in her eyes that reached out to him.

"Well?"

"I suppose we could ride by the river," Nando found himself saying much against his better judgment. He frowned and shook his head. "I don't think that the Castlereaghs would approve, though."

"Why on earth not?" Arabella bristled.

"It's primitive riding at best," Nando hedged. "No paths, marshy, overgrown."

"Are you questioning my equestrian ability?" Arabella asked as she lifted her eyebrows just a shade.

"It is not a socially acceptable place for a young lady of unblemished reputation to go riding." Nando shifted a little in his saddle. "Especially if she is unchaperoned."

"Ah." Arabella grinned. "That sounded very toplofty, you know." She leaned over and patted his sleeve lightly. "But don't worry overmuch, I don't suppose you're too old to learn better."

He could not restrain a smile. Even as the words had left his mouth, Nando had known that he sounded like a pompous ass. "You really are an impertinent miss, you know?"

Arabella pressed a hand to her chest in mock outrage. "How can you say that, sir? I've been the very model of decorum." Arabella tapped a slender finger against her cheek. "In fact if I don't do something about that, I shall probably go into a terminal decline."

"We wouldn't want to have that, would we?" Nando said, realizing that he was beginning to relax and enjoy her cheeky banter.

Suddenly Arabella was serious. "Are you vexed that I've maneuvered you into riding with me?"

"No, I'm not vexed," Nando said and found to his surprise that he meant it. "If you knew me better, you would know that I am well past the age of doing what women want me to do if it doesn't correspond with my own inclinations," he added, his tone harsh.

Arabella did not shrink from his rough tone and pressed on. "Then why…"

"Shall we ride?" Nando interrupted her unchivalrously. He had no intention of trying to answer the question he knew Arabella was going to ask. How could he ever explain why he had avoided her for so long?

Simultaneously they turned their mounts to the left and set off toward the river. Riding in companionable silence along the outside curve of the ramparts, each was satisfied for the moment to watch the other.

Arabella felt the breeze pick up as they crossed the river, and she lifted her face toward it. She longed to tear off her bonnet and let the wind blow the pins out of her hair.

In a surge of high spirits, she tapped the horse's flank with her crop and laughed aloud with pleasure as it lunged forward. The gallop was short, since Arabella soon reached the edge of the marshy forest that bordered the river, but her face was flushed with her enjoyment of the speed. She had almost forgotten how marvelous it felt to have the wind in her face. She reined in the frisky horse and turned.

"Just what do you think you're doing?" Nando demanded angrily when he reached her a few seconds later.

"Overtaking your snail's pace." Arabella made a face. "Wasn't it obvious?"

"Damn it, I thought your horse had bolted." Nando tried to crush the memory of the sharp taste of fear that had been in his mouth when Arabella's horse had surged ahead of him.

"I'm sorry," she said repentantly. "I didn't mean to startle you."

The openness of Arabella's dark blue eyes touched something in him, and Nando's taut muscles relaxed against the finely tooled Spanish leather of his saddle. "And I apologize for doubting your equestrian ability." He let his smile reach his eyes.

She let Nando lead the way, and soon they found themselves in a wonderful, junglelike world. It seemed unbelievable that they were just a short ride away from the cultivated paths of the Upper Prater. Lianas and garlands of moss hung from the trees, and the chirping and chattering of birds and waterfowl filled the air, which was humid and aromatic with the smells of the river.

At first their pace was slow to allow Arabella to look her fill at her surroundings. They stopped for a moment in a small clearing that opened onto the water, so close that the skirt of Arabella's riding habit brushed Nando's boots. One of the horses whinnied, and the sound sent several wild swans into flight.

"Oh, look. Isn't that lovely?" Arabella exclaimed, instinctively putting her hand on Nando's arm to share the moment with him. "Thank you for bringing me here." She craned her neck to follow the flight of the swans, not looking at Nando as she spoke, but her hand remained on his arm.

"You're welcome," Nando said gruffly, trying to deny the tenderness her childlike enthusiasm had tapped. A tenderness he had believed long dead. A tenderness he did not want to feel.

"Are you ready for the gallop you wanted?" Nando's voice was testy, as his anxiousness to escape the moment grew.

"Oh, yes."

"Well then . . ." Nando moved his stallion away from her to give both horses enough room.

"Just a minute," Arabella called out.

"What is it?"

But instead of answering, Arabella reached upward, loosened the ties of her bonnet to let it flop on her back and removed pins and ribbon from her topknot of curls, letting her hair cascade down her back. She'd never be able to redo it herself properly, but right now it was not something she could make herself care about.

"Well, what are you waiting for?" she called out with a laugh.

For a moment Nando stared at her, wondering if she was real or if she was a forest sprite. The sun found bluish highlights in her shiny black hair, which was already curling into a mass of fine ringlets in the humid air. Would it feel like silk if he buried his hands in it? Nando swore under his breath and wheeled Sultan around, touching his spurs to the horse's flanks.

The river lapped at the shore, and the afternoon sounds of a marsh forest and its inhabitants were all around them. It was a serene symphony that should have been soothing, but instead it served to accent the tension that was strung between them—so intense that it was almost palpable.

Arabella tried to concentrate on filling her lungs with an adequate quantity of air as they sat side by side on a log close enough to the river to be able to observe a group of ducks diving for their dinner. The exhilaration she felt was more than just the pleasure a gallop always brought to her blood. There was a sharp, expectant thrill that Arabella had never felt before, and it was this that was keeping her breathing so ragged.

A tuft of spiky marsh grass just beyond Nando's black boots seemed to be holding his attention, and Arabella took advantage of his apparent absorption to observe him. A long, slightly jagged scar marked the side of his face from temple to jaw. It was an old scar that the years had made pale and flat, but Arabella wanted to touch it, to give Nando comfort for pain long past.

Nando felt Arabella's eyes on his face, scorching his skin like coals. Suddenly her fingers were on the long-healed scar on the side of his face, and he went completely still. It occurred to him that he was doing exactly what a defenseless animal in the wild would do. He was playing dead.

"I'm sorry. Was it very long ago?" Arabella asked so softly that the words were almost carried away by the breeze.

"Austerlitz, nine years come December." His voice was curt, but Arabella's fingers didn't move and Nando found himself continuing. "It was my very first battle and although I held an officer's rank, I was greener than the greenest recruit." He couldn't control a shiver at the memory. "It was cold. So very cold."

Arabella almost cried out at the thought of Nando lying on the winter ground. Bleeding. Afraid. Wanting to comfort him for that long-past pain, she cupped her hand to his face.

Sharply Nando moved away and gripped Arabella's wrist so roughly that she made a small sound. "What do you think you're doing?" he demanded.

Arabella wanted to tell Nando that it was only compassion that she was offering. That all she wanted to take from him was his pain and bitterness. But no words came to her lips. She shook her head helplessly.

"You fool." Nando dragged air into his starved lungs. "You little fool." The fragrance of lily of the valley and warm, damp skin swirled around him. The satin skin where his fingers still held her wrist beckoned.

The anger in Nando's face faded as he fell into Arabella's sapphire gaze. God, there was so much warmth in those dark blue depths. Warmth enough to cancel out all the years of chill and indifference. All the pain and the memories that came to haunt him in the night. And he found himself wanting that warmth so desperately.

Arabella saw the anger give way. The familiar fire that touched off an answering flame inside her was there, but it was underscored by an anguish that cut into her like a knife. With her free hand Arabella gently pried Nando's fingers from her wrist, and when they fell away, she raised both her hands and framed his face with them, willing him to take from her whatever solace he craved.

Nando stilled under her touch. For a moment it seemed that he had ceased to breathe. But then he moved. Bending toward Arabella, reaching for her, pulling her to him, his mouth rough on hers.

For a moment his violence shocked Arabella into stillness, but then the flame he had sparked took over. Her hand slid from his face into his hair and her lips parted under Nando's voraciousness, giving even before he could take.

His tongue seduced with a ruthless expertise, but Arabella wanted no part of one-sided seduction. Her hands twisted greedily in his hair. As her mouth began to make demands of its own, she made a small sound deep in her throat. A sound of pleasure, of welcome.

The soft moan penetrated some still-rational portion of Nando's brain, and thinking that he had hurt her, frightened her, he pulled away. But Arabella's hands tightened in his hair. For a moment they remained like this, forehead against forehead, mouth near mouth, their rapid breath mingling.

"Don't go, Nando. Please."

Arabella felt Nando stiffen, but he did not push her away. She raised her mouth a fraction and wondered at her own temerity as she touched the tip of her tongue to his lower lip. Her hands absorbed the shudder that ran through him, and the way Nando's fingers tightened on her shoulders gave her a sense of her own power.

"Do you know what you're doing?" Nando rasped.

"Yes." Arabella's mouth curved against his. "I'm asking you to kiss me again."

Nando held Arabella away from him and gazed down into her face. He looked for selfishness, but saw generosity. He looked for wantonness, but saw innocent desire on the threshold of blossoming.

Slowly his mouth descended. This time Nando schooled himself to control and explored Arabella's lips with a gentle tongue. Sweet. She tasted so sweet.

She opened instinctively for his kiss, but Nando did not respond to her invitation. Instead his mouth wandered away from the lips to taste its way up her jaw, to nibble at the sensitive skin just below her ear.

The sensations Nando's mouth was creating were exquisite, and Arabella bit her lip to keep herself from crying out at the sheer pleasure of it, but it was his mouth on hers that she wanted. She wanted to taste his mouth again with its faint trace of coffee and tobacco. Arabella's hand tightened in Nando's hair and pulled gently to urge him back to where she needed him most.

This time Nando gave in to the temptation of entering her sweetness. Slowly he sampled the soft, inner part of Arabella's lips before sliding beyond her teeth to probe farther. Her tongue did not recoil from the touch of his, and pressing his advantage, Nando curled around her with ever intensifying pressure.

Arabella gave herself up to the kiss, her last lucid thought that perhaps she was dreaming. She was in a world where only sensation existed. Her fingers twisted in the rough silk of his hair. His scent was suddenly the only scent in the world. His taste the only taste. The whole surface of her skin was tingling and deep inside her body an ache had begun to throb, spreading a dangerous languor to her limbs.

Her tongue began to return Nando's pressure, and soon all gentleness, all tentativeness were gone as they dueled in a spiraling whirl of pleasure.

Nando's hand slid downward and the encounter with the luxurious curve of Arabella's breast jolted him out of the sensual euphoria where he had lost himself. Realizing what he was doing, how far he had allowed himself to go, he dragged his mouth away from the sweetness. Forcing himself out of the sea of sensation where he was drowning, Nando opened his eyes.

Arabella lay in the curve of his arm, her lips parted, her skin flushed, her breathing shallow and rapid. Nando passed his tongue over his lips. Her taste was still there. The sweetness that was like no other. He watched her as she lifted her lids, and the slumberous heat in her dark eyes caused a further tightening of his already aroused body.

No virgin could possibly react with such intensity, such license, Nando thought. He almost welcomed the icy feeling that closed around his heart, effacing the tenderness. But his blood still ran hot. Arabella was just like all the others, and he would take her, he told himself. He would take her and purge himself, after all.

Arabella saw his eyes turn from molten silver to ice, and a quiver took the place of the sensual tingles along her spine. She had been honest and once again it was going to cost her.

Nando shifted Arabella upright, his touch insulting in its sudden casualness, its superficiality. His eyes slid beyond her to some distant point.

No! The silent cry rose within her. Arabella felt the quicksilver change of Nando's mood cut into her. *Why is he doing this?* she cried to herself. *What have I done to deserve this sudden coldness?*

"Do you always punish people for honesty?" Arabella's voice was still breathy from the kiss they had shared.

Nando faced her. "What do you mean?"

"I was honest with you and now you're punishing me. Why?" Arabella asked, the hurt vivid in her eyes. "Do you have a reason or do you do it just for the pleasure of it?"

"I don't know what you're talking about," Nando snapped and turned to stare over the river. Could Arabella see how much he wanted her and how vulnerable the desire made him? Could she see that he was terrified of that very vulnerability because he had the scars to prove how fickle a woman's desire was, even when she called it love?

Anger began to simmer within her as Arabella waited in vain for him to face her. "Young ladies of the unblemished reputation do not react like that to a kiss, do they?" she snapped back, needing an outlet for the tension within her. "They blush and simper and fall into a faint. God forbid that they should show pleasure." She paused and narrowed her eyes. "Or was it not pleasure that you wanted to give?"

Nando spun around to her, and his hands bit into her shoulders. "Damn you, you black-haired witch."

His hands twisted in Arabella's tangled hair. Holding her in a purposely hurtful grip while his mouth savaged her lips, Nando sought to punish her for reading his thoughts. To punish her for making him desire her with a sharpness that was painful. To punish her for seeming so different from all the others, when he was so sure she was the same.

But her slackness beneath him where so much pulsing life had been before jolted Nando out of his momentary madness. He released Arabella's mouth and pressed her face against the front of his tunic, unwilling to let her see the torment and self-disgust on his face. But her hands pushed persistently against his chest until he was forced to loosen his grasp.

Arabella did not move away from him as he had expected. Instead she leaned her forehead lightly against his chin and left her hands to lie flat against his tunic.

"I will not lie to you, Nando," Arabella said softly. "I have been kissed before, but never have I felt what I did

when your mouth touched mine. I am not asking you to believe me now, but in time you will know that it is the truth."

Arabella's breath flowed onto his neck over the top of the
stiff collar of his uniform, sending a shiver down Nando's
spine. He leaned away and looked down at her. The mouth
he had bruised with his kiss was curved in a gentle smile, and
her eyes held that enticing warmth that he wanted to believe in so badly. God, she was beautiful! He had punished
her for other women's sins, and the shame of it washed hotly
over him.

"I'm sorry, Arabella."

Her hand touched his mouth gently, silencing him. "No
one should have to apologize for lashing out in pain. No
more words now," Arabella whispered, meaning what she
said, but hurting nevertheless.

They rose, dusted the bark and moss from their clothes
and walked in silence toward their horses.

Nando helped Arabella mount, and when he looked up at
her the hint of a smile played around his lips. "I shall be on
my best behavior when we ride tomorrow."

Arabella shook her head. "I'm afraid I have other plans."

"Your orphanage?"

Arabella's eyes widened. "How did you know?"

Nando felt disappointment at her display of surprise.
"All of Vienna knows by now that you play at being Lady
Bountiful at some orphanage."

Arabella lowered her lids to hide the hurt she knew would
be in her eyes. So that was how he saw it.

"Come along sometime and see for yourself."

Nando looked into Arabella's dark blue eyes for a long
time. Beneath the warmth and softness there was a determination that challenged and dared him. Was she an innocent or a seductress? he wondered. No matter, he told
himself. He could not afford to trust either.

Chapter Six

"Did I understand you correctly that you weren't able to follow them?" Prince Nikita Volkonsky's voice was deceptively soft.

"Your grace. It was impossible." The sallow-faced man in the dark frock coat furtively wiped his palms on his breeches. "They rode away from the bridle paths." He straightened, heartened by Prince Volkonsky's calm demeanor. "Even if I had had a mount instead of the carriage, I could not have followed them without being observed."

Volkonsky stared out the window, methodically cracking one knuckle after another. "I'm paying you an exorbitant sum of money to get me what I want." Suddenly he whipped around like a cobra ready to strike. "I will not accept excuses." The soft tone was gone, and every word was like a whiplash.

"B-but, your grace." The man resumed his subservient posture.

Volkonsky silenced him with a choppy movement of his hand and paced to the window. He had been stalking the Douglas girl for two weeks and had not been able to so much as corner her in an empty hallway for a few minutes. And along came Berg and went riding with her in a place so secluded they could not be followed. It was ridiculous. And he wouldn't stand for it.

He whirled around, hooking his thumbs into his belt. "I want to know exactly where the girl goes, whom she sees and what she does. And I want no excuses next time."

Casually he reached toward the small tray that held a copper pot with a cup of steaming Turkish coffee beside it and flicked it to the floor. Shifting slightly, he brought his booted foot down on the cup. With a twist, Volkonsky ground the porcelain into the Oriental carpet, not breaking eye contact with the man he had bought. When he spoke, his voice was soft again, belying his feral smile. "Do we understand each other?"

The man's Adam's apple bobbed as he nodded, then bent to the waist in an obsequious bow. Keeping that position, he backed out of the room.

Arabella was dressed to leave for the orphanage when a footman brought the message that she had a caller. Her heart took up a staccato beat as she ran down the stairs, barely remembering to slow her steps before she started down the last flight.

It was to her credit that she kept her disappointment from showing on her face when she saw Prince Volkonsky lounging in the doorway to the salon. He had showered her with attentions, flowers and compliments since the masked ball at the Hofburg, and while Arabella was conscious of the prince's handsome, dark looks, the memory of the ruthlessness of his smile when she had stood between him and Nando lingered.

"Good day to you, Prince Volkonsky."

"You become lovelier every time I see you." His dark eyes traversed her face leisurely before he bent over Arabella's hand. Instead of stopping shy of her hand as good manners demanded, Volkonsky pressed his lips to the soft skin. She jerked away, but he was prepared for her movement and his fingers tightened, keeping her hand imprisoned in his as he straightened. An insolent smile curved his sensuous mouth as his thumb brushed back and forth over her knuckles.

Annoyed with herself for having taken Volkonsky's bait, Arabella forced herself to let the hand he held go limp and schooled her expression to cool indifference. "May I have my hand?"

"Of course. My apologies, Mademoiselle Douglas." The heels of his boots snapped together. "Will you do me the honor of accompanying me on a carriage ride, *mademoiselle?*"

"I am afraid I cannot, prince," Arabella said, relieved that she would not have to lie. "I was just about to leave."

"Your orphanage?" Volkonsky's inflection was just a shade disparaging.

Arabella sighed. It was no use trying to deny a fact that apparently half of Vienna was privy to. "Yes."

"Then may I accompany you there, if I can enjoy your company no other way?"

Realizing that Volkonsky would persist no matter what she said, Arabella nodded her assent and took the proffered arm.

Nando had not slept well, and the fact that it was Arabella's image that had kept him awake annoyed him far more than the loss of sleep. Finally he had risen from his rumpled bed to await the dawn at the window.

She was beautiful, and he desired her with an intensity that made him ache. That much Nando acknowledged freely. But what he did not admit was that it was the memory of the hurt in her eyes that had not allowed him to sleep. Hurt he had put there.

He had apologized, Nando reminded himself angrily. There was no need to flay himself for his words. Besides, she was no better than all the other women who had peopled his life. Surely she was just as false, just as treacherous. She was simply a better actress.

Nando told himself all that and more in the gray hours of the dawn, and yet he found himself wishing that her innocence and radiance were real. For if they were, perhaps he could begin to believe in the beauty of life again. At some point, as he watched the pinkening sky, he felt within himself the faint stirrings of hope.

But with daylight came control and common sense, and as Nando went about his morning business, the visions that had kept him awake faded. At least that was what he told himself. And yet he rose suddenly in the midst of a meeting with the administrator of his Styrian estates and ordered his horse saddled.

Damn it, he'd apologize again and salve his conscience, he told himself. Once he had, perhaps then he could get back to the business of his life.

But Arabella was not home, so he rode toward the narrow street near the city walls by the river where he knew she spent her days.

A thin girl with startled eyes directed him down a long, dark corridor.

A hall window opened onto the courtyard, and the first thing Nando saw was Prince Volkonsky in his tight blue and white uniform leaning against a wall buffing his nails. A sense of betrayal rose in his throat like bile, but cruelly he reminded himself that he had been expecting nothing less. He swore and almost turned back. Almost. But then he caught sight of Arabella.

She sat on a stool in the one sunny corner of the courtyard, surrounded by children of assorted sizes, all of whom were looking at her with adoring wonder, as if not quite sure whether she was real or a vision that would disappear the next moment. A grimy toddler clung to her skirts while she combed and braided a small girl's hair.

Nando stood there for a long time and watched. Watched how Arabella had a smile and a gentle touch for every child. Watched how Volkonsky approached her again and again, only to be dispatched with a word and a haughty look. Watched how Arabella gathered each child in turn into her arms and wiped away the tears as she made ready to leave.

Outside, he mounted Sultan, feeling like an absolute fool. No one noticed him as the small group left the building. Arabella walked quickly, her arm threaded through Jeanne's, and Volkonsky brought up the rear looking highly dissatisfied.

When the carriage moved off, a rider emerged from a nearby alley and set off at an easy trot, matching his pace to that of Volkonsky's horses. Nando felt a cold shiver skip down his spine. So he been right the other day after all. Someone was stalking Arabella.

He touched his spurs to Sultan's flanks.

"Will you come riding with me today?"

The words greeted Arabella as she walked into the salon. She had come downstairs reluctantly when a footman had announced that she had a caller. She had been sure that it was Prince Volkonsky again. But when she saw Nando, she walked forward quickly, a welcoming smile on her face.

"Will you come?" he repeated.

She had planned to go to the orphanage, but as Arabella looked into Nando's silver eyes, which for once had a ghost of a smile in them, she knew there was only one answer she could give.

They rode only as far as the clearing where they had sat two days before.

"I came to see you yesterday, but you weren't home."

"I was—"

"At the orphanage," Nando finished.

Arabella's eyes were full of questions, but she remained silent, waiting for Nando to continue.

"I felt the need to apologize to you for—" Nando swallowed "—for the last time we were here."

"And I told you—"

"Damn it, I know what you told me, but the look in your eyes would not let me sleep." Nando halted, horrified at what he had admitted. "And now I find myself in the damnable position of needing to apologize to you again. This time for accusing you of playing Lady Bountiful."

"What do you mean?"

"I watched you. I stood at the window in the corridor and looked down into the courtyard and saw you with those children. Saw you play with them, touch them, put your arms around them." Nando's voice was husky with self-reproach. "And I had assumed you were merely playing at philanthropy."

"Is what I am doing so strange then?" Arabella asked.

"Yes . . . no." Nando gestured impatiently. "One of the first lessons my mother taught me was that one should help those less fortunate. And she always did," he explained. "But an army of servants accompanied her on her missions of mercy, and she did little but direct the dispensation of largesse." He shook his head. "I think that she would have been horrified if she had actually been forced to touch someone."

"I don't have any largesse to distribute." Arabella opened her hands palm upward and shrugged. "I only have myself."

Nando sprang up from the log where they were sitting as if he had been stung, knowing that had he remained seated, he would not have been able to keep his hands off her. She couldn't possibly be so selfless, Nando insisted, furious at himself for being so touched. It was a fiction she was maintaining. It had to be.

Arabella looked up at him, at the line that had formed between his brows, and wondered why her words had made him angry. Wanting to soothe, she smiled and patted the log beside her. "Tell me about your mother, Nando."

He ignored her invitation to sit, but he responded to the beguiling gentleness in her voice and began to speak almost despite himself.

"My memory is of a sad, wraithlike creature. People who knew her as a girl say that she was different then—vivacious and merry, always surrounded by people, always laughing."

For a moment Arabella wondered if Nando had been that way himself once. "What happened?" she prompted.

"She married my father," Nando said simply. "He was a dour, cold man. His watchwords were duty and obligation. There was no room in his life for gentler, more cheerful pursuits. He buried himself and my mother in the most godforsaken corner of our estates and she . . ." Nando had not thought of his adored mother for a long time, but now he found his throat closing. "I suppose wasted away is as good an explanation as any."

Arabella longed to go to him, to touch him, to share his pain, but she was afraid that Nando would not take kindly to sympathy.

"He died within months of her death." Nando's voice was soft and toneless. "But then he never found life very worthwhile after Karl was killed anyway."

"Karl?"

"My brother. He was the elder son, the good son." Nando's voice took on a hard, bitter edge. "The zealous hunter, the born soldier. Born to do his duty, no questions asked. He was killed at Ulm in 1805, so then it was I who had to carry on the holy Berg traditions. I found myself at Austerlitz a scant two months later." His head snapped up as if he had just then remembered whom he was talking to. "But then you already know that story."

Nando stared at Arabella. She sat, her hands folded tightly in her lap, her eyes bright, her teeth worrying her lower lip. What had possessed him to tell her all that? he wondered. He had talked about things he hadn't thought of in years. Things he had never confided in anyone.

What a ridiculous thing to do, Nando thought with amazement as he turned away from her. To lay old and secret hurts open before someone he didn't trust, just because he had seen her embrace a child.

It was the stunned expression on Nando's face that finally forced Arabella into movement. She had welcomed his words, not out of curiosity, but because she knew intuitively that what he had told her had not often been shared with anyone. But then he moved away, and she knew she could not permit him to turn away from her with that look in his eyes.

Jumping up, Arabella grabbed his arm with both hands and pulled him around so that he faced her.

"Don't you dare," she said fiercely and shook him a little. "Don't you dare turn away from me as if you were horrified that you've showed me a piece of your soul. It's human to feel pain, to need to share it with someone. It's not something to be afraid or ashamed of. Don't you understand?"

Arabella's onslaught jarred Nando out of the shadowy realm of memory and he saw the girl before him—her eyes a deep sapphire blue, huge in her pale face, her nostrils trembling lightly with emotion, her lips parted. As he let his gaze wander over her face, Nando felt rather than heard her breathing change. A pulse in her neck sprang to life. Her hands tightened briefly on his arm then fell away.

Nando brought his hands up so they framed Arabella's face. "This," he breathed against her lips, "I understand this."

He crushed her mouth again his, and Arabella lifted her hands to his wrists to push him away. But then his lips gentled and began to coax rather than to take, and Arabella's hands stayed on Nando's wrists to hold rather than to repulse.

Nando filled himself with her sweetness. She was like a drug, he thought dazedly. If he allowed her to get into his blood, he would never be free of her. And yet he let the boundless vibrancy, the irresistible warmth pour through him like a healing balm.

A whicker from one of their horses and the rustle of branches and leaves broke into their world. Immediately alert, Nando pushed Arabella behind him and moved toward the noise.

Not understanding what was happening, she started after him, but Nando hissed, "Stay where you are." Quickly he moved toward the edge of the clearing, but before he reached the forest, the sound of hoofbeats told him that whoever had intruded on their idyll was gone.

He needed to share his suspicions with Arabella, he thought. To warn her to be careful. But when Nando reached her, she stretched her hands out to him and smiled and he forgot everything. Everything but the need to kiss her again.

Chapter Seven

Arabella shifted her riding crop to her right hand and dug her fingers into a spot between her shoulders and her neck to massage muscles that had knotted with tension.

"Is something wrong, Arabella?" Nando's voice held the same polite but distant friendliness that had been there since they had last ridden in the marsh forest a week ago.

Arabella's head snapped forward and her eyes flew to Nando's. Her fingers stayed hooked over her shoulder, although they slowed, then forgot to move altogether.

She opened her mouth to make a polite denial, but suddenly the dam broke. "I can't stand this excruciating politeness anymore," she burst out. "It's driving me mad." There, it was said. Now she waited for the friendly concern in Nando's eyes to ice over. Nothing prepared her for his low, wistful chuckle.

"You have courage, Arabella. More courage than I do."

Arabella did not bother to try to disguise the surprise in her face.

"We...I," Nando corrected himself ruefully, "have been whispering around something I have not been able to face. And so I've been terribly unfair to you."

Arabella's eyes beckoned to him with such warmth, such openness that the words nearly died on Nando's lips. Everything would be over when the words were said. Everything. Then even the dubious pleasure of tantalizing himself with her nearness, her velvet voice, her fragrance, when he knew that a casual touch was all he could permit himself, would no longer be his. Nando wondered vaguely when he had given up the notion of ruthlessly seducing Arabella. Perhaps he had never really entertained it at all.

Nando remembered exactly how Arabella had felt in his arms. Had it really been only a week ago? It seemed like years. She had been soft, yet strong in her pliancy. Her mouth had tasted sweet, yet it had carried the tang of passion. The memory would have to be enough, he told himself.

"I have been acting like a suitor and I will never be that. I cannot."

He never would have believed it so difficult to meet someone's gaze. Carefully Nando steeled himself against sulkiness, against tears, but there were none. Instead Arabella's sapphire eyes sent a shower of sparks over him.

"What did you do?" she snapped, "marry a serving wench on one of your campaigns?"

The quick, angry words veiled the unexpected pain his words caused. Arabella had not given thought to marriage to this beautiful man so filled with complications, scars and bitterness. Perhaps she had unconsciously forbidden it to herself. But now that she had heard the words, Arabella knew how much she wanted Nando. She wanted him in every way. Permanently.

"No," Nando said, when he had recovered from his surprise. "I will never marry, but even if I were to do so, it could never be to you." He almost reached out to touch her. "You are so young, Arabella. So alive. And I have nothing to offer you." Suddenly he felt unbearably tired.

She opened her mouth to protest, but the sad, weary look in his eyes stopped her, and Arabella realized that he was utterly convinced of the truth of his words.

"It would be better for you if you found someone else to go riding with every day. Someone who can offer you more than I can."

Arabella cursed to herself until the considerable vocabulary she had acquired in her grandmother's stables was exhausted. Damn him for trying to make her decisions for her. Damn him for trying to escape her just because he did not dare to act on his feelings.

Her chin rose. "How very kind of you to be so concerned with my welfare."

Arabella's haughty tone was all the spark the dry tinder of his mood needed. Nando's hand shot forward and his fingers closed around her wrist like a steel vise. "Damn you, Arabella, don't you understand? I will not marry you, not ever. But if you push me far enough—" he pulled her closer "—if you push me far enough, I will make love to you."

For a moment Arabella was speechless as her breath hitched in her throat. This was the passion, the wildness she had only glimpsed by the river. Her blood heated and the excitement began to pound within her as the vision of what it would be like to see it unleashed teased her.

"How far?" she whispered.

"What?" Nando's voice was hoarse.

"How far will I have to push?" Arabella's shallow, quick breathing made her sound winded.

The grip of the fingers around her wrist loosened and became a caress as Nando's thumb began to rub the throbbing pulse point. "Not far, Arabella. Not far."

Arabella held his stormy eyes and knew she wanted him. For a friend, for a husband. For a lover—her breath tripped at the thought—if she could have him no other way.

Her lips parted in unconscious invitation, and Nando leaned toward her until he was so close that his breath mingled with hers. Arabella thought she felt his mouth graze her lips, but he drew back so quickly that she never knew if he touched his mouth to hers.

Closing her eyes for a moment, she gathered strength. Then she shrugged with what she hoped was elegant nonchalance. "Despite your surliness, I've grown accustomed to your company and I have no need for another riding companion." A wicked gleam came into her eyes. "Unless, of course, there's someone you'd like to suggest—" Arabella paused a beat "—like Prince Volkonsky, perhaps?"

Nando's heart slammed into his ribs and he had to restrain himself not to reach out and shake her. "Damn your eyes, Arabella. You will ride with me."

Slowly Arabella smiled and a silent, heated message passed between them. "Yes," she said simply.

Arabella paced in the corner of her room where she knew the floor boards did not creak. Jeanne was snoring lightly in the next room, and she didn't want to chance waking her. There would be too many questions, too many worried looks.

Was Nando asleep, she wondered? Or was he staring out into the starless Viennese night? Lost in thought, Arabella carelessly strayed out of her corner and a board groaned, the sound unnaturally loud in the stillness.

"Arabella? Is something wrong?"

She could hear Jeanne sitting up in bed.

"I only wanted a drink of water, Jeanne" she called out. "Go back to sleep."

Impatiently Arabella waited until her maid had settled down again, her breathing even. Then she tiptoed carefully toward the door, taking her dressing gown with her almost as an afterthought.

The marble steps were cold against her bare feet and she ran down the stairs quickly. She would go to the library, she decided. There she could pace in peace.

The moment Arabella stepped into the library, she knew something was wrong.

The door to the suite used by Lord Castlereagh and his staff was open, and through the aligned doors Arabella could see a faint shimmer of light in the farthest room.

Warily she tiptoed into the first room. She tested the floor with her toe before she took the next step, not daring to exhale until she was sure that a creak of the floor would not betray her. The closer Arabella got to Lord Castlereagh's study, the better she could hear drawers opening and closing and the rustle of papers.

Ignoring the knot that formed in her stomach, Arabella took another step and then another. She wasn't afraid, she told herself. She was a little light-headed with surprise, with the need for caution, for silence. She balanced herself against a desk, and her hand rested for a moment on something hard. The bronze paperweight felt comfortably heavy in her hand, and Arabella took it with her.

As she reached the study door, Arabella took a careless step and a board squeaked. She braced herself, but the shadowy figure that leaned busily over the desk did not look in her direction. Exhaling, she felt her uneven breath tremble against her lips, and a flash of irritation with herself helped her to take another step.

The man at the desk turned his attention to a pile of papers, and the light from the three-pronged candelabra fell across his face. The intruder was a footman, Arabella realized. One of the few servants hired locally.

Concealing the hand with the paperweight behind a fold of her dressing gown, she took another step and decided that this was as good a time as any to try out the German she was learning from the children at the orphanage.

"Was macht Er da?"

The man's head whipped up and his hands gripped the edge of the desk. For a long moment he was motionless, his mouth round with surprise. The first things that moved were his eyes, skipping down the row of windows, all securely shuttered for the night. Arabella stood squarely in front of the only door out of the room.

Slowly, his hands still gripping the edge of the desk, the man rose. Arabella moved one step forward. His eyes lowered to the desk and skimmed over the papers there. A hand reached out to one pile.

"Nein." The calmness and volume of her voice took Arabella by surprise.

The man jerked his hand back, and with a foolhardy sense of triumph obscuring her common sense, Arabella moved forward.

Suddenly the footman exploded into movement. With an agile handspring, he levered himself over the desk and toward the door. Toward her. Something flashed in his hand, and Arabella belatedly recognized a dagger.

For the space of a breath Arabella went still with shock, but then her fingers clenched on the paperweight. With what seemed to her to be excruciating slowness, she brought her hand up and hurled the paperweight at the advancing figure.

With a sound that made the bile rise in Arabella's throat, the bronze figure made contact with bone. The dagger clattered against the floor. For a moment all movement, all sound ceased.

Her hands at her mouth to stifle a cry, Arabella watched the man bring a hand to his battered nose. The hand came away full of blood. Then with a strangled, inarticulate sound the man was pushing past her, roughly thrusting her aside so that she fell, striking her head on the arm of a chair as she went down.

Dazed, she scrambled up and started running, stumbling over the hem of her dressing gown. Just as she reached the corridor, the door downstairs fell closed with a mighty crash.

It would be useless to follow him, Arabella realized. She could hardly pursue him in her dressing gown, and by the time she roused someone, he would have long disappeared in the warren of streets around the Minoriten Square. Breathless, she leaned for a moment against the door and closed her eyes.

Suddenly the past few moments appeared absurd, as if they were part of a dream, a hallucination, and Arabella lifted her eyelids, wondering if she had perhaps dreamed them. Then her gaze fell on the bloody handprint on the white sleeve of her dressing gown.

She would not faint, Arabella told herself. She would not. Her throat seemed to close as she tried to fill her lungs with air, but she fought the constriction and in a few moments her breath was shuddering in and out.

As she mounted the stairs, a feeling of dizzy euphoria overtook her and she giggled aloud at the thought of what the Castlereaghs would say.

The euphoria began to fade as she reached the Castlereagh apartments, and by the time she was sitting in Lady Castlereagh's dressing room with a glass of vile-tasting brandy in her hands, she began to shake.

"What you did was very brave, Arabella, but not very wise," Lord Castlereagh said in his serene, absent way. "We assumed that the man was a spy, you see, when he turned up so propitiously. So every letter, every document that is of any importance is removed every evening. There was nothing there that could possibly be of use to his masters."

"Then I injured the man for nothing," Arabella whispered, remembering the sickening crunch when the paperweight had hit the man's face.

"Your conscience need not trouble you, Arabella, my dear." Lord Castlereagh passed a gentle hand over her hair. "If you had been the injured one, I don't believe that the thought would have kept Prince Metternich awake at night."

"Prince Metternich? He was responsible?"

Lord Castlereagh nodded. "Most probably. Vienna is full of spies and informers, but by far the largest portion of them answer to Prince Metternich and his chief of police, Hager."

By the time Arabella appeared at a soirée at the French embassy that evening, she had gotten most of her color back, and the events of the past night truly seemed like a bad dream. But she was jumpy and irritable, for once annoyed at Lulu's barrage of questions about Nando.

"Well, what's your next step?" Lulu asked point-blank, since her discreet inquiries weren't getting her anywhere.

"Don't you have any words of wisdom?" Arabella snapped.

"You're asking the wrong person for advice, my dear," Lulu drawled. "I'm the one who is twenty-six and unmarried, remember?"

"Don't be ridiculous, Lulu," Arabella retorted. "I am not a stable hand, but I know what to do when a horse is lame."

Lulu raised an eyebrow. "An apt metaphor."

Suddenly Arabella felt the weariness creeping up on her, and she leaned against the back of a rococo chair. "Oh, Lulu, I don't know what to do. How to reach him. Was he always like this?"

"Lord, no. When I think of those summers, I remember him always laughing. He'd let my sisters and me tag along with him and Franz." She laughed ruefully at the memory. "All three of us were a little in love with him."

"Franz? I thought his brother's name was Karl."

"Franz was the son of one of the Berg tenants on the estate in Styria. The two were inseparable, and Franz naturally grew into the role of Nando's servant. I think that nowadays he's the only one Nando allows to come close."

"Nando's told me about his brother," Arabella said softly. "About how his father forced him to take Karl's place. He's never said so in so many words, but he hates it." She pressed a hand against her middle as the knowledge of Nando's pain churned within her. "I know he does. He hates the brutality, the killing."

"So he's let you see that far," Lulu said thoughtfully.

Arabella smiled a sad little smile. "I don't think he meant to. I don't think he even realizes he has. Oh, Lulu, why did he let them do this to him?"

"That's a question you will have to ask Nando. But do not underestimate the power that a sense of duty and honor and family has over a man like him." Compassion welled up in Lulu as she looked at her young friend. All her emotions were there on her lovely face to be read. Lulu wondered if

Arabella realized she was in love with Nando, or if she was still hiding that knowledge from herself.

"But that's not all, is it?" Arabella whispered. "That's not really why Nando shuts out anyone who wants to come close."

Lulu frowned. "I could tell you, since it is more or less common knowledge, but perhaps you should ask Nando. It's his story, after all." She broke off when she saw Prince Metternich at his most elegant approaching them.

"Countess Thürheim. My compliments. You are looking enchanting tonight." Metternich executed a bow that was just short of mincing.

Lulu acknowledged the greeting with a curt nod. She shared the antipathy of much of Austria's aristocracy toward the German-born chancellor, but she had personal reasons to dislike him, as well.

With an expectant calm, a tactic he had honed to perfection, Metternich remained standing in front of the two women until there was no way for Lulu to avoid introductions.

"Miss Douglas." Metternich bowed low over Arabella's hand. "I am enchanted to meet you."

"Prince Metternich." Although Arabella inclined her head gracefully and smiled, she eyed him with suspicion, remembering what Lord Castlereagh had said last night.

"You will forgive me, my dear Countess Thürheim, if I steal Miss Douglas away from you for a few moments?" Metternich's voice was suave. "I believe that she and I have mutual acquaintances in London."

"Indeed?" Arabella fought to gather her wits, almost losing the battle when she looked into Metternich's pale, soulless eyes. Just barely, she suppressed a shiver. He was measuring her, she realized. Although his eyes were utterly without expression, she knew that he was measuring her.

Arabella felt Lulu's touch on her arm and she acknowledged the warning.

"I shall speak to you a little later, Lulu." Arabella nodded to her friend and with a smile that was a shade too bright, she turned to place her hand on Prince Metternich's proffered arm.

They strolled through the salons, occasionally returning a greeting. Prince Metternich said nothing. They stopped for a moment in the music room to listen to a string quartet. Prince Metternich said nothing. They strolled to the main drawing room. And still Prince Metternich was silent.

Arabella wondered what kind of trap he was laying for her. Was he trying to throw her off balance, to make her nervous? Already she could feel the unsteadiness she had felt last night and this morning returning. Because she needed to mask this unsteadiness, she spoke.

"I do not think that we have mutual acquaintances in London, Prince Metternich. What was it that you wanted to speak to me about?" Arabella kept her voice brisk, afraid that it might tremble if she spoke more slowly.

Prince Metternich turned his curled, powdered head toward her, but this time Arabella was prepared for the impact of his terrible, blank eyes. "Are you always so direct, Miss Douglas?"

"I try to be."

"Indeed." Prince Metternich's thin lips curved. "It would seem that your words are as direct as your aim."

Arabella's gaze did not waver, although she had to fight to keep it that way. "Fortunately so."

"You have cost me the services of an excellent agent for many weeks. That upsets my plans."

Arabella gasped softly at his frankness.

"I see you were not expecting my openness. Well, my dear Miss Douglas, there are times when even I have uses for it."

Off balance, Arabella narrowed her eyes. "What do you want from me?"

"Information."

"Are you mad?" The words were out before Arabella remembered that she was speaking to one of the most powerful men in Europe. She stopped and fought to keep her voice down. "Do you actually think I would..."

Metternich raised an elegant hand to stem Arabella's flow of words. "Hear me out, my dear Miss Douglas." His politely bland voice took on a shade of malevolence. "Please."

They resumed their stroll through the salon, but Arabella could not bear to put her hand on Metternich's arm again.

"I am informed that you are not wealthy. I would pay you well," he continued in a tone so conversational that he might have been talking about the weather.

"Do you think I would take your filthy money?"

"So you cannot be bought with money." Metternich stopped and turned to face Arabella. "Perhaps you can be bought with something else, then?"

"If you will excuse me, Prince Metternich, I have an urgent need for some fresh air." Arabella turned to walk away.

"Can you be bought with Count Berg's safety?" The insidiously soft voice crept after her like a poisonous snake.

Arabella stopped, not believing she had heard him correctly. Her skin was crawling. She needed to escape from him and yet she turned around and retraced her steps.

"What do you mean?"

"I am not at liberty to tell you all the details, but I can tell you this." He tapped his fingertips together. "Count Berg has pursued activities that can damage both his career and his reputation." Metternich paused. "With proper persuasion, the responsible authorities will overlook what has transpired."

"What activities?" Arabella demanded. "He would never do anything dishonorable!"

Metternich spread his hands in a gesture of regret. "As I said, I am not at liberty to say."

Arabella tightened her finger around her fan. "How do I know that you're telling me the truth?"

"You will just have to trust me in this, won't you?" Metternich lifted a shoulder in a elegant shrug.

Incapable of speech, Arabella concentrated on evening her breathing. She would not show nerves in front of this slimy creature.

"May I count on your cooperation, then?" he pressed.

She would find a way out. Arabella thought feverishly. If she had a little time, she would be able to figure out what to do. "I need time to make my decision."

Metternich smiled his cold smile. "Take some time then, Miss Douglas. But not too much."

Arabella whirled around and, using all her control to keep herself from running, left the salon.

Chapter Eight

Nando paced the drawing room as he waited for Arabella. He had watched her talk with Metternich last night. He had seen her anger, her agitation. But she had disappeared from the room before he could speak with her.

"Damn her," Nando swore. From the very first moment he had looked into Arabella's eyes, he had had a terrible premonition just how dangerous to his hard-won peace of mind she would be. He had struggled to stay away from her, but she was a magnet and her invisible force pulled him in every time he tried to escape her.

Now he was caught, Nando realized with dismay. Caught in a web of his own making. He could have walked away from desire, perhaps even from need, but he had trapped himself. Trapped himself in the reluctant concern for Arabella he had foolishly allowed to grow. Trapped himself in the responsibility he felt for her safety.

Just a few weeks ago, his days had passed in untroubled boredom. Now he was all nerves. Edgy because his instincts told him that Arabella was in jeopardy. Edgy because desire for her kept his blood running hot. Edgy because he was beginning to feel a tenderness for her that persisted no matter how hard he tried to deny it. A tenderness he knew would cloud his judgment. He pressed his fingers to the base of his nose to stem the beginnings of a headache.

"Nando? Is something wrong?"

His head jerked up, and it took all of Nando's self-discipline not to close the gap between them and take Arabella into his arms—whether to shake her or to kiss her senseless, he was not sure. She was pale today with a bruised look around her eyes, and he felt a murderous rage at Metternich rise up in him. He forced himself to take a deep breath before he spoke, yet the roughness of his voice betrayed everything he was feeling.

"What were you talking about with Metternich yesterday? And why?" Nando demanded and braced himself for a clever evasion, a flirtatious excuse. Instead Arabella's eyes widened guilelessly and again he found himself hard put to keep his hands off her.

"Later," she said. "When we can be certain that we won't be interrupted. Or overheard," she added softly.

By mutual consent they rode beyond the city walls toward the outlying districts at the foot of the gentle, rolling hills of the Vienna Woods. Most of the vineyards were already bare of fruit. Only the few vines whose fruit would be left until after the first frosts to make the heavy, sweet ice wine were still laden with thick bunches of grapes.

Neither of them tried to make conversation as they rode. The skin across Nando's knuckles was stretched white as one thought chased the next. And Arabella felt despair like a heavy cloak around her shoulders as she wondered how she would make him believe her.

On a different occasion, Arabella would have been delighted with the tavern where they stopped—a freshly whitewashed building with boxes of late-blooming flowers under the windows and a bunch of evergreen over the green door to indicate that new wine from their own vineyard was being served within. As it was she barely noticed the taproom with its sanded plank floor and smoke-darkened beams, nor did she pay attention to the great, old walnut tree in the rear courtyard that spread its branches over the simple trestle tables. Automatically Arabella reached for the mug that was set down in front of her and her eyes flew upward when Nando's hand closed over her wrist.

"Drink it slowly," he admonished. "It tastes perfectly harmless and will get you drunk faster than brandy."

"What is it?" Arabella asked and looked at what appeared to be a cloudy wine for the first time.

"Grape juice that has just begun to ferment, and believe me, it's not called *Sturm*—storm—for nothing." A faint smile curved Nando's lips.

Arabella took a tiny sip and was pleasantly surprised by the sweet taste with just a hint of tartness. "It tastes delightful."

"That's what makes it so lethal."

Arabella ran her fingers nervously down the nubby surface of her mug. She saw the barely bridled impatience in Nando's eyes and knew that time had run out.

"I want your promise that everything I say will remain between us only."

Nando's lips thinned. "Do you take me for a gossip?"

Arabella sighed and decided to ignore the question. "I mean that it remains between us in every way." Very deliberately she held Nando's gaze. "It can have no consequences. You cannot act upon what I tell you."

"What do you want? My promise that I won't strangle Metternich in his bed? Or challenge him to a duel?" Nando demanded with a mirthless smile.

"I want your promise, Nando—" Arabella laced her fingers together tightly "—that this matter ends here at this table. That you will do or say nothing because of what I tell you."

Nando looked into her eyes, so dark, so serious. With dismay he watched them fill with tears and knew that he would give her his soul if she asked for it.

"All right then, I promise," he said gruffly. "Now talk."

"I went down to the library the night before last and found a footman rummaging around in Lord Castlereagh's desk." Arabella began to draw circles on the table with her fingers without realizing that she did so.

"You didn't confront him, did you?" Nando leaned forward and controlled the desire to reach out and touch her.

"Well, actually—" Arabella's mouth curved in a lopsided grin "—I believe I broke his nose."

Nando pressed the heel of his hand to his forehead and tried to discipline the desire to shake Arabella until her teeth rattled. "Do you have any conception of just how foolhardy you were?"

Arabella wrinkled her nose at him. "I've been told that repeatedly, thank you."

"Is that what Metternich wanted to talk to you about?" Nando's eyes narrowed as suspicion dawned.

"Yes. It appears he felt that since I'd put one of his agents out of commission, the least I could do is to take over the job for him."

"What did he offer you?" Nando anticipated her words in his mind and they were like icy fingers trailing along his spine.

"A generous allowance and—" Arabella licked her suddenly dry lips "—and your safety."

"What?" The exclamation was like a pistol shot in the quiet courtyard. Nando's fingers closed like a vise around Arabella's wrist. "Explain!"

"You're hurting me," Arabella murmured, even though she did not try to struggle out of his grasp. Nor did her eyes move even a fraction of an inch from his.

The anger did not fade from his eyes, but Nando's fingers loosened and began to stroke Arabella's wrist where he had gripped it so forcefully.

"Metternich said you were involved in activities that could damage your career and your reputation. If I helped him, this would be conveniently overlooked."

"Did he say what those activities were?" Nando's soft voice gave no indication of the fury beginning to boil within him.

Arabella shook her head. "He said he was not at liberty to say."

"Do you believe him?"

Nando's fingers on her wrist still stroked, and Arabella was finding it more and more difficult to think clearly. Gently she extricated her hand from his.

"I don't believe you would do anything dishonorable, Nando. But I needed to tell you this because that man is capable of twisting something perfectly innocent for his own ends." Arabella's voice was calm.

"So sure?"

"Yes. You are an honorable man, Nando. I know that." Arabella looked him in the eyes and wanted to say more.

"Are you very sure about that, Arabella?"

Suddenly they both knew that what they were talking about had nothing to do with Metternich and his machinations.

Arabella lifted her chin and allowed herself a faint smile. "Yes."

Nando looked away from the trust in Arabella's eyes. Unable to sit still any longer, he rose and began to pace. He didn't want to know what she was going to do, he told himself. It was none of his affair, now that he had cleared up the rubbish about his endangered reputation. And yet—and yet he needed to know. He needed to know very badly.

The gravel crunched under his boots as Nando whipped around and faced Arabella. "Well? What are you going to do?"

"Do?" Arabella's gaze was blank with puzzlement.

"About Metternich's proposal."

She started to laugh, but the sound caught in her throat when Arabella saw how grim Nando's face was. "What do you think?" Her voice was barely audible.

Nando stepped closer and placed his hands flat on the table. "Whatever you do, I want to make perfectly sure that both of us are quite aware that your decision has nothing to do with me."

Arabella recoiled as if he had struck her. Gripping the edge of the table, she stood. "How dare you?" she asked. "How dare you apply your mean, warped thoughts to me?" She moved back a step and felt the bench tip and fall over behind her.

Nando pushed himself back from the table and stood straight, his arms at his sides. Both the rage and the hurt lay openly on her face, and in that moment, he would not have been surprised if she had attacked him bodily. On some level, he might even have welcomed physical pain.

She had been patient, Arabella thought as she stormed around the table like a fury bent on vengeance. She took the corner too closely and felt the sharp edge of the table bite painfully into her flesh. She had waited and made excuses for Nando every time he had retreated from her. Every time his bitterness had hurt her. But this she could not ignore. This so very basic insult to her personal integrity.

It was Nando's absolute motionlessness that slowed Arabella. Then she saw the resignation, the defeat in the line of his shoulders, the misery that had darkened his eyes from silver to slate. And everything that had provoked her, offended her disappeared in the wave of tenderness that was so all-consuming that her step almost faltered.

She stepped up to him—so close that her skirt brushed his knees—and slowly lifted her hands to frame Nando's face.

"Who was it, Nando?" Arabella whispered. "Who hurt you so badly that you believe only in lies and betrayal?"

"Don't." Nando tried to turn away, but found that he lacked the strength to free himself from Arabella's hands, which held him so lightly. "Talking about it won't change anything."

Arabella let her hands slide down until they rested flat against Nando's chest. "I told you today that I believe you to be an honorable man, Nando. Unless you want to make a liar out of me, you will tell me what ghosts I'm fighting."

"Arabella, I have told you again and again that I shall never—" Nando hooked his thumbs under her palms, wanting to dislodge her hands, but seduced by the warmth and softness, his hands stayed where they were.

"I have not asked you for anything you can't give me, Nando. You can give me this."

Arabella's eyes were so limpid, so gentle, and he still felt the heaviness of guilt for his words. What harm would it do, Nando thought, to humble himself a little? Keeping his eyes on hers, he nodded. Then, releasing her hands, he turned and walked toward the low, tile-covered wall that bordered one side of the courtyard.

Nando heard Arabella's footsteps behind him on the gravel, but he did not turn toward her. Instead he stood looking out at the gentle, green countryside and his skin crawled as he remembered.

"I was twenty-two when I met Princess Katharina Bagration. Her beauty dazzled me. The past eight years have not been kind to her, but then she really did look like an angel. Apparently Katharina liked what she saw, too, for she fell into my bed so quickly that it made my head spin."

Nando's mellow voice took on a disgusted tone. "I was utterly besotted with her and made an absolute fool of myself." He leaned both hands against the tiled ridge of the wall and found the sharp pressure on his palms oddly comforting.

"I chose to ignore the fact that she had an impressive trail of discarded lovers from St. Petersburg to Paris, several children with different fathers, and a husband besides. Instead I chose to believe all the whispered promises." He lifted one shoulder in a shrug. "It was a stroke of good fortune for me that the affair was brief and ended rather suddenly when I found her in bed with our revered Prince Metternich." Nando laughed an ugly little laugh. "It's incredible how little dignity a man possesses when his breeches are unbuttoned."

Arabella's shocked gasp did not escape Nando. "I'm sorry if I've offended you. I would not have chosen to burden you with this sordid little story."

"Oh, Nando..."

Nando felt more than heard Arabella move toward him and he stepped away, afraid that he would fall apart if she touched him now.

"That little tidbit of gossip amused half the salons in Europe for months. Everywhere I went I heard the rumors, the innuendo, often enough even open questions." Nando shrugged. "After a while I even learned to laugh about them."

Anger and impatience warred with the compassion in Arabella's heart and for just a moment the anger won. "Was it then that you decided to measure all women with the same yardstick?" she demanded.

"Oh, no. I needed another lesson. This time from a very proper young lady." Nando pushed himself away from the wall.

"Just before the invitations to our betrothal ball were to be sent out, the young Countess Hohenstein decided it was more appealing to marry one of the Esterhazys instead," he said tersely. "After all, they own more land in Hungary than the emperor himself, and trace their lineage straight down to Adam."

Arabella's heart grew heavy as she listened to Nando. This was what he was looking for in her. He was waiting for her to say or do something that would prove to him she was just like the others. Now she knew what that wary look she had occasionally surprised in his eyes meant. Perhaps she would have to settle for being Nando's friend after all. But that last thought was pushed away almost before it could form.

"Well, are you satisfied now?" Nando finally turned to face Arabella.

She ignored his question and moved to lessen the gap between them. "I was wondering when you would look me in the face."

The gentleness in her eyes was still there, but the fire was not far away. He had thought to discourage her, but there was nothing even remotely like disenchantment in Arabella's face.

"Where do you get your nerve to lump me in with those poor excuses for women?" She tilted her chin up pugnaciously, bringing her mouth to within an inch of his. "If I were a man, I would call you out."

Despite himself Nando started to laugh, the tension and the old, ugly memories falling away from him like an old skin being shed. Then he inhaled Arabella's fragrance and his hands reached out to cup her face.

Nando marveled at the richness, the lack of reserve with which she offered him her mouth. And he took. He took unhesitatingly, selfishly, rationalizing that he was taking only what was being freely given. In a more lucid moment he would chide himself bitterly for taking advantage of Arabella's innocence, but now, when he had just laid his soul and its old wounds bare before her, there was no way he could have resisted the healing warmth she offered. He would not have admitted it, but it was the gentle warmth Arabella offered that he found himself needing as much as the heat of her untried passion.

With an inarticulate sound Nando took her mouth.

Arabella had been kissed before. But never, never had she felt the wild excitement, the insane pounding of her blood as when this man took her mouth so unceremoniously, with such barely contained violence. The audaciousness of Nando's caresses set her innocent body on fire. But it was the tenderness that was never completely absent from his touch that stole her heart.

There were so many textures to his kisses, Arabella thought as Nando's mouth moved over hers. So many tastes. The smoothness of his lips when he touched them to hers. The wet roughness of his tongue when it slipped into her mouth. The caressing tickle of his mustache against her skin. He tasted of tobacco and coffee and a deliciously heated flavor that was all his own.

Even as she allowed Nando to pull her still closer, Arabella knew full well that this was unacceptable behavior for a well-bred young lady. But for these few moments when he held her close, when his mouth moved so enticingly over hers, there were no recriminations, no suspicions. She wanted to soak up his nearness like a sponge, needing to remember every sensation, every emotion for the rest of her life.

Nando looked at Arabella, her eyes closed, her lips parted and still wet and glistening from his kiss, and the dark voice inside him whispered, *She's just like the rest of them, just more beautiful, more desirable and cleverer than the others,* and he began to draw away. But then Arabella opened her eyes and the dark voice was forgotten.

What would it have been like, Nando found himself wondering, to have been the kind of man who could take a woman like Arabella and dare to build a future, a life? To make plans? To watch children of your own body come into the world and grow? He shook his head lightly, as if to clear it of such forbidden thoughts.

Arabella saw the shadows in his eyes and reached up to touch his cheek, needing to have this moment last a little longer. "Kiss me again, Nando."

And when Nando again lowered his mouth to hers, the world and his memories disappeared.

By eleven o'clock Arabella had surreptitiously looked at the clock a dozen times and wondered why Nando had not put in an appearance at the soirée. She had grown so accustomed to seeing him that she could not help wondering if he was avoiding her.

"My dear Miss Douglas," a deep voice murmured behind her, interrupting her thoughts. "You grow lovelier every time I see you."

"Thank you, Prince Volkonsky." Arabella recognized the voice and the heavy, opulent scent of ambergris even before she turned around.

"Since your shadow appears to have deserted you this evening, may I have the pleasure of your company?"

Arabella smiled as graciously as she could and placed her hand on Volkonsky's arm. As they turned, she caught sight of Nando. As discreetly as possible she sent an exasperated glance heavenward, hoping that he would understand the message. She would have to explain to him that Lord Castlereagh had gone out of his way to ask her to be pleasant to Volkonsky. He was having enough trouble with the Russians as it was, he had confided.

But when she next looked, she saw that Nando's face was a blank mask, his eyes ice. Oh, God, she thought, this was the fear she had so vividly felt yesterday in the tavern courtyard. The fear that Nando would look for and find something—anything—that would enable him to put her in the same category as the women who had hurt him so deeply.

Nando told himself that the suite of rooms the Prussian ambassador entertained in was simply too small to avoid Arabella, but he knew he was lying. He watched her chat and laugh with Volkonsky, sometimes catching himself straining to read her lips, completely unprepared for the feelings that assailed him. The anger he might have understood. But how could he understand that intense protectiveness? And beneath it all was a jealousy so overwhelming, so primitive, that Nando began to realize just how thin a veneer civilization provided.

Suddenly the full force of his fury hit Nando like a tidal wave and it took all his considerable discipline not to follow them when they moved to the next salon.

Pride stiffened his spine as he turned to watch a game of whist. And wait.

Being friendly to Prince Volkonsky was hard work, Arabella thought as she tried to smile casually although her teeth were on edge. If he bent to brush his extravagant mustache against her ear under the guise of whispering compliments one more time, she would be hard put to keep her good manners.

"Would you like some refreshment, Miss Douglas?"

"That would be wonderful." Arabella sighed gratefully. Perhaps that would give her the opportunity to get rid of him. If Nando knew how eager she was to escape the prince, she thought, he would probably find it vastly amusing.

With a tiny nudge, Volkonsky bowed Arabella through a door and it was not until it fell very audibly into the lock and Volkonsky leaned back against it that she realized that they were in a deserted corridor.

Arabella stifled a brief flash of alarm. After all there was a roomful of people just beyond the door. "I take it that this is your idea of a joke, Prince Volkonsky," she said with all the imperiousness she could muster. "I fear I must fault your taste."

Volkonsky said nothing, but leaned against the door, his eyes glittering like polished jet.

"Let me pass." Arabella took a step toward him. "Let me pass, I tell you." She lifted her hand to push Volkonsky away, but he caught her wrist.

"My dear Miss Douglas, I shall be very generous and allow you to enjoy my company a little while longer." Volkonsky's teeth were very white in his swarthy face. "Or did you think you'd made my friend Berg jealous enough already?"

"How dare you?" Arabella twisted her arm, trying to free herself, almost as furious at his words as she was about finding herself in this predicament. But the movement only served to bring her closer to Volkonsky. He grasped her other hand and brought her closer until Arabella was almost lying against him. Realizing that struggling would make her rub her body suggestively against his, she went still.

"Ah, that's much better. I'm pleased that you're being so sensible."

Volkonsky lowered his head, but Arabella twisted her head aside, at the same time managing to lever one foot back to kick at his leg.

"Oh, dear—" Volkonsky shook his head "—not sensible after all."

Agilely Volkonsky angled himself upright without letting go of Arabella's wrists. Suddenly his smile was gone. With quick, efficient movements, he maneuvered her backward. The more she struggled, the tighter his grip became. Just as she opened her mouth to scream for help, he shouldered a door open and pushed through into an unlit cubbyhole.

Not bothering to shut the door behind him, Volkonsky backed Arabella up until she slammed into a wall, the impact knocking the breath out of her. Only a dim band of light from the corridor fell into the alcove, but Volkonsky's black eyes seemed to gleam in the dark like a cat's as he lowered his mouth toward hers.

When Nando saw that Arabella was nowhere in sight even though the Castlereaghs were preparing to leave, he went looking for her. Cursing himself for his weakness, he strode impatiently from salon to salon, noting with increasing anxiety that Volkonsky was nowhere in sight, either.

Again Nando paced through the rooms, and this time an unobtrusive door at the far end of a drawing room caught his attention.

He had barely stepped into the corridor when Nando heard the muffled sounds of a struggle. After nine years of war, he would have said that he was inured to human suffering, but the moment he heard Arabella's cry, Nando felt such acute terror that the blood seemed to leave his head.

But panic did not slow his reactions. He moved toward the sound, sending the door to the cubbyhole crashing against a cabinet.

Surprised by the noise behind him, Volkonsky let Arabella go and pivoted around. As he did, Nando grabbed the front of the Russian's tunic and flung him to the side. Made clumsy by lust, Volkonsky fell to the floor.

Robbed of the support of Volkonsky's hands, Arabella slid down the wall until Nando caught her shoulders and brought her upright again. In that first moment of relief, Nando forgot that he was angry with her. He forgot that she was as full of deceit as the others. In a confusion of relief and tenderness and guilt that he had not protected her better, Nando's arms slid around her and cradled her against his chest, a hand stroking her disarranged curls.

Just as Arabella's breath began to even, Nando heard Volkonsky scrambling to his feet behind him. Gently he leaned her against the wall and swung around to face the Russian.

"You're very fortunate, Volkonsky. I don't wish a scandal, so I suggest you disappear as quickly and as discreetly as possible."

Volkonsky remained motionless until Nando took a threatening step toward him. Then he straightened his blue tunic.

"You have won this battle, Berg." Volkonsky shrugged indifferently, as if classifying the incident as a trifling setback in his amorous pursuits. "But the war? Who knows?" He executed a bow that bordered on insolence in Arabella's direction. "My apologies, mademoiselle, for my—" he paused "—boldness." Passing a hand over his thick, black hair, Volkonsky left.

The click of Volkonsky's boots on the parquet floor of the corridor was still audible when Nando turned to face Arabella.

"You should not play games, Arabella, when you're not prepared to deal with the consequences." Nando's tone was brisk and his eyes wintry, all trace of tenderness gone. "When you flirt with a man like Volkonsky, it's your own fault if you end up getting mauled in an alcove like some chambermaid."

Arabella stared back at him. What did Nando want from her? Did he expect a lighthearted comment? An apology? Some kind of excuse? Well, he would get none of them. Resolutely, she tipped up her chin.

"I'm sure you know best about games and consequences, Nando." She pushed herself away from the wall and came to stand in front of him. "Thank you for the rescue. I'm properly grateful."

Her head high, Arabella walked out of the small room, praying that she could keep her tears at bay until she was in the safety of her own room.

Chapter Nine

Nando watched the gracefully swaying line of Arabella's back, glad that the teeming marketplace made riding abreast impossible for a few minutes.

What sorcery had she worked on him? he wondered. After the incident with Volkonsky, he had sworn that he would stay away from her. But the memory of Arabella's proud bearing, despite the hurt in her eyes as she left the small room, had robbed him of the paltry remainder of his tranquility. So today he had called on Arabella, intent on apologizing for his words, even though he still wasn't quite certain that she hadn't truly deserved them.

He hadn't been prepared for the simple yes with which she accepted his apology. He had expected a tantrum, or insults, or at best that haughty glare she was so very good at. When he had said as much, she had given him an incredulous look. "Why should I? You apologized. I accepted your apology. As far as I'm concerned, that's the end of the matter."

"Most women would have milked the situation for all it was worth," Nando said, his tone mild but his mouth cynical.

Arabella's black brows had come together and she stepped closer to him. "This may come as a shock to you, Count Berg, but I am not other women." She stabbed her forefinger at Nando's chest. "I am me—Arabella Douglas. *Versteht Er das?*"

Before Nando could reply, a dazzling smile had wiped Arabella's frown away. "Now do you want me to go riding with you, or shall I be annoyed with you after all?"

He had nodded silently, feeling the magic of her gentle smile. If he could have, he would have fled, for both his own sake and hers, but he found he could not. Arabella was like quicksand, he thought, and had a brief vision of himself sinking into her.

In his reverie, Nando hadn't noticed how far behind he had fallen. He realized that they were separated by swarming peddlers, children and dogs darting amid the carts and stout housewives with baskets over their arms. Only when Nando heard a high-pitched scream that carried above the noise around them and saw Arabella slide from her saddle did the realization register that he could not reach her as quickly as he wanted to.

The stallion reared as Nando's spurs dug into his flanks with far more force than necessary or advisable. He cursed the crowd around him loudly and they fell back, in awe of both the stallion's wild hooves and Nando's commanding voice.

Within moments he reached Arabella's mare and had jumped to the ground, just in time to see Arabella bodily push back a florid-faced, thickset man with one hand while she brandished her riding crop at him with the other.

The rush of blood within him subsided so suddenly when Nando saw that Arabella was safe that for a moment a black curtain descended in front of his eyes.

"What are you doing?" she cried. "Don't you dare hit that child again."

Arabella's German was accented and a bit faulty, but perfectly understandable, and Nando saw the man color more deeply and mutter something under his breath. Nando stepped forward quickly, putting one hand at Arabella's back, one on her arm.

"What's going on here?" Nando demanded.

"Nando! This monster was beating the child." Arabella freed herself from Nando's grip and reached out, pulling the sobbing little girl against her hip.

Grateful that she had reverted to French, Nando squeezed her arm, wordlessly asking for her silence. He turned to speak in low tones to the man.

Arabella knelt in front of the little girl, paying no attention to the fact that her skirt swept the refuse-strewn cobblestones. She produced a lawn handkerchief, wet it with her tongue and rubbed the child's face where rivulets of tears had made grayish-white paths in the grime. Her stomach tightened when she saw the broad, red marks on the girl's skin where she had been slapped.

Holding the girl until her sobs had subsided, Arabella was achingly aware of how the child's fragile bones seemed to be barely covered by flesh. Then she rose and, her arm still around the girl's shoulders, she approached a cart loaded with apples. Arabella handed the vendor a coin and put a red-cheeked apple in the child's hand and several more into the large pocket of her ragged, dirty apron. With a furtive glance at the man, the girl ducked her head and bit greedily into the fruit.

Arabella did not try to talk to the girl, asking only her name.

"Poldi," the child mumbled, her mouth full. "Leopoldine."

Nando spoke to the man while Arabella stood apart with the girl who stuffed the last of the apple, core and all, into her mouth and immediately started on the next one. She saw a coin exchange hands and the sullen look on the man's face lightened somewhat.

"Komm' her." Nando turned and beckoned to the child.

The girl moved forward, automatically obeying the quiet command, but she glanced back at Arabella with something resembling wistfulness. When she reached Nando, he crouched down, smiled and said something to her softly.

Poldi did not smile back, but the apple hung forgotten in her hand as she listened to him. Then Nando rose and gave her a little push toward the man who had beaten her, and she went without demur.

The man gripped the girl's arm and turned away with a last glower in Arabella's direction. Without adjusting his long steps, he dragged the child after him down the street. Once or twice the girl glanced over her shoulder as she did her best to keep up with the man's steps. She was apparently resigned to her lot and there was no fear in her face, only a curiosity about the people who had helped her.

Nando felt Arabella's hand curl around his arm. "Will he beat her again?" she asked softly.

"Probably." He felt her hand tighten and reached to stroke it with his. "Not because of you." He laughed shortly. "It was too profitable a day for the bastard for that. But he will hit her again some other day. Men like that always attack those who are weak and defenseless."

Nando looked down at Arabella quizzically. "You descended upon him like a fury. Whatever possessed you to interfere?"

Arabella's gaze still followed the two mismatched figures. "Instinct, I suppose. I heard the child scream and the next thing I knew, I had a piece of the man's coat in my hand."

Then she glanced up at Nando, but only briefly before she shuttered her eyes. "I'm sorry I put you in an uncomfortable situation."

Before Nando knew what he was doing, his fingers were clasping Arabella's chin and tipping her face up to his. "Don't you dare apologize for doing what was right," he whispered fiercely.

The bruised look in Arabella's eyes hit him like a fist to his middle. Unconsciously Nando's fingers moved to cup her pale cheek. "What is it, Arabella?"

She closed her eyes, forgetting the old pain, feeling only Nando's muscular arm beneath her fingers, his breath against her skin, his hand against her face. She shook her head, more to intensify the contact than to deny his question.

"Tell me."

Arabella remained still, her cheek still cuddled into the curve of Nando's large hand.

"Tell me," Nando whispered again.

"This reminded me of another escapade of my misspent childhood." Arabella opened her eyes and attempted a smile. "I decided to masquerade as a beggar child one day. My father happened to see me and whipped me with his riding crop right in the middle of Mayfair." Her tongue passed over dry lips as she relived that awful day.

"I had welts all over my body for weeks. I don't think Papa has *really* looked at or spoken to me since." Arabella's voice petered out to a whisper. She had almost forgotten how badly some memories could hurt.

Nando fought down the useless fury at the thought of anyone raising his hand against Arabella. He felt her pain and gently his arms went around her and brought her against the wall of his chest.

Arabella let her eyes close and allowed herself to lie quiescent against him, her head on his shoulder, her hands flat against his hard chest, breathing in his scent. Oh, she would give the world to stay like this for an hour. A lifetime. There could not possibly be more that life could offer her.

Then something changed. Arabella's palms picked up the changed heartbeat, the tension that echoed her own, and reluctantly she raised her head.

"I'm afraid we're making a spectacle of ourselves," Nando murmured.

Arabella looked around and indeed the people on the street seemed to have stopped going about their business and were staring openly at them.

But instead of letting Arabella go, Nando intensified the pressure of his arms around her. They stood like that for a long, throbbing moment before they returned to their horses and resumed their ride.

Arabella kept her eyes averted from Nando's face, afraid of what she would find there. She knew instinctively that he had been as aware as she of that delicious moment when their blood had begun to pulse more quickly and she did not want to see the cool withdrawal or the angry accusation that she remembered so well from the riverbank. It was so much sweeter to remember Nando's gentle hand against her cheek.

How long would she be able to play this terrible game that Nando demanded of her? she wondered. How long could she pretend that she wanted nothing more from him than an amusing hour or two of his company? Could she make these stolen hours last at least until she had to leave Vienna? These stolen hours that were so sweet, so bitter.

Nando watched Arabella's face, its pallor accented by the spots of color on her cheekbones. God, he wanted her. His self-discipline had controlled the physical urge for the past weeks, but these moments when he had held Arabella against him had been enough to leave it in shreds. Yet the desire was tempered by a tenderness he did not care to examine more closely, and he knew that no matter how his body goaded him, he could never take Arabella just for his own pleasure. She wasn't like the others. That was the rub. But the ever-present dark voice within him whispered evilly, *Yes, she is, yes, she is*.

Swearing, Nando touched his spurs to the stallion's flanks, beckoning to Arabella to follow him.

Chapter Ten

It had been a difficult task to persuade Lulu to accompany her to the Gypsy encampment, Arabella thought with a mischievous smile as she skipped down the steps. Even when she had insisted that the only way she could afford to attend Metternich's costume ball was if she bargained a costume from the Gypsies, Lulu had demurred.

"I'll pay your dressmaker's bill, my dear. Have her make you a proper costume."

"Please, Lulu. I can't start having my friends keep me. Come with me, please." Arabella had paused. "If you don't, I'll go by myself. I mean it."

Finally, Lulu had given in. Arabella grinned again, looking forward enormously to the expedition. She stopped to let a carriage pass. But the carriage drew to a halt in front of her and Princess Katharina Bagration leaned out.

"*Bonjour,* Mademoiselle Douglas," she said, her soft mouth curved in a meaningless smile. "You look very pleased with yourself this afternoon."

All trace of her smile disappeared and Arabella answered the princess's greeting with a nod and a curt, "Your grace," and even that cost her. Every instinct in her longed to attack Katharina and exact some small measure of vengeance for the pain and humiliation the woman had inflicted on Nando.

"May I offer you a ride to wherever you're going? I would enjoy the pleasure of your company." Katharina laughed, the malicious, throaty chuckle at odds with her little girl's voice. "After all, we do seem to have a great deal in common."

"No, thank you, your grace." Arabella managed the polite words, even though her tone left something to be desired. "I prefer to walk. And we have nothing in common." With the barest suggestion of a curtsy, Arabella walked briskly away.

Nikita Volkonsky pulled Katharina back from the carriage window by the scruff of her neck.

"I've never found you particularly intelligent, Katya," he snarled as he flung Katharina against the leather squabs. "But now I'm certain you're a fool." Pushing past Katharina to look outside, a smile briefly touched his lips when he saw that his hireling was turning a corner just behind Arabella. His contingency plan was working at least. Satisfied, he turned his attention to his companion.

"Did you really expect the girl to go with you when you remind her that the man she's been making calf's eyes at has lain between your legs?" He gave Katharina a little shake. "Answer me, damn you. Or did you do it just to spite me?"

Katharina pouted prettily. "Perhaps. I really don't see why all of you are lusting after the little slut—" she drew her diaphanous white muslin shawl closer and sniffed "—when there are others around."

"When the *others*—" Volkonsky spat out the word "—have lain with half of Europe, they tend to lose their charm."

With a muttered curse, he let himself fall back against the cushions. But out of the corner of his eye, he caught the venomous look Katharina sent him and he knew this time he'd gone too far. After all, he would still need Katharina's cooperation once the girl was in his power.

Volkonsky leaned forward again and began to mend his fences, his large hand splaying carelessly on a muslin-covered breast.

"You know how it is, my dove," Volkonsky soothed, his tone suddenly cajoling and seductive as he bent his head to nip at Katharina's neck. "We all want something new." Volkonsky rubbed the soft, plump underside of her chin with one finger. "So do you. Right, love?"

Katharina shrugged away Volkonsky's touch and snapped, "No, as a matter of fact, this time I'd like a repeat performance." She lowered her eyelids voluptuously and the tip of her small pink tongue passed over her lips. "I want another taste of Nando." Katharina leaned forward to toy with a button on Volkonsky's dark blue tunic. "You see, Niki, he was the best. The very best." She leaned a little closer and smiled spitefully. "You really should have the English girl before Nando does, Niki. Before she knows the difference."

Volkonsky fought down the flash of rage at Katharina's words and hid behind an arrogant grin. "Then we understand each other, Katya. From now on you—" he tapped his forefinger against her chin "—do exactly as I tell you, and when I've had my fill of that black-haired witch, I'll serve you Berg on a silver platter. The rest will be up to you."

When he saw Katharina lean out of her carriage, Nando had almost spurred his mount forward to pull Arabella away.

She had laughingly told him yesterday that she was going shopping with Lulu today and he would definitely be a fifth wheel. Still he had woken with an odd feeling of foreboding that had propelled him to follow her.

But even when Arabella emerged from the Thürheim town house arm in arm with Lulu and they set off in a carriage accompanied by coachman and footman, Nando's skin did not stop crawling.

The carriage headed toward the main promenade in the Prater, and Nando's tension began to ease a little in the peopled surroundings. But when the coachman veered onto a narrow road that ran closer to the riverbank, Nando swore, knowing that the only thing at the end of the road was marsh forest and a clearing Gypsies were allowed to use for their camp.

He had almost reached the turn-off when Nando found his way hampered by a carriage and rider and had to slow down to pass them.

Suddenly a familiar voice hailed him. "Hello there, Berg. What's the hurry?"

Nando reined in his mount and saluted his commander, General Prince Schwarzenberg, the only sign of his impatience a glance toward the road along the riverbank.

"You haven't haunted my audience chamber for weeks, Berg." Schwarzenberg smiled broadly. "May I assume that you are finding Vienna pleasant after all?"

"Indeed, your grace." Nando's smile was sincere despite his uneasiness. Schwarzenberg was a man who truly cared about the men who served under him.

"Ride with us a ways, Berg, and tell us how you've been passing the time." The words were an invitation, but Schwarzenberg's tone left no room for doubt that he expected as much obedience now as he expected on the battlefield.

Nando bowed, but his gaze swerved to the narrow road in time to see the dark-clothed man he had seen before round the bend behind the Thürheim carriage.

Schwarzenberg's wife, a tiny, pert brunette, leaned out of the carriage window and smiled up at Nando. "You can catch up with her later." She gestured with her chin in the direction the carriage had disappeared and her dimples deepened. "You see, we're not quite as uninformed as my husband wants you to think. But do keep us company for a little while anyway."

Nando cursed violently to himself as he matched Sultan's stride to that of Schwarzenberg's mount, the taut skin across his knuckles and a nervous muscle in his jaw betraying his tension.

Reluctantly Arabella handed the footman the unwieldly package. It had cost but a few coins and was wrapped in a shabby piece of cloth of questionable cleanliness, but it was the most exciting purchase she had ever made. It had been such a fascinating experience to sit between the colorful wagons, drink aromatic Turkish coffee and bargain with the dark-haired, dusky-skinned Gypsies that she was loath to let go of her wonderful treasures.

She turned to Lulu with a merry smile. "Now do you still say I should have had a mere dressmaker make my costume?"

"I'm sure it wouldn't have been more colorful." Lulu lifted an eyebrow. "Or more eye-catching."

"But?" Arabella prompted, hearing the reservation in her friend's voice.

"Well—" Lulu pursed her lips "—I predict that you will cause quite a stir. And I suspect Nando will have something to say about it." She sent Arabella a sly smile. "Are you perhaps planning to give him a subtle push?"

Arabella shook her head. "Not really. I wanted to pinch a few pennies and not wear one of the dozens of Austrian, Hungarian or Transylvanian peasant costumes that are sure to be there into the bargain." She answered Lulu's sly smile with one of her own. "But it is a tempting thought."

The two young women laughed and hooked arms as they fell into step. They had left their carriage on the road out of sight of the Gypsy encampment, having agreed that the luxurious Thürheim carriage would be an impediment to successful bargaining.

Laughing and talking, they paid no attention to where they set their lightly shod feet until Lulu slipped and lost her balance, gasping.

"Lulu, what's wrong?" Arabella cried, managing to keep her friend upright. "Anton," she called to the footman. *"Help Er."*

"I'll be all right, Arabella," Lulu remonstrated. "I've just turned my ankle a bit." She tried to take a step, but the pain was too great and she collapsed against Arabella.

The footman reached them with several long strides and Arabella took charge.

"Anton, you will carry the countess back to the carriage."

"No," Lulu protested. "There's no need."

"Don't argue, Lulu. You can't possibly walk on that ankle." Arabella's voice was brisk. "Give me my bundle, Anton, and go ahead with the countess."

The footman handed the bundle to Arabella without demur and with an apologetic look in the direction of his mistress, picked Lulu up gingerly and strode off.

Within moments Anton's broad-shouldered figure had disappeared beyond a curve in the road. Reproaching herself for dragging Lulu out here, Arabella looped the string that held the bundle together around her wrist and moved after him, the package bumping awkwardly against her leg.

So carefully did she pick her way through the mud-filled potholes and slick stones that she did not hear the horseman until he was almost upon her. Just as Arabella turned to see who it was, the dark-clothed rider swooped down on her and, picking her up easily with one brawny arm, slung her unceremoniously in front of him across the horse's back.

Panic closed Arabella's throat, making it impossible for her to scream for help. Making it even difficult for her to breathe. But she began to struggle, fighting against her fear as much as against her abductor.

She twisted sideways, trying to free her hands, struggling against her own weight and against the bundle that still hung from her wrist, effectively shackling her. When the string caught on a saddle buckle and tore, leaving her hand mobile, she managed to turn sideways. Ignoring the possibility that her movements could easily cause her to slip off the horse and under its hooves, she began to pummel her abductor.

"Damn you," the man shouted, his voice muffled by the dark scarf he had tied around the lower part of his face. "Be still. I won't hurt you unless you force me to." He managed to grab hold of Arabella's wrist and twisted it cruelly.

The pain shot up her arm and Arabella cried out, but still she managed to bring her elbow diagonally upward to connect with the man's midriff. The blow caught him by surprise and he grunted with pain as he let her wrist slip out of his grasp.

Disquieted by the struggle on its back, the horse whinnied nervously and began to rear, forcing the man to divert his attention from Arabella to his mount and giving her some freedom of movement. But the respite lasted only a moment before the man had his horse under control again and his hand closed again on Arabella's wrist.

Suddenly she felt something sharp scrape along her throat and realized that the heavy silver closure of her cape had opened and was yet another source of danger. She strained to reach it with her free hand, but her own body had pinned her arm at an angle that made reaching the brooch impossible.

The sharp point pressed into the hollow of her throat more insistently, and she squirmed desperately. The man's hand was at the back of her neck, and Arabella realized with a flash of panic how much more power over her he had now that her movements were no longer directed against him.

The man's rough fingers began to squeeze her neck, and in a sudden flash of inspiration, Arabella levered herself forward far enough to give her hands access to the brooch, then went limp. The man gave a satisfied grunt, and his grip loosened, then let go completely, allowing her to slump over the horse's back.

Aware that she had only a few precious moments to carry out her plan before her abductor spurred his mount to a gallop, Arabella raised her right arm, using her own body as a shield for her movement. With a tug, the brooch was in her hand.

Apologizing mentally to the horse, she drew the brooch's pin along its hide just hard enough for the animal to protest by rearing again. The man swore. His attention diverted, Arabella raised her arm as far as her position allowed her and sunk the pin into his calf.

The man jerked and roared with the unexpected pain and the horse reared again. Knowing that this was her only chance, Arabella tucked her chin into her chest and pushed both palms against the horse's flank. Letting herself fall forward, she rolled away in a wobbly somersault.

She came down on her back and the hard landing knocked the breath out of her, but within a moment she was up and running. She let her cape fall on the ground and, holding her skirts up away from her feet, she ran. The man shouted something she did not understand, and in the same moment Arabella saw Anton round the curve and come running toward her.

The horse whinnied loudly in protest as the man reined it in cruelly. As she collapsed against Anton, Arabella heard the sound of hoofbeats pounding away from them.

"*Fräulein!*" Anton cried. "Are you all right?"

Arabella could not do more than nod jerkily, and she pressed the back of her hand against her mouth in a vain attempt to stop the hiccups that began to come now that she was safe.

The footman helped Arabella to a log that lay at the side of the road and gently set her down. Within minutes, he was back with her cape and the bundle. He had even found the silver brooch, its pin now bent, and Arabella turned away from the sight, a ball of nausea uncurling in her stomach.

Lulu gave a cry of alarm when she saw Arabella. "*Mein Gott,* what happened?" She gripped both of Arabella's hands as Anton helped her into the carriage. "Are you all right? Oh, my God, Arabella. Answer me." Lulu patted her friend's pale cheeks.

"I will be in a minute, Lulu," Arabella whispered. "Truly."

Lulu reached under the seat and pulled forward a small leather satchel. Quickly she took out a bottle, poured and held out a small glass to Arabella. "Here, drink this."

Arabella shook her head as the fumes of the brandy rose to her nose, but Lulu insisted and lifted the glass to her lips. "Drink."

Gulping down the amber liquid, Arabella shuddered as the brandy burned its way down her throat. It settled in her stomach like a small fireball, but gradually the relaxing warmth began to travel through her veins. Closing her eyes, Arabella concentrated on her breathing until it finally evened. Suddenly, without warning, her fingers flew up to her mouth and she began to laugh.

Fearful of a bout of hysteria, Lulu slipped an arm around Arabella's shoulders and with her other hand dug into her reticule for the smelling salts.

"It's all right, Arabella," she soothed. "You're safe now."

Arabella opened her eyes and tried unsuccessfully to still her giggles, pressing her fingers against her lips. "I'm sorry, Lulu, I'm not being hysterical," she said not quite truthfully. "Truly I'm not." Arabella tamped down a new bubble of laughter. "But first the intruder in Lord Castlereagh's study and now this. It seems that I keep fighting off men and then getting that vile-tasting brandy poured down my throat. If this continues, I fear I shall become a drunkard."

"Perhaps you should be more careful." Lulu pulled Arabella's head down to her shoulder and resolved to talk to Nando, even though she did not relish the thought of his anger. "Do you think it could have been the same man? Or was this one of the Gypsies?"

"No. Neither, I think." Her eyes fluttered closed. "It was all probably just a coincidence."

Arabella had relaxed a little against Lulu when the sound of hoofbeats caused her to sit up sharply again. Her heart began to pound out of control and she pressed herself back into a corner of the carriage. But as the hoofbeats approached swiftly, the alarm changed to fury. She had almost been a victim twice now and, by God, she would not be a victim again.

"Damn it," Arabella cried. "I refuse to be so helpless. If I were a man, I would make mincemeat out of all of them."

Her gaze flew around the carriage as if looking for a weapon and lit on the satchel at her feet. Resolutely, Arabella reached down and grabbed the brandy bottle. "The devil with it," she swore, ignoring Lulu's cry of alarm. "Just let him try anything and I'll cut his face to ribbons."

Holding the bottleneck, she swung the bottle against the side of the carriage. The wood splintered, but the bottle held. Again she swung it, aiming for the metal door handle. This time the thick glass cracked and gave and Arabella winced as the brandy ran over her hand, forming a puddle at her feet.

The hoofbeats came closer. Shaking off Lulu's restraining hands, Arabella leaned forward. She held on to the door with one hand and brandished the bottle in the other, preparing to greet their attacker with a thrust of the thick, jagged glass.

By the time Nando was able to extricate himself from the Schwarzenbergs' company, his nerves were taut enough to snap. Disregarding all etiquette, disregarding the outraged looks of the occupants of the carriages and landaus, he galloped down the chestnut-tree-lined drive, Sultan's hooves raising dust and scattering the finely crushed gravel.

For once he did not question what he was doing, nor his motivations. Too urgent the need to make certain that Arabella was safe. Too keen the metallic taste of fear on his tongue.

Nando didn't slow his mount even when he saw the carriage coming toward him. Only when he was almost abreast of it did he rein Sultan in, at the same time gesturing to the coachman to stop. He saw the footman jump from his step at the rear of the coach, and if he wondered about the defensive stance the man took up near the carriage door Nando did not stop to think about it.

He had dismounted and turned toward the carriage when his step almost faltered. What was he doing here, making a fool of himself? Opening himself up to all the possibilities for pain and ridicule that he had safeguarded himself against for so long? But everything paled beside the need to know that Arabella was safe, and Nando stepped closer.

When he found himself facing the jagged edge of a broken bottle a moment later, Nando's finely honed instincts had him gripping the hand holding it before he realized that the hand was Arabella's.

They stared at each other, Nando's fingers gripping Arabella's wrist, her hand clutching the bottleneck.

She had lost her bonnet. Her hair had come undone, half her black curls hanging down past her shoulders. There was a smear of mud on her face and a nasty scratch near the hollow of her throat. All of this Nando took in in the space of a breath.

"My God, what happened, Arabella? Are you all right?" Nando's voice matched his pounding heartbeat.

Arabella stared at him, her eyes wide and almost black with only a narrow sapphire rim around the huge pupils.

Nando's fingers eased their pressure. "Are you all right?" he repeated.

"Yes." Arabella's voice was somewhere between a croak and a whisper. "Yes, I'm all right." Her eyes veered to the bottle she clasped tightly then returned to Nando's face. "I almost cut you." She swallowed with difficulty and passed her tongue over dry, bloodless lips. "If you hadn't stopped me, I would have slashed your face."

"But you didn't." Nando's thumb began to soothe the spot where his fingers had seized her. "You can let go now."

But it was as if she hadn't heard him. Her gaze kept wandering between Nando's face and the jagged edge of the glass. The shock of having come within a hair breadth of slashing Nando's face had managed to frighten her as even the attack moments before hadn't.

Gently Nando began to pry her ice-cold fingers from the bottleneck one by one. Then he took it and flung it aside.

Lulu stuck her head out of the window. "Arabella was attacked, but she managed to free herself. She thought her attacker was coming back."

The anger that flashed into Nando's eyes colored his voice. "And where were you, Lulu? And your servants? And what were you thinking of at all to come here?"

Nando's tone snapped Arabella out of her state and she flew to her friend's defense. "It's not Lulu's fault. I was the one who wanted to come here."

"And what were you doing here, pray tell? There's nothing back there but the Gypsy encampment."

Arabella bristled at Nando's tone. "I had an errand there."

"What, damn it?" Nando's already thin patience snapped as relief bred anger. "Did you want your fortune told? Or a potion mixed?"

"It's none of your business." Arabella's eyes flashed sparks. "You're not my keeper, Nando."

"I'm certainly glad of that, although, God knows, you need one." Nando realized with a start that he was still holding Arabella's wrist, and he let go so suddenly that her hand fell against the window frame.

"You will forgive me for bothering you, I trust." Nando's icy gaze swept over the two women. "Good day."

Nando wheeled and swung onto his stallion.

It was not until she heard the pounding of Sultan's hooves that Arabella moved. She fell back against the leather squabs and covered her face with both hands as everything rushed at her all at once and the tears came.

Chapter Eleven

Arabella twirled in front of the mirror. The Gypsy skirt of bold red and black swished around her exposed ankles and accented the curve of her hips. Although she had used the drawstring to make the neckline of the embroidered white blouse as modest as possible, it clung to her curves as lovingly as a chemise. Now that she was dressed, apprehension brushed her nerve endings despite the secret, little thrill she felt. Smiling at her reflection, she tossed the black hair that fell down her back in its natural tumble of curls, bound by only a narrow red ribbon.

Doing her best to ignore Jeanne's muttering behind her, Arabella stuffed the contents of the white velvet reticule she ordinarily used for balls—handkerchief, rice powder, a vial of scent, a few coins—into the roomy pockets of her skirt.

Jeanne stepped up to Arabella with her evening cape over her arm. But instead of holding it for her to slip into, she shook her head. "How could you do this? If your mother knew, she would be sick at heart."

"Oh, come now, Jeanne, there's no need to go that far." Arabella tamped down the impatience that threatened to surface. "Besides, you know very well how few coins are left in my box, and since the invitation requested that the ladies dress in costumes of the Habsburg realm, I would not have been able to attend otherwise."

Sniffing, Jeanne shrugged. "Well, if a man is too bold with you tonight, it will be no more than you deserve."

"*Bonne nuit,* Jeanne," Arabella said quietly, not wanting to quarrel, and closed the door softly behind her.

"Arabella? Is that you?"

Arabella turned toward a figure in a golden mask wearing the festive dirndl dress of an Upper Austrian peasant girl, complete with the fringed square scarf of fine silk and cap edged in exquisitely worked gold braid. She grinned behind her red mask, with black lace trim that fell to her mouth.

"Of course, it's me, Lulu. You were with me when I bought this, after all."

"Just making certain," Lulu said dryly. "Have you seen Nando yet?"

Arabella shook her head. She had not seen Nando since that day near the Gypsy encampment and she honestly wondered if he would bother speaking to her at all.

Lulu moved back a step and sized up her friend. "Good. I think I'll linger by your side and watch the fireworks."

"I'm not sure if he's on speaking terms with me. Besides, he wouldn't dare," Arabella said, her eyes unconsciously scanning the crowd. "He has no right." But even as she spoke, her heart leaped with a heady mixture of nervousness and pleasure.

"Of course, he doesn't. But something tells me, my dear, that *that* is not going to make any difference." Lulu squeezed her arm and turned away to greet someone on her left.

Arabella sank her hands into her pockets and smiled to herself as she swished her full skirt, lazily watching the dancing master scurry around, arranging the sets for a quadrille. Suddenly her view of the dance floor was blocked.

"Just what do you think you're doing?"

Nando bit out the words with such fury that for a moment Arabella was silenced. But she recovered her aplomb quickly, and as she did, her own emotions came to a boil. She balled her hands into fists, grateful for her pockets, and swallowed the overpowering desire to scream at Nando like a fishwife.

"I am trying to observe the dancing and *monsieur* is blocking my view." Her voice was just a shade breathless.

"Very amusing. Arabella—"

"Tsk, tsk, *monsieur*. No names, please."

"Are you mad to wear a costume like that?" Nando stepped closer. "And you risked your life for those indecent rags?"

Arabella looked up, her eyes wide behind the mask. "Are there no Gypsies in the realms of the Habsburgs, *monsieur?*" Her voice was deceptively sweet, as she deliberately misunderstood his questions.

"You know perfectly well what I mean," Nando barked. "Your costume is an invitation to every man here tonight. A most unambiguous invitation." He was absolutely furious and he hated the violence of his reaction as much as he hated his inability to conceal it.

The satisfaction of having reached beyond Nando's reserve receded before his summary behavior, and Arabella felt her nostrils begin to quiver. Some things she wouldn't take—not from him, not from anyone.

"How kind of you to be concerned about the virtue of a Gypsy girl," she drawled with more sangfroid than she was feeling and reached up to toy provocatively with the laces of her blouse.

"Arabella..." Nando began again and reached for her shoulder.

Nando's movement triggered her temper and before Arabella could consider her words she snapped, "Leave me alone, Nando. You have no rights to me."

Nando looked down at Arabella. Her sapphire eyes were blazing defiantly at him from behind the red mask, but her teeth were worrying her lower lip. She was a picture in contrasts, and he felt something soften within him.

He had been unfair to her tonight, as he had been so many times before. Arabella's costume was hardly more immodest than so many of the others. And could she be faulted that her slender yet lush body was set off to perfection by the colorful silk? That her unbound blue-black curls invited a man to sink his hands into them? That her graceful movements presaged other movements, other pleasures? Nando felt the familiar tug of arousal, an arousal that masked a deeper and more basic need, and looked away.

Suddenly a heavy hand descended on Nando's back in the guise of a friendly greeting.

"How now, my dear Berg. You are being most unfair, hiding such a charming Gypsy from the rest of us."

Volkonsky's eyes slid greedily over Arabella, and she felt a shiver of repulsion at his openly avid gaze, remembering all too well how his hands had explored her body that evening in the alcove.

Leaving one hand on Nando's shoulder, Volkonsky propped the other one on his hip. "Gypsies are very much *en vogue* in Russia. Did you know that, *mademoiselle?*"

Arabella lifted a hand and flung a heavy strand of hair over her shoulder. "Gypsies are very much *en vogue* everywhere, *monsieur.*" It amused her to use the prerogative of the masked ball to deprive Volkonsky of his title.

Volkonsky leaned forward, took her hand and with a lazily insolent gesture lifted it to his lips. But instead of breathing a kiss over the tips of her fingers as etiquette would have required, he turned it and kissed the inside of her wrist. "And fair game everywhere, as well." His thumb moved leisurely over the marks still visible on Arabella's wrists. "As you have apparently already learned. *Hein?*"

Arabella curled her fingers and twisted her hand away. "I have learned no such thing," she snapped. "The only ones who are fair game are those who let themselves be."

"Ah, yes," Volkonsky drawled. "And are you certain that you know which ones you belong to, *mademoiselle?*"

"Volkonsky, I warn you..." Nando snarled and jerked the Russian away from Arabella.

Volkonsky turned slowly, his hand going to the hilt of his sword. With the silky gesture of a lover he caressed the gilt metal. "You warn me?" His sensual mouth thinned. "Please do continue, my dear Berg, I would relish a reason to make an early morning outing along the river with you."

Arabella felt the blood leave her face. It was well and good for the two of them to bandy words and strut around like peacocks, but to even _hint_ at a duel was unbearable. Acting on intuition, she thrust her hands between them and pushed the two men apart as hard as she could. Her gesture took them both by surprise, and the breach between the men widened.

Stepping forward, Arabella planted her hands on her hips and had opened her mouth to tell them what she thought of them when the gap between the two men was filled by Prince Schwarzenberg.

"You will excuse us for a moment, _mademoiselle._" The prince bowed. "Volkonsky." Without waiting for a reply, he took Nando's arm and drew him away.

Her heart pumping madly with fear, Arabella whirled, barely escaping the hand Volkonsky reached out for her. She had to keep him safe, Arabella thought wildly. She had to keep Nando safe. Moving quickly, she slipped through the crowd to look for Lulu.

Arabella found Lulu laughing and flushed from a quadrille and plucked at her sleeve. "I need your help," she whispered.

Lulu excused herself from her partner, and when they were a few steps away she sniffed. "I hope you have a good reason for this. Count Allendorf is one of the few men in Vienna who do not treat intelligent women like lepers."

"I'm sorry, Lulu, but this is urgent." Arabella pulled her friend behind the chairs and _canapés_ that had been set up in the gallery. "Did you hear them?"

Lulu shook her head. "Just the beginning of Nando's tirade. What happened?"

"Volkonsky made a few of his choice remarks and Nando decided to defend my honor. That beast Volkonsky dared him to go on and hinted at a morning outing along the river."

"Oh, no," Lulu exclaimed. "And the fool would have to pick Volkonsky, when everyone knows that the man's second-favorite pastime is dueling and he always shoots to kill."

"Lulu, you've got to find Nando for me. Please."

"What are you going to do?"

"Talk to him."

"Talk? Are you serious?" Lulu demanded. "To a man wanting to defend his honor? Or yours?"

"Please, Lulu."

Lulu sighed. "Where is he now?"

"Prince Schwarzenberg took him aside." Arabella tugged at Lulu's sleeve again. "Lulu, please. Tell Nando that I'll meet him at the bottom of the stairs that lead to the dining room."

"But no one will be there now."

"Exactly."

Arabella ran down the curved staircase and leaned against the wall to catch her breath. Pressing her hands against her middle, she tried to compose herself. But standing still only served to aggravate her agitation, so she began to pace, her black lace-tied slippers tapping lightly on the parquet floor.

What if Lulu hadn't found Nando? What if Schwarzenberg had not detained him long enough? What if Nando had met Volkonsky again and she was too late? The questions whirled in her brain until she was ready to scream with frustration.

"You wanted to see me, Arabella?"

Arabella jumped and whirled at the sound of Nando's mellow voice. Her pacing had blocked out the sound of his steps on the carpeted stairs, and he was standing so close behind her that when Arabella turned around, she was almost flush up against him.

Nando caught her by the shoulders. "What's the matter? You're trembling."

His voice was gentle and held none of the impatience or anger she had feared. Arabella's hands flattened against his chest. "You're not going to fight him, are you, Nando? You're not going to let him provoke you into a duel? Tell me you aren't. Please." She knew that there had to be a better way to say this, but she had no patience for preliminaries.

Nando allowed a smile to curve his mouth. When was the last time a woman other than his mother had worried about him? He couldn't remember.

"Don't you dare laugh at me." Arabella's hands curled into fists. "Tell me."

Nando did not answer at first, but instead reached up and leisurely tucked a stray curl behind her ear. It felt like silk, and he was sorely tempted to see if the rest of Arabella's hair felt the same.

"Would it matter so much?" he questioned softly and for a moment the softness was reflected in his silver eyes.

The touch of Nando's fingers on her ear almost made Arabella forget why they were here. But then the heels of her hands pushed at his chest. "Answer my question," she demanded fiercely.

"We haven't fixed a rendezvous yet." Nando shrugged carelessly. "But probably only because Schwarzenberg kept me occupied until Lulu dragged me off."

Arabella's body went limp with relief within his grasp.

"But you're not going to. Tell me that you're not going to fight him," she whispered. His chest felt hard and warm beneath her hands, and the thought of this body cold and still because of her was unbearable. "Please."

The last word was an almost soundless movement of her lips, as for the first time Arabella put a name to the emotion that lived within her. How was it that she had not seen before that she loved him?

Her stomach plummeted so quickly that her eyelids fluttered closed. Vaguely she registered a pain in her chest, but only when she dragged in a lungful of air that was more a sob than a breath did she realize that she had forgotten to breathe.

Arabella opened her eyes and they widened as she took in every plane and angle of Nando's chiseled face. It was as if she was seeing him for the first time, and she felt her eyes moisten with tears of wonder as the initial feelings of helplessness and panic receded and joy began to fill her.

Suddenly Nando needed to see her face, and his hands tangled feverishly in Arabella's hair, ripping at the ties of her mask. When it had fluttered to the floor, he framed her face with his hands. The emotion he had fled for so long blazed in her eyes and he felt it burn through his soul as an arrow burns through flesh. Closing his eyes against the unbearable sweetness, he leaned his forehead against hers.

"No, Arabella. Please, no," Nando begged, each word bringing a physical pain. He was starving and yet he must refuse the life-bringing sustenance. What would it be like to take what he saw in her sapphire eyes into himself? To accept it, to savor it, to treasure it always? But even as the pain of loss drilled through him, the persistent voice of Nando's evil spirit whispered malignantly that it was only poison he was refusing. Poison hidden in the sweetest of receptacles.

Nando's words caressed her skin. They were a denial and yet for one visionary moment, Arabella knew they were a plea, a confession, as well.

Almost absently, Nando began to move his thumbs on the satin skin of Arabella's chin, slowly inching upward until the pads were stroking the generous line of her lower lip. Her lips parted, but he continued the gentle touching, making no move to take the invitation.

He was so close that his thumbs filled the space between their mouths completely and Nando felt his nails graze his own lips as his fingers moved along the soft pillow. Arabella's sweet breath flowed against his fingers, his lips, and Nando felt the desire surge and ripple through his blood. And yet he made no other move but to continue the feathering strokes.

Arabella squeezed her eyes shut and tautened her muscles against the terrible, burning ache at her center. Why was Nando torturing her like this? Would he never kiss her? Her tongue darted out to moisten her upper lip, and Nando's thumb brushed its sleek, wet underside.

Nando stilled as that random touch spurred his body to full arousal. He drew his head back one inch, two, so that he could look into Arabella's face. The long-lashed curtain lifted from her sapphire eyes. The softness was still there, the... No, damn it, he would not put a name to the emotion he saw there. The emotion that was surrounded by a flame he had ignited. A bright, hot flame that burned for him alone.

Arabella looked into Nando's stormy eyes and with an instinctive knowledge she knew that what she saw there was the mirror image of the wildness that raged within her. But she, in all her innocence, accepted the storm, just as after that first panic-filled moment she had accepted the love.

With all the need, all the hunger of her nineteen years Arabella wanted Nando. She wanted everything Nando could give her, and in this first, magical moment, she believed she would be satisfied with however much or little it would be. And she knew she would die if he did not kiss her.

Locking her eyes into his, Arabella uncurled her tongue and deliberately slid it along the joint of Nando's thumb to the tip.

As glass breaks when the temperature climbs too high, so the tenuous control Nando had over himself snapped at that simple touch, so incredibly arousing in its very subtlety. He lowered his head and with a groan that could have been her name he melded their mouths together. His tongue plunged into her mouth, probing, tasting. And the fire within him grew.

She took him within her and marveled at the burst of sensation Nando's tongue evoked as it circled her own, then slid along the edge of her teeth, as if inviting her to close and keep him prisoner in her hot, sweet wetness.

Her hands worked their way from between them and slid around his middle, bringing them flush against each other. The hardness of his arousal met her belly as if there were no clothes, no barriers between them, and Arabella did not withdraw from that new sensation. Instead her mouth closed around Nando's tongue in response, in acceptance of the passion that surrounded them like a flaming curtain.

His hands moved away from her face, threading through her hair and sliding downward, wanting to mold her to him. But the coolness of the silk Arabella wore after the seductive warmth of her skin brought him back from the utter intoxication of the senses and he drew away.

He was still touching her, but Arabella felt cold and bereft without Nando's mouth on hers, without his strong, hard body pressing its stamp into her softness.

"You don't know what you're doing," Nando rasped.

"I am not a fool, Nando." Her fingers curled into the cloth of his tunic to keep him from slipping away.

"No, you are not a fool, Arabella, my sweet. But you are so very young," Nando said ruefully and briefly touched his fingertips to her cheek. "You need a man. And he need not necessarily be me."

He saw the pain surge into her eyes, but he denied it, as he denied his own. "You're young and strong and you need to try your strength," he went on as one corner of his mouth lifted in a lopsided grin.

Arabella stepped back, and Nando's hands fell away from her shoulders. Carefully she tried to sift through the sensations, the emotions of the past minutes, so new, so earthshaking. Was he truly making light of this? Had that one clairvoyant moment when she had seen into his heart been a mirage? No, Arabella insisted to herself. Nothing in her life had ever been as real as that one diaphanous moment.

Then her chin lifted as her pride asserted itself and with the optimism of her youth Arabella smiled. "Yes, perhaps I do."

Retrieving her mask from the floor, she moved past Nando toward the staircase. She wanted to stay and move into his arms again and yet she felt that she needed some distance, just as much as he did.

But she had only begun to climb the stairs when Arabella gripped the white and gold banister with both hands and looked down at Nando. "Promise me that you will not fight Volkonsky."

Nando tilted his face upward and looked into her sapphire eyes for a long moment, a heady warmth filling him. A warmth that he savored and for once refused to question.

"Yes, *ma petite,* if it means so much to you, I promise."

Arabella looked into the gray depths and, satisfied that Nando spoke the truth, she nodded briefly and ran up the stairs.

Chapter Twelve

After two months of festivities, many of the hundred thousand people who had gathered in Vienna for the sole purpose of being present during the congress were becoming sated with the endless succession of balls, masquerades, soirees, musicales and *tableaux vivants*. But as November came to a close, even the most jaded palate felt the excitement that was generated by the incredibly elaborate preparations for the Carousel, a medieval tournament to be reenacted in the Imperial Riding School.

Nando despised having to take part in what he considered gross exhibitionism. But even more than that, he despised the thought that Princess Katharina Bagration had been assigned as his lady.

Scowling into the mirror, Nando adjusted the richly embroidered silk sash in Katharina's colors. The sash had arrived accompanied by a note perfumed with a nauseating amount of scent and containing an unsubtle invitation to renew their acquaintance.

Damn her! Nando swatted at a tortoiseshell brush, sending it clear across the room. It repulsed him to handle what she had touched. He grimaced. What he needed was a charm to counteract the vile, filthy feeling that wearing her gift gave him.

His gaze skimmed over the dressing table and fell on the white mask Arabella had so ingenuously invited him to ask for at their first meeting. He had taken it then, fully intending to discard it at the first opportunity, but somehow the scrap of silk had resisted. He reached for it now and raised it to his face. Nando's eyes fell shut. Even after all these weeks, it still carried a faint fragrance of lily of the valley. For a sweet moment he forgot the tournament, forgot Princess Katharina Bagration, forgot even his own cynicism.

Not stopping to consider this uncharacteristic attack of whimsy, Nando carefully worked the material into the folds of the sash, leaving enough showing so that he would know it was there. He saw Franz watching him with undisguised curiosity and he averted his gaze, color touching his prominent cheekbones. Muttering something distinctly uncomplimentary about himself, he snatched up his hat and strode from the room.

Arabella gripped her fan tightly in her lap to keep her restless hands still. The prospect of this evening's entertainment had cast a pall on her mood that her own good sense could not dispel. With only half an ear, she listened to Lady Castlereagh's running commentary on the people present and amused herself by examining the hall.

The twenty-four Corinthian columns that circled the Imperial Riding School each carried the crest of one of the twenty-four young Austrian noblemen participating in the tournament. With a smile Arabella noted that she was sitting almost directly opposite the column that carried the Berg crest—a black panther with a gold crown on a background of red and green.

The bells of the nearby St. Michael's Church had just begun to chime eight o'clock when the first fanfare sounded and the wide doors opened to admit the twenty-four ladies, heavily veiled from head to toe with gold-edged gauze.

At the sound of a second, more elaborate fanfare the audience rose to greet the royalty with enthusiastic applause, and at a sign from the Lord Chamberlain, the ladies removed their veils to salute the rulers. When the veils fell, a murmur went through the audience.

Vienna was no stranger to luxurious gowns, but the tableau that presented itself at that moment beggared description. The shades of the velvet gowns in the baroque style had been limited to four colors—black, dark red, sky blue and emerald green—but the precious stones worked into the bodices, the profusion of brooches, clasps, necklaces, bracelets and tiaras that caught and refracted the light of the candles that turned night into day were truly dazzling.

The brisk military music began and Arabella felt her heartbeat accelerate as the knights appeared. There he was, his stern beauty a foil for his ornate, bejeweled costume. Her heart flew out to him.

On their ebony chargers, the riders approached the monarchs' tribune two by two to pay homage. Then, wheeling around sharply, they nudged their horses into a brisk trot to cross the hall to the ladies' tribune to pay homage again. Smiling graciously, twenty-four ladies stood to curtsy and return the greeting.

Nando's glance flickered dispassionately over the group and settled on Katharina, her porcelain beauty coarsened by her black velvet gown. Small wonder that ʌ ʌ affected the virginally white muslin gowns as a disguise for ʌ e vulgarity that years of debauchery had brought to her face.

The sight of Katharina's smug smile brought the bitter taste of bile to Nando's mouth. Not thinking, not considering the consequences, knowing only that he needed a glimpse of Arabella's face to see him through this farce, he turned his head sharply to the left and looked up, his eyes searching the first row of the gallery.

There she was. A heated rush of pleasure ran through him as he looked at Arabella—her blue-black hair a perfect foil for her dusky pink gown, not a jewel to detract from her loveliness. Her mouth was serious, but the moment their eyes met, her sapphire gaze grew soft and liquid. Nando felt a rush of possessive pride as his eyes rested on her face for one more moment. *Mine,* he thought unreasoningly. *Mine.*

Nando smiled, his heart lighter, and lowered his head fractionally in greeting. Then he turned to the tribune and saw that Katharina had lost her smile. Her nearsighted gaze went from him up to the gallery. She could not see that far, he knew, but there would be more than enough people who would hurry to inform her.

Arabella smothered the gasp that rose in her throat and felt the hot flush flood her skin. But her chin remained high even as she felt people craning their necks to see who had been the recipient of Count Berg's salutation.

She sat there quietly, although her heart sang and her blood pounded in time with the horses' hooves, which suddenly accelerated from a measured walk to a trot, then to a canter and finally to a gallop.

Then the tournament began in earnest as the knights, their fiery Hungarian chargers in full gallop, exhibited their prowess with one feat after another. They picked rings off wooden poles with their lances. They proved their aim by throwing spears at elaborately painted wooden Saracen heads then severing the heads from their anchorings with one swipe of the sword. Then, their stallions moving in formation, they cut through rope after rope from which apples dangled and split the fruit with their swords in one dexterous maneuver.

Other, more dangerous jousting games followed, and Arabella breathed a sigh of relief when the finale came, the young noblemen leading their mounts through a series of complicated equestrian steps in time to the lively music.

With endless babble and not a little confusion, the whole party adjourned next door to the Hofburg for supper, where strolling minstrels sang plaintive old melodies to the accompaniment of the harp.

"How dare you humiliate me like that?" Katharina lashed out at Nando the moment they were seated.

Nando turned his icy gray gaze toward Katharina and felt only disbelief that he had once loved this woman to the point of madness. "How dare *you* indulge in God knows what intrigue to be paired with me?" he replied with quiet, detached contempt. "This spectacle was quite grotesque enough as it is."

Katharina smiled smugly and cocked her head to admire her beringed hands, fluttering her fingers to make the ostentatious stones catch the light. "It was really very simple. I had a word with Tsar Alexander. And he had a word with Court Marshal Trautmannsdorff."

"It must be comforting to have such a powerful protector after all those years when no court would receive you," Nando sneered.

"How dare you?" Katharina demanded with a singular lack of imagination.

"Smile, Katharina, my dear." Nando leaned a little closer, catching an overpowering whiff of her scent, which seemed so vulgar next to the memory of the fragrance of lily of the valley and warm skin. "We are being assiduously watched, and you wouldn't wish people to think you were bothered by a trifle like that, now would you?"

"Who were you looking at?" demanded Katharina, her voice petulant.

"Ask your friend Metternich, why don't you. I'm quite certain his spies have it all written down," Nando drawled with deliberate carelessness and reached for his crystal wine goblet, full of amber Tokay wine, missing the look of pure, unadulterated hatred in her limpid aquamarine eyes.

She would pay him back, she swore. She would find a way to cause him pain.

Even though Nando ignored Katharina for the remainder of the supper, there was no way he could escape dancing the opening quadrille with her at the gala ball. After they had executed the final figure, Katharina anchored her hand on Nando's arm as the dancers dispersed toward the sidelines.

Automatically Nando adjusted his stride to Katharina's tripping steps and blanked out his mind, needing a moment of relief from the revulsion that was turning his stomach. Not paying attention to where they were going, he allowed her to choose their direction, and only when he felt Katharina's nails sink into his arm did he realize that they were approaching Arabella.

"Ah, Miss Douglas." Katharina moved squarely in front of Arabella. Nando felt her wobble and realized that she was standing on tiptoe, attempting vainly to minimize the fact that she was almost a head shorter than Arabella.

Arabella inclined her head with impeccable elegance. "Your grace."

Katharina's nearsighted eyes swept downward and back up to Arabella's face before she spoke again. "So much lovely jewelry here tonight, do you not find it so?"

"Indeed, your grace." Arabella managed a noncommittal smile and prayed for control, realizing how important it was to avoid further confrontation.

"I declare that I have seen far more jewelry here in Vienna than in London," the princess declared airily, her perpetually pouting lips curling with disdain.

The lock on the muzzle that Arabella was keeping on her tongue snapped. "That is hardly surprising, your grace."

"How so?" Katharina's aquamarine eyes were blank with uncomprehension.

"Britain has been paymaster to the alliance these many years, your grace." Arabella's indigo eyes flickered over the glittering necklace of obscenely large diamonds and rubies that almost covered the princess's sizable *décolleté plongeant*. "Apparently while the English invested in cannons, the other allies put their money in diamonds."

Katharina preened as if she had been complimented and stroked her necklace lovingly. "If I had known that you had no jewelry to wear, Miss Douglas, I would have lent you something of mine," she purred.

Arabella took a deep breath to calm the wave of disgust and hate that swept over her. She did not care what the princess said to her, she told herself. She knew that Katharina was a stupid woman. But she could not forget that this was the woman who had hurt Nando so deeply. "Thank you, your grace, but there is no need." Arabella paused to allow her mouth to curve in a cool smile. "My mother always said that it is only the old, shabby paintings that need a bright, new frame."

The smile on Katharina's face blurred and ran like a butter sculpture in the sunlight. She opened her mouth once, twice. *She will pay,* Katharina swore to herself. *I will make the chit pay.* Turning sharply, she moved away, dragging Nando along with her.

When Nando finally claimed Arabella for their first waltz, he felt as drained of energy as if he had fought a major battle. Holding her a bit more closely than etiquette allowed, he sought to cleanse himself of Katharina. For once, the evil voice inside him was still.

Arabella grinned mischievously. "You know, I'm expecting the wrath of God to descend on me any minute. I have told more lies in the past hour and a half than in as many years."

He invited her to continue with a raised eyebrow.

"I have lost count of the people who have inquired if I was the object of Count Berg's salutation when he should have been acknowledging his lady's curtsy." Her lips curved in a self-deprecating smile. "My denials carried just the right touch of delicate indignation." She wrinkled her nose. "But of course after that little scene everyone will know the truth."

"I'm sorry for being so indiscreet." Nando felt an oddly sharp pang of guilt that he had exposed Arabella to gossip. "I just couldn't stand looking at her one moment longer." He looked at her face, the smile on her generous mouth so gay and tender, the mischief in her sapphire eyes so appealing. For a moment the pain of wanting her, wanting her body and soul, was more than he could bear.

For the first time he wanted to give her the words. But there were no words he had the right to speak. How could he tell her that she was a candle in the deepest, darkest night? A fire at which his cold soul warmed? The treasure he dare not reach for?

What would it have been like to have been the kind of man who could take a woman like Arabella and dare to build a future, a life? Nando wondered. But he was a cynical, cold bastard, he reminded himself brutally, who would take everything and at best give physical pleasure in return.

Arabella felt her heart plummet as she watched the bleakness take over Nando's features and make his eyes utterly colorless.

"Nando?"

But then the music drew to a swirling, graceful close and Nando executed a perfect bow over Arabella's gloved hand. Suddenly he knew that he had to escape quickly to avoid giving away more than he had already. Before he made more of a fool of himself. Before she discovered the barren wasteland that was his soul. Before she found the need for a bit of human warmth that still lived in some intact corner of his being.

"Nando, talk to me. Tell me what's wrong," Arabella pleaded as she dragged at his arm. But his brisk steps propelled her forward, her heelless dancing slippers giving her no purchase on the polished parquet floor. But he ignored her.

A jumble of emotions surged inside her. Anger, impatience, fear because he would not take what she so wanted to give. Love that gave her the courage and the confidence she needed.

Her fingers dug mercilessly into his arm, and he finally stopped and looked at her, resentment marring his handsome face.

"Is this the only way to get your attention? With pain?" Arabella demanded, returning his stare boldly. "Is pain the only feeling you understand?" She squeezed his arm again, more gently this time. "Oh, Nando, don't you understand that I don't want anything from you you can't give me?"

Nando shook his head, forcing himself to meet her eyes squarely. "There is nothing I can give you, Arabella. Nothing," he said bleakly.

Arabella felt her confidence falter. She had been sure, so sure that somewhere beneath all the barricades he had erected over the years there was a wellspring of feeling that belonged to her alone. But if that was so, how could Nando look at her with such desolation in his eyes?

Before Arabella knew what was happening, Nando had returned her to where Lady Castlereagh sat. With a bow, a glib word, he was gone.

Chapter Thirteen

The cold wind snapped Nando's cape around him as he walked to the Schwarzenberg palace. He had spurned his carriage, but the short distance across the ramparts and the Glacis was hardly enough to satisfy his restless need for movement.

There had been no sleep for him this past night. After returning from the ball in the early hours of the morning, he had had Sultan saddled and had ridden for hours, trying to bring some kind of clarity and order into his mind.

Nando had become accustomed to the life where nothing ruffled the frozen surface—not fear in battle, not emotion in passion. Both battlefields offered exercise of which he habitually acquitted himself with exquisite flair and prowess. Only a faint self-disgust had always lingered—as a foul smell lingers long after its source has disappeared.

But now a strange discomposure seemed never to leave him. Time was out of joint for him. Even his dreams were fraught with images of Arabella. Dreams from which he awoke, his flesh throbbing with unfulfilled desire.

So much had changed in two short months. So much more than the surface of his life had been ruffled. His guard had begun to slip. Old, long-forgotten yearnings had begun to surface. Yearnings he knew were destined to remain just that. And even though he had cursed Arabella as he had spurred his stallion through that ghostly hour just before dawn when the night is at its darkest, he knew that she was a bright beacon in the blackness, and in some secret corner of his heart he was grateful.

In all her youthful joy and optimism, Arabella believed she would win. When Nando looked into her eyes, he saw the joyful innocence that believed in fairy tales and happy endings. She did not know that every finer, gentler emotion had been cut out of his soul as surely and as cavalierly as limbs are amputated on the battlefield, that evil voices lived within him and reminded him constantly that perfidy is always the other side of beauty.

And yet there were moments—too many moments—when the voices were silent. Moments that allowed Nando to believe that this woman was different from all the rest. And they were the hardest of all to bear. They were the moments when his hands held the pure gold an alchemist's miracle had transformed from a dark, base metal, yet he *knew* that he could not keep it. That he must lay this priceless treasure down to be picked up by another.

When Nando had reluctantly returned to his palace, Franz had met him in the stables, holding a note sealed with a splash of red sealing wax and Prince Schwarzenberg's crest. The note had been delivered before dawn, he said. The message was brief and to the point and contained not a politely phrased request but an order to appear at eleven o'clock.

Now he stood at attention before the pacing prince.

"Apparently I was mistaken in my belief that your discipline qualified you for any assignment." Schwarzenberg spun on his heel and glared at Nando. "*Any* assignment."

Nando inclined his head briefly. "With all due respect, your grace, there are assignments difficult to reconcile with either the honor of a man or that of an officer of the Imperial Austrian Army."

Prince Schwarzenberg looked at his subordinate with a grudging respect. "Well said, Major Berg, but in this case not relevant, I'm afraid. As you well know, the life of our society functions by its own set of rules."

Yes, Nando thought bitterly, he knew that well. Too well.

The two men were the same height and their eyes locked as Schwarzenberg went on. "I *request—*" his emphasis gave no doubt to the fact that request was a mild expression indeed "—that you apologize to Princess Katharina Bagration. Personally. And credibly." He barked out the words. "I have no wish to see this matter blown out of proportion until it becomes a full-fledged diplomatic incident." He hooked his thumbs into his gold-fringed sash. "Do I have your promise, Major?"

"Your grace." Nando bowed in reluctant acquiescence, the stiffness of his posture telling Schwarzenberg all he needed to know.

The prince visibly relaxed and walked to a round table whose surface was decorated with exquisite marquetry work and poured two measures of brandy into heavy crystal snifters.

"At ease, Berg," he said as he handed the glass to Nando. "I don't mind telling you that this is a sticky business. We can only be grateful that Tsar Alexander was ill yesterday and did not attend the Carousel. I shudder to think what would have happened if he had witnessed your snub to a, ah, lady under his protection with his own eyes. It would be prudent, I think, to remove your presence from Vienna for a time," Schwarzenberg continued. "Meeting Tsar Alexander in society would not be propitious."

Nando tensed.

Schwarzenberg held his glass toward the light and swirled the amber liquid, squinting at the colored refractions. "Our divisions in Lombardy and Tuscany need inspection. It is logical that I entrust this duty to one of my most reliable officers."

Nando knew that without realizing it, the prince was offering him an escape from the turmoil of his soul. Wasn't this what he had been searching for last night as he had ridden his horse to exhaustion? But he also knew that despite everything he did not want to go. But generations of hard discipline told.

"When do you wish me to leave, your grace?"

"I shall expect you here this afternoon to collect some letters you will need." He leveled his gaze at Nando. "You can reach Gloggnitz today and get an early start over the Semmering tomorrow morning. The mountain roads are tricky at this time of the year."

Nando nodded and stood. He was almost at the door when Schwarzenberg called out. "Berg?"

"Yes, your grace?"

"You will not forget the apology?"

Nando raised a fine eyebrow. "I have a reputation for executing orders efficiently, your grace."

Schwarzenberg allowed himself a faint smile. "You also have a reputation for modifying those orders to suit your own ideas."

Nando looked Schwarzenberg directly in the eyes. "Indeed, your grace. That is a reason you have pinned more than one decoration on my chest." Without waiting for a reply, he bowed and left the room.

The girl on duty at the orphanage door jumped up and ran toward her the moment Arabella entered the dim vestibule. The vague disquiet that had plagued her all morning vanished as Arabella looked into the angular young face, the eyes wide with excitement.

"Oh, *Fräulein,* you're so good to us," the girl bubbled.

Arabella patted the girl's cheek and smiled. "Thank you, Anni, but you really shouldn't exaggerate like that."

"Oh, but you are. You sent us that wonderful basket."

"What basket? What are you talking about, child?" Arabella asked gently.

"The basket that came this morning. It's so beautiful. And huge. The director called us all together and let us look at it. There are biscuits in there and jam tarts," she went on breathlessly. "And there are enough chocolate bonbons for every single one of us." Her voice lowered and became reverent. "His excellency said that if we behaved we would each get one after mass on Sunday." Anni paused for a moment. "I had a chocolate bonbon once. But it melted in my pocket and I had to lick it off the cloth."

Frowning slightly, Arabella shook her head, wondering who had sent the basket. It must have been someone who had wanted to please her, for few things could give her greater pleasure than to do something for the children at the orphanage. She smiled again, hoping that it had been Nando.

Giving the child's cheek another pat, Arabella said, "Why don't we go see what else is in this mysterious basket? Come along, Anni."

The girl bit her lower lip and blinked back tears. "But I'm on duty, *Fräulein*. I will be punished if I leave the vestibule."

"Come along, Anni." Arabella could not bear to see the girl left out. "I shall tell the director that I wished you to come." She turned briskly down the hallway toward the communal room where the children always spent the afternoon hours.

Nando swore silently as he paced Princess Katharina Bagration's drawing room. She was making him wait, enjoying the petty power she possessed by way of the men who shared her bed. He slammed his fist into his palm in frustration.

He stopped at the window to look out at the gray November day. Two months ago he would have been grateful for this assignment, he mused. An assignment that would take him away from the shallow pleasures of the capital. But now, even as a part of him was relieved that he would be free of Arabella's drugging presence, Nando's stomach tightened at the thought of leaving her completely unprotected. Not that he had done a particularly fine job of protecting her up to now, he thought, kicking at the curved leg of a nearby sofa. He recalled all too well the look on Arabella's face when he had finally caught up with her carriage near the Gypsy encampment. Still...

His spine stiffened as his keen ears picked up movement in the adjoining room. Deliberately Nando crossed his arms across his chest and turned toward the window. He heard the door behind him open, and a draft propelled Katharina's opulent, cloying sweet scent toward him. Feeling perversely stubborn, he remained at the window, deciding that the price of an apology could well include just another touch of discourtesy.

The moment stretched. Then the door fell closed and Katharina's little-girl voice sounded. "Nando! What a surprise."

With insolent slowness Nando turned and allowed his gaze to travel from Katharina's blond curls to her slippers before he bowed. "Your grace."

Katharina tittered, a hand fluttering briefly to her mouth. "Such formality between old friends. Nando, really..."

Suddenly she turned away and Nando saw her fingers twine briefly at her waist before she moved to rearrange the porcelain figurines on a shelf. His eyes narrowed at this uncharacteristic behavior. Where was the sulky flirtation? The invitation that always seemed to lie in her nearsighted blue eyes? Nando took a step toward her. If he hadn't known better, he would have sworn that Katharina was nervous. He shifted his position so that he could see her face.

"I have come to apologize, your grace, for any behavior on my part yesterday that could be construed as a slight of any kind." Nando recited the words languidly, trying to repress just how much they galled him. "But as I'm sure everyone in Vienna knows, it is impossible to insult a lady of your reputation." He added the last, certain that even Katharina's limited intelligence would grasp the innuendo, but certain, too, that she would not be able to react to it without compounding the insult herself.

"Oh." Katharina's white hands fluttered at her ample bosom. She turned to face Nando but did not look at his face. "So that's why you've come."

Nando felt an inexplicable chill run down his spin. "Why did you think I'd come?" The bored smoothness was gone from his voice.

Katharina fingered the pearl and diamond necklace at her throat. "How should I know?" Her shrug was casual enough, but her aquamarine eyes darted round the room, refusing to settle on Nando's face, and her voice was shrill.

She was hiding something. Nando felt a warning pressure at the pit of his stomach. He moved toward her.

"Why, Katharina?" Nando took another step, crowding her against the back of a sofa.

"Don't be tiresome, Nando. How should I know why you've come to call on me?" Katharina wound the ends of her gauzy shawl around her fingers.

Her voice was even breathier than usual, and Nando felt a pulse begin to beat in his temple. Whatever she was hiding, he knew it was imperative he find it out. Abruptly he changed tactics and backed away.

"*Eh bien.* Now you know why I've come to call." Nando smiled slightly. "I was just following orders."

Katharina's control snapped then as would a tautly pulled string, and she moved toward Nando, brandishing her fan like a weapon. "Damn you," she shrieked. "It's the English bitch you were fawning over yesterday. At least twenty people went out of their way to tell me that."

Nando moved nimbly out of her reach, his body language taunting her to keep talking.

Her pouty mouth distorted with rage, Katharina pursued him. "Well, don't you worry, you bastard. This is the last time that black-haired witch has had the best of me." She was screaming.

Nando grabbed Katharina's arms and shook her violently, but, her gaze unfocused, wild, she did not react to it.

"She's done for now, that stupid, naive chit. I have cooked her goose and there's nothing you can do about it. Nothing." Suddenly Katharina began to laugh.

The pulse in Nando's temple began to feel like a drumbeat and his hands slid up toward Katharina's neck.

"What have you done, damn you?" he shouted, shaking her again. "Talk."

Katharina's laughter shrilled again. "Poison, *mon ami*. We Russians are very good with poison."

"How? Tell me." Nando could see his fingers pressing into the soft, white flesh of Katharina's throat. But he felt nothing but the fear for Arabella that drummed in his blood and left an acrid taste in his mouth. Her eyes bulging, Katharina gagged and for a moment the terrible laughter stopped. But as soon as his fingers loosened, the hysterical sounds began again.

Relentlessly, Nando pushed Katharina against a wall. He had always hated violence, but at this moment, he found himself an inch away from committing murder.

"If you've harmed Arabella, nothing will save you, Katharina." He was breathing hard. "Not the Tsar, not Metternich." Nando pressed her against the pastel brocade, stretching her white neck as he roughly cupped her chin. "I swear, if you've harmed her, I will take the greatest pleasure in killing you. Personally. Slowly."

Flinging Katharina away from him, Nando ran from the room. The last sound that he heard was the dull thud of Katharina's soft body hitting some piece of furniture as it fell.

There was a moment of silence when Arabella entered the large, cold room, as every single one of the children stopped whatever they were doing. Then a babble of childish voices arose and the children seemed to spring up as one and crowd around her, jostling each other for a place at her side.

Embarrassment and guilt that it had not been she who was responsible for their delight warred with pleasure and, as Arabella looked at the smiles and shining eyes, pleasure won. Even the staff seemed to have entered into the joyful mood, as for once they let the children laugh and cavort without admonishing them to be quiet and mind their manners.

Finally, one of the older boys made himself heard above the clamor with an uneven, raspy voice obviously in the throes of mutation. "The director said we could have something from the basket once you came, Fräulein." He paused. "May we?"

The voices quieted as the children waited for Arabella's reply.

"Of course, you may."

There was a collective sigh of relief. Someone took hold of Arabella's hand and pulled her toward a chest of drawers where a wicker basket stood.

It was indeed huge and it proved heavy as Arabella carefully lifted it down to the floor. There were braided rolls and sausages mixed with tissue-wrapped packages with the jam tarts and biscuits Anni had mentioned. And standing on end were two large flat boxes of chocolates.

Quickly Arabella unwrapped several of the packages while the children automatically lined up according to size as they had been drilled to do whenever anything was being distributed. Then she went down the line with a sugar-dipped jam tart and a smile for each child.

Within minutes of leaving Katharina's drawing room, Nando was dashing up the steps of the British embassy. Shoving the footman at the door aside, he was running toward the staircase as the head butler rounded the corner.

"Where is Miss Douglas, Rogers? Where is her apartment?" Nando's fingers bit into the butler's arm, disregarding all the proprieties.

"Miss Douglas is not in, sir." Rogers tried to disengage his arm without the indignity of struggling.

"Where is she? Tell me."

Radiating disapproval, Rogers pulled himself as upright as he could. "Miss Douglas does not confide her whereabouts to me, sir."

Nando closed his eyes for a moment in an attempt to gain control. "I realize that, Rogers. But I need to find her immediately." His fingers on the butler's arm tightened briefly as he remembered the wildness in Katharina's eyes, in her laughter. "Did something come for her today? A package, flowers, anything?"

"I don't believe so, sir." The butler looked to the footman at the door for confirmation. "No, sir, nothing." Rogers succeeded in extricating his arm from Nando's grasp and pulled at his cuffs.

"Was Miss Douglas alone when she left?"

Rogers's mouth puckered like a dried prune. "Indeed, sir."

Nando turned away from the butler, digging the heels of his hands into his eyes. Somewhere in the house, a clock struck two. She could have gone anywhere. For a walk. To the dressmaker, the milliner. To visit Lulu, anyone.

He rubbed his temple, where a pain had begun to throb, as if there were an idea there trying to get out. Suddenly he knew. The orphanage. Of course, the orphanage was the most likely place to look for her. Nando started for the door, but stopped before he reached it and returned to stand in front of Rogers.

"Should anything come for Miss Douglas, Rogers, keep it in a safe place and do not give it to her. Do you understand me?" Nando grasped a handful of gold-braided livery and shook the man. "Anything."

Taken aback by Nando's urgency, Rogers could only nod. He was still standing there when Nando slammed the heavy oak door behind him.

"My dear Fräulein Douglas." The door to the communal room opened just as Arabella had finished distributing the jam tarts and the director entered, his thin, normally sour face wreathed in smiles. "I was hoping that you would come by today so that I could thank you."

"I'm afraid you've come to the wrong address with your thanks, Herr Weigelt. I did not send the basket." Arabella smiled regretfully. "It must have come from someone who knows of my interest in the orphanage."

Herr Weigelt waved his hand. "Whatever. We are most grateful." He gestured toward the basket. "It was most thoughtful of you, pardon me—" he coughed "—of the donor to include a bottle of wine."

He folded his hands together almost prayerfully. "I have taken the liberty of putting it in my office. Perhaps you will do me the honor of joining me in a glass?"

"Gladly. In a moment." She turned to the children. "I suggest that you eat your tarts now. It would be a shame if they got lost or crumbled." Arabella said the words reluctantly, hating to cut short their anticipation of such a rare pleasure, but she knew that unless they ate their treat immediately, the smaller, weaker children would get nothing once she had turned her back.

Finally satisfied, she turned to the director and took his proffered arm for the walk down the long, winding corridor to his cubicle of an office.

Herr Weigelt handed her into a slightly shabby armchair and Arabella watched him bustle merrily around the small office, his monstrously fat white pug, which she privately thought looked more like a huge slug with legs than a dog, following him everywhere.

He brought glasses, uncorked the wine, making a production of sniffing the cork, talking expansively the whole time. Did it truly take so little to make a jolly man out of a dour one? she wondered.

At last he filled plain, cut-glass goblets to the rim with the ruby-colored wine and sat across from her.

"Since you refuse to admit your generosity, Fräulein Douglas, may I propose a toast to our noble benefactor." He leaned forward and touched his glass to hers. "*Prost.*"

GET 4 BOOKS

Return this card, and we'll send you 4 brand-new Harlequin Historical™ novels, absolutely *FREE!* We'll even pay the postage both ways!

We're making you this offer to introduce you to the benefits of the Harlequin Reader Service®: free home delivery of brand-new romance novels, months before they're available in stores, **AND** at a saving of 80¢ apiece compared to the cover price!

Accepting these 4 free books places you under no obligation to continue. You may cancel at any time, even just after receiving your free shipment. If you do not cancel, every month, we'll send 4 more Harlequin Historical™ novels and bill you just $3.19* apiece—that's all!

Yes! Please send me my 4 free Harlequin Historical™ novels, as explained above.

Name

Address   Apt.

City   State   Zip

247 CIH ADGV (U-H-H-11/91)

DETACH ALONG DOTTED LINE AND MAIL TODAY! – DETACH ALONG DOTTED LINE AND MAIL TODAY! – DETACH ALONG DOTTED LINE AND MAIL TODAY!

Get 4 Books FREE

SEE BACK OF CARD FOR DETAILS

FREE MYSTERY GIFT

We will be happy to send you a free bonus gift! To request it, please check here, and mail this reply card promptly!

Thank you !

BUSINESS REPLY CARD

FIRST CLASS MAIL   PERMIT NO. 717   BUFFALO, NY

POSTAGE WILL BE PAID BY ADDRESSEE

HARLEQUIN READER SERVICE®

3010 WALDEN AVE
P O BOX 1867
BUFFALO NY 14240-9952

NO POSTAGE
NECESSARY
IF MAILED
IN THE
UNITED STATES

DETACH ALONG DOTTED LINE AND MAIL TODAY! – DETACH ALONG DOTTED LINE AND MAIL TODAY! – DETACH ALONG DOTTED LINE AND MAIL TODAY!

"*Prost.*" Arabella smiled and concentrated on balancing the full glass to her mouth without spilling the wine.

Suddenly there were loud voices and footsteps outside the door. Herr Weigelt grumbled, put down his glass and rose just as the door burst open and swung back on its hinges so violently that the draft it generated made Arabella snap back her head.

Before she had registered that the man who paused for a split second in the doorway then vaulted into the room was Nando, he had reached her. Still moving, he lashed out and hit Arabella's forearm, knocking the wineglass to the floor.

Her cry at the impact of the blow was both surprise and outrage, but before she could form any words, Nando had lifted her up from her chair by her shoulders.

"Has anyone eaten or drunk anything from the basket that came?" His voice was tight with the control he was exerting over himself in order not to explode. "Have they? Answer me."

Nando's voice was so intense that the anger Arabella had felt faded and was replaced by a chill that lingered along her spine.

"Jam tarts," she whispered. "The children all had jam tarts."

"You," he gasped. "Did you eat or drink anything?"

Arabella shook her head. "No. No, I didn't."

The words were barely out of Arabella's mouth when Nando charged out of the room, pulling her after him.

"What's going on, Nando?" she panted as she struggled to keep up with him, holding her skirts up with her free hand.

"Later. Just show me where the children are."

Within moments they burst into the communal room and skidded to a stop. All movement stopped and forty pairs of eyes stared at them.

"Do any of you feel ill?" Nando asked, fighting to keep the desperation under control.

But all the children were feeling fine, and after instructing the two supervisors to report immediately if a child felt ill, Nando took the basket and turned to leave the room.

Herr Weigelt was standing in the doorway watching them, a sour look on his face. "May I ask you what is going on here? I believe you owe me an explanation, your grace." He was obviously irritated, but the habit of obeisance toward his betters was strong and his tone and stance were respectful.

Nando guided Arabella out of the room. Once the door closed behind them, he set the basket down and went to stand in front of Herr Weigelt.

"First of all, I need the promise of your discretion, sir," Nando said, grateful for the semblance of control a brisk, businesslike tone gave him. He had come harrowingly close to panic when he had arrived at the orphanage and had heard about the mysterious basket from one of the servants he had encountered during his search for Arabella.

Herr Weigelt nodded.

"From information I—I happened to come across, I have reason to believe that something in the basket is poisoned." Both Arabella and Herr Weigelt opened their mouths to speak, but Nando held up his hand to silence them. There was no way he could hint at who was responsible.

"Please do not ask me how I came by this information. Suffice it to say that I have." Nando dug in two fingers at the base of his nose, trying futilely to relieve the pressure gathering there. "Shall we continue this discussion in your office?"

Shocked and incredulous, Herr Weigelt nodded and led the way down the hall. He opened the door and, stepping aside, he let Arabella and Nando pass.

Nando stiffened and immediately moved in front of Arabella to shield her, but the jerky movement of her hand to her mouth and her muffled gasp told him that she, too, had seen the hideously contorted corpse of the pug, bloodflecked foam at its mouth, lying beside the puddle of wine.

There was a hoarse, choking sound behind them, then Herr Weigelt rushed past them and knelt next to the dog. His trembling hands stroked the white fur as he sobbed, babbling incoherent words.

Staring at the puddle of wine and the dead dog, Nando felt bile rise from his stomach. That wine had come from the glass Arabella had been holding. The glass he had knocked out of her hand a moment before she had touched it to her lips. A vision of what would have have happened had he stormed into the room just a minute later flashed through his mind, cutting off his breathing as if he had just taken a blow to his diaphragm.

As Nando turned toward Arabella, she lifted her gaze to his and any words of comfort that he might have spoken died in his throat as he watched the understanding dawn in Arabella's sapphire eyes, which were glazed with shock.

Powerless. He was powerless. Comprehension struck Nando, bringing the bitter taste of self-disgust to his mouth. He had been unable to protect Arabella. He would not be able to avenge the attempt on her life. He could not even keep the stunned realization of how close she had come to losing her life out of her eyes.

The helpless rage burned within him and yet the habit of years sent Nando behind his well-mannered, cool veneer. Only his hands, which he kept clenching then forcibly relaxing, bespoke his feelings. "Are you all right, Arabella? Can I get you something?"

A shudder went through her. Arabella could feel it as it started at her knees and traveled up her body. She was helpless to stop it and yet she fought it, knowing that if she gave in to the weakness, she would never stop shaking. Forcing herself to breathe deeply, she steadied herself. Only when she was certain that she would not collapse into his arms did Arabella slowly raise her gaze to Nando's face.

But when her eyes took in the calm, cool features that might have been carved in marble, the distant gray eyes, Arabella realized how much more than a polite inquiry after her well-being she wanted. She could stand alone. She knew that. But what wouldn't she give for a little warmth from Nando at this moment. For a little of the heat that had been in his eyes last night when he had saluted her at the Carousel in front of half of Vienna. For a shadow of the desperation that had been in his face as he had knocked the wineglass out of her hand.

Arabella stayed perfectly still as she held his gaze and she did not move when she spoke softly, the words more an invitation than a plea. "Hold me, Nando."

Nando reached for Arabella and pulled her roughly to him, pressing her face against his tunic for a moment before sliding his fingers into the hair at her nape and pulling her face up to his. He watched her eyes widen until he could see his own reflection in the dark pupils, and Nando knew that now she was no longer seeing the ugliness around them, but only him. A strange sort of satisfaction swept over him just before the desire took hold. Perhaps he was not powerless after all, Nando thought. Perhaps he could with his hands, his mouth, affirm to Arabella just how alive she was.

As Nando's mouth moved over Arabella's skin, as her taste, her fragrance flooded his senses, the memory of just how close he had come to losing her went through him as a bullet tears through flesh and he almost cried out. She would leave Vienna and him someday soon, but he needed to know that she was somewhere in this world. Smiling. Living.

The events of the past half hour receded as Arabella went into Nando's arms. He filled her vision completely. She felt only his hands, his mouth, and it was as if the universe contained only the two of them.

Fueled by hopelessness and desperation, Nando's mouth took hers again. There was no finesse, no gentleness in his kiss as his tongue plunged into Arabella's mouth, invading, inciting, until her tongue moved to tangle with his in a primitive mating dance. Their skin heated. Their bodies pressed so close that they felt their heartbeats as one. Only when it seemed that their breath was at an end did the greedy kiss stop. But they stayed open mouth to open mouth, as if each needed to draw the next life-giving breath from the other. His palms pressed against the sides of her face, Nando whispered Arabella's name against her mouth as if it were a prayer. And perhaps it was.

Later, ignoring the still sobbing Herr Weigelt, Nando methodically went through the basket.

"What are you looking for?" Arabella whispered. "Do you think anything else was poisoned?" She put a cold hand on Nando's arm. "Who did this?"

Nando shook his head and lifted a package out. As he transferred it to his other hand, something fell to the desk with a bright tinkle. The gold gleamed from the clutter on the desk and he did not need more than a fleeting look at the bauble to identify the earring that had once been his gift to Princess Katharina Bagration. Nando's hand closed over it and he felt a grim satisfaction. He might not be able to take any open steps against Katharina, but his find would help him put enough pressure on the bitch to restrain her from a repeat performance.

They were silent on their way to the Dietrichstein Palace, and it was only when they were safely inside that Nando drew Arabella into a salon and handed her into a chair while he paced.

"I have received orders to inspect our troops in Italy. Punishment for my misbehavior last night, you understand." Nando's voice was flat, expressionless. "I should have been on my way hours ago."

The ache of loneliness already beginning, Arabella asked softly, "How long will you be gone?"

"I don't know. Weeks." Suddenly he stopped in front of Arabella, crouched and took her hands in his. "Will you promise me that you will be careful while I'm gone? Do not go out by yourself. Watch who you are alone with."

"Can't you tell me what's going on, Nando?"

Nando wished he could find some comfortable, protective lie, but a glance into Arabella's limpid eyes told him that she would see through it and him. Slowly he reached into the pocket of his tunic and extracted the earring he had found. Not saying a word, he opened his hand.

Arabella stared at the earring, a love knot with a bell attached, its clapper in the form of the letter K, unable to look away until Nando closed his hand again. Only then did she look up to meet his eyes.

"She is under the protection of the Tsar and a Russian subject besides, so the Austrian police will not—cannot—move a finger against her. But I shall pay her another visit before I leave Vienna." Nando's fist tightened on the earring so that he could feel the fluted edges of the bell cutting into his palm. "Katharina is not a brave woman, and I shall be quite explicit about what I will do to her if anything, *anything* happens to you or anyone close to you while I'm gone."

A cruel smile curved Nando's mouth and Arabella shivered.

Nando saw the tremor and knew that it had been aimed at him. His hatred for Katharina rose another notch. He rose, wanting to relieve Arabella of his presence as quickly as possible.

He took her hand in both of his. "Promise me that you will be careful."

"I will."

Nando breathed a kiss over Arabella's hand. "Adieu."

He was almost at the door before Arabella realized that he was leaving without kissing her goodbye.

"Nando."

He stopped and looked at her over his shoulder.

"Do you really think that I'm going to let you leave me this way?" Arabella smiled and held both hands out to him.

Nando covered the distance between them in two steps and crushed Arabella to him. For a moment they clung to each other. Then Arabella lifted her face to him and offered him her mouth.

The desperation of an hour ago was still there. But now Nando harnessed the passion, wanting to give Arabella a moment of gentleness to remember him by. His tongue glided into her mouth and he explored her with a provocative slowness. She made a soft sound of pleasure and Nando took it into himself to keep and to cherish.

But suddenly the rhythm changed. The flames erupted and soared, spinning them into a whirlpool that left them breathless and gasping.

"Tell me that you will miss me and mean it," Arabella whispered against Nando's mouth.

Nando brought her a breath closer so that she could feel his aroused body. "Do you doubt it, my sorceress?"

"Hurry back."

Nando captured Arabella's face between his hands and held her still for a long moment as his eyes traveled over her, as if committing every feature to memory. He wanted her. That he understood. But the ache he felt every time he looked at her, that was another matter.

He skimmed over Arabella's mouth one last time. "Think of me."

And then he was gone.

Chapter Fourteen

The days passed. But they passed with painful slowness that rubbed every nerve in Arabella's body raw. Couriers came. But it was never the courier she was waiting for.

Suddenly all the amusements Arabella had enjoyed because Nando had been there became shallow and left the taste of ashes on her tongue. She began to hate the daily round of social activities. She began to hate the chime of the clocks that marked off yet another hour without him. Even her work at the orphanage became a routine that did not quite satisfy.

More and more often the memory of the little girl she and Nando had saved from a beating haunted Arabella. Why did she remember that day so much more clearly than others? Perhaps because Nando had been with her. Perhaps because he had held her with such unquestioning tenderness. But no matter what the reason, one clear, crisp December morning Arabella knew that she was going to look for that child.

Within an hour she had charmed the cook into giving her a basket of food, donned a dark bonnet and simple wool cape, hired a day carriage and was on her way.

She worked her way through the market, stopping often to question the buxom women who stood behind stalls or carts hawking their wares. Suspicious of her accent and her appearance, some refused to answer. But even those who did answer knew nothing of the girl named Poldi. Hours later, Arabella had nothing to show for her efforts but a collection of black and blue marks from being jostled by passersby.

Returning to the end of the marketplace, Arabella saw an apple cart that had not been there before. Her pulse accelerated as she recognized the woman from whom she had bought fruit for the child.

"What d'you want from her?" the woman demanded, her crafty eyes becoming slits within the folds of red-veined fat.

"Do you know her?" Arabella asked eagerly.

"Maybe, maybe not. Why are you looking for her?"

Cursing inwardly that her inadequate German forced her to use the simplest of sentences, Arabella said, "I am looking for a maid. This girl pleased me."

The woman snorted. "She'll steal you blind, Fräulein." She closed her eyes a little further, already calculating how many *Kreuzers* Baric would pay her if she made sure he got to keep the stepdaughter whose light fingers kept him in drink.

"So you do know her." Arabella ignored the woman's words. "I will pay you if you tell me where to find her."

Opening her eyes, the woman straightened her bulk. "How much?"

Arabella dug into her reticule and gave her a coin.

The woman examined the piece and tucked it away in a pocket beneath her grubby apron. Then she folded her arms across her huge bosom and stared at Arabella brazenly. "Maybe I know. Maybe not."

Another coin exchanged hands and when that, too, was put away, the old woman regarded Arabella, gauging whether another coin might be forthcoming. Then she shrugged and jerked her head toward the far side of the marketplace.

"The second alley beyond the fountain. Her name's Nagler, but she lives with her stepfather." Her gap-toothed smile angled overtly for a reward. "His name's Baric. He unloads kegs for the brewery." She chuckled unpleasantly. "When he's sober."

The greedy old woman repulsed Arabella, but she was so glad to reach her goal that she thrust another coin at her before she turned away.

Arabella took a step back as she turned the corner. The width of the alley would barely have allowed three people to walk abreast and the stench was almost unbearable. The gutters ran with every imaginable kind of filth and would probably overflow underneath the half-rotten doors at the least provocation.

A door creaked open, revealing an old woman. A hunched shoulder made her hold her head at a grotesque angle, reminding Arabella of the gargoyles she had seen on the cathedral in Paris.

"*Wo wohnt Baric?*" Arabella demanded.

"Baric?" The old crone eyed her for a moment then poked her chin in the direction of an entry diagonally across from hers and retreated behind her door.

Arabella felt a shiver travel from the nape of her neck down the length of her back. She felt as if she had woken up from a nightmare to discover that it was reality, but the fear and disgust she felt only strengthened her resolve.

A shuffling noise behind her made Arabella spin around and she found herself face-to-face with Poldi.

The girl jumped back a step in surprise, then the handle of the large bucket she was holding slipped out of her red, chapped hands and the pail tipped over, inundating both her feet and Arabella's. Helplessly, the girl watched the water puddle at her feet and her chin began to tremble.

Unmindful of the filth, Arabella knelt and gathered the child into her arms. The gentle touch loosed the girl's tears, and Arabella held her close until her sobs died down to hiccups then stilled. Leaving her arm around the thin shoulders, Arabella rose and let the girl precede her into her dwelling.

Nothing Arabella had seen had prepared her for the sight that awaited her. Compared to this hole, the mean, little thatched huts occupied by the village poor in Surrey whom she had visited with her grandmother were luxurious abodes indeed.

Something scurried across the floor as they entered and Arabella saw the long, naked tail of a rat disappear under a crude wooden partition. The room had an earthen floor covered in places with pieces of brick and tile. In one corner there was a hearth that looked as if it had not seen a fire in a long time, and the only furniture was a plank table and in place of chairs, several kegs that still reeked of beer.

A sound of shock mingled with disgust escaped her and Arabella felt Poldi stiffen beneath her hands and step away, tugging at the ragged woolen shawl that was knotted around her shoulders.

"It's not so bad," the girl said defiantly. "Lots of people don't have a roof over their heads at all." Tears still glistened in her hazel eyes, but the angular chin was thrust out, her expression mutinous.

"Why are you looking for me?" she demanded, her natural mistrust gaining the upper hand now that Arabella's gentle touch was no longer undermining her belligerence. "I didn't pick your pocket, even though I could have. Or the officer's pocket, either."

Arabella controlled her shock at Poldi's impudent words and searched for some plausible reason, feeling the need to salvage the girl's pride.

"I wanted to bring you something." She held out the basket. "Because... because it will be Christmas soon."

Poldi went very still and stared at the basket as if it were a living thing.

"Go ahead and open it," Arabella prompted. "It's all for you."

The girl slanted an uncertain glance at her, like a puppy that has been kicked too often, and when she realized that she would not be punished for her eagerness, her fingers flew to unpack the basket. A jam tart that Arabella had added on her way out of the kitchen lay on top, and Poldi immediately stuffed it into her mouth with both hands. When she felt Arabella's hand on her shoulder, she started and looked around guiltily as she wiped her mouth with the back of her grimy hand.

"Not so quickly, *Kleines,*" Arabella admonished gently. "The basket stays here with you."

The girl's eyes filled with tears again, but she blinked them back determinedly. Arabella's heart went out to the child and she resisted the impulse to embrace her again, realizing that Poldi knew far better how to cope with blows than with tenderness.

But the girl's spirit had not been cowed. Her eyes were bold and proud beneath the glitter of tears. How long would it take for her spirit to be broken? Arabella wondered. How long before abuse and perpetual hunger took their toll? How long before she would start walking the streets either by choice or by force?

Suddenly Arabella knew that she was going to get Poldi out. She had no idea how she was going to do it, but she would.

Taking Poldi's red, chilblain covered hands in hers, she sat on one of the kegs and drew the girl closer. "I'm going to find another place for you to live, Poldi. Would you like that?"

The girl's eyes widened a little, but she remained silent.

"A place where you will have enough to eat. Where you could learn a trade perhaps."

The girl let her hands be held, but there was no response either in her face or in her touch.

Puzzled, Arabella asked, "Do you live here with someone you don't want to leave? Your mother? A brother or sister?"

Poldi shook her head once. "My mother died last winter."

The girl's bald, seemingly emotionless statement moved Arabella more than tears would have. Perhaps because she sensed Poldi's sense of loss and her loneliness as if it were her own.

"And you've been alone ever since?"

She shook her head again. "Not alone. Baric lives here. Sometimes." Her thin shoulders twitched with an uncontrollable shiver.

"Are you afraid of him?"

"No!" The answer was quick and Poldi's chin came up for emphasis, but the fear flashed into her eyes.

Arabella squeezed the small hands. "I'll be back for you as soon as I can."

The girl looked at her with a blankness that could have been either lack of understanding or disbelief.

"I promise."

Poldi stared back at her and said nothing.

But there was no place for Poldi. The director at the orphanage, coldly polite at best since the incident with the food basket, refused point blank to take her in, pleading rules he could not break. The girl had a stepfather, after all.

At the Thürheim town house, she was told that Lulu and her sisters were not expected until late that evening.

And she knew that Lady Castlereagh would never allow her to bring the child to the British embassy.

"Wohin, Fräulein?" asked the cab driver as Arabella climbed into the hack.

Trying to think, she gestured at him to be silent, and he shrugged and pulled his hat down toward his forehead.

She closed her eyes for a moment and saw Poldi's thin face, pale underneath the grime, her eyes large and disbelieving. Suddenly Arabella began to shiver, but it wasn't with the cold that had begun to seep through her wet shoes and damp cloak. Her skin crawled with the memory of the filthy, vile-smelling hole, the scurrying of the rat and the thick-necked man who might choose this night to abuse the child again.

Arabella leaned forward and jerked the driver's coattail. "Back to the Naschmarkt," she said. "Quickly."

The drive seemed to take forever. It had begun to rain—an icy rain that threatened to turn into sleet at any moment, but Arabella did not feel the cold. She felt nothing but the need to reach the child as soon as possible.

Arabella jumped out of the cab even before it had quite stopped and gathered up her skirts to allow her to move more quickly. This time she noticed neither the filth nor the stench in the alleyway as she sped around the corner. She was within a few steps of the entry when she heard the scream.

Her breath spilling raggedly from her lungs, she lunged toward the crude door handle, but the door would not give. Calling on reserves of strength that she did not realize she possessed, Arabella rattled at the door. With a dull crack the porous wood gave way just as something resembling the snap of a whip sounded, followed by another muffled cry.

Arabella paused in the doorway, unable to see more than vague shapes in the darkness of the room. All movement seemed to have stilled, the only sound an occasional sob from the direction of the hearth. Realizing that her only advantage was the element of surprise, she moved toward it quickly and was relieved to feel the girl scrambling toward her.

Clutching the child's arm, Arabella pushed her toward the door. Suddenly the man let out a bellow of rage and lumbered toward them. Her progress slowed by a keg, Arabella kicked at it and darted after Poldi.

There was a crash behind them, followed by inarticulate swearing, and Arabella grabbed Poldi's hand and pulled her toward the marketplace.

Moments later Arabella half lifted, half pushed Poldi into the carriage and managed to gasp, "Drive. Quickly," before she tumbled onto the worn seat.

After she had disentangled her cloak and managed to sit up, she threw a nervous glance behind them, but everyone was apparently far more concerned with getting out of the cold rain as soon as possible than their flight. Baric was nowhere to be seen, and Arabella breathed a heartfelt sigh of relief.

"Are you all right?" Arabella turned to Poldi, opening her cloak to spread it around the girl's shoulders. "Did he hurt you, little one?"

Poldi shook her head. "He tried to whip me with a leather strap, but he only caught me on the arm a couple times. He was drunk and his aim was bad."

The girl spoke with such incredible matter-of-factness that Arabella shivered. Her only acquaintance with corporal punishment had been that long-ago whipping from her father, and yet the memory was still vivid enough to raise gooseflesh and cause a wave of nausea. But for this child it was apparently no more than an everyday fact of life.

Arabella tried to pull the girl against her to share body warmth, but Poldi resisted and remained sitting stiffly beside her.

"*Wohin, Fräulein?*" the cab driver barked from his seat, obviously eager to be rid of his passengers and out of the rain.

"The city," Arabella said and leaned back.

She had been acting purely on instinct all day, but now she needed something more tangible than that. Forcing herself to think clearly, Arabella went over her options, realizing finally that she had only one.

With a little sigh she closed her eyes and said a little prayer that Nando's housekeeper was a softhearted woman.

Realizing her bedraggled appearance, Arabella ignored the haughty look that the footman in the green and white

Berg livery gave her. But the man straightened immediately when he heard her name, and within minutes a comfortably plump woman had appeared and was smiling in welcome.

"Please. *Kommen Sie, bitte.*" She cast a questioning look at Poldi, but said nothing.

The impressive bunch of keys at the housekeeper's waist jingled as she led the way to a huge kitchen with a vaulted ceiling. The room was warm and redolent with the fragrance of herbs—lovage, parsley, marjoram—which hung in neat bunches to the side of an enormous stove.

"Please, sit down." She gestured toward a bench that went around two sides of a solid oak table with a finely sanded surface. "Shall I have someone see to the child?" she asked and reached toward her as if loath to tolerate a grimy guttersnipe in her spotless kitchen.

Arabella felt the girl's almost imperceptible movement against her side. "She can stay here." Keeping her arm loosely around the girl's shoulders while allowing her enough room, she sat down.

The woman's eyes held a certain watchfulness, but they were kind, and Arabella decided to come straight to the point. If the answer was no, she would have no time to waste.

"This is Leopoldine Nagler, and I need a place where she can stay until I find a permanent place for her. Her mother is dead and her stepfather abused her."

A frown creased the housekeeper's smooth forehead. This was obviously not a situation she was used to handling.

Arabella drew a deep breath and gave Poldi's shoulder a reassuring squeeze. "Count Berg knows this child, and I'm sure he wouldn't be angry if you looked after her for a little while. I will discuss a permanent arrangement with him when he returns."

"I don't know." The woman's glance skimmed over the girl. "If you've taken her away from her stepfather without permission, he could bring a charge against you."

Arabella put a hand on the woman's arm. "Please. On my responsibility. I'm sure the man will not go running to the police. When Count Berg returns, we can settle any problems."

The housekeeper remembered Franz had said this was the young woman who had made Count Berg smile for the first time in years. She nodded and Arabella and Poldi exchanged a smile.

Arabella stayed while Poldi was settled into a small room in the servants' wing. After the grime had been washed away, the girl turned out to be a pretty little thing with curly ginger-colored hair and freckles.

Poldi had been very quiet, but as she sat cross-legged in the middle of the clean bed with a bowl of warm milk and a thick slab of bread and butter, her eyes began to sparkle with natural vitality as she began to realize that she was warm and safe from harm. Arabella sat on the edge of the bed and watched her, pleased with her day's work.

"Who is this Count Berg?" Poldi asked between bites.

"He's an officer and a friend of mine."

"Friend?" She shot Arabella an appraising look that was knowing beyond her years. "You mean your lover?"

Arabella felt the heat rise into her face. She had forgotten that the German word *Freund* could mean either friend or lover.

She compressed her lips. "No, he is not my lover. And how old are you to know the meaning of the word, anyway?"

"Twelve. Is Count Berg the handsome officer who was with you that day in the marketplace?"

"Yes."

Poldi smiled mischievously. "Then you prob'ly wish he was."

Arabella shook her head, but she felt a coil of heat spread within her beneath Poldi's frankly appraising gaze. Thoughts of Nando had receded behind her quest for the child, but suddenly he was with her with such clarity that it took her breath away.

What would he say when he found Poldi ensconced in the servants' wing of his palace? Arabella wondered. Would he be irritated, angry? Would he demand that she leave? Would he go to the trouble of having his solicitor even out any legal wrinkles? But then she remembered how he had crouched and spoken gently to the girl in the marketplace. She didn't think he would disappoint her. She hoped not.

Resolutely she pushed his image away and moved a little closer to the girl. Taking her chin between thumb and forefinger, she said, "You won't be hungry here, Poldi, and I want you to promise me that I won't regret bringing you here."

They looked at each other for a long time, both remembering Poldi's comment about picking pockets.

Poldi nodded solemnly and slid down under the quilt.

Chapter Fifteen

Christmas came and went with almost no public festivities, for at Christmas all Austrians, even the imperial family, retreated within their closest family circle.

But despite these tranquil, hushed days everyone flocked to the salon of Baroness Fanny Arnstein, who had imported a German tradition to Vienna and filled a good portion of her drawing room with a huge fir tree decorated with apples, nuts and candles. Even the Castlereaghs were induced to go, although they usually avoided the baroness's salon, uncomfortable in its literary, witty atmosphere.

Arabella stood in a window enclosure, apart from the conversation and the laughter, and gazed at the candlelit tree with the wonder of a child, blissfully ignorant of two pairs of eyes that were watching her carefully.

"She's quite lovely, Niki, isn't she?" Princess Katharina Bagration whispered as she glided up to Prince Volkonsky. With supreme effort she kept the venom out of her voice. She tilted her head to look into his face and laughed with soft malice. "You're salivating, my friend. Have you had her yet?"

"You damn well know I haven't. No thanks to you." Volkonsky's greedy gaze didn't swerve from Arabella.

Katharina tapped her fan against her short upper lip as she watched him. "You'd better make good use of the time you have left," she murmured. After her unsuccessful trick with the poisoned wine, she had decided it would be much less dangerous and vastly more amusing to help Volkonsky have Arabella after all. Especially after the way Nando had threatened her.

"What do you mean?" Volkonsky growled.

She stood back and gauged him, her innocent-looking, nearsighted eyes suddenly focused and sharp. "I have it on good authority that Nando will be back soon." She chuckled. "And we both know what your chances will be then."

"Shut up, Katya."

She saw the muscle in Volkonsky's jaw twitch and carefully fanned the fire she had started.

"Who knows if she'll be worth the trouble. Virgins seldom are." She gave him a little shove with her elbow. "But it would please you to take it before she gives it to Berg, hmm?"

Volkonsky licked his dry lips. His body had already been heavy and aching with the thought of what it would be like to take Arabella, and Katharina's suggestive words only increased the ache—and the hatred, because he knew that she was right.

Katharina drew her arm through Volkonsky's and steered him to a quiet corner of the room. "Niki, my friend, your black-haired English witch just can't appreciate you properly." Her fingers kneaded his arm and her little-girl voice turned husky. "Yet."

Volkonsky felt a ripple of excitement in his loins and wondered if she could be right. Would the skill he had practiced in countless bedrooms and brothels from St. Petersburg to Paris perhaps melt the ice princess once she got a real taste of it? It was a heady thought.

"You'll just have to spirit her away and give her a little object lesson, *mon cher.*"

Volkonsky shot Katharina a nasty glance. "You think I haven't tried?" he fumed. "But the world is apparently populated by idiots who've managed to bungle it every time."

"I see," she murmured. "Perhaps I can help you."

"How? When?" Volkonsky grabbed her arm.

"Not so fast, Niki," Katharina purred. "You do remember your promise, don't you?"

"What promise?" Volkonsky looked at her blankly.

"Berg," she snapped. "You promised me Berg." Katharina reached out and pinched her former lover savagely.

Volkonsky winced. "Of course I remember, Katya, my sweet. Now tell me what your plan is," he demanded.

"I have heard just *en passant* that the fat lady and her husband are going to Prague. They are leaving in a few days and will be gone for at least a week. If you are clever, this should give you enough opportunity to get what you want and return her—" she paused suggestively "—only slightly used."

The familiar rush of blood he felt when the hunt—any hunt—was coming to a climax heightened the already ruddy color of Volkonsky's face. Eagerly his eyes sought Arabella again in the crowded salon.

Arabella examined her hair in the oval hand mirror and grinned. Poor Jeanne would have an attack of vapors if she could see her. But Arabella had no patience tonight to tame her naturally curly mane into the requisite knot of well-bred curls. She fastened her hair with several combs and let it fall below her shoulders in a natural, riotous cascade.

She knew she could have waited to have Nanette, the Thürheim maid, do her hair, but the poor girl was busy enough getting the three countesses and their maiden aunt ready for Prince Razumovsky's ball without taking care of her, as well.

Despite herself, Arabella was enjoying being away from her maid's overwhelming affection, eagle eye and constant questioning for a few days, and now that Jeanne had almost recovered from her inflammation of the lungs, Arabella had stopped feeling guilty about it. And being Lulu's guest for the week or so that the Castlereaghs were spending in Prague gave her the freedom to spend as much time as she wanted with Poldi without having to account for her comings and goings to anyone.

Lulu peeked into her room and beckoned. "Shall we go? Konstantine is quite impatient to show off the pearl and diamond necklace that Prince Razumovsky presented her with for Christmas. If he keeps this up, she will own her weight in jewels by the time she becomes his wife."

A luxurious carriage with Prince Razumovsky's crest waited for the five ladies. Two footmen stood on a small ledge at its back to protect the passengers and guard the pitch torches in the iron rings on either side of the carriage. A third held the door open, keeping one arm at the requisite angle to be used as a mounting aid.

The Thürheims piled into the carriage with much chatter and laughter, but Arabella felt a shiver along her spine, and suddenly she had no wish for bright lights and flirtation.

The Razumovsky Palace had been turned into a garden of delight. Throughout the salons and ballrooms, potted orange, lemon and cherry trees, flowering shrubs and arrangements of the most exotic blooms from the Razumovsky hothouses made a lie out of the fact that tomorrow would be the thirty-first of December.

What seemed like thousands of candles in the crystal chandeliers and the candelabras of silver, gold, brass and porcelain illuminated the rooms, bringing out the details of the ornate ceilings, the finely ornamented moldings, the friezes with superbly elegant Greek motifs. Precious paintings by old masters decorated the walls, and statues of pure white Carrara marble by Canova glowed with their own special fire.

The heat intensified the potpourri of fragrances from flowers, perfume and heated bodies, and Arabella found herself longing for a whiff of the chill, crystal-clear December air almost before the evening began.

"Good evening," murmured a smooth voice just behind her left shoulder. "Is that lovely ice-blue of your gown indicative of your mood tonight, *mademoiselle?*"

Arabella turned and encountered Prince Volkonsky's gleaming obsidian eyes. A chill traveled through her and she laughed to mask the moment of discomfort. Suddenly she found herself wishing she had not promised Lord Castlereagh to tolerate Prince Nikita Volkonsky's attentions. "Have I been complimented or insulted, prince?"

"I have only compliments for you, *ma belle dame sans merci*. And you? What do you have for me?" Volkonsky's voice sank to an intimate whisper and he shifted a little closer, his hand coming up to brush the back of her gown, sliding just under her hair.

Arabella's smile faded a little. If there was anything she disliked, it was this encroaching on her personal space under the guise of whispered compliments. She moved out of his reach with a motion too obvious to be ignored.

"Was that a rhetorical question, prince? Or would you care for a reply?"

"Only if you think I will like what I hear." His laugh was a little forced, and without giving her a chance to answer, he held out his hand to lead her onto the dance floor.

It was almost midnight when the carriage jolted to a stop in the courtyard of the Berg Palace. For a moment Nando remained slumped in a corner, even after the door had been opened. When he finally moved to rise, every bone and muscle protested the movement. He picked up the sword, which he had unbuckled as a sole concession to comfort, and stepped to the cobblestones. Taking a deep breath of crisp air, he stretched pleasurably to remove the kinks that a journey of three days and two nights had put into his long limbs.

Despite the late hour, Menzel, Nando's steward, was in attendance within minutes of their arrival.

"Why don't you go back to bed, Menzel," Nando said, as he began shrugging out of his travel-stained clothes. "I imagine any news will keep until tomorrow."

"Of course, your excellency."

Menzel bowed to the waist, his lean body seeming to bend on a hinge. As always when Menzel executed his bow, Nando waited for the creak of wood upon metal.

"Your excellency had an invitation for this evening."

"Spare me." Nando sat down on a chair and began pulling off his boots. But without wanting to, he wondered if Arabella would be there and his hands stilled. He looked up to find that Menzel hadn't moved. "Well, what is it?"

"A ball at Prince Razumovsky's."

Razumovsky, Nando mused. He gave the most glittering affairs in Vienna. Of course Arabella would be there.

He had thought of her. More than he had wanted to. Much more. Enough to keep him awake at night. Enough to wake up unrefreshed, his body heavy with desire. Enough to sleep alone all these weeks.

Hundreds of kilometers away Nando had found that he was even more vulnerable to her than when he had known she was nearby. Perhaps that was why he had resisted the urge to write to her, knowing that all the unwanted thoughts and emotions and desires would find their way into the ink drops and deprive him of his last defense.

He had just shaken the bathwater from his hair like a young dog and wrapped himself in a linen bath sheet that had been warmed by a hot brick when Franz entered the room with a tray of food.

"Good God, Franz," he exclaimed, "you are as tired as I am. Leave that to the others."

Franz smiled, but continued with his work, placing several platters with different kinds of sausage, thinly sliced roast pork and wedges of cheese and a carafe of golden wine on the table near the high stove made of glazed, heavily ornamented porcelain tiles.

Suddenly realizing how hungry he was, Nando picked up a piece of meat with his fingers and stuffed it into his mouth, the flavors of pepper and caraway tangy on his tongue.

"Go get some sleep, Franz," Nando instructed, "and send me someone who knows his way around my wardrobe."

"Your excellency is going out?"

"The Razumovsky ball."

Franz said nothing, but went into the other room, where Nando heard him opening doors and drawers. He slipped into a robe, grabbed a piece of bread and a wedge of cheese and went to lean against the doorjamb.

"What's the matter? Don't I get a lecture on the merits of rest?"

Franz spread a lawn shirt carefully on the back of a chair and his lips twitched barely with the beginnings of a smile. "You do what you must."

Nando grinned. The tiredness from the journey was gone, and he felt younger and more vital than he had for a long time. "Come in the barouche to collect me around five o'clock. We'll drive to Uncle Johann's and say hello to the old man."

"So early?"

"I want to be back by noon. I may want to go riding."

Unable to hide the smile that spread over his face, Franz turned away.

With an arrogant possessiveness he had never before manifested quite so blatantly, Volkonsky monopolized Arabella so completely that she began to feel a distinct sense of confinement. But halfway through a wickedly lavish supper, between the jellied duckling and mousse of smoked pigeon, his knee invaded her space just a little too much and she lost patience.

"Perhaps you should ask our host to change the design of his tables for his next affair." Arabella favored Volkonsky with thin smile. "Apparently it does not offer you enough room for your legs."

Arabella did not bother keeping her voice down, and there were several snickers from those within hearing distance.

"My apologies." Volkonsky bent to kiss her hand more to hide the rush of fury than anything else. Damn her, he thought. Tonight she would pay. She would pay twice for every time she had let him feel the sharp side of her tongue.

As Volkonsky bent down, Arabella felt a frisson of expectancy, of pleasure that had nothing to do with the damply eager lips touching the back of her hand. But the vibration at the back of her neck did not dissipate. Instead it began to thrum like a violin string that is pulled taut then plucked with a fiery movement. Slowly Arabella turned her head to look over her shoulder to search for the source of heat and saw Nando.

Nando felt an unreasoning rush of joy when he caught sight of Arabella. He strode down the gallery, hurrying to see if the same joy was reflected in her eyes. Then he stopped so suddenly that he had to steady himself against the brilliant green of a malachite-faced pillar.

He watched Volkonsky slip his hand under Arabella's palm and lower his head. Watched her hold still for the touch of his lips on her hand.

A sharp pain stole his breath as his heart pounded against his ribs. But within moments the iron discipline of so many years prevailed. His pulse slowed. Nando felt a brief chill as the ice returned to encase his heart, but he welcomed it. He was safe now.

Then Arabella turned to face him. For a moment her lips parted as if to speak, and her face, her eyes seemed to light up like the sunrise, and Nando felt all the emotions that he had banished to the darkest part of his soul begin to fight their way to the surface again. But just as suddenly as it had come, the light in her eyes died away, and he wondered if he had perhaps imagined it in his exhaustion.

Their eyes held for a heartbeat and then another. Arabella turned away and Nando knew that it was over.

Chapter Sixteen

Arabella was walking a tightrope without a net, knowing she could not afford a misstep, a moment of imbalance. She could not afford to look at Nando again and see that glacial indifference in his eyes, for she knew it would splinter her into a thousand fragments. Despite her confusion, her hurt, she refused to provide him with the satisfaction of knowing he could reduce her to a defeated, pathetic little heap.

She did not try to question what had happened to make Nando look at her with that terrible, inhuman detachment. That would be for a private time of grief when she could let go of the pride that was the only thing that still held her upright.

Her feet moved in time with the music and she concentrated on one more minute, one more dance, one more hour that she had to survive.

She was so fully absorbed with her relentless task that she saw neither the glance nor the signal that passed between Volkonsky and Princess Bagration. But with some sixth sense, she felt the burning sensation that Nando's gaze brought to her skin ease. The unexpected relief flooded her limbs with a dangerous lassitude, numbed her mind like a drug. She called on yet another reservoir of strength and nodded to Volkonsky's solicitous suggestion that he have her cape fetched so they could take some air.

* * *

"Nando, what are you doing here?"

He felt a hand on his arm and turned reluctantly to face Lulu. Pulling his mouth into a fair imitation of a smile, Nando tried for humor. "I received an invitation, just like you did."

"When did you get back? How long have you been here? Have you spoken to Arabella? Doesn't she look especially lovely tonight?" The questions bubbled for a moment then fizzled to a stop. Lulu stared into his bleak eyes. "What's wrong?"

He looked back to the dance floor, his gaze scanning the thinning crowd. Damn, where was she? He couldn't see her.

Lulu clutched his arm. "Nando, what's wrong? Tell me?"

"Nothing is wrong, *ma chère.*" Nando brought his eyes to Lulu. "Everything is in perfect order." The pain he thought to have mastered washed over him again. As he struggled to keep it out of his face, he cursed himself for allowing Arabella the power to inflict such pain on him, unaware that there was no way in the world he could have kept that power from her.

"It's Volkonsky, isn't it?" Lulu narrowed her eyes. "You saw her with Volkonsky and you're jealous."

He said nothing.

"She's done nothing wrong, Nando."

An eyebrow curved upward. "I'm not blind."

"You're a fool," Lulu spat and flounced away.

Princess Bagration glided up to Aunt Therese von Thürheim, who was fussing with the bejeweled peacock feathers that ornamented her graying hair. "May I trouble you for a moment, *ma chère comtesse.*"

Aunt Therese blinked owlishly as she recognized the blond beauty beside her.

"I just wanted to tell you that I've persuaded your lovely guest to be unfaithful to you for a few days."

"Our guest? Arabella?" Therese von Thürheim's pudgy cheeks jiggled in surprise.

"Yes. She has agreed to keep me company."

"Arabella? You mean Arabella Douglas?" the old woman repeated, confused. She distinctly remembered Lulu telling her that the princess hated Arabella. Didn't she? But the smile was so friendly, so sincere, the voice so sweet that she decided she must have mixed things up in her memory after all.

"I just wanted to tell you that I'm taking her with me tonight. So you needn't worry. She'll be in the best of hands."

Aunt Therese nodded a bit dazedly and watched the blond vision in white float away.

"What was that all about?" asked Lulu as she came up behind her.

Aunt Therese smiled. "Such a charming lady."

Lulu gave an unladylike snort and reaped a disapproving glance from her aunt. "Charming viper, would be more like it. What did she want?"

"I thought I remembered, but I must have been wrong..." She fluttered her fan and peered at her niece. "I don't know why I thought...well, anyway, the princess said that Arabella would be staying with her for a few days."

"What?" The word exploded and a few heads turned. "What else did she say?" Lulu's fingers bit into the old woman's flaccid flesh as she gripped her arm.

"Nothing. But what..." The older woman's words petered out as Lulu whirled away.

Prince Volkonsky instructed a footman to bring them their capes and turned to Arabella. "Would you like to sit down? I'll have a refreshment brought."

Arabella ignored the proffered chair as she ignored the hand that slid up her back under her hair. She was holding herself upright, but she was numb. Her body. Her mind.

Volkonsky smiled as his hand skimmed over velvet. The realization that this body he had lusted after for so long would soon be at his mercy sent a sharp flash of desire coursing through him, coupled with a feeling of triumph. He had not thought it would be so simple at the end.

He put a glass in her hand and automatically Arabella took a long sip, but the almond milk tasted bitter beneath the sweetness and she set the glass down.

She had no idea how much time had elapsed when her cape finally settled around her shoulders. Arabella's fingers fumbled with the frogged closure and she shook her head at her clumsiness. Then without warning the world around her exploded with cries, screams, shouts.

Before she could look around her, she was being swept outside, and Arabella's last memory was Volkonsky's devilishly smiling face with a halo of orange flames behind him.

Lulu rushed back to where she had left Nando a few minutes before, but he was nowhere to be seen.

Heedless of the curious looks, she hurried on, cursing the trees and shrubs that obstructed her vision. She darted from room to room like a doe on the run. The fear that something terrible was happening to Arabella welled up and harshened her breathing, and for a moment she leaned against a table to press a hand against the stitch in her side. Then she saw him.

Half sliding across the well-waxed parquet floor of the partially deserted salon, she stopped herself by catching his arm. "Thank God, I've found you," Lulu gasped. "You have to go... it's Arabella... she..."

With his hand on her shoulder Nando silenced and supported her. "Go away, Lulu. Go away and leave me alone. I am no longer interested in Arabella."

The stridently enunciated words fell on her like bullets, but she still held on to his arm. "You're not only a fool, Nando, you're a liar." Her fingers tightened. "Listen to me. Princess Bagration told Aunt Therese that Arabella would be visiting here for a few days, that she was taking her to the Palm Palace with her."

The hair at the back of Nando's neck stood on end at those words. Surely Katharina wouldn't dare.

Mistaking his silence for indifference, Lulu shook his arm impatiently. "Don't be stupid, Nando. Think."

Suddenly pandemonium broke loose around them. At first there was only a rumble of voices that rolled through the rooms with a stunning velocity, gathering momentum and volume like an avalanche. But within moments it erupted into shouts and cries that seemed inarticulate. Someone bellowed, "Fire." There was a high, drawn out scream. Then another.

Lulu pushed Nando away. "Go. I can take care of myself."

Alarm exploding in his brain, he ran. Dodging scurrying guests and servants, Nando tore down the staircase to the main entrance where a row of imperturbable footmen stood ready to fetch cloaks for those guests who had the nerve to wait for them. Collaring a footman, he pushed him against a wall with a strength that was all the more dangerous for its carelessness.

"Prince Volkonsky. Have you seen him?"

"Y-yes, your excellency." The man rolled his eyes toward the hand that threatened to cut off his air.

"Where? When?"

"He l-left a few minutes ago."

"Alone?"

"No," he gasped. "A young lady was with him."

Cursing, Nando pushed through the knot of people clogging the entrance and scanned the crowd that milled around outside with the dangerous aimlessness of a herd of cattle about to stampede. The drive was jammed with carriages. Coachmen tried to quiet nervous horses. Voices called names, orders. There was shouting, crying, screaming.

The lawn with its light covering of snow was full of black silhouettes running from the palace. Nando glanced behind him and saw that orange flames were already coming out of the upper windows, licking greedily at the wooden frames.

The bell of a nearby church began to clang out the alarm. A team of horses reared at the sound and bolted sideways. They took the low hedge and raced downhill across the lawn, the carriage careening crazily behind them.

Nando ran down the drive toward the street, scanning the passengers of every carriage. Nothing.

In front of him a pair of horses reared as several wagons loaded with firefighters and huge barrels of water squeezed through the gate at full gallop. A dark-haired man thrust his head out of the carriage window and shouted something incomprehensible. Then he turned toward the burning palace to shake his fist at the wagons that had veered off into the lawn, and his eyes connected with Nando's.

For a moment both men went still, freezing in the middle of a movement. Then, as if on cue, they exploded into motion simultaneously. Volkonsky's fist came down on the carriage door and he shouted to the coachman, who cracked his whip, sending the already nervous horses bucking through the gate. Nando dashed down the drive and skidded to a stop in the street just in time to see the carriage clatter around a corner.

He spun and started back toward the gate, determined to commandeer a carriage or a horse, but Franz's voice called his name.

With one leap Nando was in the barouche beside Franz. Before he had settled in the seat, they were moving. More bells had begun to ring, and the quick, warning peals seemed to accentuate the bedlam on the street.

"Volkonsky, the damned swine, has abducted Arabella," Nando shouted over the din as the barouche took the corner leaning precariously to one side. There was no doubt in his mind that his words were true. He had seen the hatred mixed with fear in Volkonsky's eyes. But still he asked himself just what she had done to encourage him. Had she perhaps gone with him willingly?

Suddenly the passage was barred by a group of cavalry, to make way for a police patrol. The police were armed with thick batons to keep the sensation seekers a safe distance from the fire. The necessity for this was emphasized almost immediately by a group of men in baggy workers' clothes who emerged in the street crying, "*Gemma Feuer schau'n,* let's go look at the fire," with unabashed glee.

Nando roared a command, and the soldiers saluted and prodded both police and curiosity seekers aside to let the barouche pass.

By the time the barouche bumped onto the Franzens Bridge, its springs violently protesting the speed, they had managed to close the distance to barely the span of the Danube. But a new wave of onlookers, enticed by the orange glare against the blue-black sky, surged toward them, slowing their pace to a crawl.

Nando leaned forward, his hands pressed against his thighs. If Volkonsky turned right after the bridge toward the Prater woods and its tangle of paths, Nando would need an army to find them.

But when the carriage swung to the left, Nando expelled the air so sharply from his lungs that he realized with a jolt of surprise that he had been holding his breath. The wave of humanity coming toward them thinned a little, and with a grimace, Nando cracked his whip above their heads. He winced at the ugly sound and at the way the people scattered right and left, cursing him with half-audible mutters, but he cared nothing for sensibilities of any kind at the moment.

"They're probably going toward the Vienna Woods," Nando muttered half to himself as they raced down the Taborstrasse. "There are enough lodges and farms out there." He gave Franz a grim look.

For a moment Nando let himself lean back against the leather seat, but immediately his body shot forward again. The moment of respite from his fierce concentration on the chase had allowed Arabella to slip into his mind again. Was Volkonsky touching her now? Did he have his hands in the glossy, midnight hair that spilled over her shoulders? Were his lips on her creamy skin? Her mouth?

Nando's hand tightened on the hilt of his sword and his stomach rebelled at the direction his thoughts had taken. "I'll kill him," he swore through clenched teeth, ignoring Franz's stare. "If he touches her, I swear I'll kill him."

Volkonsky hung on to a strap and tried to focus his gaze. The wild rocking and jolting motion of the carriage made it almost impossible. He was certain that it was Berg in the carriage following him.

"Faster," he shouted to the coachman. "Faster, damn you! *Bistreya!*"

A curve pressed him back into the seat and Volkonsky looked at the young woman who lay crumpled in the corner like a rag doll. Her cape had opened and her dress had slid off one shoulder, exposing an expanse of skin that gleamed like fine pearls even in the murky interior of the carriage. Even in unconsciousness, with all animation gone from her face, her beauty was undiminished.

Then he remembered that Berg was somewhere behind him, and the rage rose to obliterate the desire he felt. Volkonsky's mouth turned down as he reached to touch Arabella's shoulder. Her skin was cool and she showed no sign that she was in any way aware of his touch. Angrily he thrust his hand into her bodice. The soft flesh that gave under the hard grasp of his fingers aroused him without giving him any sensual pleasure.

Suddenly he regretted having drugged Arabella. If she were awake and kicking and screaming, at least he would be occupied, instead of thinking about that whoreson Berg who was snapping at his heels. Volkonsky cracked his knuckles one by one and swore. If he had known that a fire would break out at Razumovsky's palace, he need not have bothered with a drug. It would hardly have attracted a great deal of attention if he carried out a hysterical female in a situation like that.

Unwilling to wait any longer, he lunged toward Arabella.
Her hair had fallen across her cheek, and he wrapped the
ebony curtain around his hand, pulling her close. Curling
the hand into a fist, he pushed her chin up. Her head lolled
back, and he lowered his mouth to hers.

Her slack lips presented no barrier to his tongue. Brutally Volkonsky tasted her, filling her mouth, but there was
no pleasure to be had from a limp body, no matter how
tempting. With a curse, he flung her into a corner.

With a thump, Arabella's shoulder hit the side of the carriage and she moaned softly as she slid to the floor, her
movement abetted by the jolting of the carriage. Quickly,
Volkonsky scooped her up and angled her on the seat again.
He passed his tongue over his lips eagerly as he curved his
hand around her chin. Perhaps she would awaken more
quickly with a little assistance.

He shook her shoulders. "Wake up, Arabella." He shook
her again.

Arabella's head fell back and lolled from side to side as a
low sound of protest formed in her throat.

Volkonsky's fingers bit into her cheeks. "Wake up, my
sweet. I did not go to all this trouble to have a cadaver in my
bed," he whispered, conveniently forgetting that it was the
drug his valet had obtained from a Turk that had put her in
this state.

Her eyelids fluttered and with tiny movements—a flick of
a hand, a quiver, a sigh—Arabella started the journey back
from her twilight sleep. Volkonsky watched her struggle to
consciousness with a greed he could taste on his tongue. Her
breathing grew less shallow, and he could see her flesh move
temptingly with each lungful of air.

Volkonsky thrust his hand under Arabella's gown and
tore at her drawers until his fingers touched the smooth skin
of her thighs. His excitement growing, he groaned and his
mouth clamped down on hers again.

Arabella surfaced from her drugged senselessness as a
body surfaces from water, bobbing up for a brief moment,

then sinking again. She wanted to go back to the warm place where soft, sweet-smelling grass pillowed her head and Nando's face filled her vision. With a sigh she plunged into the welcome depths.

Nando. She was granted only a glimpse of his face before she was swept into the cold. Her first sensation was a pain in her temples that throbbed in time with her heartbeat.

She tried to move, but her limbs were too heavy. Slowly other perceptions reached her. A weight on her chest. A pressure on her stomach. She opened her mouth to breathe, but it was full of something wet and moving, and fear gave her the strength to lift her hands and push.

"At last, my black-haired witch, you are awake."

Then her mouth was free and the weight lifted from her chest a little. The words were a murmur of sounds that ran together in her ears, and Arabella moved her lips to question, but the only sound that came was the whisper of her breath.

The pressure she could not identify slid down from her stomach, along her legs and returned upward, and her mind grabbed at wisps of memory. The ball. Lights. Orange lights that hurt her eyes even though she knew they were closed. Then she remembered, and a desolate sound rose in her throat. Her parched lips moved. "Nando."

Suddenly there was a new pain in her arms and shoulders to distract her from the throbbing in her head.

"No, it's not your Nando, you bitch. Open your eyes and look at me."

Arabella struggled to the surface and her eyelids half-lifted. The images that penetrated her eyes were blurred and moved with a crazy rhythm, but she recognized anger in the disjointed sounds that reached her brain. She retreated from the ugly sound and was submerged again in the blackness.

Nando. She smiled and reached out her hand. Their fingertips touched, but this time he did not come closer. Instead his figure dissolved until he was only a diaphanous image and then not even that. Arabella opened her eyes, wanting to reach for him, to hold him, and the shape before her came slowly into focus.

Her first reaction was one of puzzlement, for she did not recognize the distorted features above her. Where was Nando? Before the puzzlement became panic, she felt the pain in her shoulders again.

"Damn you. I am Nikita Volkonsky and before I'm through with you, you will well know who I am."

The words grated harshly on her ears, sending another volley of pain through her head. One by one the words fell into place, and with an ominous clang like the closing of a dungeon door the full realization of her situation hit Arabella. For a moment the recognition paralyzed her and the only part of her that moved were her eyes, which grew wider and larger as she stared at the man above her. But then the fear and the adrenaline rushed through her system, and not knowing that this was exactly what the man holding her wanted, Arabella began to struggle.

Seemingly oblivious to her hands, which pushed and flailed and scratched, Volkonsky began to run his hands over her body. His touch was greedy and hurtful, and no matter how she tried to twist away from him, he found her. The carriage bounced through a rut, the movement hurling them both to the floor. Volkonsky held her fast with his body, and his mouth began to travel over her, leaving wet, slimy trails on her skin.

Little by little Arabella felt the energy that had pulsed through her begin to flag. Some force was pulling her under again. A silent scream built in her throat as she battled the shape above her for one more moment before the sweet, welcome darkness enveloped her. She slipped downward, unaware that all movement around her had suddenly ceased.

The December wind blew in Nando's face and yet he could feel the sweat trickle between his shoulder blades. He had long since taken the reins from Franz, needing at least to occupy his hands. But what earthly good did that do, when his thoughts raced far ahead of their horse and pictured scenes that made his palms slick with moisture?

How much farther did they have? The mare was tiring, slowing down. They neared another turn, and Nando felt Franz's hand on his arm.

"Here."

He looked at the ground lit by a diffuse half-moon and saw the fresh tracks of a carriage that had cut the corner sharply. Nando clucked sharply to the horse, and feeling that the end of the journey was at hand, the mare picked up speed.

Light shone through the trees, and as the barouche broke out of the woods, Nando saw a large farmhouse with several outbuildings. The pungent odor that blew toward them bespoke of cows, perhaps a few pigs.

His stomach tightened as he saw Volkonsky's carriage in the light of several pitch torches, its door open. Throwing the reins to Franz as they entered the yard, he jumped down. The muddy ground sucked at his boots as he ran toward the coachman who was standing somewhat irresolutely at the carriage door.

"Wake up, damn you. Wake up." His face distorted by a demented rage, Volkonsky knelt on the floor of the carriage, and was shaking an obviously unconscious Arabella.

Nando felt the fury and the pain rise within him like a liquid coming to boil. "Bastard," he cursed hoarsely as he swooped down on his prey.

Volkonsky looked up and as his hands fell away from Arabella's shoulders, she collapsed onto the floor. Nando needed all his control to guide his hands to the front of Volkonsky's uniform tunic and not his neck. With a jerk he pulled the Russian out of the carriage and flung him to the ground.

Sliding inside the carriage, he gently cradled Arabella in one arm while the other hand looked for and found the pulse in her neck. Suddenly it was impossible to swallow past the lump in his throat. Impossible even to breathe. As

Nando's hand trembled over her cheek, she shifted in his arms and opened her eyes.

"Nando?"

"Yes. Hush now. You're safe."

Her eyelids fluttered shut, and the relief Arabella felt was so great that she almost slipped back into the black void that hovered on the fringes of her consciousness. Nando's arms tightened around her, and she stepped from the edge, forcing herself to open her eyes again to reassure him.

Their eyes met and held, saying what was long overdue. Time stood still, and Arabella gazed into eyes that were a shining, molten silver. Eyes that mutely held the answer to all her questions. She chided herself for wanting the words as well.

"Did he hurt you?" Nando's hand was still curved around her neck, his thumb on her uneven, shallow pulse.

Arabella tried to curve her lips into a smile. "Nothing irrevocable, I think."

His arms tensed around her and Arabella let her eyes fall closed again. Vaguely she was aware of something warm and furry being wrapped around her and of being lifted to the carriage seat.

"Will you be all right? I'll be back to take you home as soon as I can."

There was an urgency underneath the gentleness of his tone and her eyes flew open. Her hand struggled out of the robe to grip the front of Nando's uniform. "Where are you going?"

There was only silence, and suddenly Arabella knew with a terrible certainty what he planned to do.

"Please, Nando, rio," she begged. "Don't do it. Don't make me go through this."

"You stopped me once before. If you hadn't, you might have been spared this. This time you cannot stop me."

Nando cupped her face in his hands, and his thumb stroked lightly over her bruised lips. He bent forward, wanting to take a taste of her mouth with him as a talisman. But Arabella's eyes widened and he stopped a breath away from her lips, cursing himself for his thoughtlessness. She had suffered enough tonight without him forcing his kiss on her, too. He contented himself with a quick, featherlike touch to her cheek.

"Don't worry, *chérie*," Nando said lightly. "I will be back."

Lithely, he sprang from the carriage and strode to where Volkonsky stood swearing at his coachman, who was doing his awkward best to remove the mud from his master's uniform jacket and white kidskin breeches.

"Tell him not to bother, Volkonsky." The words cracked through the chill predawn air like a whip. "You will be down in the mud again before long."

"You filthy…" The Russian started forward, but Nando whipped his sword from its scabbard so quickly that Volkonsky almost stumbled into it.

"Don't," Nando barked. "Don't make it more difficult than it already is for me not to kill you on the spot like a mad dog."

Casually taking aim, Nando pressed the tip of his sword into a silver uniform button. Volkonsky stumbled and Nando gave him another poke in the chest, which sent him backward again. Satisfied, he stepped back, unbuckled his belt and swiftly unbuttoned his uniform tunic. Flinging his things to Franz, he fixed Volkonsky with his cool eyes.

"I fear we shall have to violate the *règlement,* prince. The choice of weapons and place is mine." Nando's words echoed through the unearthly stillness of the yard.

Nando rolled his shoulders briefly to relax the knots of tension that had built there over the past hour. Then he drew himself up very straight and saluted his opponent, his sword flashing silver. "*En garde,* Volkonsky."

Chapter Seventeen

Arabella angled herself to the window, her heart beating in her throat. The yard had filled with the inhabitants of the farm, some dressed, some wearing nightclothes. Several of the menservants were holding pitch torches. There was not a sound. No one moved. But the flickering light made the shadows weave—a ghastly caricature of the *tableaux vivants* that were performed so often in Viennese salons.

For a moment her gaze turned inward and Arabella slowly raised her hand to her mouth. Nando had almost kissed her. Oh, how she had wanted that kiss—to cancel out the shame, the ugliness. To make her forget. But she had seen the disgust in his eyes. Disgust he had quickly masked behind concern.

Of course Nando felt disgust, she thought. Even she was filled with revulsion for her body, which had been touched and demeaned and befouled. She rubbed the back of her hand harshly against her lips, but nothing could erase the vile taste that seemed to cling to them.

For the first time that night, Arabella did not struggle against the tears that filled her eyes. Then the tableau in the yard broke into movement. She wanted to look away, but instead she gripped the window frame. As the scene unfolded before her, she forgot her personal misery as fear for Nando clogged her throat.

Nando was standing perfectly still and straight, the light glinting off his sword as he waited. The wind ruffled the loose white shirt that was tucked into his tight scarlet breeches. Once he glanced over his shoulder and sent her a smile that briefly relieved the grim lines of his face. Arabella knew that he had never looked more beautiful and that she had never loved him more.

Volkonsky threw off his coat and drew himself straight, albeit with difficulty. "I shall be satisfied with first blood," he stated.

Nando looked his opponent in the eye. "I shall be satisfied when you beg for mercy."

Volkonsky shrugged arrogantly, the movement of his shoulders masking the shiver that went through him. "As you wish."

The two men exchanged the formal salute, and although there were no seconds to referee the duel, they stepped forward and raised their swords in regulation manner to cross them at the tips. Then, as one, they fell back and engaged, their swords clicking lightly.

Volkonsky would have liked to circle his opponent for a while to get used to the feeling of the weapon in his hand. To measure the skill of the man determined to bring him to his knees. After all, the sword was not his favored weapon. But he was given no opportunity. Within seconds he was parrying a full attack.

The two men were well-matched in size—both tall and broad-shouldered. Only where Nando was lean and firmly muscled, Volkonsky was padded with mementos of easy living. But they both moved with a grace that made their duel a *danse macabre* of terrible beauty.

Volkonsky feinted, leaving his side without defense, and Nando lunged, eliciting a gasp from the spectators. But he did not complete the lunge and sink the tip between his opponent's ribs as he could have. Instead he suspended his forward motion with exquisite control and sliced through the lawn of Volkonsky's shirt with a fine, upward flick of the wrist.

That gesture of contempt enraged and unnerved Volkonsky far more than a direct hit would have. He launched a wild attack, which Nando parried with cool, easy elegance. And when Nando countered with a riposte, he again reached past Volkonsky's defense and cut another slit through his opponent's shirt without so much as scratching his skin.

Both men seethed with rage. But Volkonsky's fury made him rash and clumsy, while Nando was able to harness his anger and use it as an advantage. Perhaps because he knew that if he did not, he would not be able to restrain himself from slaughtering his rival.

Never in his life had Nando felt such hatred, such blood lust. Never in his life would he forget Arabella's pale face and the bruised look in her eyes when he had picked her up from the floor of the carriage. How he wanted the satisfaction of feeling Volkonsky's flesh give way under his sword. But he knew that whatever his own inclination, he could not spill Volkonsky's blood. He could not do that to Arabella.

Arabella. Nando wished that he could spare a moment to look at her. To reassure her. But he knew that the best reassurance would be to get this over with as soon as possible.

He attacked mercilessly, no longer looking for dropped defenses and openings to lunge so that he could tease or humiliate. Nando's priority was to exhaust and disarm his opponent and to do it quickly. Pressing forward, he drove the Russian backward step by step across the yard.

Nando saw where they were heading, and if he could have spared an ounce of concentration, he would have smiled. His swordplay tight and precise, he pressed. One more step, then another.

In the middle of a backward step, Volkonsky's boots hit the brick rim of the pit that caught the runoff water from the dung heap next to it. His hand opened as his arms flailed for balance, sending his weapon to the ground, but it was too late. With a cry he tumbled backward into the foul-smelling liquid.

At a gesture from Nando, several servants ran forward with a length of rope and pulled the sputtering, swearing Russian onto the ground. His clothes stained and dripping, he roughly pushed away the men who had helped him out, sending them sprawling in the mud.

As soon as he had cleared the water from his eyes, Volkonsky reached down for the weapon he had dropped, but Nando stepped forward and flicked it out of his reach with the tip of his sword.

"I have no intention of fighting you any more tonight, prince." Nando's voice took on a heavily sarcastic tone on the last word.

Volkonsky managed an arrogant laugh. "I thought you wanted to hear me beg for mercy."

"It is enough that I could have killed you tonight several times over." Nando allowed himself a disdainful smile. "Besides, you smell much too vile for me to come close enough to fight you."

"Damn you, Berg," Volkonsky snarled. "My seconds will call on you."

"You're welcome to call me out." Nando's tone was mild. "I will enjoy sharing this little scene—" he made a small circular movement with his sword "—with our mutual acquaintances in the city." Nando saluted Volkonsky with his sword and inclined his head in a mockery of a bow. "Adieu, prince."

Nando's step was springy as he strode toward the carriage. He abhorred violence, but tonight, for the first time in his life, Nando had had the satisfaction of knowing what it was like to battle for a woman's honor and win.

With a single leap he was inside the carriage. Putting gentle hands on Arabella's shoulders, Nando smiled at her. "You see? I told you it would be all right."

Arabella nodded and tried to smile, but the fear that had paralyzed her during the duel still gripped her. Nando had fought for her, and yet she knew that he would never be able to touch her again without remembering this night. Not wanting to see the disgust in Nando's eyes again, Arabella lowered her head.

Nando's scent drifted up to her—musky and male. It would be so tempting to press her face against his shirt-front, to feel his heartbeat against her cheek. But she did not dare.

Feeling how stiffly Arabella held herself away from him, Nando thought she still feared being touched. He decided to tease her out of her anxiety. Gently, ever so gently he tipped her face upward with thumb and forefinger and let his thumb slide upward to rest against her lower lip.

"Is that any way to greet the conquering hero?" Nando asked softly, his eyebrows slanting in self-mockery.

To his dismay tears filled Arabella's eyes. Filled until they spilled over to run down her cheeks in thick rivulets. Nando braced himself against her sobs, but she made no sound. Only the silent tears continued to fall, coupled with an infinitesimal trembling of her lip against his skin.

"Arabella," Nando whispered, cupping her face. "Arabella." The name was an endearment, a caress.

As he watched the tears run down her face, Nando felt something inside him crack and break apart, freeing a flood of emotion he did not know how to cope with. Grimly he wondered how many of those tears should be laid at his doorstep for what he had done to her tonight.

"Tell me what to do. What you need," he pleaded. "I want to help you. I need to help you."

Arabella freed her hands from the furry lap robe and slid them over his. "Kiss me."

Slowly, afraid to frighten her, Nando bent his head and pressed his lips against her wet cheek. He could taste the salt of her tears and he took their flavor within himself to keep forever.

He drew back and Arabella looked into his eyes, searching for the revulsion she was so sure would be there. But she saw only gentleness and... She closed her eyes for a moment, not daring to put a name to what she saw there. When she opened her eyes, Nando was smiling at her, and the warmth gave her the courage she needed.

"Kiss me again," she murmured. "Really kiss me."

Nando came closer by degrees, wanting to give her the time he thought she needed, knowing nothing of the impatience, the need that pulsed within her.

Her lips were salty where the tears had flowed over them, and as his mouth glided against hers, he felt the stiffness leave her body little by little until she lay against him soft and pliant. Still her hands stayed on top of his as if to hold him fast. But withdrawal was the furthest thing from Nando's mind as, with exquisite care, he brushed the last traces of salt from her lips with his tongue.

Nando's tongue slid along the seam of Arabella's lips in the gentlest of quests. A beckoning. A plea. Her lips parted. An invitation. An avowal. This and much more they read in each other's eyes before their eyelids fell closed and they merged in an intimate kiss.

He probed with care, still fearful, still unsure of his welcome, but Arabella was greedy. Greedy for the absolution, the cleansing that his kiss represented. Greedy for Nando's taste she had gone so long without.

For endless moments Nando explored all the sweetness Arabella's mouth had to offer. He wanted to go slowly, but somewhere in the course of their kiss, his control slipped away unnoticed by them both and he possessed her mouth with no less passion than he would possess her body.

Still, Arabella did not capitulate. Her mouth blossomed beneath his. Provoked. Pursued. Responded. And gave, endlessly.

Nando felt arousal tauten his body, and as the pleasurable ache brought a measure of sanity, he dragged his mouth from Arabella's, his chest heaving.

"I'm sorry. I didn't mean to fall upon you like a beast," he whispered into her hair and pressed her face against his shoulder.

Arabella felt an incredible weakness, as if her bones were made of water, but she smiled into his shirt and her fingers stroked his wrists before they fell still. For a long while she was incapable of moving. When she could, she tipped her head back to look at Nando.

"You didn't, you know. Not like . . ."

Her eyes clouded and Nando knew that Arabella was remembering. "Shh." Gently he stroked her face until the hunted look began to dissipate.

Carefully, as if she was the most fragile, most precious porcelain, Nando slid his arms around Arabella and picked her up. "Come, I will take you away from here."

He moved easily, as if she weighed nothing. She turned her face into his shoulder as they crossed the yard. Perhaps it was cowardly, Arabella thought, but she did not think that she had the strength to look at Volkonsky now.

In the barouche, Nando settled Arabella next to him and pressed her head to his shoulder.

When they had finally left the flickering light of the farmyard behind them and were surrounded by the black and silver of the night, Arabella felt the events of the past hours fall away from her like a long-past nightmare and she stirred against Nando.

"Where are we going?"

"I'm taking you back to Vienna."

"Vienna?" She said it as if it were a foreign word. She had no wish to return to Vienna. She would have liked nothing better than to stay like this forever, cradled against Nando's strong, lean body, rocking with the motion of the carriage. To stay in this wonderful world that seemed to belong to the two of them alone.

"Must we?" she murmured.

"I can hardly rescue you from one abduction only to make you victim of another."

Arabella nodded. "It's a pity though," she said. "It's so lovely here in the country. I've been in cities for so long that I wish..."

"You wish?" Nando prompted, wanting, no, needing at this moment to lay every wish at Arabella's feet.

"I wish I could have a holiday away from the city."

"A holiday away from the city?" So surprised was Nando at her words that he mimicked them stupidly. Why would Arabella possibly want to spend time in the country where there was no one to admire her beauty or her clever tongue?

"Mmm. Look at all the lovely trees around us." Arabella raised her face to the tall pines that wore a light covering of snow. "Listen to the stillness." She held her breath, and indeed the only sound was the beat of the horse's hooves and the light creaking of the carriage springs.

She smiled at Nando. "You still don't know me very well, do you?" The sadness crept into her eyes. "Despite everything, you're still not quite convinced that I'm not a featherbrain whose only care is how I will look at the next ball." Arabella angled herself against him, the movement of her body innocently causing Nando a sweet agony. "Admit it."

Even in the dark, her smile dazzled, tempted, and Nando felt his pulse accelerate. A crazy idea took hold of him. *This is absolutely insane,* his mind told him. But his lips said, "If you really mean it, we could send Lulu a message that you're all right. That she needn't worry."

Arabella went still.

"Franz and I were going to drive out to Trautenstein to visit my great-uncle." Nando went on quickly, before the sane portion of his mind had a chance to stop him. "He lives in a marvelously medieval castle in the middle of a forest. We could spend the day there and go back to Vienna this evening or even tomorrow."

Nando laughed as an untypical lightheartedness took hold of him. Suddenly he felt as carefree and foolish as he had felt when he and Franz were planning some boyhood prank. Something forbidden. Something tempting.

"Would you like that?" Nando touched his fingers lightly to Arabella's cheek.

"More than anything."

Nando gazed into Arabella's face, needing reassurance. "You're sure? Uncle Johann will be a most proper chaperon."

Arabella shook her head as if at the antics of a small boy, but her heart was singing. "Tell me, Nando, which one of us are you trying to convince?"

Johann von Berg's castle was located halfway up a thickly wooded mountain. When the narrow road, full of sharp curves and turns, ended without warning, Arabella found herself looking at a sheer wall, its pale gray contours fuzzy in the fog that had come with the dawn. At each corner of the castle was a rounded tower with long, narrow embrasures. It was easy to imagine a crossbow being aimed out of such an opening.

There was a creak of metal on wood as the huge doors were pulled open by invisible hands, and slowly they passed through the arched entryway.

"Nando!" The vigorous voice rang across the square courtyard, and both Nando and Arabella turned toward it. A tall, white-haired figure strode toward them, his arms outstretched, and the two men embraced warmly.

"Uncle Johann, may I present Miss Arabella Douglas."

"A lovely surprise for an old man." Johann von Berg bowed elegantly over Arabella's hand and kept it in his when he straightened. "I am very pleased to meet you."

Their eyes met and they measured each other, finally giving their approval with a candid smile. Both knew that they were bonded together by the love they felt for the man who stood between them.

Within minutes a footman had been dispatched with a message for Lulu and they were settled in front of a roaring fire. A servant brought coffee for the two men and tea for

Arabella and a large plate of fresh crescent rolls with butter and apricot jam, which smelled of summer.

Arabella did not listen to the slightly abbreviated version of the events of the past hours that Nando gave his uncle. But the sound of his voice was comforting, as was the appearance of the gaunt old man who sat across from her. She smiled with the knowledge that this was precisely how Nando would look fifty years from now.

The remainder of the drug, the warmth of the room, the feeling of safety seemed to tug at her consciousness. She forced herself to sit straight and massaged her temple where a faint pain had returned to throb.

"My dear." The old man leaned forward and took her hand. "Would you like to rest a little?"

"I apologize for being such poor company. I'm afraid I still haven't quite recovered from the drug," Arabella said, enunciating very carefully, afraid that she would slur the words.

"Drug? What drug?" Nando's voice was sharp.

"Volkonsky drugged me." Her eyes focused on Nando in sudden irritation that he would think she had gone with the Russian of her own free will.

"He drugged you?" Nando repeated in a hoarse whisper. "Why didn't you tell me?"

Struck by the sudden fire in Nando's eyes, Arabella could do nothing but shrug silently.

Nando put his hand on Arabella's arm, as if needing reassurance that she was all right. "I would not have let the bastard off so easily had I known," he murmured, steel audible underneath the softness.

"Do moderate your speech, my boy," Johann von Berg reprimanded Nando mildly, but at the same time a smile softened his imperious features.

Arabella awoke to the rustle of clothing and looked up to see a young woman with a coil of butter-yellow braids around her head carefully arranging gowns on a daybed with a curved back. Hearing Arabella move, she turned and bobbed a curtsy.

"*Fräulein*. Count Berg sent me to help you bathe and dress when you awoke. My name is Lisl."

"Good morning, or should I say good afternoon?"

"It's just past one o'clock, *Fräulein*."

Arabella sat up and stretched luxuriously. She had slept for over four hours and she felt refreshed, her head clear. The only reminder of the night before was the ache in her arms and shoulders from Volkonsky's brutal hands.

Lisl chatted easily as she washed Arabella's hair and helped her bathe, clucking over the bluish marks that marred her skin. The clothes she had brought belonged to Johann von Berg's wife, who had died seven years ago, she explained.

"The gentlemen thought you might like to go riding this afternoon. That's why I brought the riding habit," Lisl said as she held a silk stocking ready for Arabella's foot. "If you do, Count Berg suggested you wear it down to luncheon. Young Count Berg," she added with a smile that dimpled her plump cheeks.

Arabella balanced against the bedpost as Lisl smoothed the stocking up her leg. She let the young woman's voice swirl around her like the soothing burble of a brook and wondered what she would see in Nando's eyes this time.

The first thing she saw was a warm flicker of pleasure, and she almost sighed audibly when it disappeared instantly behind a polite smile.

"I see Lisl's managed to make you look like a real Austrian Fräulein." Nando turned Arabella and looked at the thick, black braids that had been smoothed into a coil, leaving only a few curls at her temples, making her look very young and demure. His hands itched to unbraid her hair, to bury themselves in its softness as they had last night. But the heady insanity of the night before was gone, his control was in place and he was determined that it stay there.

They rode after lunch. The silence of the wintry forest was eloquent and they did not break it except for the occasional desultory word until the gray walls of the castle loomed in front of them again.

They were still within the shelter of the old beech trees when Arabella reached out to put a hand on Nando's sleeve.

"Where have you gone, Nando?" she asked when he turned to face her. "You've been a polite stranger all afternoon. You've gone out of your way not to touch me." She thought she saw the beginnings of cool withdrawal in Nando's eyes and hurried on. "You've been acting as if last night never was. As if you never fought for me. Never kissed me."

"And do you know why?" Nando rasped, his hands tightening visibly on the reins. "Damn you. Do you know why?"

"Tell me." The fire in Arabella's eyes challenged him. "Show me."

In one fluid motion Nando swung down from his horse, pulled her from the saddle and crushed her against him. For a long time they stared into each other's eyes.

"Because I want you," he finally whispered against her mouth. "Because I've wanted you for months. Because I need every ounce of discipline not to take you to my bed and let the consequences be damned."

The moment stretched. The temptation, the desire grew, a living thing within him. Then Nando pressed Arabella's face against his chest, no longer able to look into her eyes without opening his heart.

"I have nothing to offer you, Arabella," he whispered against her temple. "Nothing but a few moments of pleasure, and you deserve more. Much more."

"Why can't you let me decide what I deserve?" Arabella pushed her head against his imprisoning hand and tipped her face upward.

"Because I . . ."

She watched the pupils of Nando's eyes dilate as the message from his heart reached his mind.

"Know best," he finished on a unsteady breath.

But Arabella had seen the truth flash into his eyes, and she tucked it into her heart as she stepped out of his arms.

When they returned from their ride, the table had been set for tea. Yet Arabella discovered a few moments later that it wasn't just tea but a full-blown country *Jause,* the Austrian equivalent of high tea, that Count Berg had insisted be prepared for her benefit. And she did her best not to disappoint the old man who took such obvious pleasure in urging her through several different kinds of sausage, thinly sliced pork roast and succulent cured ham, followed by all manner of pastries.

"You must try at least one of each," Johann von Berg insisted. "It's days like this that I know why I bother paying a fortune for a pastry cook from Bohemia."

Nando sat withdrawn and silent as she chatted with the old man. When Count Berg left them alone, Arabella would have wanted to go to Nando, but his stance was so forbidding that reluctantly she turned away and sat down in the deep embrasure of a window to stare out at the treetops that were fast disappearing in the falling dusk.

It was the same dream she had had last night, and Arabella fought against waking up, remembering somehow that when she did, reality would be cold and ugly and painful. But one by one, perceptions seeped into her awareness. She was warm. She was lying on something soft that gave way beneath her back. There were hands on her shoulders, but they were gentle. She felt safe. She felt right.

Lips touched her mouth, and the velvet touch burrowed through her body to lodge as a burning ache deep within her. She felt her blood heat and she knew then that the dream was not a dream at all. Her eyelids fluttered open and

Nando filled her vision, his eyes closed as he tasted her mouth.

Arabella lay still, fearing that Nando would retreat should he realize that she was awake. But the moment came when she could no longer be still. When her breathing became just a little uneven. When her lips parted under his mouth. When her body shifted to better accommodate his.

As she had known he would, Nando sat up as if he had been scalded. Arabella put her hand on his clenched fist, which lay on his thigh.

"Last night when I was unconscious, I dreamed," she said softly. "I kept seeing your face, and every time I awoke, it wasn't you who was there. Except the last time."

Nando's silver eyes did not move from her face, but he said nothing, as he let the sound of Arabella's sleep-husky voice flow over his skin.

"I was dreaming again now and I was afraid to wake up until I realized that the dream wasn't a dream after all."

"Go back to sleep now, Arabella." Gently he brushed his knuckles against her cheek and moved to stand.

But her fingers closed around his wrist. "No."

The word was spoken softly, but it reverberated in Nando's head like a mad drumroll. Arabella's eyes were dark, almost black, in the dim light. They penetrated him, held him. Was this what Odysseus had felt like when Circe had beckoned with her siren song?

"You don't know what you're saying."

Still holding his wrist, she sat up. "I'm not a backward child, Nando."

"But I've told you..."

"I know what you've told me, Nando." Arabella released his wrist and brought both hands to his face. "I want whatever you have to give me. Do you hear me?" She gave Nando a little shake, the heels of her hands digging into his jaw. "And I want it now."

Chapter Eighteen

Nando knew he had no right to make love to Arabella, to claim her innocence for himself. He knew that guilt would hang heavy on his soul. There would be pain for both of them. His mind knew all this and more. Yet what was logical thought at a moment like this? A moment that was measured by the warmth of Arabella's hands on his face, the softness of her body, the need that trembled between them like a crystal dewdrop on a rose petal.

All that and the love Nando would not acknowledge gave him the strength—and the weakness—to accept what Arabella was offering.

Afraid he would elude her at the last moment, Arabella kept her hands on Nando's face even as he cradled her in his arms and lowered her onto the feather bed. Her arms went around him as he lay against her, and she turned her head to nuzzle the dark gold hair that fell over his neck. For the space of a breath she was suffused with the serenity that comes when a momentous decision is made, the final, irrevocable step taken.

But just as the moment of calm that comes before a storm is frayed by the inexorable wind, so did Arabella's serenity begin to dissipate as one sensation after another crept in. The thin lawn of Nando's shirt, warm with the heat of his skin, beneath her fingers. The rough silk of his hair against her face. The scent of tobacco and leather and male skin.

It was this last that touched Arabella like an intimate caress and caused a tremor of incipient desire to shiver through her. Feeling her tremble, but not knowing what occasioned it, Nando raised himself on an elbow to look at her. But there was nothing in Arabella's face that spoke of fear, of doubt.

And there were none of these emotions in her. For Arabella knew that if this hour, this night was all that she would ever have, she would take it and make it be enough. Enough to give Nando what she would never want to give another.

Cupping her cheek with his hand, he feathered his thumb over her lush mouth. Desire was stirring strongly within him, but the passion lay in check as Nando let his fingertips absorb the texture of Arabella's skin. He was still in command, not quite beyond the possibility of pulling back, and for a moment a scrap of rational thought returned to haunt him.

Arabella watched his face as he moved his thumb over her mouth. The touch held a seductive sensuality that was echoed in his gaze, hot and just a little unfocused with arousal. Then the smooth stroke seemed to stumble, and for a moment she thought to see the heat in Nando's eyes ebb. Fear that he would retreat shot through her, and desperate to pull him within a magic circle of desire from which he could not escape, she nipped at his thumb.

The sharpness of the pain startled him, but instead of pulling back his hand, Nando lingered, his flesh pressed against her teeth. Slowly the pain changed, clarifying and distilling itself to become the purest pleasure.

If Arabella had not been watching Nando so carefully, she might have missed the tension that flowed beneath and tautened his skin. But even in the dim light of the single candle, she would not have missed the change in his eyes. She saw how his pupils dilated, leaving only a narrow gray rim around the black center, and she almost smiled with the knowledge that she had pushed him over the edge of caution. He was hers. Even in her innocence Arabella knew. For tonight Nando was hers.

His eyes still open, Nando touched his lips to hers, meaning to go slowly, but Arabella's taste, her fragrance rose to his head like strong brandy. When he had wanted to dip inside her mouth to leisurely sip at the sweetness she offered, he found himself invading it with the utter ruthlessness of a man on the brink of starvation.

He filled her vision again and she waited for the touch of his lips on hers. Arabella knew the textures, the tastes of his mouth. She knew the sweet pleasure it wrought. But when Nando's tongue plunged past the barrier of her teeth to fill her, Arabella found she had known nothing.

The urgency, the desperation of Nando's possession became her own, and his wildness whipped through her to merge with her own need. Arabella opened her mouth for his invasion, and every fiber of her body exulted as she stayed with him, breath for ragged breath, taste for hungry taste, touch for greedy touch.

Without releasing her mouth, Nando sat up, bringing her with him, and his hands dived in her hair. Hairpins flew as his impatient fingers undid the coils and he greedily ran his hands through Arabella's hair to unravel the braids. The sleek strands seemed to heat at his touch, and the hot, black silk drove him to yet another peak of arousal.

His hands closed roughly in her curls, pulling her head back, but his mouth slid down to her throat in gentle counterpoint. Nando tasted the translucent skin under her chin, and when his lips settled on the pulse at the base of Arabella's throat, he could feel its rhythm flow into him and match his own heartbeat.

Arabella's fingers caught in Nando's hair as he teased the frenzied pulse with his tongue. She didn't know what it was that she needed so desperately.

"Please, Nando," she moaned.

He lifted his head to look at her, afraid he had hurt her, frightened her. Afraid she was asking him to stop. Afraid he would not be able to. Afraid he would. But Arabella's mouth was soft with invitation and her sapphire eyes were glazed with desire.

"Please what?" Nando ran his fingers over her face, as if her skin would give him the answer. "Please what?"

Arabella's lips parted, but it was a moment before she whispered, "Please make love to me," spacing the words as if they were difficult for her to say. Her hands released his hair and slid forward to lie against his cheeks. "Will you?"

The wave of tenderness that rushed through him was so foreign to him that he did not recognize it. But in that moment Nando knew he had come home. He turned his head and whispered his answer against Arabella's palm.

He stood then and pulled Arabella up with him. They faced each other, her hands curled into his. Only their hands touched and yet they both felt the liquid heat that was flowing through their bodies, welding them together.

He freed one hand and reached beyond her to snuff the candle, but Arabella's hand was quicker.

"No," she whispered. "I want to see you. I want to watch you make love to me." If this night was all she would have, then she would not give up a moment of it to darkness.

Nando felt a new wave of desire swell his body at her words. At the picture they conjured up. But he forced himself to stand still under her hands, which were imprisoning his. Gradually she released her grip until his hands lay loosely on her palms.

They stood still for a long time. Then he lifted his hands away and hers fell to her sides. Slowly Nando began to remove Arabella's clothes.

Keeping his eyes on her face, he took away her garments one by one, waiting for her protest. But there was none. When he had loosened the straps of her chemise, Nando held the lace-trimmed edge, not allowing it to slip away. Her lips curved in a tender smile as Arabella acknowledged his hesitation, and her hands covered his. She worked his fingers away from the cloth, and the shift slithered down her body with a soft rustle to lie in a white pool at her feet.

Nando's fingertips feathered over Arabella's skin as he knelt before her. He kept his eyes fixed on her face as his fingers loosened the fastenings of her drawers and slid them over her hips as if he needed the distraction from the soft curves he was exposing. And he did.

But at some point his gaze slid from Arabella's face and traced downward. Her skin was opalescent, and the light of the candle behind her gave her a glow that invited his touch, his kiss.

Slowly Nando leaned forward and touched his mouth to the pearly softness of her belly. He felt more than heard the sound Arabella made and he started to pull back, reproaching himself for frightening her. But then he felt her fingers tangle in his hair, and her warmth came closer and closer until his face was pillowed against her fragrant flesh.

The flames erupted everywhere at the touch of skin on skin. Nando's mouth opened and the moist warmth fanned the fire that already seemed to be consuming her. Arabella never knew if her knees buckled or if some hidden instinct bade her to drop to the floor.

His mouth trailed hotly up her body until their lips were separated by mere inches. Nando put his hands on her waist and let them drift upward until they came to rest along the soft outer curve of her breasts. The tremor that went through him quivered onto Arabella's skin and into her until they were both seized by the vibration.

"You are a sorceress," he murmured. "You work your magic on every man who comes close."

Arabella stretched up, bringing her naked body against his still clothed one. Even the soft material of his shirt seemed abrasive on the sensitized tips of her breasts, and a moan of pleasure rose in her throat. "No," she whispered against his mouth, "only one. Only you."

With a fluid motion he tipped her into his arms and stood. Levering her against him, Nando threw back the feather quilt and lowered her onto the mattress.

Only half aware of the brazenness of her posture, Arabella made no attempt to cover herself or to disguise the yearning for his touch that filled her to overflowing. Nor did she avert her gaze for even a moment as Nando divested himself of his clothing with a speed that bordered on desperation.

His sleek body gleamed golden in the candlelight, and Arabella knew she had never seen anything even remotely as beautiful. For a moment he was Apollo descending from his sun chariot to make love to a mortal woman.

Nando approached the bed and she saw the myriad scars that crisscrossed his body. The pain shafted through her, and for a moment she wondered if those scars were why he had wanted darkness. The marred beauty that bespoke of so much suffering made her suddenly shy. Arabella rolled onto her side, and her knee flexed automatically up to shelter her femininity.

Nando cupped her face and turned it toward him. "Arabella?" The question needed no elaboration for either of them.

She reached for him then, hungry to test the texture of his skin as he had tested hers, but her hand hesitated and stopped just short of touching him. A moment of indecision passed then Arabella's hand fluttered down to lie on the sheet between them.

"Teach me, Nando. Show me how to touch you. How to bring you pleasure." Her whisper was husky, and her gaze caressed him as her hand had not dared.

A liberating emotion swept through Nando, and with a twitch of surprise some still lucid part of his brain identified it as relief. The realization registered that up to this moment he had not truly believed that Arabella was coming to him untouched, unschooled by any man. And the infinite gratitude that it was so released the pent-up air from his lungs.

He covered her hand with his. "Later. I will teach you later." His voice was a raspy whisper.

She looked a little lost, a little disappointed, and Nando smiled as his hand curved around her neck. "Your first loving must be beautiful, my heart. If you touch me, I may not be able to give you what you need."

My heart. The endearment washed over Arabella, and she wondered briefly if Nando realized what he had said. Then all thought fled as his mouth came down to hers.

He teased her mouth until her lips parted, willing prey to his tongue. But this time Nando savored what he had taken so ravenously before. He slid his tongue into her mouth and traced his way over every ridge and contour. And he trembled with desire barely held in check when Arabella's tongue rose to meet his.

When they broke apart, gasping for breath, Nando's hand traveled over her shoulder, down her arm to rest on her hip, and his eyes followed its progress.

"So beautiful," he murmured, and his gaze swept again. "I was wrong. You're not a sorceress, Arabella, but a goddess. A goddess made to be worshiped."

His words released a coil of heat deep within her, and Arabella shifted and pressed her legs together to still the sensation. But her movement served only to tantalize it, and it curled and stretched, snaking through her flesh.

The movement was not lost on Nando. Wanting to acquaint her with his touch, he slid his hand from her hip to lie flat on her belly and his body pulsed as he registered the instinctive arching of her hips to meet him. Inch by inch he moved up the satin skin. When his hand finally closed on the soft globe of her breast, the small sound Arabella made deep in her throat was almost his undoing.

The slight roughness of Nando's palm against her breast set off fierce vibrations in places Arabella had not known her body possessed. Intuitively she moved against him.

Suddenly her mouth was being taken again. "Yes," Nando breathed between kisses, "show me what you want. Tell me."

"Everything," Arabella gasped. "I want everything."

IIis hand moved from her breast, and without warning it was replaced by his mouth, and his hand slid down, down to find the moist heat that was waiting for him.

Greedily Nando watched her face as the pleasure swept her up into its madness. The slick heat of her made his own arousal painful, but he was hardly aware of the ache as he stroked and fondled her. He took every panting breath, every movement, every moan like a gift. And when he felt Arabella begin to tremble with the first beginnings of the earthquake, he was so full of joy that he could have shouted with it.

Arabella was certain she was dying. No one could possibly feel such pleasure and survive. But she did, and the pleasure expanded and surged within her on and on until the world exploded in blinding ecstasy.

When she opened her eyes, Nando was smiling at her. Arabella tried to return the smile, but instead her eyes filled with tears that overflowed when she lowered her lids to hide them. Nando said nothing, but he gathered her against his flank and let his fingers leisurely wander her face to absorb her tears of joy.

"I thought I was dying," she whispered into his shoulder.

Nando nuzzled a kiss into her hair. "The French call it *la petite mort,* the little death."

"But you..." Arabella lifted her face to his. "What...how?" Her teeth closed over her lower lip and she felt heat rush over her face. "You didn't die the little death." She took a deep breath. "I want you to."

Nando caressed the corner of her mouth with a butterfly kiss. "So I will, my heart. I will die inside of you."

She looked at him with a question in her eyes.

"I want to take you with me on that journey," Nando explained gently. "And we will wait until you are ready to go."

They lay together until his hand, which still curved around her femininity, moved again. Slowly he provoked, incited, unleashing again that reservoir of sensation within her. With exquisite care Nando brought her to the very edge, knowing that he would not be able to answer for his control once Arabella sheathed him.

On a wave of pleasure Arabella felt his fingers probe her, stretch her, then Nando was kneeling between her legs, lifting her, fitting her to him. She expected pain, but there was none. Only the brief discomfort of never-used muscles stretching to accommodate the fullness within her. Then he was touching her again, moving within her, and the pleasure rose and rose and finally crested as she cried his name over and over again.

His control did not desert him. Even as her silken sheath began to flutter around his flesh, Nando held back his own release to watch her grasp the pleasure he was giving her. But when Arabella closed around him in a final spasm, he could hold back no longer. He thrust once, twice, and with a cry spilled his heat into her softness.

Nando was still hard when he took himself out of Arabella's body many minutes later, but his arousal seemed a mild form of excitement compared to the painful desire that had gone before.

She shifted to make room for him beside her. Her gaze fell on the sheets, and her eyes widened and flew to Nando's face. "Why didn't I bleed?"

"There need be no blood, no pain, my sweet. If a man is gentle enough, there need be nothing but pleasure for a woman. Even the very first time." Nando's hand lifted to her face as he realized that Arabella needed reassurance that he believed her to have come innocent to his body, and his eyes gave it to her.

Arabella cuddled her cheek into his hand and let herself be drawn into the warm, hard curve of his body.

He traced a lazy caress on her back. "Sleep now."

She shook her head as she looked at him. "I don't want to miss a single moment of this night." Her smile was bright and brave, but Arabella fought against an ache that had already begun to build within her. She wanted to hold this night, to stop time, to halt the passage of the moon in the sky, to keep the sun below the horizon forever. "Will you stay with me all night, even if I fall asleep?"

His arms tightened possessively around her. He wanted to stay. He wanted to sleep with Arabella and wake up with Arabella and make love to Arabella. Not just tonight, but forever. "Yes, I will stay," he whispered fiercely into her hair. "Tonight is ours."

The sky had taken on the vaguely grayish cast of a winter dawn when Arabella awoke. She stretched out her hands for Nando, but the sheets beside her were cool.

He stood at the window, his stance tense. She could almost see into his brain, full of recriminations for himself. Perhaps for her as well. She wouldn't allow that, she thought, and slipped out of bed.

The high tiled stove in the corner still warmed the room, but the hardwood floor was cold against her bare feet and she shivered as she walked toward Nando. He started when she leaned her forehead against his back and spread her fingers on his cool skin, and she realized that he had been so sunk in thought he had not heard her approach.

He began to move away, but her hands slid around him, anchoring him in place. She stepped closer and a sigh of pure pleasure escaped her as skin met skin. Again he shifted away, but Arabella's hands tightened.

"I won't allow it," she whispered against his back. "Do you hear me? I won't let you do it."

Nando tried to ignore the satin of her skin against his. He tried to disregard the way the tips of Arabella's breasts hardened and pressed against him. He tried to detach himself from the warmth that her breath spilled on his back.

"I won't let you twist last night into a mistake." Her hands loosened and fell to lie lightly on his waist. "Turn around, Nando. Turn around and look me in the eye and then tell me it was wrong. That you regret it." Her nails bit lightly into his skin. "I dare you."

Nando turned within her grasp and her sleep-warm beauty took his breath away. He let his lids fall closed, his only defense against the invitation that lay in her dark eyes. He had piled enough guilt on his head in a moment of passion last night without compounding it in the light of day.

Arabella saw the self-reproach, the bleakness, and she spread her fingers on his skin in a gentle caress meant more to comfort than to arouse.

"I knew what I was doing last night, Nando. You did not seduce me with wine or promises." Arabella's chin came up proudly. "If any seduction was practiced, it was I who practiced it. If any contrition is to be felt this morning, it is I who must feel it." She smiled and her hands curved over his hipbones and tightened. Confidently, boldly Arabella stepped forward until she connected with his awakening flesh. "And I do not feel contrition."

The accusations Nando had been leveling at himself flew out of his head as if they had never been as their bodies met. His arms went around Arabella, crushing her to him. She was a drug in his blood, Nando thought, and he knew that he would barter away his life, his soul to make love to her one more time.

"I've said it before," he gasped. "You are a sorceress, Arabella." He buried his face in the fragrant tumble of her curls.

She longed to tell him that it was not sorcery she practiced. That the only magic she wielded was her love for him, but she knew that today she could give him only her desire, her body. Her love would have to remain unspoken.

Nando's flesh burned between them, branding them both, and Arabella gloried in the realization that he could not control his desire for her.

"You promised to teach me," she whispered against his skin. "You promised to show me how to bring you pleasure."

Still he did not move.

Arabella tilted back her head. "Are you going to make me beg, Nando? I will, you know."

The words were humble, but the innate pride in her voice was not lost on him. And it was that pride more than his own desire or hers that Nando bowed to as he picked Arabella up in his arms to keep his promise.

That first day of 1815 was a lovely, lazy day, and Arabella was content to take what life offered.

Yet that night there was a desperate edge to their lovemaking as Nando came to her again and again. They both knew morning would bring the end of their magical interlude, and each sought what he or she needed most. Arabella fought to fill Nando with her essence, her love, so he would never be able to forget or forgo her. And Nando sought to drink of her so he would have enough for the desert that the rest of his life would be.

In that darkest hour before dawn Nando lay awake, watching her. Arabella's face was soft in sleep, a hint of temperament visible only in the willful curve of her mouth.

He had been a realist and a cynic for so long that he had forgotten what wishes and dreams felt like. But in this moment Nando allowed himself the small luxury of imagining what it would feel like to awaken at any hour of the night for the rest of his life and see and touch this lovely girl who lay beside him. To watch her ripen to womanhood. To see her bear his children. To grow old beside her and someday to sleep the eternal sleep at her side.

But like all wishes and dreams, that was all it could ever be. She was so young, so full of joy. How could he risk this joy by tying her to him, a man who had lost any gentler virtues he might ever have possessed long ago? A man who would never be capable of giving her the warm love without which she would wither.

Nando woke Arabella in the early dawn and she took him into her, greedy, desperate, for she had seen the love in his eyes, yet she knew it was not enough to make him want her permanently. And she loved him too much to try to keep him against his will. One last time she arched into his embrace and took what the moment offered.

It was a silent drive to Vienna, as both Nando and Arabella wrestled to fit the past two days into the tangled weave of their lives. But when the tall spire of St. Stephan's Cathedral appeared, the view jolted Arabella out of her meandering and she realized with a guilty start that she had completely forgotten about Poldi. Possibly Nando had no idea that she had installed the girl in his palace.

Her nervous movement did not go unnoticed, and Nando rubbed his thumb on the back of her shoulder in silent encouragement to speak.

Arabella glanced at him and her teeth worried her lower lip. "I have something to ask of you, Nando. A rather large favor, in fact."

The wrench Arabella's words gave him came automatically. Too thorough was his acquaintance of women who asked for favors after a few nights in his bed. The warmth he still carried in him began to seep away.

"And what?" Nando's mouth twisted a little, as if the words left an unpleasant taste on his tongue.

"Do you remember the little girl in the marketplace? The one we saved from a beating weeks ago?" Arabella spoke quickly, aware of the sudden chill in his eyes.

"Yes." His voice was cautious.

"While you were gone, I went looking for her."

"You what?" Nando's hand tightened inadvertently on her still-bruised shoulder, causing Arabella to wince. "Don't you know how dangerous that could be? Didn't I tell you to be careful? Did you go alone?''

She related the whole story with increasing confidence, realizing that the growls of disapproval that regularly punctuated her words were not directed at what she had done, but at the fact that she had ignored his instructions.

"So now she is installed in your servants' wing, learning her letters and how to stitch a neat row." Arabella put her hand on Nando's sleeve, wanting to dissipate his grim countenance. "And for the first time in her life she's not cold or hungry or afraid."

"Don't look at me as if you thought me the devil incarnate," Nando flared suddenly. "Did you actually believe for a minute that I would be capable of throwing her out on her ear?" The unreasoning irritation he felt had much more to do with himself and the conclusions he had jumped to than her words.

Arabella shrugged. "I believed I could depend on you to help her in some way, but I thought you might be less than pleased to find her living in your palace."

"Your trust in people is going to get you between the devil and the deep blue sea one of these days. Did you consider the perils of taking in a street child like that?" he demanded.

"Yes." Arabella smiled at the surprised look that greeted her simple admission. "Poldi and I reached a clear understanding the very first evening."

Nando chuckled. "If the family silver is missing, I will lay the blame at your door."

The early winter twilight was beginning to close in on the city when the doors of the Berg Palace swung open to admit the barouche. Wanting to reassure Poldi about her future, Arabella led the way toward the servants' quarters. Two chambermaids flattened themselves against the wall to let them pass, aghast at the sight of their master below stairs, and Arabella couldn't repress a giggle at the incongruity of the situation.

But all levity in her died when Nando blocked her way as she raised her hand to open the door to Poldi's room and she found herself staring into the cold, distant face of a stranger.

"We must talk, Arabella. You know that."

Arabella passed her tongue over lips that had suddenly gone dry with dread. She tried to interpret his words, his expression, and as she did, quietly her heart began to break. "Yes—" she jerked her head in a quick nod "—we will talk by and by." She pushed past him before her eyes could fill.

With difficulty Nando stopped himself from taking Arabella into his arms to wipe the look of shock off her face. But he did not dare touch her, now that he had finally gathered the courage to talk to her about their future. They needed to talk seriously, he thought, without interference from that fatal chemistry that sprang up between them at every touch.

Poldi greeted Arabella with an enthusiastic yelp that died away abruptly as she saw Count Berg behind her friend and took in his serious expression.

"Count Berg has come to tell you that you may stay." Arabella ruffled the girl's hair and tried to smile.

Poldi's gaze darted briefly between the two adults. "Are you sure?" she whispered in Arabella's direction.

Nando moved to stand beside Arabella. "Yes, Leopoldine, you may stay."

The girl snuggled closer to Arabella while keeping her eyes on Nando's face. "I don't have to go back to Baric? Ever?"

Arabella put a reassuring arm around her shoulders, and with a sudden movement Poldi turned toward her and pressed her face against Arabella's hip. Taken aback by this unaccustomed reaching out, Arabella knelt and took Poldi's still thin, trembling form into her arms, taking comfort and reassurance even as she gave it.

Nando watched Arabella's spontaneous gesture of affection with uneasiness and more than a little envy. "I shall wait for you downstairs," he said and backed out the half-open door.

He paced the entry hall, periodically pounding a fist into his open palm. He could give her so little, he told himself. He could not even begin to return the unconstrained affection that Arabella gave so easily. Only in bed could he give her a small measure of what she needed. But God, he was selfish. He could not bear the thought of letting her go. Could he do it? he asked himself. Could he ask Arabella to accept a husband with so many scars on his soul?

Arabella heard the echo of Nando's boots on the marble tiles long before she saw him, and her heart accelerated to an almost unbearable speed. His face was grim, his mouth thin and hard as he paced. She watched him slam a fist into his open palm and wince.

He didn't want her, she thought. Or he didn't want to want her. It was all the same. Had she really seen love in his eyes? Or had she only seen what she had needed to see so badly? After all, no words had been said. She had no proof except the memory of his eyes warm with love and tenderness.

The wave of despair threatened to engulf her before Arabella forced her back to straighten. She would set Nando free, she told herself. If nothing else, she would keep her memories untainted by bitterness.

Nando's mien softened when he heard her approach. "Well, how did you find your protégée?"

"She's doing splendidly." Arabella's smile did not touch her eyes. "As you said, Nando, we need to talk."

"Of course." He looked askance at her, taken aback by the flat tone of her voice and her set, wooden expression. Opening the door to a salon, Nando bowed Arabella inside.

"May I offer you some refreshment?" He winced inwardly at his insipid words.

"No, thank you. I had hot chocolate with Poldi." Unable to look at him, Arabella turned away to stare unseeing at the gathering dusk beyond the window.

"I shall ring for the candles to be lit."

Nando's movement toward the bell cord roused her more than his words, and Arabella put out a hand to stop him. She had to say this quickly before she lost her courage.

"Please do not trouble yourself. What I have to say won't take long."

A leaden feeling of dread settled in the pit of Nando's stomach and he wanted to cry out, to stop her, to kiss her until she had no breath to speak, and yet he could not move. He stood still and waited for Arabella's words to fall as a condemned man waits for the fall of the executioner's ax.

"I am well aware that you didn't want this to happen between us, Nando, and I—"

"Are you certain that you want to say this, Arabella?" Nando interrupted, not quite able to accept his fate silently.

"I must." Desperately Arabella tried to blank all emotion from her eyes. "You have no obligation to me. I wanted you to know that."

How very brave she is, Nando thought. How gallant. "And if I wished to have obligation?" he asked softly.

Her eyes narrowed, wondering what kind of a game he was playing with her. "You do not. Or if you do, it is only a temporary aberration sprung from a guilty conscience, which you need not have."

He raised an eyebrow at her clipped tone. "You seem very certain of what is going on in my head."

"You make it rather easy for me. As I apparently do not."

"Are you reproaching me?"

"No, Nando. I am simply stating a fact." She suddenly felt so very tired. *Oh, my love,* she thought, *let me get through this quickly.*

Slowly Arabella walked to Nando and put her hand on his sleeve. "Let us not fence."

He could feel her slipping away from him, and the panic rose in his throat to choke him. *This is what you want, you fool,* his brain screamed. *She's offering you your freedom.* But the thought gave no comfort.

Suddenly the thought hit Nando with all the power of a pistol fired at point-blank range. She had not told him she loved him. Not at the height of passion. Not in moments of tenderness. She had let him make love to her, but she had never once said that she loved him. How foolish, he thought. How very foolish of him to assume that she did.

There was a curious lack of pain after the first excruciating blow, and Nando was reminded of his first battle and how he had watched his blood pool and seep into the half-frozen ground. But the pain could not be held at bay for long. No. It began to batter at him in enormous, implacable waves, and he marveled distantly at the instincts that were still functioning despite the savagery that raged within him.

He threw off her hand and turned to grip her shoulders. "What do you want, Arabella?"

Was that need in his eyes? Desire? Love? Arabella closed her eyes against it. She could not afford confusion now that she had made her decision. "Nothing," she whispered, remembering too well the moment when she had told him she wanted everything. "I want nothing."

Nando's hands dropped away. Arabella swayed and it was only with the utmost willpower that she did not fall when his support was withdrawn.

"You are dismissing me?" His voice was hoarse with disbelief.

Arabella closed her ears against the note of hidden entreaty in Nando's voice, telling herself that what she was hearing was incredulity that she was relinquishing the hold she could have had on him with a little cleverness.

"To be able to dismiss presumes that one must have had. I never had you, Nando." Arabella raised her eyelids, heavy with unshed tears. "Not really."

"And what were the last two days?" His eyes narrowed as the distrust returned to prick at his back. "Or did you merely wish for my services?" Nando spat the last word at her.

Arabella's abraded nerves snapped, returning some of her lost energy. "Stop it. Just stop it," she cried. "How dare you? Ever since I've known you, you've told me that you are not the man for me. That you could never give me what I need. And now that I've decided to believe you, you are offended."

Suddenly Nando felt every emotion drain from him as blood drains from a wounded body, leaving him empty. He stared at Arabella. "Believe what you will."

She almost moved toward him then, but before she could, Nando spun to stare out a window. Quickly, before the tears began to flow down her face, Arabella ran out of the room, not bothering to close the door behind her.

Chapter Nineteen

Arabella had dreaded her return to the British embassy. Dreaded the questions that would be asked. Dreaded the lies she would have to tell. But she found that the Castlereaghs had returned early from Prague, and with the confusion of their arrival compounded by the news of a peace treaty ending the war between England and their recalcitrant former colony in the New World, little attention was paid her. A celebratory ball was decreed, and the household was thrown into a frenzy of preparations.

Grateful for the diversion, Arabella marshaled her energy into helping the disorganized Lady Castlereagh make the necessary arrangements—invitations, flowers, refreshments—hoping to distract herself. But no matter how busy she kept, her emotions and thoughts allowed her no peace.

Through one sleepless night after another, she relived those moments in the dark, empty salon, recalling every word, every glance. She remembered the disbelief, the desolation in Nando's eyes when she had told him she wanted nothing from him, and finally reached the terrible conclusion that she had been wrong. She had pushed herself into Nando's life, torn down the barriers he had erected, she realized. And once she had succeeded, she had trampled on his new vulnerability in the worst way, if with the very best intentions.

She remembered how he had told her that he could give her nothing, and she could not help wondering if she had made it so.

Dizzy with fear, she crossed the courtyard of the Berg Palace the next day, the sound of her shoes on the wooden cobblestones reverberating in her ears like whipcracks.

She was well aware of the impropriety of her behavior as she mounted the stairs toward the vestibule. It was bad enough that she came here almost every day to visit Poldi, even though she always took pains to be discreet.

There was no one around at this early hour, and remembering a chance remark of Lulu's that Nando's apartments were on the third floor, she resolutely climbed the wide curved staircase.

The dim corridor was deserted, and Arabella looked at the row of doors. Which one was his? Then a door opened at the far end and a footman emerged carrying a tray. Not wanting to be seen, she pressed herself against the wall in the shadow of a large marble statue.

The footman was muttering when he passed her, the tray laden with bottles, and when he had disappeared down the staircase, Arabella ran toward the door, her heart pounding, sure that Nando was near.

Nando raised his hand toward the crystal goblet half full of burgundy, but suddenly it no longer seemed worth the effort. He wasn't succeeding in drinking himself senseless anyway. With a frustrated sound he dropped his hand to his thigh and tipped his head back.

He stared at the ceiling of richly carved dark wood. How long had he been drinking? he wondered vaguely. One night? Two nights? A week? He couldn't remember. Absently he ran a hand over his whisker-rough chin. It really didn't signify, he thought bitterly. The only thing that signified was that the reason for the drinking was still too much with him. The pain he had wanted to dull with bottle after bottle of wine was still stiletto-sharp.

And like the pain that never seemed to end, Arabella was still there. Her image was everywhere, taunting him. Even when he closed his eyes, it was there, branded on his eyeballs. Her voice was within his head. And the soft laugh that sounded like the notes she coaxed from the pianoforte. Even her fragrance did not leave him alone—that blend of lily of the valley and warm skin.

A staccato rap on the door bounced off the pain behind his eyes. Then a voice in the corridor registered somewhere on the blurred fringes of Nando's consciousness. Her voice. He shook his head. It couldn't possibly be her voice. It was only the memory that lived in his brain. Or maybe he had finally drunk himself into oblivion. He lurched forward and pushed himself upright, not even noticing when the chair he had been slumped on tipped and crashed onto its back.

Arabella stood in front of the door, her hands damp and trembling. Then she reached for the ornate door handle and pressed it down. The door held. Locked. She knocked once, twice, then a third time. No answer.

"Nando, it's me. Arabella. I must speak to you." She stiffened at the sound of movement on the other side of the door, followed by a crash. "Please," she persisted. "I know you're there, Nando. Open the door. Please." Arabella put both palms flat against the door and leaned her forehead against an edge of gilt molding, as if to absorb Nando by touching the cool wood. She willed the door to open, willed him to listen and forgive.

"I love you, Nando," Arabella whispered, her pride forgotten. "Talk to me, please."

Stiff-kneed, Nando walked toward the door and slouched against the jamb, letting his head slide along the wood until his temple pressed against the gilt molding, aggravating the pain within. He welcomed it. At least that was something tangible to hold on to. Not like a disembodied voice come to mock him.

He did not understand the words, but he heard the sadness in Arabella's voice, the entreaty, and his fingers crept across the wood. Perhaps her voice was not just a figment of his wine-clouded brain. Perhaps she was real after all. He reached to unlock the door.

As his hand closed over the key to turn it, Nando felt the door tremble slightly on its hinges, and before he could move, the light, quick tapping of leather against marble told him that if she had been real she was now gone.

Arabella moved automatically through the festivities. She kept her eye on the servants, checked that refreshments were plentiful, listened, smiled, made appropriate responses and allowed herself to be led away for an occasional dance when her duties permitted.

Princess Katharina Bagration lowered herself onto a window ledge, her narrowed eyes following Arabella's movements. Her fan began to beat in time with the waltz that was being played. Soon, she thought. Soon she would have her revenge.

"Have you forgotten our bargain, my dear?" Volkonsky sidled up to her.

Katharina sent Volkonsky an arch look. "I have not forgotten, *mon ami*. In fact, I've been very busy."

"And what *have* you been doing, pray tell?"

"Gathering information, Niki. Very interesting information." Katharina smiled smugly and slid an arm through his. "And I have been spreading information, as well."

"Do elaborate, *ma chère*."

"For instance, the child she has settled in the Berg Palace. The child she visits every day."

"So what?" Volkonsky pushed her away. "That's something anyone with a few coins at his disposal can find out."

"But it's not commonly known, dear Niki. And I am making certain that as many people as possible learn that

Miss Douglas visits the Berg Palace every day." She laughed softly. "Believe me, they do not assume it is a child she visits there."

"So?" Volkonsky narrowed his eyes, unable to follow Katharina's logic.

"Don't be a fool, Niki," she said, her smugness gone. "If her reputation is gone when you make your move, *if* you ever make your move, no one is going to care this much—" Katharina snapped her fingers "—about what you do to her."

Volkonsky looked at Katharina with a new respect. "It would appear that I have underestimated you, Katya."

"That is a mistake not only you have made, my friend," Katharina snapped and turned away.

"Good evening, Arabella. May I speak to you for a moment?"

Arabella hid the shiver that went through her at the sound of Nando's voice by rearranging her cashmere shawl. It had been weeks since she had seen him except from afar. How could she possibly still react to him this way?

"Of course." She kept her hands curled tightly in the corners of her shawl, knowing that she wouldn't be able to keep them from trembling and at the same time too proud to let him see this weakness.

Heels together, Nando bowed formally. So she wasn't even going to offer him her hand, he thought, amazed at the pain that such a minor thing could inflict. His gaze flickered over her face, searching for something, anything that would give him the right to say what was in his heart. But all he saw was cool politeness. Even the dark circles under her eyes, cleverly disguised with rice powder, escaped him.

"I wanted to tell you that Leopoldine's future is assured. I have made arrangements for her adoption."

"Arrangements?" Arabella interrupted. "I thought you..."

Nando spread his hands in a gesture of regret. "The law forbids me to adopt her, since I am titled."

"A curious law." She tightened her shawl around her. "But quite understandable. To keep the strain pure, I assume."

Nando scanned her face, but found only mockery in the thinned lines of her mouth. "I have had papers drawn up by which my steward, Menzel, and his wife will be her adoptive parents," he continued. "And I will provide funds so that she is financially secure. Her stepfather has already signed away his rights, and I expect no problems to arise."

"Oh, thank you." Arabella's smile lit up her face for a moment and she almost reached out to touch him. But then Nando's frosty gaze reminded her that he wasn't doing it for her, but to fulfill a promise. To a count, it was a matter of honor to always keep his promises. She lowered her lashes. "I am most sensible of your kindness."

Her smile blinded him like a ray of bright sunlight, but it was gone so quickly that he was sure he had imagined it. No, it couldn't have been Arabella outside his door, he thought. It had been only a phantom of his drink-muddled brain. This cool, remote creature could not possibly have come to his door to plead with him. She could not possibly be the same woman who had been liquid fire in his arms.

Arabella's gaze fell on her hands, which still clutched her shawl convulsively, the skin white over the knuckles, and pride forced her to loosen her fingers. Pride forced her to meet Nando's eyes. She looked long and hard at the ice there, searching for a breach, a crack, anything that would give her a glimpse of the warmth she had seen there a lifetime ago. But there was none.

"Thank you again," she murmured and turned away.

Under Lulu's worried eyes Arabella crumbled one biscuit after another. Her tea had long grown cold, and when she finally brought the cup to her lips, she grimaced at the taste.

"Now that you've ruined ten perfectly good vanilla crescents, would you care to tell me what's on your mind?" Lulu inquired, letting her vinegary tone mask her concern.

Arabella took a deep breath, but she couldn't bring herself to begin to talk. Her conversation with Lady Castlereagh this morning had struck her like a bolt of lightning, and the shock was still with her. But when Lulu sat down on the settee beside her and put a gentle arm around her shoulders, she stiffened and pulled away.

"Please don't be sympathetic with me, Lulu. I won't be able to bear it, if you are."

Lulu withdrew her arm, but remained seated. "Arabella, don't you think that it's past time you talked to me?"

Arabella stared at a watercolor on the wall. "Did you know that it really is true what they say? That the subject of gossip is always the last to find out about it?"

Lulu sighed. "So you've heard."

"Why didn't you tell me?"

"I knew it wasn't true, and you were miserable enough as it is." Lulu smiled ruefully.

"But you see, it is true in a way." Arabella looked at her companion. "I have been observed entering the Berg Palace almost every day, and I can't even deny it." Tonelessly she recited Poldi's story to Lulu, as she had recited it to Lady Castlereagh earlier that day.

"And you know what the most grotesque thing is? For the first time in my life, I actually tried to be discreet." A bitter laugh escaped her. "The Castlereaghs have been very kind to me, and I didn't want to hurt them in any way. I suppose I underestimated the efficiency of the spies in Vienna."

Arabella plucked at her dress for a few moments before she lifted her head and went on. "But it doesn't really signify any more. You see, I shall be leaving Vienna soon. Lord Wellington arrives next week to take over Lord Castlereagh's duties, and we go back to London soon after." She twisted her mouth into a poor imitation of a smile. "That will solve all the problems."

Lulu covered Arabella's clenched hands with hers. "Does Nando know?"

Again there was that slash of pain that took her breath away at the mention of his name. Arabella wondered if it would always be like this, or if it would grow weaker in time.

"That I'm leaving? No. But there is no earthly reason for that to interest him. I have only spoken to him once since we returned from Trautenstein." She paused, aware of how winded she suddenly sounded. "A very brief, civilized conversation about Poldi."

"Tell me what happened between you two."

Arabella shook her head. "I can't talk about it, Lulu." But even as she said the words, Arabella longed to confide in Lulu. To unburden herself of everything, though she knew she could not. For within herself she was not only carrying the secret of all that had passed between Nando and herself. She was also carrying Nando's child.

Nando kicked a leather case out of his way and resumed pacing. God, he despised these watchdog duties, and Prince Schwarzenberg knew it. Still he had assigned Nando to head the escort for Tsarina Elizabeth's pleasure journey to Pest.

Franz watched surreptitiously as his master paced the room like a caged animal. Franz had been taking time with the packing, hoping for an opportunity to say what he had to, but it did not look like that would happen anytime soon. With a sigh he snapped the last case shut, pulled the straps tight and straightened. Well, he'd have to make his own opportunity.

"Countess Lulu was here yesterday." Franz addressed his remark to the desk that stood near one window, but he was keenly aware that his words had stopped his master in his tracks.

Nando folded his arms across his chest. "So? She thinks she is very clever. Since I have refused to talk to her, or rather have refused to have her talk to me, she thinks she can get to me through you." He glared at Franz. "Well, she is mistaken. Both of you are."

With his peasant stubbornness, Franz ignored his master's comment and dug in. "She told me several things you should be aware of."

"I can well imagine what they are. I'm not interested," Nando snapped and resumed his pacing.

"Not even in the rumors circulating about you?"

"Rumors?" Nando whirled to face Franz. "What rumors?"

Franz looked into the stormy eyes of his friend and master. "Arabella Douglas has been seen entering the Berg Palace every day, and people have drawn the logical conclusion."

Nando's breath caught. Hearing her name made him feel as if he had been kicked in the ribs.

He walked to the window and stared out, absently massaging the ever-present tension knots in his neck. No matter how hard he had tried to deny it, she was always in his mind. No reasoning, no logic, not bitter experience, not even her own words could change that.

What an incredible fool he had been, Nando thought. He had been offered the most precious treasure and he had hesitated for so long that the treasure had dissipated like a mirage in the desert. He pushed away the stray thought that perhaps it had always been a mirage.

"The Castlereaghs are going back to England within a fortnight," Franz pressed on. "They may not be here when you get back from Pest." He took a deep breath. "And Arabella Douglas will return to London as Count Ferdinand Berg's discarded mistress."

Nando stood perfectly still although his heart was suddenly a trip-hammer, pounding against his ribs, scattering the heartsickness, the sense of defeat that had been devouring him for the past weeks. Now he would take her, he told himself, the words assuming a life of their own and racing through his bloodstream. Take her and make her his. She wouldn't dare refuse him now. He would wed her. He would lock her in his bedroom and make love to her until that cool, polite look disappeared from her face forever. Until passion lived in her sapphire eyes again. Until no other man existed for her. He swore the last to himself with a vehemence that made his breathing quicken.

"Did you hear what I said?"

"I heard you, Franz."

Nando turned, and Franz stepped back in surprise. Gone was the grimness, the despair of the past weeks. There was determination in the set of his mouth and a faint smile in his eyes. He slapped Franz on the shoulder then quickly strapped on his sword and picked up his hat and cape. He was almost out the door when Franz called out to him.

"We have to be at the Hofburg in two hours."

"Yes," Nando shouted from the end of the corridor. "I'll meet you there."

Nando forced himself not to pace as he waited for Arabella. His interview with Lord Castlereagh had set his nerves on edge. The Englishman had expressed his personal satisfaction at Nando's offer for Arabella's hand and, as her temporary guardian, had given his consent, but he had made no bones about the fact that he had his doubts that Arabella would accept Nando's suit.

"I realize this may sound odd, my dear Count Berg, but my wife tells me the girl is anxious to be gone from Vienna and would rather not see you again." He had cleared his throat and looked expectantly at Nando.

Nando had disregarded the shiver of anxiety at the base of his spine and said, "I am certain that all misunderstandings can be resolved. I will speak to Miss Douglas, if you permit."

Despite his apprehension, Nando's confidence as he stood in the Castlereagh drawing room was real. At this moment he could not allow himself anything else.

* * *

It was ironic, Arabella mused, as she made her way down the stairs. A month ago she would have been senseless with joy if she knew that Nando was waiting for her downstairs with an offer of marriage on his lips. Instead, she felt she was going to her doom. Could there possibly be anything worse than having to refuse the very thing that one wanted most in the whole world?

She stopped in front of the closed door for a moment to draw a deep breath. Then she entered the drawing room and, deliberately not focusing on Nando's face, strode to where he stood.

"I will not marry you." Arabella pressed her lips together and stared at the brass buttons of his uniform tunic.

"Is that so?" Nando drawled, needing the indifference to camouflage the hot confusion of emotions that had surfaced.

Arabella could not resist the provocation of his tone and her eyes shot upward and collided with cool gray. "Yes, that's so," she snapped.

"Would you care to give me a reason?" Nando toyed with his gloves, needing some kind of distraction to stop himself from shaking her.

"I don't need a reason."

"It might be polite if you gave me one, anyway."

The cool smile that curved Nando's mouth maddened her, and Arabella allowed him to goad her, welcoming the provocation, for she knew that anger was her only defense. Without it, it would be too easy to forget that she had only his overweaned sense of honor to thank for his proposal.

"I have no intention of giving you a reason," she blazed. "And I have no cause to be polite to you, either."

Nando's heart lightened at the anger in Arabella's voice. Where anger lived, caring was not far away. It was indifference he had feared most of all. He stepped closer and laid his hands on her shoulders, forcing himself to keep the touch light. "You will marry me, Arabella. No matter how you fight it, you will marry me."

Arabella closed her eyes for a moment, letting his words touch her like a caress, letting herself pretend that she could say yes. Oh, what a temptation it was to say yes and damn the consequences. But she knew she could not. She could not allow the new life that slept within her to be touched by the unhappiness and recriminations that would surely result from a marriage based on guilt.

She lifted her eyelids and let her gaze mesh with his. One more chance, she thought. She would give herself the gift of one more chance.

"Can you give me a good reason to marry you, Nando?"

The emotion flowed toward his lips, but the caution that he had been taught at such high cost caused him to stanch it, as one would the dangerous flow of blood. "It would be the honorable thing to do. For both of us."

Arabella's hands flew upward, striking Nando's hands away from her shoulders, all thought of restraint driven from her mind in the wave of anger and hurt that engulfed her.

"And our honor must be satisfied at all costs, isn't that so? Damn you to hell, Ferdinand von Berg," Arabella cried. "You lead the life of a soldier, although the killing sickens you, to satisfy your family's, your father's honor. You take in a child you don't want to honor a promise." She twined her fingers together to stop herself from striking him. "And now you will marry me to save your honor and mine into the bargain. How dare you? How dare you do this to me?"

Suddenly all her pain surged up, destroying the last of her control, the last of civilized behavior. "Oh, damn you," she cried. "Damn you." Her fists clenched and beat against Nando's chest.

Nando stood still for a moment and let her rain blows on him. Then in a quick movement, he framed Arabella's face, the heels of his hands pressing against her cheekbones, his fingers biting into her scalp. "Do you believe that?" he demanded harshly. "Truly believe that is all it is?"

"Yes." She looked into Nando's eyes and her heart recognized the desperation. "No," she whispered.

In that split second before he lowered his mouth to hers, Nando saw the play of emotions in Arabella's sapphire eyes. He saw the anger, the pain give way to passion, to...love. It was love, wasn't it? he questioned fiercely in that moment before his mouth reached hers. Later, he thought, he would have his answer later.

His lips opened hers and Nando plunged his tongue into Arabella's mouth, keeping nothing back, not his pain, not his anger, not his love. And as he gave, he took from her, allowing her to keep nothing to herself. He could taste the love on her tongue. She could keep her eyes blank, but she could not conceal the heat, the sweetness that her mouth offered.

Enthralled, they possessed each other, surrendering nothing, surrendering everything. Their tongues twined around each other with a savage hunger. It was not a gentle moment as their breath, their taste met and mingled and became one.

When their mouths separated, their breath was still quick and hot and moist on each other's lips.

"Is this reason enough for you?" Nando whispered hoarsely. One hand curved around Arabella's head, while the other slid down her back to press her roughly against his arousal. "Or this?"

Arabella's eyes widened in the realization of how her body had betrayed her. How she had betrayed herself. And even as that awareness chilled and alarmed her, the heat of Nando's aroused body against hers pulsed through her, sweeping all her senses into a turbulence she could not withstand. Her hands, which had stilled against his chest, came to life again and pushed, but she made no more headway than if she had been pushing against a wall of granite.

"I will return within a fortnight, Arabella. And when I do, you will be my wife." He lowered his mouth again. "My wife."

When he was gone, she stood very still in the middle of the empty room. The taste of coffee and tobacco and bittersweet passion was on her tongue. The scent of leather and horseflesh and aroused male was in her nostrils. And in her body was the unbearable heat that he had created with his touch.

Carefully Arabella stored every sensation within her. They would have to last her for the rest of her life.

Chapter Twenty

Curled in the window seat in her room, Arabella watched the movement of the sharply silhouetted shadows down the Gothic archway of the Minoriten Church across the way. She had reached the end of her tether. The Castlereaghs were being kind to her, as always, but they ignored her refusal to marry Nando, treating her like a stubborn child who would obey in time.

She had gone through all the possibilities dozens of times, but she was no closer to a solution than she had been a week ago. All she knew was that she had to be gone from Vienna when Nando returned.

The door behind her opened without warning, and a tart voice spoke. "Well, if Mohammed won't come to the mountain, the mountain will come to Mohammed."

Arabella turned to see Lulu throw her cape carelessly over a chair and march over to her like a general ready to do battle.

"You've done avoiding me, my dear." Lulu plunked herself down on the window seat next to Arabella. "And I've done being silent and tactful. I shall not budge from this spot until you tell me what's going on and what I can do to help you."

Arabella shook her head, afraid that with the words the tears would come.

Lulu reached over and cupped Arabella's cheek. "Please?"

She had been alone for so long and the gentle touch, that one softly spoken word opened the floodgates.

"Oh, Lulu, Nando insists on marrying me, but for all the wrong reasons. He's just doing the honorable thing." She gripped Lulu's hands. "I couldn't stand seeing whatever he feels for me turn to hatred because I trapped him in a marriage he didn't want."

The tears she had held back for the past week filled her eyes and spilled over in fat rivulets. "Sometimes I lie awake at night and think I could accept anything just to be able to see him, hear his voice, touch him." Her voice cracked. "But I can't."

"Why not, for heaven's sake?" Lulu's eyebrows arched. "Most marriages are built on less."

Arabella took a deep breath. "I am with child."

"With child? And you intend to keep it from Nando?" Indignation crept into Lulu's voice. "How can you do that to him?"

"How can I raise my child in a marriage that will be empty of all the things that count?"

Lulu shook her head. "You want everything, Arabella. Are you sure that you aren't asking for too much?"

"Perhaps." Arabella sighed. "But I can't do it any other way."

"I'm sorry." Lulu rubbed her temple. "It's just that I love both of you."

"Did you mean what you said about helping me, Lulu?" Arabella blurted the words quickly before her courage left her.

"However I can."

"Help me get away. I need to leave Vienna before Nando returns. I can't think here because I'm terrified. When I've gone, I'll think of some way to go on for the rest of my life."

For a long time Lulu looked into Arabella's eyes. Then she nodded. "We have an estate in Upper Austria. The house is comfortable, and you can stay there as long as you want."

"What can I do for you, Prince Volkonsky?" The Russians were all barbarians at heart, Metternich thought with distaste, but his scrupulously polite tone masked his feelings. Smiling, he elegantly gestured Volkonsky toward a chair.

Volkonsky acknowledged the invitation with a curt nod, but, too jumpy to sit, he began to pace. That black-haired English witch was driving him to the edge, and the fact infuriated him almost as much as her rejection. His body seemed permanently heavy with desire for her, no matter how many other women he had. He could wait no longer to take her.

"I would ask a favor of you, Prince Metternich."

Metternich kept his lips curved in a noncommittal smile and gestured for Volkonsky to continue. He hoped it would be something easily implemented. It wouldn't hurt to have an additional favor to call in another time.

"I need the certainty that Count Ferdinand Berg will not be returning to Vienna for the next four or five days and I would appreciate your help."

"Berg is on an official mission accompanying your Tsarina, *mon cher* prince." Metternich allowed himself a discreet little shrug. "His return depends solely on her majesty's wishes." He watched Volkonsky over his steepled fingers, taking mild pleasure in forcing him to be more explicit.

"We both know that Tsarina Elizabeth could stay in Pest for another week, or she could be back in a day and a half," Volkonsky barked impatiently. "I do not wish to spend the next several days looking over my shoulder."

"Just what is it that you would like me to do?"

"I want you to take Berg out of circulation. A word from you would suffice."

Metternich chuckled self-deprecatingly. "You do me too much honor. My powers are not as far-reaching as you seem to think."

Volkonsky whirled and planted both hands on Metternich's desk. "I know exactly just how far-reaching your powers are."

Forcing himself not to recoil, Metternich raised his eyebrows "Indeed?" Then he allowed himself a small smile and nodded. "I will take the liberty of reminding you of my co-operation by and by."

"How soon?" Volkonsky leaned closer.

Metternich tapped his fingers against each other as if he were weighing possibilities. He spoke a moment before the other man's impatience drove him to ask again. "The time it takes a hard-riding messenger to reach Pest, I imagine."

Volkonsky straightened and laughed. "Excellent. I knew you would not disappoint me." He laughed again and strode to the door.

After the door had closed behind the Russian, Metternich remained motionless for a long moment before he rose and rubbed his hands together lightly in a fastidious gesture of triumph. Neat arrangements like this were very much to his liking, he thought with a gratification that was as close to glee as his character allowed. Volkonsky owed him a sizable favor. The stupid English chit would get just what she deserved. And Berg. Berg would be taught a much-needed lesson.

Metternich's lips curled in a cruel smile as he rang for his secretary.

Nando drained the last of the ruby wine from his goblet and cursed the time, which passed so slowly. The days with their insipid social duties. The long nights when he had naught to do but to survey the wreckage he had made of his life.

God, how could he have been so stupid, so blind? he rebuked himself. He had talked of making Arabella his wife

as if she were a chattel, instead of telling her that she would
be his beloved until the grave and beyond. He had hidden
behind talk of honor, instead of having the courage to tell
her that he loved her more than life itself.

When had he begun to love her? Nando wondered. When
had the simple desire to possess changed to the need to
cherish? When had she become as vital, as basic to his life
as the air he breathed?

His mouth twisted as he stared into space, and an odd resentment rose within him at the realization of just how much
he was in her power. Suddenly he was glad he had not told
Arabella he loved her. She could make his life a living hell
if she knew how much she meant to him.

The mournful, sensual Gypsy music began again and tables were pushed aside. The rhythm picked up tempo and a
Gypsy girl leaped into the cleared space with the agility and
grace of a cat and began to dance.

Nando watched her dance through narrowed eyes. She
was pleasing to the eye with her lush curves and her tumbled ebony mane. Her bare feet stamped on the earthen
floor of the *csarda,* the tiny bells on her ankles an almost
innocent counterpoint to the blatant sexuality of her dance.
The music swept higher and higher in a frenzied crescendo,
and the girl sustained the tempo, twisting and whirling, her
tambourine beating the heated rhythm, her disheveled hair
falling over her face.

The energy, the speed, the intensity of the music and the
pagan dance swelled, peaked and stood suddenly still. The
music stopped so abruptly that the silence was a charged
thundercloud before lightning erupted. Into the silence the
Gypsy uttered a hoarse cry, threw back her head and fell to
her knees, her arms outstretched as if to welcome a lover.

Applause and cheers erupted from the officers lolling at
the plank tables. A cacophony of laughter and calls broke
out as each man tried to outdo the other in lascivious invitations directed at the Gypsy girl. Nando remained still as
he watched the scene, flicking his hand imperiously toward

the innkeeper to refill his goblet with more of the dark red wine of the Hungarian plains.

The Gypsy rose slowly and spread her fingers on her hips. The movement made her damp blouse cling even more snugly to her breasts, which were still heaving with exertion, and she surveyed the tavern with her heavy-lidded black gaze once, twice. Hands still on her hips she began to move purposefully, one step at a time, as if it was still part of the dance. Each step brought her heel down onto the earthen floor with a soft thud, and the bells on her ankles tinkled a soft accompaniment.

Without taking her eyes off Nando, she picked up the pitcher of wine from the counter. Slowly she moved forward to where he sprawled carelessly, filled his goblet and set the pitcher on the table with a bang. Then she straightened, her hand returned to her hip and she waited.

Nando ignored the half-jeering, half-envious calls of his fellow officers and reached for the wine. Only then did he look up and let his gaze travel over the girl who stood in front of him with such impudence.

She had the ripe beauty of a full-blown rose even though she probably wasn't older than sixteen. Her scent, of some sweet perfume, sweat and smoke, was earthy. Her luxurious curves invited the touch. Her red mouth was slick and her hips promised pleasure.

Perhaps she was just what he needed tonight, Nando mused as he drank deeply. If he didn't look too closely at her face, he could almost imagine that the luscious body, the tumbled black curls belonged to someone else. Perhaps she would still the ache, soothe the anger that had festered within him since Arabella had pushed him away, her lips still swollen from his kiss.

He let his gaze roam the Gypsy's body again and waited for the first stirrings of desire. But he felt nothing except an acrid taste in his mouth from disgust and too much wine. He focused his eyes on her face again. "Get out," he growled, slamming the goblet on the table. *"Verschwind'..."*

But the Gypsy did not move away from him. Instead she leaned over and picked up his hand, which was splayed on the rough planks. She stared at it then traced her fingers lightly over the palm.

The touch roused Nando, and he snatched his hand away from the girl. "Goddamn it, you baggage, I told you to leave me in peace."

The Gypsy smiled. "You have no peace, my friend."

Nando's head snapped up and he saw eyes that were like polished pieces of jet. Eyes that shone with insolence and a secret fire.

"What's the matter, Berg?" a high, slurred voice broke into their exchange. "Have you had too much to drink to manage a hot piece like her? I'll be glad to take her off your hands."

Nando silenced the man with a murderous look.

"There is a black-haired woman in your life," the Gypsy said in a contralto husky with wine and smoke.

His lips curled in a contemptuous smile. "Don't you have a more imaginative way to get me into your bed?"

"Oh, I know you are not for me." Her breasts shifted as she shrugged indifferently and tossed her hair over one shoulder. "What you have between your legs is only for the other one. The one who robs you of sleep even when you are alone in your bed."

This is ridiculous, Nando thought, but he could not prevent his pulse from accelerating. Nor could he tear his eyes away from her.

"You were not looking for her, but you found her," the Gypsy whispered, her eyes suddenly glazing over as she bent forward.

Nando stared at her.

"And you were not looking for what is in your heart, either, but it is there. And it will be there forever. It will not be easy for you. Beware. There is danger. For you. For her. For the child." She paused, her breathing quick and shallow.

Suddenly the Gypsy was pulled away from Nando.

"Since you're not interested, Berg, I'll take her off your hands."

Disregarding the man standing behind the girl, Nando shot forward and closed his fingers around her wrist. "What child? Who is the danger from, damn you? Who?"

The girl shuddered and her eyes focused on Nando's face again. "You're hurting my hand."

Nando's fingers loosened only marginally. "Tell me what you saw." His voice was gritty.

"The vision is gone."

Suddenly Nando was jerked back by the collar of his uniform. Before he could turn, he heard a voice intoning, "I arrest you in the name of His Majesty, the Emperor."

He pulled himself free and spun around, all his instincts alert, muscles tensed for movement, his hand shifting automatically toward the hilt of his sword. Two burly armed guards stepped smartly on either side of him. Nando ignored them, although his hand dropped to his side. He had not survived nine years of war by taking foolish risks. He assessed the thin man in a black cape before he spoke.

"Indeed? May I inquire what the charges are?" He clenched his jaws in the attempt to control the muscle that he felt twitching in his cheek. What he felt was not fear. At least not fear of the dark-clothed, sallow-faced man who had several armed men to do his bidding. But the Gypsy's words had stirred some source of uneasiness within him.

The man's long, thin fingers toyed with his walking stick. "The charge of brawling in public will suffice for the moment."

Nando's pale eyes flicked coolly over the slight figure, indifference masking the alarm that tugged at his nerves. "For the moment? Surely you can be more specific."

"Count Berg will learn the specifics by and by."

Nando took a step forward and was immediately pulled back roughly by the guards.

Realizing that he had no choice, Nando slowly unfastened his sword and placed it hilt forward into the thin man's hand, his outward calm revealing nothing of the storm within. Who was behind this? To what purpose?

The Gypsy's words nagging at his brain, he slowly walked through the silent *csarda*, the two guards close enough behind him for him to feel the prod of metal in his back.

Chapter Twenty-one

Arabella looked around the bare room. Everything had been packed in the trunk and valises that she had sent ahead with Jeanne earlier that evening.

So many dreams, Arabella thought, as her gaze drifted around the room for the last time. So many hopes. Scattered and left to wilt like flowers after a feast.

There was sadness in her heart, but she was free of regrets. Arabella's hand drifted to her middle and her mouth curved in a gentle smile. Even in the midst of her heartache, fate had been kind to her. She would have Nando's child to keep the pain of loss at bay.

She tiptoed down the stairs toward the servant's entrance, speeding her steps when she realized that the carriage was waiting. Tears blurred her vision a little as she slipped out the narrow door, and she did not notice that neither the footman nor the coachmen were wearing Thürheim livery.

When she felt the carriage make a sharp turn and stop a few minutes later, Arabella leaned forward to speak to the coachman. But before she could say anything, the carriage door opened and Prince Volkonsky vaulted inside.

He cupped her chin in his hand. "You're looking a bit pale, my dear. But lovely as usual." His tongue moved over his lips. *"Ravissante."*

Arabella knocked his hand aside, swearing at herself for her delayed reaction. "How dare you?" she said. "Get out! Immediately!" She leaned forward to push the door open, but Volkonsky caught her hand and shoved her into the seat.

"I would be a little friendlier if I were you, *ma chère*." His voice was a low purr. "This time Count Berg is not around to come to your aid." He smirked. "Nor is anyone else, for that matter."

"What are you talking about, you barbarian?" Arabella shot back with more confidence than she felt. "All I need to do is call out."

"I think not, my dear." Volkonsky's tone was still mild, but his black eyes glittered with a dangerous light. "But you're welcome to try."

Arabella pressed her face to the window and saw two cossacks standing at attention outside the carriage door. She whirled toward Volkonsky.

"Where are the Thürheim servants?"

He leaned back and began taking off his white gloves finger by finger. "On their way to the Dietrichstein Palace." Volkonsky smiled. "A pity you had to leave early."

Arabella stiffened and for the first time alarm tingled along her spine. Stubbornly she lifted her chin and glared. "I would greatly appreciate it if you would tell me what is going on, Prince Volkonsky." Her emphasis on his title was derisive.

Volkonsky watched her. "Information is cheap in Vienna." Lazily he flicked the gloves against the palm of his hand. "All I had to do was send my carriage early."

"For all the good it's going to do you, prince," Arabella snorted. "Do you think it will go unnoticed when I do not arrive at the Thürheims?"

"No," he agreed affably. "That's why you will write a note to the good countess, my dear, and tell her that you've made other plans."

"I will do no such thing." Arabella bristled. "Let me go immediately." She moved toward the carriage door again.

This time Volkonsky did not push her back. Instead he grabbed her by the shoulders and dragged her close until she lay across his lap. "You will do it, Arabella, believe me." His fingers dug into her flesh "It's amazing what a human being will do when a little force is applied." His fingers pressed farther. "Just a little."

Arabella could feel his breath hot on her face, and nausea began to roil in her stomach.

Then as suddenly as he had gripped her, Volkonsky's grasp slackened. Kicking the carriage door open, he half threw, half pushed Arabella out so quickly that she didn't have time to cry out. Before she reached the ground, she was swept up by a huge, bearded cossack.

Relief that she had not fallen kept her from crying out for the moment it took for Volkonsky to bark an order in Russian. A hand closed over her mouth as Arabella opened it to scream for help. The man carried her as easily as if she were a trussed chicken, and although she knew that her vocal chords were screaming, the only sound that emerged from her mouth was a distant groan.

They went up one flight of stairs, then another. The trap was closing on her, Arabella thought as a wave of panic beat at her. She started to struggle again, but the cossack gripped her a little tighter, and his hand pressed a little more firmly down on her mouth until she subsided again.

Minutes passed and suddenly Arabella found herself being dumped on a sofa like a sack of flour. She struggled to sit up, her eyes darting around the room. Horrified, she saw that she and Volkonsky were alone. The click of the key turning reverberated in her head like a roll of thunder.

Immediately she tried to stand, but her legs did not obey her and she fell back, panting from a lack of air.

As Volkonsky lazily pushed his large body away from the door and came toward her, she straightened against the back of the sofa, fighting the fear that sent chills skipping along her spine.

"I have waited a long time for this," he said as he sat next to her. "And I have done waiting." Volkonsky's hands anchored Arabella's head as his mouth descended on hers.

Desperately Arabella tried to twist her head away, but her attempts served only to increase the friction of Volkonsky's mouth on hers. Brutally he pried her mouth open and filled it with his tongue.

Gagging, Arabella brought her hands up and pushed at Volkonsky's chest, but he did not budge. His only reaction was to punish her lower lip with a savage nip. But her hands did not still, and worked their way upward until her fingers could press against his throat. The fear slid into panic, giving her a strength she had not known she possessed.

When he finally let her go, her gaze met Volkonsky's black eyes, which glinted with lust and anticipation. He was pleased, she realized. Volkonsky was pleased that she had fought him. Panic started to close in on her, and Arabella defied it, realizing that if she succumbed to the terror, she would have no choice but to submit to the man who eyed her as if she were a choice morsel prepared for his gluttony.

There was a pressure in her throat, as if the fear had chosen that part of her body to reside in. By sheer force of will, Arabella made herself swallow past the lump, forbidding her stomach to heave. A deep breath and she swallowed again. Heartened by that very small gesture of defiance, she set herself to composing her mind.

But before she could form a coherent thought, Volkonsky pulled her against him again. Arabella lifted her hands to fight him, but this time she remembered that it was precisely this that he wanted, and as his mouth closed over hers, she forced herself to go limp. Volkonsky's hands tightened painfully around her head, and as Arabella began to berate herself for her miscalculation, he released her and she fell back.

Volkonsky's full mouth was petulant as he measured her. "I thought you had more spirit in you than that."

Step by step, Arabella fought for control, as a climber fights his way up the sheer face of a cliff, handhold over handhold. This was her only chance, she realized, as her thoughts slowly began to fall into some semblance of order. She had to play games with him. Cunning cat-and-mouse games that would keep him at bay until she found a way out.

"And I thought that you had more finesse, Prince Volkonsky." Arabella managed to pull her mouth into a fair imitation of a coy smile. "Some women may relish being treated as if they were the spoils of war, but I am not one of them." She pressed her hand to her middle as unobtrusively as possible in an attempt to relieve the queasiness in her stomach.

"You will soon see just how much finesse I have, my dear. But first things first." Volkonsky stood and pulled her toward a desk. "You will write exactly what I tell you."

Realizing that she had no choice, Arabella sat down and wrote the words that Volkonsky dictated.

When he had tucked the note away in his sleeve, Arabella braced herself for another attack. But instead Volkonsky saluted her ironically.

"I shall let you rest for now, *ma chère*. I have some business to see to before I return to keep you from getting bored."

He was almost at the door when he turned around. "The only key is in my pocket. And it's a long way from the third floor to the ground." Volkonsky smiled as if he had uttered a pleasantry. "Do we understand each other?"

Arabella nodded once in assent, but her head was high.

The moment the door closed behind Volkonsky, she was up and searching the room for a means of escape.

The Gypsy danced. Her bare feet flew on the earthen floor until they were only a blur, the bells on her ankles marking the wild rhythm. Her hair veiled her face as she whirled, ever closer, until her skirt whipped at his legs. Her scent drifted ever closer to him, but Nando couldn't quite capture it, and he leaned forward to bring it closer.

The music stopped so suddenly that the quiet assaulted his ears. The Gypsy stilled and crumpled at his feet with pliant grace, the ebony curls fanning outward, their tips grazing his face as she went down. In the moment before she raised her face to him, her scent reached his nostrils—not the earthy scent he expected, but the gentle fragrance of lily of the valley and warm skin.

Then she brushed back her hair, her fingers threading sensuously through the black silk. Slowly she brought her face close to his. So close that his vision was completely filled by her eyes, which bored into his. Eyes that were not black, but the color of dark, rich sapphires.

"Beware. There is danger. For you. For her. For the child," she whispered, her breath warm and sweet on his mouth.

Nando watched himself lift his hand, felt himself twist it through her hair, wanting to bring her closer. But even as he wrapped the heavy silk around his fingers, it turned to gossamer. The face and form before him began to fade until she melted away into the darkness behind her.

Desperately, he reached for the dissipating vision. Called to her. He had to see her face again. He had to know what else it was she had to tell him. But his hand clawed only air.

Nando sat bolt upright, his eyes wide open but unseeing. Slowly he became aware of the chill that was cooling the drops of sweat on his forehead. He smelled the dank fetidness of the cell, heard the rustle of the straw pallet on which he sat.

Slowly he slid his hand down his breeches, as much to reassure himself that he was awake as to rid his palms of dampness. He shook his head to clear it, then rested his forehead on a bent knee.

The cell was a windowless hole and he had lost track of the time. How long had it been since he had been brought to Vienna under guard? Three days? Four? Nando tried to reconstruct the days. How often had he slept? How often had a tin plate of the slops that passed for food been shoved at him through the slit at the bottom of the heavy wooden door laced with iron bars? But despite his efforts to remember, the days remained a formless mass of desperation.

And what of the reasons behind his arrest? For the hundredth time Nando tried to unravel them. Who had signed the order? Not many people had the power to arrest an aide-de-camp to Prince Schwarzenberg. Why hadn't he been interrogated? The questions hammered at him, and because he could find no logical reasons, wild, irrational fears plagued him. And the Gypsy's words haunted his waking hours as well as his sleep.

With a visceral instinct he knew that Arabella was in danger. And although his logical mind half dismissed them, the Gypsy's words reinforced the feeling. But who was the child? Poldi perhaps? One of Arabella's orphans? Who had devised this perverted, vengeful plot? Metternich? Volkonsky? Katharina? Sweat broke out on Nando's forehead again as he considered the possibilities, not knowing which of them was worse. Knowing he could do nothing about any of them.

Footsteps sounded on the flagstones outside his cell, and Nando's head snapped up at the screech of a key in the rusty lock. With a flash of hope he scrambled from the filthy straw pallet, ignoring the protests of his body. Perhaps some turnkey had decided to heed his offer of gold after all.

The door opened and light from a torch spilled into the cell.

The sight of Volkonsky, dapper, smiling as he stepped gingerly over the threshold, brought to a boil the rage Nando had controlled for days.

"You!" Nando spat. "I should have know that you were behind this." His customary caution and coolheadedness long dissipated, he lunged forward, choosing to ignore the two burly men who stood to either side of Volkonsky.

At a flick of Volkonsky's hand, the two men moved forward and flung him backward with a casual violence that sent Nando crashing against the wall. The pain, sharp and clear, was almost welcome after days of darkness and nebulous fears. Nando steadied himself with his palms against the uneven bricks and stood.

"I don't suppose you would care to send your bully boys away and try your own hand at beating me, Volkonsky?"

"Indeed, I have better things to do than to dirty my hands with you, Berg." Volkonsky glanced down at his immaculate white gloves, as much to hide his irritation that even after three days in this stinking cell Berg had lost neither his courage nor his arrogance as to emphasize his point.

"I just stopped by to fill you in on the latest gossip." Volkonsky's very white teeth flashed as he smiled cruelly.

"I can imagine what you have to tell me," Nando snarled, suddenly understanding the logic behind his arrest. "Have you and Katharina found more filthy rumors to spread about Arabella Douglas? Are you planning one last charge, so to speak, and you wanted to make sure that I did not return to Vienna inopportunely to crimp your efforts?"

Volkonsky continued to smile but said nothing. He was outwardly calm, but Nando could sense his excitement. And the excitement was accompanied by an almost tangible assurance that made Nando's skin crawl with some unnamed fear.

"Your powers of deduction are admirable, my dear Berg. As far as they go." His teeth flashed again in the dim light. "But I've devised a delightful plan that goes a little farther." Volkonsky hooked his thumbs behind his belt and pinned Nando with his obsidian gaze. "Aren't you going to ask me what it is?"

"I have no doubt that nothing will stop you from telling me." Chill disdain colored Nando's tone.

"The gossips in Vienna are abuzz with the news that Miss Douglas has disappeared." Volkonsky's tone was studiedly casual. "Word has it that the notion of marriage to you was so repulsive that she has fled."

"What? What have you done with her?" Nando lunged forward again as panic clawed at his throat. "Are you mad? I will kill you!"

The two men stepped into Nando's path and, gripping him painfully, pinioned him against the wall.

"She is my guest." Volkonsky went on as if he had not been interrupted, watching Nando carefully as he spoke. "An unwilling guest for the time being, but I shall do my best to change that. If not..." He shrugged.

Rage exploded within him again, and against all odds Nando began to struggle against the two thugs holding him. Blocking out the pain in his shoulders, he managed to twist one arm free. He shoved one man and whirled toward his second captor, sending his knee into the man's groin.

Desperately he pushed forward, knowing that this was the only chance he was going to get. Nando's hands closed around the hilt of Volkonsky's sword. He had it out of its scabbard and a few inches from Volkonsky's chest when one of the thugs hooked an arm around his neck, snapping his head backward with an audible crack. His fingers loosened and the sword clattered to the floor. Dragging him back, the two thugs slammed Nando against the wall and pinned him there.

For a moment Nando's eyes fell closed as he struggled to fill his lungs with air. When he opened them, he saw Volkonsky gesture jerkily to the torchbearer to hand him his sword. It was scant comfort that his hands were not quite steady as he sheathed his weapon.

With some effort Volkonsky threw back his head and looked at Nando. "I'm glad to see that something can break through your sangfroid, Berg."

Nando heard the slight tremble in Volkonsky's voice, but he didn't try to capitalize on it. The panic rose as his mind raced from one dead end to another. Then a thought struck.

Perhaps he could sway Volkonsky not to touch Arabella if he humiliated himself, debased himself.

"Don't harm her, Volkonsky. I beg you..." Automatically he tried to straighten and was brutally shoved against the bricks.

Volkonsky grinned. "Your words are music to my ears, Berg, but I believe I have something better to do right now than listen to you."

"Don't, please." Nando's voice was raspy with emotion. "What can you gain from it, after all, except a moment of pleasure? Not even satisfaction, since you will always know you had to take what was not freely given." For a moment he could sense a hesitation in the other man and he pressed on.

"Besides, even our lecherous society frowns on rape of respectable women."

"Ah, Berg, but there you are mistaken." Volkonsky's teeth flashed briefly. "Miss Douglas's reputation is in shreds. Do you really think that anyone will believe she was forced?"

Nando swallowed with difficulty. For a few moments he silently gauged his opponent. "But you will always know, won't you?" he said softly.

"Damn you," Volkonsky snapped and pivoted. "Take his signet ring," he barked over his shoulder. "And I don't care if you have to cut off his finger to do it."

Stiff-kneed with anger, Volkonsky stalked out of the cell. Damn Berg, he thought, as he strode down the dark corridor. He should have had the thugs beat Berg senseless—before Berg robbed him of the pleasure of anticipation.

Chapter Twenty-two

Arabella sat on the bed, painstakingly plaiting and knotting the drapery cords together to form a long rope. During the three days of her captivity, she had learned that keeping her mind occupied with plans to escape and her fingers busy kept the panic at bay.

She'd gone through the room with a fine-tooth comb in her search for objects she could use as weapons—a vase, a bottle of champagne, a heavy bronze inkstand—for she knew that soon, very soon, Volkonsky would lose his taste for the cat-and-mouse game she was playing with his vanity and take what he had brought her here for. Arabella kept telling herself that when he did, she would be ready for him.

Where had she found the strength and cunning to play this game with Volkonsky? The strength to allow him to put his wet, greedy mouth on hers and remain limp and passive even though her body and mind rebelled. The guile to tease and taunt and flirt even though the urge to fight him was almost physical.

But her tactics had paid off, she comforted herself, needing to counter the rising nausea. Every time he had released her and renewed his heavy-handed courtship. So far, an inner voice reminded her.

Her hand trembled to her mouth as Arabella remembered how Volkonsky had casually tossed Nando's gold and lapis signet ring onto her dessert plate. The horror that

Nando, too, was a prisoner had been so great that it had taken a long, terrible moment for the thought to lock into place. Then she had opened her mouth to scream at Volkonsky to take her, take her and be done with it, but to set Nando free, but no sound had come.

"You seem less than moved by the fact that Berg is languishing in prison because of you, my dear," Volkonsky had said, his voice drawn out and complaining.

Arabella had quickly shuttered her eyes and hidden her nervous hands. "What did you expect me to do, prince?"

He had sprung up and begun to pace, cracking his knuckles one after another. "Cry, rant, throw yourself upon my mercy. Damn you, I don't know." Pivoting, he had stopped within an arm's length of her chair and pulled Arabella toward him. "I should have taken you that first day," he muttered.

His mouth had been close to hers, and she knew that unless she kept him talking, he would force his kiss on her again. "But you didn't." Arabella wondered at her cool tone.

"I was a fool." Volkonsky's hands bit into her shoulders. "I let myself be goaded into trying seduction. First by you and then by Berg."

He had pushed Arabella into the chair and leaned down, his hands on either side of her head. "Soon, Arabella. My patience is exhausted and I will not wait much longer."

The sound of footsteps in the hall had her scurrying to hide the almost finished rope under the pillows.

The door opened with a burst then slammed shut with a violence that had it shuddering on its hinges. Volkonsky let himself fall against it and hooked his thumbs into his belt. Even though his eyes were half-closed, Arabella could see them gleaming. A shiver ran the length of her spine, and in defiance of it, she raised her chin a notch.

Lazily he stretched to lock the door and pocketed the key. His mouth curved in a feral smile. "It's time, Arabella."

With an indolent movement of his shoulders, he pushed himself away from the wall and started toward her, his steps slow, unsteady.

He was drunk, she realized, her mouth dry. Drunk and aroused and determined. Without warning Volkonsky quickened his steps and lurched toward her. His hand reached out for her, and as Arabella jumped back, her slippers caught the hem of her gown. For a moment she fought for and almost regained her balance, but Volkonsky's hand came down on her shoulder and she fell, taking him down with her.

Eyes closed, he lay motionless half across her body. His full weight was upon her, his arousal insistent against her thigh. Suddenly Arabella was too frightened to remember the rules of the cool game she had been playing with him for the past three days, and she began to struggle.

She had almost managed to dislodge the dead weight from her when Volkonsky's eyes opened and he shifted his body to effectively trap her again. He looked into her widened eyes.

"Strange, isn't it, how confidence tends to fade when you're flat on your back?" He anchored her by splaying his hand on her midriff, the tips of his fingers just touching the curve of her breast. "You thought to curb me, my dear, but only because I let myself be curbed."

Volkonsky's voice was soft—almost the silky tone of a lover. Arabella's gaze skittered across his face and saw the ugly counterpoint. The mouth curved in a cruel smile. The nostrils flared with barely checked desire. With a desperate jerk she twisted her hands free from between their bodies and pushed at his broad chest, but he easily grasped her wrists in one hand and pinned them above her head.

"I told Berg today I had already had you," Volkonsky whispered hoarsely. "The look on his face was worth the lie."

Arabella closed her eyes as a wave of despair engulfed her, and for a moment the will to fight drained out of her.

"Look at me," Volkonsky growled, his hand moving roughly, impatiently over her body. "Because now it's going to be true, Arabella. In a minute, I'm going to spread your legs and make it true."

He lowered his head, seeking her mouth, but Arabella flinched from his brandy-laden breath. She twisted her head, but he gripped her face, his fingers biting into her cheeks. And still she struggled.

Volkonsky raised himself on an elbow to give himself more leverage and, seeking to control her, dug his knee into her abdomen. Suddenly Arabella went perfectly still.

"No." Her whisper was barely audible. "Please, don't. Don't hurt me."

Her sudden stillness and her plea succeeded where struggling and pride had failed. Baffled by her reaction, Volkonsky stared at Arabella, his black eyes muddled and bloodshot.

She sucked in her stomach to ease the pressure. "Your knee. You're hurting me."

His grip loosened and Arabella rolled away from him, bending her knees toward her belly in an instinctive movement of self-protection. Volkonsky made no move to restrain her, and she pushed herself using both hands, sliding backward over the polished planks. She pushed again, and the momentum propelled her to her knees. Pausing for a moment to steady her breathing, she crossed her arms over her stomach.

Volkonsky shook his head as if coming awake. His eyes narrowed, and his gaze moved speculatively over her.

Arabella inched back. Her toe met an obstacle, and the tinkle of glass against metal was like thunder in her ears, freezing her in the middle of a movement. But Volkonsky, still sprawled on the floor, seemed not to have heard it, or if he had, attached no importance to it.

Suddenly he rose to his knees. His half perplexed, half speculative expression was gone, and if the corner of the bed had not been at Arabella's back, she would have retreated farther. His full lips curled back from his teeth in a snarl that seemed inhuman. At another moment Arabella would have laughed and told him that he looked ridiculous impersonating a mad dog.

"You're pregnant!" Volkonsky bellowed. "Admit it! You're carrying Berg's by-blow in your belly."

For the first time during her captivity Arabella felt the panic close in on her completely. It seemed to block every one of her senses, paralyze her movements, numb every thought until even the panic itself was gone.

"The bastard." Volkonsky's voice was unnaturally high, as if he were on the verge of hysteria. "The bastard with his hypocritical talk of honor. I wanted to be the first one to take you," he shrieked. "I wanted your virginal blood on my body."

He fell forward onto his hands. "You will not have this child, Arabella." His heavy breathing spaced the words, making them sound doubly ominous. "I swear that I will couple with you until your body spews this child from it."

Volkonsky began to crawl toward her.

He came closer and closer still. Then the numbness began to fade, and even though the terrible fear returned, so did the strength. Her child was in danger. Her child. Nando's child.

Her hand slipped back to grip the long neck of the champagne bottle she had secreted behind the bed curtain. Volkonsky was beyond an arm's length, and Arabella tensed all her muscles to force herself to wait a moment longer.

He loomed in front of her, his broad body filling her vision. Arabella twisted as far as she could to give her arm momentum. Volkonsky's eyes were fastened on her mouth as he reached for her. She gripped the bottle a little tighter and swung her arm in a wide arc.

Arabella watched the scene unfold almost as if she were an observer instead of a participant. She saw the bottle strike the side of Volkonsky's head. She heard the dull crack of glass against bone, then the slightly louder thud as the bottle dropped to the floor. She saw Volkonsky's eyes widen in surprise, saw him raise a halting hand toward his temple where the blood had begun to flow. She watched him sway, then catch himself once, twice. When he tipped over like a bowling pin and fell on his face, Arabella's eyes closed in relief.

Minutes passed. She had no idea how many. Still on her knees, Arabella straightened and took a deep breath. And then another. She was all right, she realized. She was all right, and so was her baby.

But she was still a prisoner. Her gaze skittered around the room. Volkonsky was unconscious, but for how long? The fear licked at her. She accepted it and moved, determined not to lose the small advantage she had gained.

Scrambling up, she snatched the rope she had plaited from under her pillow and began to bind Volkonsky's hands behind him. Her head whipped up when he made a sound. What if he was coming round already? The first thing he would do would be to shout for the guard.

She darted toward the table and grabbed a linen napkin. That would serve as a gag, but she needed something to hold it in place. Oh, God. Arabella pressed her fist to her mouth. Why hadn't she planned more carefully? She hadn't thought farther than the few objects she had hidden around the room and the length of rope.

Within moments, she had stripped a sheet off the bed and was hacking at it with a dinner knife. When she knelt at Volkonsky's side, her courage failed her, and she was afraid that touching his bloodied head would be beyond her strength.

She had begun to loop her rope around Volkonsky's feet when she realized that she would never have enough. Somehow she would have to dispose of the guard as well. Quickly she hacked and ripped more strips from the sheet and prayed that the linen would hold.

Her gown was damp with sweat by the time she had finished tying Volkonsky's feet together and securing them to the bed. But she knew that the major part of her task was still to come.

Forcing her awkward fingers on, she knotted another piece of the rope around Volkonsky's neck. Leaving a little bit of slack, Arabella tied the other end around the claw-shaped foot of a heavy armoire. He would not be able to move more than a few inches without cutting off his air. There was a bitter taste in her mouth as she struggled with the knots. He had almost raped her twice. He had had Nando imprisoned. He had wanted to make her abort her child. And yet she still found hers a repulsive task.

Exhausted, she let herself sit on the floor. It was done. She leaned a bit closer. Volkonsky still showed no signs of wakening. Gingerly Arabella dipped her fingers into the pocket where she had seen him put the key. Nothing. She forced her fingers farther until they slid down Volkonsky's flank.

When she finally touched the key, her fingers almost shied away, so warm was the metal from Volkonsky's body. But she grasped it tightly as she moved away.

As quietly as possible, Arabella prepared for the next test of her strength. A chair behind the door would have to suffice as vantage point. The champagne bottle would have to serve again as her weapon.

Nausea was roiling in her stomach, but she forced herself to ignore it as she ignored the slight tremble in her hands. She fit the key into the keyhole, turned it and pressed down the door handle.

As the door swung open, she raised the bottle above her head. Only at the last moment did she remember the Persian lamb hat that was part of the cossack's uniform. Quickly she changed the angle and hoped that the bottle would find a spot not cushioned by the hat.

Why was he taking so long? she asked herself. She could hear noises in the hall—the scrape of a boot heel on the marble tiles, a low mutter. Did he suspect something? she wondered, and tried to swallow past the pulse that was beating in her throat.

The door opened farther and bumped against the chair on which she stood. There was a shuffle of feet, then silence. Arabella's eyes shifted, following a line from the door. Straight to where Volkonsky lay.

A sound of dismay escaped her. Later, much later, she would realize that the sound had been the lure that had saved her. The cossack swung around the door toward her and in reflex Arabella swung the bottle at his skull.

She was nearing exhaustion when she finished tying up the cossack in much the same manner as she had bound Volkonsky. Her fingers trembled as she locked the door behind her and ran down the hall.

Even as her brain urged her to creep cautiously down the stairs, her instincts drove her forward. She slung her cape around her shoulders, holding it closed with both hands so the lower part of her face was hidden. Praying that she would not encounter Katharina, Arabella ran down the stairs.

Chapter Twenty-three

Arabella dodged from door to door, darted from shadow to shadow. Somehow she had to get to Nando quickly, for she was certain that with her gone, Volkonsky would head for Nando the moment Volkonsky was freed.

She rounded St. Stephan's Cathedral and ducked down the Wollzeile toward the Thürheim town house. Suddenly she picked up the sound of running steps behind her and automatically bolted forward. She thought she heard someone call her name. If only she could reach Lulu, she thought, she would be safe. Then she tripped over a loose cobblestone and was falling.

Hands caught her a fraction of a second before she hit the pavement. She opened her mouth to call for help, but then the darkness was descending on her.

As she came awake little by little, the anxiety that still ran through her blood could not block out a feeling of safety. When she opened her eyes and Lulu's worried face filled her vision, she knew why.

"Arabella, *chérie,* are you all right?" Lulu touched her cheek gently. "Where have you been? Can you tell me what happened? I've been out of my mind with worry."

"Volkonsky." Arabella passed her tongue over her parched lips. "It was his carriage that came for me instead of yours." She drew a deep breath and let it shudder out of her before she continued. "He kept me locked in a room in the Palm Palace." She closed her eyes. One simple sentence, she thought. Just a few words to describe a three-day nightmare.

"Did he—did he hurt you?"

Arabella shook her head and almost managed a smile. "I kept him at bay until the last. When he tried to attack me, I knocked him unconscious with a bottle of champagne." A half-hysterical giggle crept into her voice. "Fitting, isn't it?"

Then Jeanne was at her side with a nightgown slung over her arm. "Come here, child." She wiped at the tears of relief that trickled down her face. "I'm putting you to bed."

"No!" Arabella sat up and gripped Lulu's arm. "No. Volkonsky had Nando imprisoned. I don't know how or where. Once he's freed, he'll go after Nando. I have to get Nando out of prison before then." Arabella shook Lulu. "Somehow I have to get him out."

"So that was it." Lulu covered Arabella's hand gently with hers. "Vienna has been buzzing with rumors about Nando's arrest. He was taken from a *csarda* in Pest by a civilian attended by two men in uniform, but no one seems to know who gave the order or where he was taken."

"I have to find out." Arabella swung her legs from the couch where she lay.

"Arabella." Lulu held her with both hands. "Be realistic. What can you do?"

"Surely you know someone who can find out where he is." Her voice was high and urgent. "Please, Lulu. You must help me. And send for Franz. Perhaps he knows something."

Having obtained Lulu's promise, Arabella allowed Jeanne to help her bathe and wash her hair. By the time Lulu returned with Franz in tow and information about Nando's whereabouts, Arabella was dressed.

"I'm going to try to bribe him out." She turned to Lulu. "Can you loan me money? Somehow I'll repay you."

"Arabella," Lulu protested, "this is much too dangerous. What you're planning is madness. What will you do?

Stroll into the prison, strew a few gold pieces around and take him out with you?''

"There has to be a way, and I will find it. I must." She paused. "I could never live with myself if I did nothing."

"Then wait, at least," Lulu pleaded. "They can't lock him away indefinitely. It will be untangled soon, I'm sure. We'll go see Schwarzenberg, Metternich, anyone."

"And if it is not cleared up? If he is not released? What is one more dead body when so many have died?" she cried out. "I must do this, Lulu. Don't you see?"

"I see that you are too stubborn to listen to reason." Then Lulu's voice softened. "Keep yourself safe."

Arabella squeezed Lulu's hand, knowing that she could not give her reassurance. Then she rose to get ready.

Within an hour, Arabella stood in front of a grim, gray stone building so huge that she had to move her head from her left shoulder to her right to take it all in. Standing well to the side of the gate, she eyed the cubicle near the entrance that housed the watchman and wondered how much gold would buy her way inside.

A trio of people hurried past, jostling her, and without knowing why, she moved forward, keeping a step behind them.

A large, burly man in the flowing black robe of an attorney spoke insistently to the couple who walked at his side. Only a few of his words floated to Arabella, but enough to tell her that they were on their way to visit a prisoner.

Her heart was beating in her throat as she walked behind them up the short incline that led to the prison entrance. As they passed the tiny guardhouse, the burly man waved a piece of paper at the watchman, who barely raised his eyes from the small block of wood and knife his hands were busy with. He nodded and murmured, *"Grüss Gott, Herr Doktor,"* before he reached for a bell and returned to his whittling.

The hard, dissonant sound of the iron bell resounded twice in the arched entry, and immediately a man, an enormous ring full of keys of all sizes chained to his waist, appeared to open the gate.

Absorbed in their conversation and their problems, the three people in front of her paid Arabella no mind, and the gatekeeper spared her no more than a cursory glance, apparently assuming her to be a part of the group. Inside the courtyard where the high walls spread a perpetual dusk she stopped for a moment, needing to quiet her breath, but the clang of the gate behind her spurred her to follow the small group through a wide arched doorway at the far end of the courtyard.

She found herself in a long corridor where the murky lighting barely allowed her to see that there were no doors, only corridors that radiated outward like the tentacles of a huge octopus. The small group she had followed had been swallowed up by one of the passageways. Now even the voices died away, and Arabella knew she was on her own.

Her heartbeat a wild drumroll in her ears, she walked forward. Footsteps approached, and a man with an armful of cardboard-bound papers emerged from one of the corridors. She whirled toward him.

"Thank heavens, *mein Herr,*" she exclaimed. "I seem to have gotten lost." Her gloved fingers stifled a nervous giggle that was only half-feigned.

She approached the man, whose craggy face was creased in a frown but was not otherwise unfriendly. "I'm supposed to see Herr . . ." Her fingers fluttered at her temple as if she were trying to recall a name that had slipped her mind, and she bit her lower lip. "I can't remember his name."

"What is your business?" the man asked a bit gruffly but without hostility.

Arabella cast down her eyes and twisted her fingers around the string of her reticule. It was easy to play the role of a distraught, helpless female, she thought, when your heart feels as if it is about to fly out of your body. "I need to ask about one of the prisoners," she whispered.

"A debtor?"

She shook her head.

"One of those held by order of the police, then?" He eyed her with something resembling pity. "We have plenty of those these days." A snort of a laugh accompanied his words. "It will be Herr Wegart, then, whom you want to see."

It could be a trick, she knew, but some instinct assured her it was not, and she nodded eagerly. "Yes, yes of course. That was the name." A little of the pressure seemed to leave her chest. "I'm sorry, I am distressed these days."

Her fingers dived into her reticule, and Arabella pressed a coin into his hand. "Would you take me to him, then?"

The glint of gold in his palm changed the man's aloof mien to something decidedly more obsequious. *"Natürlich."* He bowed low. "Please follow me, *Fräulein.*"

Arabella found her heartbeat calming as she followed him along dank passageways that never saw the light of day. It was as if she were on the stage, and now that the performance had begun, the worst of the stage fright was over. She could do it, she told herself, blocking out the insistent thought that it seemed too easy.

Arriving in front of a door that stood half-open, her guide made an impatient sound when he found the room empty. Gesturing to her to wait, he set off again. As she stood alone in the dark corridor, her fear returned, cutting off the air she needed to breathe. Assaulted by grim images, every coherent thought fled.

The time stretched, filled with images of this man on whom Nando's fate could depend. Was he a weasely creature who looked as if he spent his life eavesdropping in corners? Or perhaps a boorish, uncouth jailer with hands that looked as if they could break bones?

Then she heard footsteps and saw her guide walking a deferential half step behind a small, plump man. The roly-poly figure that had been squeezed into the green and black civil servant's uniform and the rosy face above the stiff collar were so far from all her preconceptions that Arabella almost laughed aloud in relief.

Herr Wegart pranced a little as he greeted her, gesturing Arabella inside the office with a bow. He sat down behind his well-ordered desk and folded his hands. "To what do I owe the pleasure of your visit, *Fräulein?*" he inquired affably, acting for all the world as if she had come to purchase a new bonnet or a bolt of cloth.

"I have come about one of the prisoners here, Herr Wegart." He gestured for her to continue. "His name is Berg. Count Ferdinand Berg."

He frowned. "How do you know that he's here? Are you a relative?"

The mother of his unborn child, she thought. "A friend," she said. "His manservant told me he was here."

"Ah." There was a suggestive twinkle in his eye now. "And you wish to visit him?"

Arabella looked straight into his eyes and wondered briefly if she was signing her own arrest warrant with her next words. Phrasing her words with more care than she was accustomed to, she said, "I wished to inquire what Count Berg's situation is at present. And how it can be remedied."

Wegart frowned and rose to pace around the small room. He stopped next to her chair and looked at her, then swiveled around and returned to his desk. Carefully he folded his hands again. "Can you be more specific, *gnädiges Fräulein?* I would mislike it if we did not understand each other quite clearly."

Arabella understood then and felt a little more of the tension seep out of her. He was as unsure of her as she of him.

"I am not a spy, Herr Wegart, sent to test your loyalty and incorruptibility," she said, glad to escape from diplomatic hedging to open speech.

"How do I know that you are telling the truth?"

"I have no proof." Arabella sent him her most dazzling smile. "But I assure you, I want only Count Berg's freedom."

Wegart threw back his head and laughed, the sound strangely sonorous for his diminutive size. "His freedom?" he trumpeted. "*Ich bin nicht Gott.* I am not God, *Fräulein.*"

Her hands went automatically to her middle, all the tension suddenly back, pressing like a huge stone on her chest. "But . . . but the man who brought me here said . . ."

"I'm afraid you have been misled. I am only a simple civil servant who follows orders and keeps the registers on the prisoners our worthy police bring here." He shook his head. "*Es tut mir leid.* I am sorry, I have no power to free anyone."

She would not cry, Arabella told herself. Still she could feel the telltale thickening in her throat, the pricking behind her eyes. Battling the tears, she reached into her reticule and extracted the purse Lulu had begged from her rich brother-in-law to be.

Keeping her eyes on Wegart, she deposited the purse on the desk, the momentum making the coins chink. Keeping her fingers on it lightly, she said, "Perhaps you can reconsider your possibilities, Herr Wegart?"

A shrewd light came into his pale blue eyes as he examined the fine morocco leather bulging with coins.

"Indeed," he said, "perhaps it was hasty of me." He pulled a large leather-bound book toward him. "Let me see if I can find this Count Berg of yours in my register."

Arabella watched greedily as he ran a pudgy finger down columns of names recorded in a fine, spidery hand. The finger stopped and she stiffened, waiting for him to speak.

When he looked up from the page, he resembled a melancholy clown, his eyes turned down at the corners. "A most difficult case, I'm afraid. Count Berg has not been charged as yet." His eyes returned to the book before him.

"And the order for his arrest was given by Prince Metternich himself."

"Metternich?" Arabella felt fear choking her again as she imagined Nando thrown into some oubliette and left there forever.

Wegart eyed the fat purse again and she relaxed a bit, telling herself that the little man was only being clever and trying to improve his bargaining position.

"Of course, there is much confusion these days." He shrugged and cupidity fairly shone in his eyes.

Arabella fingered the soft leather. "How much longer do you think he will be in prison? Ten days?" Without waiting for a reply, she opened the purse and one by one counted out ten gold pieces. Making two neat piles, she pushed them halfway between the edge of the desk and Wegart's hands.

With difficulty the little man tore his eyes away from the coins that shone so brightly against the dark wood and met Arabella's eyes. "A little longer than that, I fear."

"Twenty days?" Before he could answer, ten more coins joined those on the desk.

He laid his uniform cap over the four neat piles and moved to rake them toward him, but Arabella put her hand on the cap's crown.

"Perhaps you can explain your plan first, Herr Wegart."

He acknowledged Arabella's strategy with a nod and a smile, apparently finding it perfectly normal procedure. Opening a drawer, he extracted a large document with a heavy seal at the bottom and patted it lovingly.

"I have here an order to transfer a group of prisoners to the Meidling prison early tomorrow morning. It could be possible to add a name to the list."

Arabella frowned, unclear as to the advantage of this.

"It is about a league south of the city gates. If a prisoner were to escape on the way there—" Wegart briefly raised his hands and eyes toward the ceiling "—it would be most unfortunate, but, *mein Gott,* such things happen."

He folded his hands on top of the document and leaned forward. "Please listen well, *Fräulein*."

For the next half hour Arabella listened, committing everything the little man said to memory, for he was loath to let her use pen and paper. Finally he said, "I will need a little persuasion for the guard. To make certain the chains are not closed properly and the aim of the guards is poor."

Arabella lifted the cap and added another pile of coins.

"How do I know you will do as you say? That the chains are unlocked and the aim poor?" she asked.

"You do not. But I assure you that I want only Count Berg's freedom," he said, echoing her earlier words. "You have been very generous, *Fräulein*. Count Berg is a fortunate man."

Arabella said a quick prayer, realizing that she had no choice but to trust him.

Chapter Twenty-four

Pinkish stripes were beginning to creep onto the horizon when Arabella set out, accompanied by Franz and Lulu's footman, Anton.

None of the three had slept much, having spent hours going over the road they would take to Trautenstein. Although Arabella feared the memories that waited for her there, she agreed that the castle and Johann von Berg would provide suitable protection for Nando until his name was cleared.

Wegart's instructions had been amazingly precise. A rider was to walk a saddled horse toward the city. Wegart would make certain that Count Berg was the last in the line of prisoners, that his shackles were loose and that the guard's weapon would be ineffectual. It had sounded like a simple enough plan in the small office, but the escape would not end there.

Against the arguments of the two men, Arabella had insisted that she be the one to walk the horse intended for Nando, while the two men would give them cover from the trees on either side of the road.

Arabella, so easily impatient with idleness, sat her horse without a fidget as she squinted into the early morning sunlight. Occasionally she reached down to soothe her mount or the stallion next to her, but otherwise she sat with an almost unnatural stillness and waited.

So focused was she on the task ahead that she allowed no thought to enter her brain beyond their plan. If someone had put a simple, everyday question to her, she might not have been able to answer. Some men might have recognized Arabella's state of mind as one they had experienced before a battle or a duel, knowing that what they had to do was all-important and would determine the course of their lives.

So she sat when a line of men straggled into view, guarded at the front and rear by a soldier carrying a bayoneted rifle. At first Arabella did not move, but she felt her heart slam into her ribs with astonishing force as the blood began to rush through her veins. A thin layer of sweat covered her skin. Calmly, deliberately Arabella nudged her horse into a walk.

"Halt. Stehenbleiben."

The command rang out like a whip crack, and Nando's soldier's body obeyed, coming to an immediate standstill, every instinct awake, while the forlorn men in front of him shuffled to a stop, bumping into each other, the chain that manacled them together clanging dully. A man near the front of the line had sunk to his knees in exhaustion, and the front guard stepped up to him and prodded him impatiently.

Carefully Nando rotated his wrist within the iron manacle. The half-inch gap was still there. He smiled grimly. The guard who had manacled him that morning had been negligent.

Nando felt the tension gather between his shoulder blades as he waited for the guard behind him to move forward as well. There was a farm to the left, and the house and outbuildings would give him some cover. The horse that grazed contentedly nearby looked as if it might give him decent service. Now all he needed was a little distance from the guard behind him.

But the guard behind him stood fast as if he had sprouted roots, and Nando swore pungently to himself as he realized he would have to let the chance go. Even with the element of surprise on his side, he wouldn't be able to reach cover before he had a ball in his back.

The command to move sounded. Chains clanged, and the men in front of him moved off again, their shoulders round with defeat, their eyes on the road where the mud sucked at their feet. Their pace was slower now, and Nando's gaze traveled the countryside restlessly. It was then that he saw the horseman.

Her fingers stiff from her overlong stillness, Arabella reached down and fingered the pistols attached to her saddle to reassure herself that they were still there.

Raising herself slightly in her stirrups, her breathing was suddenly loud in her ears. There he was! Just as Wegart had promised, Nando was the last man in line.

A huge wave of relief swept over her as she saw that he held himself straight and walked as freely as the slow pace of the other men would allow. For the first time since she had learned that Nando was in prison she was free of the fear that Volkonsky had tortured and maimed him.

Automatically she reached over to soothe the restive, high-spirited stallion beside her. They were closer now. She could distinguish Nando's face, and she needed every ounce of her self-control to keep herself from digging her heels into her mount's sides and galloping toward him.

He had seen her. Even from a distance she could tell that his eyes had narrowed and registered her presence, but there was no recognition in his face. Arabella reined in her horse and crowded to the very edge of the road, as if she was making room for the approaching men.

She trained her gaze on Nando, greedy for the sight of him, willing him to look at her, as if she could communicate every detail of their plan to him with her eyes. She had no thought that this was the man she had run from. At this moment she only knew that her heart was full of her love for him and that she needed him to be safe.

He was so close that if she called out, he would hear her. Willing him to look at her, to move at the right time, she trained her gaze on Nando. She pressed her hand against the base of her throat where a mad pulse beat. Then his gaze moved from the stallion beside her to her face, and their eyes met.

A saddled, riderless horse! Nando narrowed his eyes, disbelieving his incredible good fortune. A burst of energy galvanized his body as he realized that his opportunity had come.

He monitored every movement the rider made, afraid the man would turn into the woods that crowded both sides of the road at the last moment. Careful to make no sound, he worked his hand painfully through the iron manacle until the only thing keeping it from dropping to the ground were his fingertips, which curved around its underside.

Then a movement of the youth's hand toward his throat drew Nando's attention to the face that was partly shadowed by a dark, battered cap.

His muscles went slack and his feet faltered as he stared at Arabella's face. The chain attached to his wrist manacle went taut, and Nando recalled the use of his muscles at the last moment before the ring slid from his fingers. Forcing his legs to obey him, he moved forward, his eyes never leaving her face.

He shook his head a little as if to clear it, but her face did not disappear. It drew closer, the features more distinct. It truly was she and not a vision come to taunt him. The realization set off a flash of almost painful joy.

How had she gotten free of Volkonsky? he asked himself. On the heels of that first burst of joy, the grim question crowded into his brain. Nando's gaze veered from Arabella and scanned the countryside for a sign of the Russian.

The mistrust of years pushed itself to the fore, the taste bitter, but then he felt himself falling into Arabella's sapphire eyes, their magic swirling around him. He was drowning. Drowning in her beauty. Drowning in his memories of her soft skin, her fragrance. Drowning in the turbulent, violent sea of his emotions.

She was even more beautiful than he remembered. The men's clothing she wore both camouflaged and molded her figure, and Nando felt the instant heated reaction of his blood. This he understood. This he could take pleasure in. But what of the painful constriction of his heart? What of the bittersweet emotions that filled it and overflowed?

Was she here to help him escape? Or was this some kind of terrible trick? The thought forced itself past the heat, past the feeling he would not name. Nando scrutinized Arabella's face for a clue, but her perfect features were set in a calm mask. Only her eyes were bright with something he could not read. His fingers, suddenly agitated, ran along the rough, corrugated edge of the loose manacle.

He was only a few feet away from Arabella now. In a moment he would be abreast of her. In a moment he would have to make the decision whether he would trust her with his life. Was it his imagination or had she moved the hand in which she held the reins of the others horse toward him? A step closer. Then another.

From down the road came the staccato beat of horses' hooves. In the forest a jay gave a noisy warning. The rasp of the guard's breath was suddenly loud in his ear.

Then the steel point of the guard's bayonet was between his shoulder blades. *"Laufen Sie. Schnell.* Run. Quickly." The words were so low that Nando would have thought he had imagined them if he had not felt the man's damp breath on his ear.

Nando exploded into action. In the space of a breath he had dropped the manacle, whirled and shoved the guard onto the muddy ground. Continuing onward in a smooth arc, he swung himself into the empty saddle.

Their horses had erupted into a gallop before shouts at their backs alerted them that the others had become aware of what had happened. Nando let Arabella ease ahead. If there was shooting, he preferred his back to be the target.

Paying the lone horseman galloping toward them no mind, they veered off the road. The horses' hooves pounded into the soft needle-strewn ground, sending little clods of earth flying. The path was narrow, the low-hanging branches often brushing their heads. They were no more than ten yards into the forest when the first shot sounded.

There was a shout behind them, the another. Arabella's stomach lurched, wondering what had happened. Had the cry come from Franz or Anton? She risked a glance over her shoulder, but her view was obscured by Nando. Knowing that she dared not stop, that she had to keep riding as fast as possible no matter what happened, she spurred her mount onward.

Nando took an almost painful pleasure in the freedom of their headlong gallop. The fresh, cool air that rippled through his hair was an elixir after the fetidness of the prison, the untrammeled movement after days of bars and chains a gift from the gods. He was certain he had never felt so alive.

No, that wasn't true, he thought as his gaze fastened on Arabella's figure, which sat the large horse so expertly. It had been those two nights with Arabella, stolen out of time, when he had truly known what life was. What it could be.

Why was she here? he wondered again. How had she arranged his escape? At what price had she bought her freedom from Volkonsky and his freedom, as well? The pain ripped at his gut as the vista of all the terrible possibilities opened up in front of him.

Every one of his thoughts, every suspicion meshed with his love, his need, and formed an absurdly unreal, dangerous state of mind. The mad pace, the wind that whined past Nando's ears, the danger at his back all blended to exacerbate his state of mind. With a violence that was foreign to his nature he swore that this time Arabella would not flee him. This time she would be his.

As his mind shaped the thought, Nando heard the crack of a pistol behind him, and a split second later felt a bullet hit his thigh.

Arabella whipped around in the saddle the moment she heard the shot, hoping against hope that she had imagined the sound. She saw Nando clutching his leg, blood oozing between his fingers, and she knew that she had not. Her gaze flew past Nando, and she could not suppress a cry as she recognized the horseman who was gaining on them.

When she saw Nando rein in his mount sharply and dismount, Arabella did not hesitate for a moment. She veered and doubled back, sliding to the ground almost before her horse had stopped.

Desperately she pulled at one of the pistols, but it caught on the reins and she fumbled with it, losing precious seconds. By the time she held it in her hand, she saw that Nando had reached Volkonsky.

Volkonsky had emptied his weapons, and now he raised a pistol to use it as a club. But before he could bring it down, Nando had gripped him and pulled him down from the saddle.

Clutching her pistol in both hands, Arabella dashed toward Nando. He whirled to face her just as she reached him. One hand flew out to capture her wrist and with the other he tore the pistol away from her.

For a fraction of a moment their eyes met and Arabella saw the accusation in Nando's silver eyes.

She wouldn't turn away, Arabella told herself. She would show no weakness, even though she could feel her lifeblood drain away and leave her empty. She held Nando's gaze and stood utterly motionless. His grip loosened and her hand fell against her side like a lifeless thing, the sound audible in the stillness of the clearing.

Slowly, deliberately Nando turned from Arabella and leveled the pistol at Volkonsky's head.

The silence was suddenly broken as Volkonsky began to whimper. "Don't," he cried softly and shielded his head with his hands, palms outward. "Please don't shoot me. *Je vous en prie.*" Volkonsky hiccuped. "Please, Berg. I lied to you. I didn't take her." His gaze darted to Arabella. "Tell him." He covered his face with his hands and began to cry.

"Put your hands down, Volkonsky." Nando's voice was as icy as an arctic wind. "Face your death like a man, at least."

But Volkonsky continued to sob and mumble pleading, disjointed words.

"Stand up, damn you," Nando shouted, rage making his voice crack. "If you do not, I will shoot you like the dog you are." He took aim.

The unreasoning fury in Nando's voice snapped Arabella out of her numb state, and she moved forward and put her hand on his arm.

"Don't do it, Nando. He is not worth it."

He jerked away from her touch. "Are you pleading for him now?" he snapped derisively.

"No, Nando," Arabella said softly, sadly. "I am pleading for you."

Nando stared into Arabella's fathomless sapphire eyes, which were clouded with pain. He forgot Volkonsky, he forgot his imprisonment, he forgot everything but the reality of Arabella standing a hand's breadth away. The violence flowed out of him like a poison purged from his blood, and he knew that even if she had betrayed him, even if she had made Volkonsky the gift of her body, he loved her too much to let her go.

The sound of hooves interrupted the stillness that had fallen over the clearing. Nando stiffened and trained the pistol in the direction of the sound. The rider came into view, and he saw Franz with a man he recognized as Lulu's groom riding pillion behind him.

Franz trotted into the clearing, an exuberant smile on his broad face despite the bloodstained cloth that was wound around his arm. He lifted his hat and waved it in Nando's direction.

"*Gott sei dank,* thank the Lord, you're safe." His gaze swept toward Volkonsky, who was still cowering on the ground. "And the vermin's been caught."

Nando stared at Franz, the truth dawning on him. She had risked her life for him, and he had dealt her the ultimate insult. He turned toward Arabella. The pain in her eyes was terrible to see, and Nando knew it was he who had put it there. He lifted his hand. It faltered for a moment before he reached out to her in a mute plea for forgiveness.

Her chin high, her back straight, she turned and walked away.

Arabella felt her energy ebbing as she walked toward her mount. She had watched Nando in the line of prisoners. She had seen all the conflicting emotions on his face. The doubt. The suspicion. And she had seen nothing of a softer, more tender emotion that might have eased her hurt. That she could have forgotten, discounted. But how could she ever forget the furious accusation, the violent touch of a moment ago? The last of her strength trickled out of her, and she leaned against her mount's lathered rump, closing her eyes against the dizziness that threatened her.

But a moment later her eyes flew open when she felt hands on her shoulders.

Nando turned Arabella around and gazed into her eyes, longing to erase the hurt, desperately searching for the soothing, healing words. He had said the word "love" in his mind. Could he say it aloud? he wondered. Would it make him whole? And would Arabella believe him? Would she forgive him? Could she?

"Arabella," he began, "I... Forgive me."

She gave him no answer, but he could feel her shrinking from his touch.

"Talk to me, Arabella." Nando forced himself to take his hands from her shoulders. "Please."

She stared past him. "What is there left for us to say?"

"Everything."

Arabella pressed her head against her horse, finding a certain comfort in the warm, pungent-smelling flesh. She rolled her head to the side, not able to bear meeting Nando's eyes. The silver eyes that now held the tenderness she would have sold her soul for half an hour ago.

How she wanted to take what he offered. But how could she when she knew with a hideous certainty that Nando was still prepared to believe the worst of her. That he would condemn her for a whore and forgive her in one breath for the simple reason that his desire was greater than his disgust.

Slowly Arabella turned to look at him. Her gaze ran greedily over Nando's beloved features, and she cursed herself that she had not resisted the temptation. Now she was caught in his eyes like a rabbit in a circle of light—aware of the terrible danger and yet unable to flee.

Powerless to resist touching her, Nando framed her face with his hands.

They both went perfectly still as the contact of skin upon skin tore through the last defenses they had against each other.

"I love you, Arabella." Nando felt something akin to relief as he spoke the words, as if a long-suffered burden had fallen from his shoulders. But the relief dissipated like snow in the springtime sun when he saw the despair in her eyes.

Nando's words were like a red-hot poker against Arabella's flesh. She had never dreamed that the words she had waited for so long would cause her such pain.

His hands tightened. "Would you deny that you love me?"

Arabella moved her head from side to side in negation, but stopped in the midst of a movement—the feel of Nando's hands on her skin too treacherous. "I deny nothing."

"But you turn away from me. I warn you, Arabella—" Nando could feel the violence he had felt earlier rising within him again "—I will not let you run this time." He leaned closer, his mouth only inches from hers. "Do you hear me? I will not let you run. Not now. Not ever."

He was so close that Arabella could feel his breath on her lips. It would be so easy to give in. For just a moment. For just the space of one kiss. But she found that there was pride even in the midst of pain, and her chin rose.

"You will have no other choice, Nando. Do you think I can bear to hear you say 'I love you' and to know there is always a qualifier behind it? 'I love you despite, although, regardless.'" A deep breath trembled through her. "You love me, but you do not trust me."

Nando opened his mouth to deny her words.

"Do not perjure yourself." Arabella's voice rose in warning. "From the beginning you were prepared to believe the worst of me, and nothing I could do or say could change your mind. You still do. The only difference is that you are willing to forgive me for it because you want me."

Appalled at her words, appalled at what he realized was the truth, Nando's hands slackened and dropped to her shoulders, but he found himself unable to break the contact with her completely.

"That's why you refused my offer of marriage, isn't it?" he whispered hoarsely as the horrible understanding washed over him. What had he done to her? What kind of terrible pain had he inflicted on her that he had driven her to this?

Arabella nodded sadly. "No matter what I say, you will never truly believe me."

"That's not true," he insisted, telling himself that he spoke the truth. "I would believe you. I would."

"A brave lie," Arabella whispered. "No, Nando. Every time you saw me with another man, you would brood. Every time you held me in your arms, you would wonder if another man had touched me just this way. And someday you would hate me for marrying you, Nando." She put her hands on his and removed them from her shoulders. "And I love you too much for that."

Arabella closed her eyes, unwilling to share her pain with him any longer. "Leave me, alone, Nando. Please," she begged. "Don't say anything."

Nando saw how close to the breaking point Arabella was, and his hold on her slackened, even though the need to pull her into his embrace was so strong that he could feel the imprint of her body across the space between them.

"Not even thank you?" he asked, an ironic twist marring his chiseled mouth.

Arabella's lids lowered in acknowledgment of his words and his hands dropped away.

Chapter Twenty-five

It was a silent group that rode to Trautenstein. Absent was the joy and the triumph that should have been theirs.

Arabella pushed their pace, burning to shut herself away and weep the grief from her heart. But when they dismounted in the courtyard and she saw that Nando's wound was bleeding profusely despite the bandage he had made, she broke into action.

By the time the men had helped Nando into the salon, she had arranged blankets on the sofa and sent servants flying for bandages and hot water.

Nando bit back a groan as the men lowered him onto the makeshift bed. "I want her out of here, Uncle Johann. I've caused her enough pain for one day."

"Yes, my boy," the old man soothed. "Be still now." Under his breath he sent one of the servants for the resident barber as he began to cut away the torn breeches.

Arabella caught her breath when the bloody cloth fell away. The wound was not deep, but the bullet had plowed a long, ugly furrow into Nando's thigh. She barely managed to stifle her cry as Nando's body arched when the barber probed the wound.

"Just a scratch," he murmured. "The bullet just grazed it. All we have to do is clean it and do some stitch work."

Tersely the barber ordered brandy, a basin, needle and thread. When everything had been brought, Arabella watched wide-eyed as he arranged Nando's head on the pillow and sent an adroit blow to the wounded man's jaw with the side of his large hand.

Arabella opened her mouth to protest, but the barber silenced her and gestured her closer. "We must work quickly. He won't be unconscious long."

Ignoring the nausea that threatened to rise within her, Arabella knelt and held the basin while the barber cleaned the wound with a piece of linen and the best cognac from Uncle Johann's cellars. By the time he had taken up the needle and thread, Nando was beginning to move restlessly.

"Have you the stomach to do a little stitching, *Fräulein?*" the leech inquired bluntly. "He'll be coming to soon."

Arabella swallowed and nodded. She would do whatever she had to. Still, she needed all her willpower to force herself to pierce Nando's flesh for the first time. She had expected resistance, but the needle passed through the flesh easily. Sinking her teeth into her lower lip, she began to stitch in earnest.

"Shh, Nando. Quiet. Lie back." Arabella pressed Nando down on the sofa.

His eyes opened and widened and he struggled up again. "Are you hurt, Arabella? What happened?" His voice was blurred with pain.

She followed his gaze, and her stomach lurched when she saw the stains on her clothes where she had wiped her fingers. "I'm all right, Nando. It's your blood. I helped the barber stitch you up."

Now that she saw he was all right, the tension she had been running on dissipated and she remembered what had passed today. "Please excuse me." Her voice was barely a whisper. "I'm very tired." She rose, careful not to look at Nando.

Count Berg moved toward her and touched her elbow. "May I take you up to your room?"

Arabella nodded and turned to go.

"Stay."

She stopped at the sound of Nando's voice, but did not turn to look at him.

"Please."

Could she refuse the plea she heard in his voice? She must, Arabella told herself. He had hurt her too often and too badly, and she could take no more. Yet she turned and took a step toward him.

Old Count Berg watched the two young people and felt the almost tangible heat that flared between them. Gesturing to the servants to follow him, he quietly left the room.

Nando's heart was a trip-hammer in his ribs, the sweat gathering between his shoulder blades as he rose awkwardly and took a step toward Arabella. She flinched from him, and the pain that shot through him was as real as the pain in his leg.

"You should not be on your feet, Nando."

"I've had worse." He tried to smile.

Unable to be still, Arabella pulled off the shabby cap she wore and began pulling the pins out of her hair until the thick braids tumbled past her shoulders. Then Nando touched her and she jumped, the hairpins she held scattering on the floor. Suddenly her heart was beating so wildly that she could scarcely breathe, but in her mind she felt an almost unnatural calm as if heart and mind were completely separate entities.

Nando's fingers lay on her arm in a silent plea and Arabella looked up. Silver and sapphire met and clung, questioning and giving answer. In the space of a breath everything was said, yet neither of them was truly aware of what messages passed between them.

"What does a man do when he finds he's been the worst kind of fool?" Nando's mouth curved into a crooked, rueful smile.

Arabella said nothing, too bewildered by the maze of her emotions to find words.

"How many times did you put happiness into my hands and I thrust it away?" Nando's eyes scanned her face, looking for the forgiveness he knew he did not deserve but needed so badly.

She shook her head, more to indicate her inability to speak than to give answer.

"Can you forgive me, Arabella?" Nando asked softly, his fingers moving tentatively toward her, then retreating.

Arabella looked into his eyes, and even as her every fiber cried out her love, she was not certain that at this moment she could speak words of forgiveness and not lie.

The silence stretched, the echoes of this question vibrating between them. Finally Nando could stand it no longer. He would beg if he had to.

"Arabella, please, *je t'en prie...*" His hands lifted to her shoulders.

She raised her hand to his mouth to stop his words. No matter what had passed between them, she did not want him to beg. When she took her hand away, she curled her fingers protectively over the spot that had touched his lips. She felt no desire for revenge, but the hurt Nando had inflicted on her, or perhaps the pride that had sustained her for so long, stopped her from making the final, absolute gesture of forgiveness.

Nando looked into her eyes, searching for the forgiveness her lips refused to give him, but he did not find what he looked for in the sapphire depths. His hands dropped to his sides and his heartbeat went from the vibrant rhythm of hope to the harsh, mournful cadence of a dirge.

Of course not, he rebuked himself. *After what I've done to her, she would be a fool to give me another chance. Another chance to hurt her.* The pain clawing at his throat, Nando started to turn away. He felt a gentle hand on his arm.

"We will talk tomorrow, Nando," Arabella said softly. "Let us sleep on it. When our minds are fresh again—" she shrugged "—perhaps we can order our lives then."

She turned and slowly left the room. The wound within her was still raw, and she wondered if it would ever truly heal.

On her way upstairs, Arabella wandered into the study, drawn by the brightly burning fire. Twisting her cap in her fingers, she stared into the flames, so lost in her thoughts that she did not hear the footsteps behind her.

"*Fräulein?*"

Arabella started and turned to find Franz standing several steps behind her.

"Yes, Franz?"

"Forgive me, Fräulein Arabella, for speaking to you like this." He took a deep breath and plunged on. "He needs you." At his sides his large hands clenched and unclenched. "So badly."

"I know, Franz. And I need him." Her eyes started to fill. "But there's been so much mistrust, so many ugly words. I don't know if we can live with that."

"Pride is a cold bedfellow, *Fräulein.*"

Arabella stiffened at Franz's blunt words, but then she remember that he loved Nando as much as she did.

"Believe me. I know." His broad peasant face seemed to sag as a sadness took over it.

She waited for Franz to continue, but he stared past her into the blue-tipped flames. Then he began to speak so softly that she had to lean toward him to catch his words.

"I had a girl once. Before I went into the army, we shared the apple, but the next time I came home, her belly was fat with another man's child."

"Shared the apple?"

The glazed look left his eyes. "It is an old custom among country folk. When two people decide to share their bed for the rest of their lives, they share an apple, for it is the sweetness that lasts into the deepest, darkest winter. It is the symbol of life, for even the most shriveled fruit yields the seed of new life. The man had left her, but I was too proud to take her back." Franz's voice grew lower. "Now she is dead and I am still alone." He was silent for a long moment. Then he retreated a few steps and bowed. "Forgive me for my words."

Before Arabella could say anything, he was gone.

Nando stood at the window, a glass of wine forgotten in his hand. The filth of prison was washed from his body. He was trying to filter away the pain from his soul.

He had not yet lost, he told himself with the urgency of desperation. But he knew he was lying. Arabella might not have taken away all hope. But what was the use, when all the terrible words, the accusations could never be unsaid. The hurt never undone. They would always be between them.

He downed the wine without tasting it. What an incredible trick of turnabout for destiny to play on them. If his suspicions had turned out to be the truth, he would have forgiven her. But forgotten? Never. And Arabella was willing to forget the pain he had inflicted on her. But forgive? He didn't think so.

He heard the door open.

"I won't be needing anything else, Franz," Nando said wearily, massaging the tense muscles in his neck with one hand. "Go to bed."

Arabella stood in front of the door to Nando's room assailed by a terrible sense of familiarity. What if he rejected her? And if he wanted her, would he want their child, too? The enormity of the step she was about to take dizzied her, and her heart beat so madly that it stirred the corsage of her gown.

She lifted her hand to the elegantly curved brass door handle for the second time. For the second time she let her fingers fall away. It had been easy in the solitude of her room. There, the realization that her love for Nando committed her to withholding nothing from him had slipped into her mind without a ripple. There, the knowledge that she had to give him the gift of her complete vulnerability had not frightened her. Everything had been so simple until this moment when she stood in front of his door and remembered that it had once remained closed against her.

Then the picture of Nando alone beyond the door rose in her mind and her heart flew toward him. The memory of the quiet desperation with which he had asked her forgiveness, the memory of how the light in his eyes had died when she had refused to give him the words he needed, surfaced, and suddenly she knew how much that step had cost his proud spirit. The fear fell away from her and she pushed the door open.

There was no answer from Franz. The only sound Nando heard was the key turning in the lock.

"What the devil..." He whipped around. "Arabella?" His voice was barely a whisper as he stared, unsure if what he was seeing was a mirage or a miracle.

She locked her eyes to his and crossed the room, her step slow but sure. She stopped an arm's length away and set the plate she carried on a table. Nando's gaze followed her movement without registering what it was she had held, returning to her eyes almost immediately, asking, searching.

"Franz tells me it is a custom where you come from for two people who decide to spend their lives together to share an apple." Her voice trembled a little and she stopped, partly to catch her breath, partly to give him the chance to speak. But he was silent. A flurry of uncertainty shivered down her spine and was put aside.

Then Nando moved and closed the distance between them, putting his hands lightly on her shoulders. "Tell me," he demanded softly, still not quite believing that Arabella had come to give him what he needed. "I need to hear the words."

"I love you." She placed her hands flat against his chest. "And I have learned that love is not a miser, nor does it bargain." Her fingers spread, as if to absorb more of his warmth, his heartbeat. "It is a bottomless well that gives forever and ever."

"Does it give forgiveness?" Without meaning to, Nando dug his fingers into her flesh.

She raised her hands to his face. "Always."

Nando looked into Arabella's eyes, which shone with love and tears, and wondered what he had done to deserve what she was giving him. When he reached for the apple she stayed his hand and waited until he looked at her again.

"There is something else I need to tell you first."

She saw a shadow flit briefly into his eyes before the cleansing fire chased it away.

Her pregnancy wasn't showing yet, but Arabella took Nando's hand and drew it to her middle, where her stomach would soon begin to round. "There will be a child soon. Very soon." She whispered. "Will you want both of us?"

She watched him, a throb of fear in her throat. She had lived two months with her unborn child and he—for she was certain that the child she carried was a son—was already as real to her as if he were lying in her arms. But he was a stranger yet to Nando.

Nando felt the blood flow out of his head as the realization that he had almost lost not only Arabella but his child, as well, swept over him. Then a second wave of what could only be described as panic overwhelmed him as he recalled how Arabella had ridden herself to exhaustion for his sake.

She saw him pale, but before she could put a name to the emotion she saw in his face, Nando had crushed her to him and buried his face in her neck. Her arms went around him and a shaft of alarm went through her when she felt him begin to tremble.

"Are you all right?" Nando whispered against her neck. "The riding. It didn't harm you?"

"I'm fine. We are both fine." Arabella almost laughed with relief and tried to pull back to look at him, but he resisted. "Don't hide from me, Nando," she implored. "Please."

Long minutes passed as fraction by fraction he loosened his grip and allowed her to tip her head and look into his face. Allowed her to see the tears that blurred his eyes. Still holding her tightly in one arm, he let his fingertips feather over her face, as if memorizing her features, the texture of her skin.

"I love you." His voice was thick with emotion.

Reaching around her, Nando picked up the apple and with a vigorous twist split it into two halves. Standing hip to hip, they ate the sweet fruit, their eyes making their vows, promising forever.

The sweetness of the fruit still lay on their lips when he lowered his mouth to hers. Just one kiss, he told himself. Just one chaste kiss to seal the pledge they had given each other.

Nando's lips pressed lightly, undemandingly against Arabella's mouth, but her lips opened beneath his, beckoning, inviting. Her warm breath heated, incited, and he was lost. The passion, the need of the long, empty, hungry weeks was suddenly compressed into the pressure of mouth against mouth, and the heat spiraled upward.

His breath was ragged when Nando tore his mouth away, but Arabella pursued him, stretching upward, her velvet-clad body sliding, whispering against his clothes.

"Make love to me, Nando. Please."

"No, not now." His erratic breath caused his words to stumble. "I'll hurt you."

She gloried in the feeling of his aroused body against hers. "No," she whispered against his mouth, "you won't hurt me. We've done with hurting." Her teeth slid along his lower lip, and when she heard his groan, she knew he had capitulated.

The hands that undressed her were not quite steady. Nando laid her on the bed and sat beside her. He let his gaze caress her, wanting to prolong the moment.

Arabella insinuated her hand into the opening of his shirt and her fingers glided along his hair-roughened skin. The textures that offered themselves to her touch tantalized, and she closed her eyes and stifled a moan of pleasure.

Nando watched her with the greediness of a starving man. He saw how she pressed her thighs together to relieve the pressure there, how her nipples puckered with her arousal, and suddenly he could not bear to wait a moment longer.

Material ripped and buttons bounced as Nando tore off his clothes. One last time he paused at the edge of the bed to look at her, and their eyes met. Then Arabella opened her arms and he lowered himself to lie beside her.

Arabella's hands slid ceaselessly over Nando's golden body as if to reassure herself that he was here. That he was hers. "Will you always believe me? Believe in me?" she demanded. Her breath caught in her throat as his clever fingers caressed and provoked.

"Yes." Nando breathed the word into her mouth, following it with his tongue to fill himself with her taste. "I love you," he murmured. "Promise me that you'll never change."

"I promise." She rubbed her thigh against his aroused flesh. "You'll have to take me as I am."

"Yes," he whispered, as he moved over and into her body. "I will. Always."

* * * * *

Author's Note

The Congress of Vienna was an extraordinary gathering that lasted months longer than it was supposed to—from September 1814 to June 1815—simply because most of the participants spent a vast amount of time amusing themselves with all imaginable diversions and hatching intrigues, both political and amorous. The population of Vienna was more than doubled during this period and the one hundred thousand visitors included almost all of Europe's reigning monarchs and princes, plus quantities of diplomats, soldiers, adventurers and adventuresses, any of whose escapades would be enough to fill a book. So it is small wonder that some of them found their way into the pages of my novel.

Although my heroine and hero are products of my imagination, some of the major characters are real historical personages. Prince Nikita Volkonsky, Princess Katharina Bagration and Chancellor Prince Clemens Metternich were prominent participants and all three were tireless in both dalliance and conspiracy. None of the incidents I describe involving these people have an actual base in reality, but they are very much in character and *could* very well have taken place.

Another historical personage is Countess Lulu Thürheim whose witty and often malicious diaries were a treasure trove of details about the period.

These few months of history are exceptionally well documented and the profusion of diaries, memoirs and chronicles is a researcher's dream. Even the reports written by the Viennese secret police are available and lead one to believe that there was at least one spy under every bed.

This colorful and rich period has become very real to me, and I hope that I've succeeded in making it come alive for my readers.

COMING NEXT MONTH

#103 THOMASINA—Marianne Willman
Dr. Brendan Gallagher balked when he discovered his
apprentice was a woman, but Thomasina Wentworth soon
managed to win his heart.

#104 A CORNER OF HEAVEN—Theresa Michaels
When Confederate Colonel Colter Saxton tried to force his
way back into Elizabeth Waring's life, she had no right to stop
him—for he was the father of her child.

#105 SILVER FURY—Isabel Whitfield
Even their love couldn't bridge the gap of suspicion that
separated Shelly Young from Dillon Ryder, until they learned
the importance of trust.

#106 KING'S MAN—Caryn Cameron
It was Nicholas Spencer's royal duty to wipe out the local band
of smugglers, not to fall in love with their leader,
Rosalind Barrow.

AVAILABLE NOW:

HARLEQUIN®
OFFICIAL SWEEPSTAKES
RULES

NO PURCHASE NECESSARY

1. To enter, complete an Official Entry Form or 3" × 5" index card by hand-printing, in plain block letters, your complete name, address, phone number and age, and mailing it to: Harlequin Fashion A Whole New You Sweepstakes, P.O. Box 9056, Buffalo, NY 14269-9056.

   No responsibility is assumed for lost, late or misdirected mail. Entries must be sent separately with first class postage affixed, and be received no later than December 31, 1991 for eligibility.

2. Winners will be selected by D.L. Blair, Inc., an independent judging organization whose decisions are final, in random drawings to be held on January 30, 1992 in Blair, NE at 10:00 a.m. from among all eligible entries received.

3. The prizes to be awarded and their approximate retail values are as follows: Grand Prize — A brand-new Mercury Sable LS plus a trip for two (2) to Paris, including round-trip air transportation, six (6) nights hotel accommodation, a $1,400 meal/spending money stipend and $2,000 cash toward a new fashion wardrobe (approximate value: $28,000) or $15,000 cash; two (2) Second Prizes — A trip to Paris, including round-trip air transportation, six (6) nights hotel accommodation, a $1,400 meal/spending money stipend and $2,000 cash toward a new fashion wardrobe (approximate value: $11,000) or $5,000 cash; three (3) Third Prizes — $2,000 cash toward a new fashion wardrobe. All prizes are valued in U.S. currency. Travel award air transportation is from the commercial airport nearest winner's home. Travel is subject to space and accommodation availability, and must be completed by June 30, 1993. Sweepstakes offer is open to residents of the U.S. and Canada who are 21 years of age or older as of December 31, 1991, except residents of Puerto Rico, employees and immediate family members of Torstar Corp., its affiliates, subsidiaries, and all agencies, entities and persons connected with the use, marketing, or conduct of this sweepstakes. All federal, state, provincial, municipal and local laws apply. Offer void wherever prohibited by law. Taxes and/or duties, applicable registration and licensing fees, are the sole responsibility of the winners. Any litigation within the province of Quebec respecting the conduct and awarding of a prize may be submitted to the Régie des loteries et courses du Québec. All prizes will be awarded; winners will be notified by mail. No substitution of prizes is permitted.

4. Potential winners must sign and return any required Affidavit of Eligibility/Release of Liability within 30 days of notification. In the event of noncompliance within this time period, the prize may be awarded to an alternate winner. Any prize or prize notification returned as undeliverable may result in the awarding of that prize to an alternate winner. By acceptance of their prize, winners consent to use of their names, photographs or their likenesses for purposes of advertising, trade and promotion on behalf of Torstar Corp. without further compensation. Canadian winners must correctly answer a time-limited arithmetical question in order to be awarded a prize.

5. For a list of winners (available after 3/31/92), send a separate stamped, self-addressed envelope to: Harlequin Fashion A Whole New You Sweepstakes, P.O. Box 4694, Blair, NE 68009.

PREMIUM OFFER TERMS

To receive your gift, complete the Offer Certificate according to directions. Be certain to enclose the required number of "Fashion A Whole New You" proofs of product purchase (which are found on the last page of every specially marked "Fashion A Whole New You" Harlequin or Silhouette romance novel). Requests must be received no later than December 31, 1991. Limit: four (4) gifts per name, family, group, organization or address. Items depicted are for illustrative purposes only and may not be exactly as shown. Please allow 6 to 8 weeks for receipt of order. Offer good while quantities of gifts last. In the event an ordered gift is no longer available, you will receive a free, previously unpublished Harlequin or Silhouette book for every proof of purchase you have submitted with your request, plus a refund of the postage and handling charge you have included. Offer good in the U.S. and Canada only.   HQFW-SWPR

HARLEQUIN® OFFICIAL
SWEEPSTAKES ENTRY FORM

4-FWHHS-4

Complete and return this Entry Form immediately – the more entries you submit, the better your chances of winning!

- Entries must be received by **December 31, 1991.**
- A Random draw will take place on **January 30, 1992.**
- No purchase necessary.

Yes, I want to win a FASHION A WHOLE NEW YOU Classic and Romantic prize from Harlequin:

Name _____ Telephone _____ Age _____

Address _____

City _____ State _____ Zip _____

Return Entries to: **Harlequin FASHION A WHOLE NEW YOU,**
P.O. Box 9056, Buffalo, NY 14269-9056   © 1991 Harlequin Enterprises Limited

PREMIUM OFFER

To receive your free gift, send us the required number of proofs-of-purchase from any specially marked FASHION A WHOLE NEW YOU Harlequin or Silhouette Book with the Offer Certificate properly completed, plus a check or money order (do not send cash) to cover postage and handling payable to Harlequin FASHION A WHOLE NEW YOU Offer. We will send you the specified gift.

OFFER CERTIFICATE

Item	A. ROMANTIC COLLECTOR'S DOLL	B. CLASSIC PICTURE FRAME
	(Suggested Retail Price $60.00)	(Suggested Retail Price $25.00)
# of proofs-of-purchase	18	12
Postage and Handling	$3.50	$2.95
Check one	☐	☐

Name _____

Address _____

City _____ State _____ Zip _____

Mail this certificate, designated number of proofs-of-purchase and check or money order for postage and handling to: **Harlequin FASHION A WHOLE NEW YOU Gift Offer,** P.O. Box 9057, Buffalo, NY 14269-9057. Requests must be received by December 31, 1991.

ONE
PROOF-OF-PURCHASE

4-FWHHP-4

To collect your fabulous free gift you must include the necessary number of proofs-of-purchase with a properly completed Offer Certificate.

© 1991 Harlequin Enterprises Limited

See previous page for details.